ZWINGLI

ON PROVIDENCE
and other essays

ON PROVIDENCE
and other essays

ULRICH ZWINGLI

Edited for Samuel Macauley Jackson
by William John Hinke

THE LABYRINTH PRESS
Durham, North Carolina

Library of Congress Cataloging in Publication Data

Zwingli, Ulrich, 1484–1531.
   On providence and other essays.

   Reprint. Originally published: The Latin works and the correspondence of Huldreich Zwingli, volume two, with variant title: The Latin works of Huldreich Zwingli, volume two. Philadelphia: Heidelberg Press, 1922.
   Includes index.
   1. Theology—Addresses, essays, lectures. I. Jackson, Samuel Macauley, 1851–1912. II. Hinke, William John, 1871–1947. III. Title.
BR346.A25   1983   230'.42   83–19612
ISBN 0–939464–17–9 (pbk.)

CONTENTS

CONTENTS

VI

The Works
of Huldreich Zwingli

I.

DECLARATION OF HULDREICH ZWINGLI REGARDING ORIGINAL
SIN, ADDRESSED TO URBANUS RHEGIUS.

(August 15, 1526)

[DE PECCA- | TO ORIGINALI DECLARATIO | Huldrychi. Zuinglij,
Ad Vrbanum | Rhegium. | 48 unnumbered octavo pages, of which pp. 2,
45-48 are blank. Signed on p. 44: *Tiguri quintadecima die Augusti.*
An. | *M.D.XXVI. Tigvri. Ex Aedibus Christophori Froschouer, i. e.,*
"Zurich, August 15, 1526. From the press of Christopher Froschouer."
Printed in *Opera Zwinglii*, tom. II, fol. 115b-122b; *Jo. Oecolampadii et*
Huld. Zwinglii epist. libr. IV (Basileae, 1536) fol. 54b-61b; Schuler and
Schulthess ed., Vol. III, pp. 626-645; Finsler, *Zwingli Bibliographie*, No. 72.
The following English translation, based on one made by Mr. Henry
Preble, was revised throughout by the editor.

This pamphlet was in answer to a letter of Rhegius to Zwingli, which
has not been discovered thus far. (See Zwingli's *Werke*, Vol. VIII.
(1914), 633, note 4). Rhegius had some doubts as to the soundness of
Zwingli's views regarding original sin. This appears from a letter which
he wrote on January 14, 1526, to Ambrose Blaurer of Constance, in which
he expressed himself rather vigorously: "I am sorry Zwingli was not at
Baden [*i. e.,* the Baden Disputation, May 21-June 18, 1526]. He would
have defeated all the Papists once for all, except in the matter of original
sin, which he seems to treat in a very unsound fashion. In regard to the
Lord's Supper, though he might be criticized, he certainly could not have
been defeated by those counterfeit theologians." Nor was his mind

1

altogether set at rest by this treatise, for he expresses in a letter of September 28, 1526 (*Zwingli's Werke*, VIII, 726-8) the fear that Zwingli might be accused of Origenism. Zwingli tried to remove his doubts by a letter dated October 16, 1526 (*Werke*, VIII, 737-9).]

HULDREICH ZWINGLI TO URBANUS RHEGIUS,* PREACHER OF THE GOSPEL AT AUGSBURG.

GRACE and peace through Jesus Christ, our Lord. You wrote me very recently a letter which, though it was very long, was not long enough, most learned Urbanus, for it so abounded in new and learned things and showed with clearness that you had been in no way offended by the letter which I had combined with the one in which I discuss the Eucharist with Billicanus in no unfriendly way†, as I think.

Yet I have not been able to answer before those things which I think ought by no means to be passed over in silence, though I have constantly and eagerly desired to answer them. I am so badly driven by occupations, nay by those furies, who, kindling everywhere the fires of contention, will some day suffer a punishment worthy of Castor and Pollux. But now, having secured, or, if the truth may be told without shame, having stolen, a little leisure time, I will do my best to say at least something if not altogether enough with regard to the question you raise in your letter. For you are not the only one who thinks that I hold and write an unusual doctrine with regard to the pollution of human descent. There are other great men who entertain the same idea. I have myself seen letters of certain men to myself and to others, some of which beg me to explain my view more clearly, while others warn their friends not to

*The reformer Urbanus Rhegius (Koenig) was born in 1490 at Langenargen, near Lindau. He studied at Freiburg and at Ingolstadt. At the latter place he became professor of poetry and rhetoric. In the year 1520, he became cathedral preacher at Augsburg, where he accepted the principles of the Reformation. In 1530, he was called as superintendent to Celle and as such was the reformer of the Duchy of Luneburg. He died March 23, 1541. His works appeared in 1562 at Nuremberg, four volumes in German, three volumes in Latin. His biography was written by Heimbuerger (Gotha, 1851) and by Uhlhorn (Elberfeld, 1861).

†See the *Responsio H. Zwinglii*, to the letters of Theob. Billicanus and U. Rhegius, Schuler and Schulthess ed., III, 646-670.

suffer themselves to be dragged to destruction by me. They are both of them overcautious, not to say anxious. For those to whom the question is so clear that they think I need to make a declaration of doctrine, ought to bring out publicly their own clear teaching forthwith, for I do differ somewhat with those who have so far been thought to have hit the nail on the head in this matter; and, on the other hand, those to whom my view seems so dangerous that they think they ought to warn their friends to beware of it, should caution all men, or at least try to make me explain like those who were before me. I will, therefore, with the help of Christ, try to make all men see clearly that what I have said upon this matter briefly but plainly, was not said at random or without authority from the sacred Scriptures; and that, on the other hand, much has been said by many people in regard to this matter which has little foundation in the truly sacred [canonical] writings. For what could be said more briefly and plainly than that original sin is not sin but disease, and that the children of Christians are not condemned to eternal punishment on account of that disease? On the other hand, what could be said more feebly or more at variance with the canonical Scriptures than that this disaster was relieved by the water of baptism, while through want thereof it was intensified, and that it was not only a disease but even a crime? Therefore, my dear Urbanus, believe that I treated such reasoning so concisely and lightly in my work upon Baptism and Catabaptism* because otherwise the book would have grown to interminable length. For I had determined even then, to treat the whole subject more at length and with greater precision if circumstances should demand it. But I had a hope that the thing would be settled by those few words, for in these days men's minds are so happily constituted that if you offer them a slight opportunity or give them a handle to take hold of, they straightway press on to the very end. Yet some are of a more sincere spirit than others. We often say we do not understand a thing when we do not want to understand it. Or we are ashamed to appear ignorant. We sometimes forget both God and our-selves,—that it is impossible for anything to escape Him or for us to know everything.

But do thou, to come at length to the subject, most fair-

*See Zwingli's *Werke*, Schuler and Schulthess ed., vol. II, 1, p. 287.

minded priest of the truth, accept my argument in this manner: Let us first of all come to an agreement as to these terms, "sin" and "disease." Then let us define the disease itself, and attempt to discover the appropriate name for it, and show how it damns and whom. Thirdly, let us show that it cannot be cured by any other medicine than the blood of Christ, the Son of God, so far am I from denying Christ's efficacy. Therewith I shall also search out whether the evil can be averted by anything else than that blood, for instance, by the water of baptism.

That "sin" is properly used of a wrong committed through negligence or thoughtlessness, I think everybody is aware, such as the Greeks call παράπτωμα ἀπὸ τοῦ πταίειν,* the Latin theologians "delictum a deliquendo vel negligendo," the Hebrews "asham," like those wrong-doings from which St. John says no man is free†, and which Christ bids us atone for by constant prayer, saying, "Forgive us our debts."

For since they are of daily occurrence, they drive the pious man, like constant goads, to self-debasement and depreciation of his faults. Or it is used for the misdeed which any one commits and enters into knowingly and with his eyes open, after mature deliberation and thought, such as the Greeks call ἁμαρτία,i. e., a failing or fault, because, if we may believe Origen, it is done "contra conscientiam," in conscious opposition to conscience, while the Latins call it "scelus," "crimen" or "flagitium." In this category are included highway robbery, homicide, war (voluntary sins these), treason, excessive lust, mercenary judgments, oppression of the innocent, and all this class of monstrous wrongs, such as the sins of David, Ahab and Judas.

Now the word "disease" I do not use here according to the pattern of those learned in the law, who, as Gellius tell us,‡ distinguish it from "defect" only in that the first is temporary, the other lasting; I use it as combined with a defect and that a lasting one, as when stammering, blindness, or gout is hereditary in a family. Such an infirmity or natural defect we are in the habit of calling "einen natürlichen Bresten" in German—a natural infirmity. On account of such a thing no one is thought the worse or the more vicious. For things which come from

---

*i. e., a false step from the verb *ptaiein*, to fall.
†Probably I John 1: 8 is intended.
‡A. Gellii Noctium Atticarum Libri XX, Bk. IV, 2.

nature cannot be put down as crimes or guilt.

For this reason, I have said that the original contamination of man is a disease, not a sin, because sin implies guilt, and guilt comes from a transgression or trespass on the part of one who designedly perpetrates a deed. I will give an example. To be born a slave is a wretched condition, but it is not a fault nor a crime in him who is so born, for when born one has not yet committed any trespass or transgression. If, then, any one should say, "But his ancestors' acts caused them and their descendants to be reduced to slavery, hence there was wrong-doing involving fault, and slavery followed it as fine or penalty," he would be right assuredly. I say so, too. The sin involved in the wrong-doing of our first parent is called "original sin," not in the real sense of the words but metaphorically, and is nothing else than a condition, wretched to be sure, but much milder than the crime deserved. For as prisoners of war, when they might have been slain with impunity, have sometimes been saved through mercy and grace on condition that they and all their descendants shall be slaves, so the originator of the human race, having deserved utter destruction,* was by the goodness of God driven into exile, and made subject to death, and so was exiled not only from a most charming garden, but from the most delightful sight of the divine countenance and the glad companionship of the angels.

And this disaster fell upon his descendants also. For a dead man cannot beget a living man, nor a slave a free man. Adam, therefore, being justly dead and an exile, could not generate offspring who should be living in the sight of God or a citizen or heir of the heaven from which he had utterly fallen.

Now, what I say shall be proved by the testimony of Paul. In Romans 5 [: 14],† he says: "Death reigned from Adam to Moses, even over them that had not sinned after the similitude of Adam's transgression." By these words it becomes plainly apparent that Adam perpetrated the crime upon which the

* πανωλεθρία. Zwingli put the Greek words into the text. We prefer to add them as footnotes.

†The verse division of the Bible, that is, the numbering of the verses, was first introduced into the Latin Bible in a small octavo edition, printed by Robert Stephanus, in 1555. Hence the earlier quotations are usually by chapters only. We have added the verses in square brackets.

penalty of death was so rigorously inflicted that it clung to all his descendants, but that they who afterwards died in consequence of this defect of birth did not sin as Adam had sinned. The disease, therefore, and defect, brought upon man by the fault of the first parent, is what has vitiated the offspring, the offspring did not vitiate itself. When, therefore, it is called "sin" in the Scriptures, it is clear enough, I think, that this is done by metonymy. Hence, when you also, most learned Urbanus, quote the testimony of Paul, Rom. 7 [: 17], "Now then it is no more I that do it, but sin that dwelleth in me," and show that Paul also called that disease "sin" rather than serious disorder, and ask then why I, too, will not suffer it to be called "sin," as Paul and all have called it, you are right to ask it. But now, I hope, you see clearly that I am not contending for a name, but wish to bring out the thing itself a little more plainly and significantly. I allow you, therefore, and everybody who is not satisfied with calling this disaster a sin to call it a heinous, criminal, and disgraceful offense, but on the understanding that by these terms are meant the disease, defect, or condition of mortality, and that boundless tendency to self-love of which I shall speak later. And this is not contradicted by what Paul again says, Rom. 3 [: 23], "All have sinned," for in the same way the word for sinning is used figuratively, so that the meaning is, "All are in this wretched condition of having been deprived of the glory of God through the fault of their first parent." Thus far, I think, we have come to an understanding or an agreement if you prefer, that I shall suffer this defect of human depravity to be called "sin," but you shall understand by this term a condition and penalty, the disaster and misery of corrupted human nature, not a crime or guilt on the part of those who are born in the condition of sin and death.

Now we have come to the place to define the disease itself and to give it a name according to the definition, which I undertook to do as the second part of my task. If, then, we can find the source of this evil, we shall by one and the same stroke reach the definition and the name. The source, then, *ab ovo,* as they say, was this: When the Creator of all things had installed in paradise, as in the palace of Alcinous,* that man

---

*The king of the Phaeacians, whose gardens had become proverbial. Mentioned in the Odyssey, Bk. VII, 112-132.

whom he had set over all living things, He bound him to Himself by this law, "Of every tree in the garden thou shalt eat without fear, but of the tree of knowledge of good and evil shalt thou not eat, for on the day thou eatest thereof thou shalt die." [Gen. 2:16-17].

This law he suddenly transgressed in this wise. That supreme Architect had built woman from a single rib of Adam —while he slept, an exceedingly unpropitious omen. For what will not woman dare in the hope of deceiving and eluding her husband, after having at birth seen him sunk so deeply in sleep that he did not feel it when his side was torn open and a rib taken out? Having discovered her nature the Devil determined to attack the man through her, and though he believed her capable of any recklessness, he yet saw that newly born she was still unacquainted with wiles. Hence, the clever pleader got around her by the ambiguity of the name of the tree. For inasmuch as God had forbidden them to eat of the tree of the knowledge of good and evil with the intent that they should never try to know anything of themselves, but should depend upon Him alone in all their thoughts and reflections and designs, the Devil distorted the reason for the name of the tree into this, that it received its name of "the tree of the knowledge of good and evil," because he that should eat of it would straightway become thoroughly skilled in good and evil. He also charged God with treachery in that he had said that immediate death would threaten those that would eat. The foolish woman, therefore, forthwith began to be suspicious of God, as if He had been insincere in forbidding a thing from which such advantage would arise and as if He feared for His dominion. Beside this, the rare beauty of the tree allured her, the fruit whetted her appetite, the desire to know good and evil drew her on, and being at once insolent, glad, and filled with great hopes, she seized the apple and persuaded her husband to try how these hopes would issue, having promised him everything that was most fair. And he, overcome not so much by the blandishments of the woman as by his eagerness, both to know good and evil and to become equal with God, put his teeth into the fatal fruit, and immediately his eyes were opened, not to see what he had hoped, but to gaze upon the whole band of evils that awaited him, and straightway he fell. What other cause can we think this most indiscreet act had than self-love? Adam viewed himself with admiration, thought himself not unworthy of greater dominion than that which he had, over the beasts namely, searched his mind and found it capable of more than he thus far knew. Nay, overstepping and surmounting all things, he represented himself in imagination as a sort of judge and dictator in the matter of good and evil. These expressions captivated his ear; these arguments shattered the law in regard to not eating; these battering-rams leveled the citadel of innocence with the ground, and the fate the Lord had foretold fell upon the thrice and four times wretched creature. For he had perished utterly, having deserved the extreme of all punishment, and as the Hebrews say, had died the death, only the Lord in His own kindness, rather than because of Adam's deserts, found a means of propping up the fallen, of which I shall speak in the third part.

We have now the source of the transgression, namely φιλαυτία, that is, self-love. From this have flowed all the evils which exist anywhere among mortals. Given over to death by this, man must by no means be thought to have begotten sons unlike himself, any more than a wolf begets a sheep or a crow a swan. For thus it is written, Gen. 5 [: 3], "And Adam begat a son in his own likeness, after his image, etc." The children of the first parents, therefore, were in no more excellent condition than they themselves, and so with all their posterity. And Adam was made the chattel of sin by transgressing the divine law. For he that doeth sin, is the slave of sin. Into the same condition, therefore, we have all been born after him. Hence, whatever we meditate for our own sakes, we consult only our own interests, and simply walk through the universe eager to have all things our own, serving us, and eager to be ourselves over all things. Hence, again, the Lord says, Gen. 6 [: 3], "My spirit shall not always strive with man, for that he also is flesh." Flesh, therefore, scorns God and loves itself. And a little later he says, "And every imagination of the thoughts of the human heart is only evil continually."* Again God reiterates the same thing, Gen. 8 [: 21], "I will no more curse the earth for the sake of man; for the imagination

*Gen. 6: 5, slightly changed by Zwingli.

and thought of man's heart are prone to evil from his youth."*

All these things tend to prove this one point that our nature was vitiated in our first parent, so that it is constantly sinning through excessive self-love, and if God should leave it to itself, could meditate nothing sincere and generous, any more than runaway slaves. This propensity to sin, therefore, from self-love is "original sin;" the propensity is not properly sin, but is a sort of source of and disposition to it.

I have used† as an illustration, a wolf still a cub. It is in all respects still a wolf as far as its disposition is concerned, and is an animal that would slaughter everything in its savageness, but it has not yet carried off any plunder because its age prevented it. The hunters, therefore, no more spare it than they spare the wolf, from whose jaws they rescue its prey, because its nature, though it is so young, is so well known to them that they are sure it will follow the instincts of its kind when it grows up. The disposition, therefore, is the original sin or defect, the plundering is the sin which flows from the disposition. The sin itself consists in the act, which recent writers call, "actual deed," and this is properly the sin. And this Paul explains most clearly of all in the fewest words, Rom. 7 [: 14], "I," he says, "am carnal," (here you have the "flesh" of Genesis and the disposition of the young wolf), "sold under sin," (here you have the condition of slave, the corrupted nature, the propensity to sin, and, in a word, the defect or disease). "For that which I do, I allow not"—the Hebrews use the word for knowing all the time instead of the word for approving or allowing,‡ as in Psalm 1 [: 6]. "The Lord knoweth," i. e., approveth, "the way of the righteous," and Psalm 36 [: 18].** "The Lord knoweth the days of the upright," and Num. 14: 31, "and they shall know the land which ye have despised," (where we read "et videbunt, and they shall see," but wrongly, for there is the same word

*Thus according to the Vulgate, which Zwingli quotes.

†Zwingli used this illustration in his book on Baptism, see Schuler and Schulthess ed., Vol. II, pt. 1, p. 288.

‡Paul was writing Greek, not Hebrew. Hence the Vulgate and English version translate correctly, "I know not." The Greek word ought not to be translated "I allow not."

**Psalm 36 in the Vulgate; but Ps. 37, in the Hebrew and English translations. The difference is due to the fact that in the Septuagint Pss. 9 and 10 are counted as one Psalm.

יָדַע [to know] in all the passages). "For what I would, that do I not; but what I hate, that do I. If then I do that which I would not, I consent unto the law that it is good. Now then it is no more I that do it" (that, namely, which I hate in my inner man) "but sin that dwelleth in me. For I know that in me (that is, in my flesh), dwelleth no good thing, etc." [Rom. 7: 15-18].

Now the sin that dwelleth in us is nothing else than the defect of a corrupted nature, which from self-love constantly desires things contrary to the spirit. For the spirit strives for the general weal, the flesh for its own particular welfare. For God does not take thought for Himself, but for those He has created, for He needs nothing but all things need Him. Thus all flesh, however much it pretends to be good, in as far as it is flesh, attributes all things as for its own good; but if it perceives a different sentiment in itself, it should attribute it to God as His blessing and gift. For the works of the flesh are manifest. The flesh, then, is one thing, its works another, and the flesh is not sin, but that which the flesh doeth is sin. The flesh, therefore, the disposition of man, the original defect or sin, this propensity, is that which desires things contrary to the spirit. But this desire is not without a cause, and since no man hath such desire except for his own sake, this propensity can only come from φιλαυτία, that is, self-love. When Catiline lavishes his possessions, he is striving for a reputation for liberality; when he plunders what belongs to others, his aim is the same. See by what opposite means the defect pushes its way to its own desires. In a word, self-love devises and combines all these schemes; it is itself the disease or defect from which all our ills come forth as from a Trojan horse.

Now that we have searched out the source of our ills, and the name of the disease or defect, the next thing is to inquire, as the thesis of this second part of our work, whether this disease condemns all mortals to the woes of everlasting death. In considering this question I think we should not fail to note the following:—The bliss of everlasting life and the pain of everlasting death are altogether matters of free election or rejection by the divine will. Therefore, all who have ever discussed this question seem to have drawn the lines rather incautiously in damning all infants or all grown persons who have not been circumcised or washed with the water of baptism. For what else is Paul after, in Romans from the ninth to the twelfth chapter, than to show that blessedness cometh to those elected of God, not to those who do this or that? For he loved Jacob and, according to the words of the prophet [Mal. 1: 3], hated Esau, when they were still being formed in their mother's womb. Since, therefore, everlasting life belongs to those who have been elected to it by God, why do we form rash judgments about any, since God's election is hidden from us? Were we in His counsels when He made the election, so that He might not rashly pitch upon some unworthy person unawares, forsooth?

Again, as to those who have grown to mature age, why do we in our indiscretion damn those who have not been marked with the external sign? For again Paul says in Romans 2 [: 25], that he whose foreskin is intact, (for he calls him ἀκροβυστία, that is, the foreskin [or the uncircumcision]) is preferred to and excels him who boasteth of a circumcised foreskin, if only he doeth what the law enjoins. For he shows that the works of the law are written in his heart when he doeth that which the law enjoins. But who writeth upon the human heart anything worthy of God, but He who created him, as Jeremiah 31 [: 33] witnesseth? When, therefore, we see the uncircumcision do what the law directs, why do we not recognize the tree by its fruit? Why do we not perceive that God hath engraved the works of the law upon his heart? If, therefore, he doeth the work of God under impulse from God, why do we damn him because he has not been baptized or circumcised, especially when, again, the apostle attributes to such accusation or absolution of conscience in the day of judgment [Rom. 2: 15-16], and it is nowhere written, "He that is not baptized, is damned;" and the words in Gen. 17 [: 14], "the uncircumcised man-child whose flesh of his foreskin is not circumcised, that soul shall be cut off from his people," were said unto the people of Israel in order that no one should omit that sign, not in order to destroy a man (by whatever accident it was that the sign had not been received) nor to indicate that the sign had any power. But all things occurred to them under figures, and God ordered rites of this kind of them that they might be constantly reminded of spiritual things. He demanded circumcision of the heart, and therefore directed that that member be circumcised, which was the fittest symbol of the passions, that men might be always reminded of the internal circumcision. He wished the law to be ever before their eyes in every thought and every act, and therefore He ordered them to make phylacteries.*

This nation alone, therefore, which was descended from Abraham or lived with his descendants and, confessing the same faith, made one Church with them, was prohibited from omitting the sign of the covenant and not because a merciful God had so bound His grace and spirit and election to that sign that he refused to draw unto Himself any but those that were signed with this sign.

Since, I say, (to come back to the main discourse) everlasting life has nowhere been promised on the terms that unless one has been circumcised or baptized he shall in no wise attain it, there is no reason why we should at random consign to the lower regions them that have not been marked by these signs. All these things are gathered from the second chapter of Paul's Epistle to the Romans. Nor did Christ say, "He that is not baptized, shall not be saved." I have brought forward these arguments for the purpose of showing that they are wrong by the whole diameter of heaven† who, even if they have names not only great but ancient, are in the habit of consigning to everlasting damnation, now the children of Christians when they have not been baptized, now all those whom we call "the Gentiles." For what do we know of the faith each one has written in his heart by the hand of God?

Who does not admire the faith of that holy man Seneca, as his letter XXXIV to Lucilius‡ discloses it? He says, "We should certainly live as if our lives were in plain sight, think as if some one could look into our inmost souls. And some one can, for what profiteth it that a thing is kept secret from man? Nothing is closed to God. He is present in our minds and in the midst of our thoughts. So in the midst of them, I mean, as never to depart from us." Thus Seneca.

Who, pray, wrote this faith upon the heart of man? Let no one think that these things point to the taking away of Christ's office, as some men charge me with doing; they magnify

*They are supposed to be referred to in Deut. 6: 8.

†i. e., they are entirely mistaken.

‡In the edition of Hense (1914), it is Letter LXXXIII.

His glory. For through Christ must come all who come to God. On this a little later. Hence I do not even suspect that the father-in-law of Moses came to God by any other way than through Him who said, "I am the way, and the truth, and the life" [John 14:6], as also Moses and all men came. For the words, "He that believeth not shall be damned" [Mk. 16:16], are not to be understood absolutely, but only of those who having heard the Gospel refuse to believe. Hence children and those who have not heard the Gospel are not bound by this law, but with grown persons the point is whether the law of God is written on their hearts or not. For thus again they stand or fall unto the Lord, through Christ Jesus the only way to salvation.

And this is also the case with those who, like the children, have not heard, Rom. 9 [:11], "that the purpose or ordination* of God according to election might stand," and, "I will have mercy on whom I will have mercy" [Rom. 9:15], and "It is not of him that willeth, nor of him that runneth, but of God that showeth mercy" [Rom. 9:16]. For Christ himself says: "If I had not come and spoken unto them, they had not had sin" [John 15:22]. Let their ignorance, therefore, not be counted against them to whom none hath come to preach the mystery of Christ. They stand or fall unto the Lord. Paul treats the same point, Rom. 10:18, (and this is not against me, but on my side), "Have they not heard? Yes, verily, their sound went into all the earth." This counterblast† the apostle hurled at the Jews and thereby took away from them the opportunity to answer by making a pretext of ignorance and saying, "We have not heard; we do not know." "The whole world," he says, "resounds with the Gospel, and ye have not heard?" In a word, election is unshaken and the law written on the hearts of men, but so that those who are elect and do the works of the law in accordance with the law written on their hearts come to God through Christ alone. For he is the son for whom the master of the house prepared the wedding and invited many [Lk. 14:16]. And if any man ask me whether we should not make a statement concerning those about whom we have the declara-

---

* πρόθεσις.
† ἀντιπίπτον.

tions of the divine word, I answer, "By all means, but where have we this word, 'Every child, nay, every mortal, who was not circumcised of old or washed with the water of baptism in modern times, shall be consigned to the lower regions?' For it is damnation to have been born in this condition." To the solving of this problem, I now turn (for there was a second part to this thesis)—whether the inborn corruption condemns all mortals to the woes of everlasting death?

To this question I answer without difficulty, first of all by the words of the Lord Himself, in which He foretold that as soon as man should eat of the forbidden fruit, he should straightway die. He ate; hence, he is dead. For as he became the slave of sin by transgressing, he could not beget children who were in a better condition. From a sinner we are all descended as sinners. If sinners, therefore, enemies of God; if enemies, therefore, also damned.

Again we are damned by the testimony of the prophets, of which I will content myself with a single example, Psalm 14: 2, "The Lord looked down from heaven upon the children of men, to see if there were any that did understand, and seek God. They are all gone aside, they are become unprofitable altogether." Finally, Paul in many passages and in many words touches this question, especially in the Epistle to the Romans:—"Yea, let God be true, but every man a liar" [Rom. 3: 4]. "All have sinned," that is, have become the slaves of sin and death through the guilt of the first parent. "As by one man sin entered into the world, and death by sin; and so death passed upon all men, for that all have sinned" [Rom. 5: 12], that is, have been born in sin, or, as he says in another place, "sold under sin" [Rom. 7: 14] (by pollution of birth). And that "to have sinned" and "to be dead" are used by Paul for "to be damned," he himself shows, Rom. 5: 18 [5: 16]. "For," he says, "the judgment was by one" (sin, namely) "to condemnation, but the free gift is of many offences unto justification." And a little later,* "Therefore as by the offence of one judgment came unto all men to condemnation; even so by the righteousness of one the justification of life came unto all men." As far, therefore, as the force of sin is concerned, the first man and all

*Following the reading of the Vulgate, Rom. 5: 18.

who are descended from him are damned by it.

From this answer, in which I grant that by original sin all that is born infected with it is damned, a two-fold objection arises against me, first, for what reason I said a little while ago that those ought not to be rashly damned who have not been circumcised or baptized, when they are of tender years or show by their works that the law of God is written on their hearts, while I now damn all men altogether, second, for what reason I said in the book on Baptism that original sin does not damn. To the first I answer that I have thus far spoken of the nature and force of original sin in such terms to show according to my poor ability what it is, whence it is, and what its power is; in order that we may understand thoroughly that which we are discussing. But I have not yet begun to speak about the remedy by which this disease is met. However, justly do I condemn those who, without having thoroughly studied the disease or the remedy, damn what they do not know.

Original sin damns, to be sure, so far as its force and nature are concerned, but a very present remedy saves and supports, and it has been applied not too late but just in time. We are all going to destruction through original disease, but we are on the way to restoration to safety through the remedy which God has discovered against the disease. Given over to the flesh we consider only the things of the flesh; filled with the divine Spirit we are lifted up to the things of heaven. When we speak of the nature of the flesh, all is lost and ruined, nay, deplorable and hopeless; when of the grace and light of the Spirit, all things are bright in the gladness of sure hopes. It is not strange, therefore, if I have said, that as far as the force of original sin is concerned all are damned by it, but that, since a remedy has been found which restores every thing, they are wrong who rashly damn all men. For I am going to show that this remedy has so abundantly restored all things as the disease would have ravaged all things far and wide, if it had not been checked. On this, therefore, now hear first my opinion, or rather the voice of truth.

God had said to the man, "The day thou eatest thou shalt die the death" [Gen. 2: 17]. Thus spake the true Zeus, whose orders all the things that are obey so implicitly that they would rather be destroyed than not fulfil them. The man, therefore, died, for what He had foretold had to be. Let us, then, gradually trace the death he died. It was not that death of the body or flesh which an impious but vigorous speaker might perhaps say had been better than propagating such a disaster-laden race. For he lived more than nine hundred years longer. Everlasting death, therefore, followed, as far as the deed itself and guilt are concerned, that is, he deserved not only the death of the body but everlasting death. And this his fear and the display of nakedness show. For when Adam said, "I was afraid when I heard thy voice, for I was naked" [Gen. 3: 10], he betrayed by his fear the guiltiness of his conscience which accused itself of its treachery, and in its self-love trembled at the death of which it felt itself worthy. Yet he still ventured to make up a new pretext, to deceive Him, forsooth, who knew that the man was going to do this before He created him, and said, "I am naked." What of it? He had created him naked. "Let Him see me naked," should have been his thought. But all this is the reasoning of a despairing conscience, which by its fear and vainly-sought escape admitted its damnation righteous.

We have then a transgressor and a runaway who is damned by his own judgment. For if he had not been damned in his own eyes, he would not have taken to flight. Then the goodness and mercy of the Creator brought out the remedy which it had provided before man fell. Through sinning he had deserved eternal death by the righteous judgment of God. God had determined to satisfy His righteousness by the death of His Son who cannot sin, that we might see at once most clearly His righteousness and His mercy—His mercy in that He hung upon the cross His own Son for fallen man, His righteousness in that He redeemed him at such a price, for He shows that it could not have been satisfied more cheaply. He thus enters upon the path of clemency, in order to set us the example of doing nothing rashly or impulsively:—He turns immediate death into lasting disaster; He banishes from Paradise, where all things sprang up unsown,* to a rebellious and intractable land, that what should have been at hand in a moment might be drawn forth by long toil. For this belonged to man's discipline.

But the everlasting death, for which He found no remedy

* ἄσπαρτα.

(since all things in the visible world were less than man, and all things in the invisible world were less than that price which His inviolate righteousness demanded), He remedied with His own Son. And that at just the right moment, as some prophet—(or is not a Christian poet a prophet? I say he is)—once sang, "He Himself then marked out the wood [the cross] to undo the damage of the wood" [the tree in Paradise].* Presently, when supreme wisdom saw that man was going to make shipwreck by wood, it determined to throw him wood to cling to and bring him to shore, and promised that there should be born of woman one who should bruise the head of the general enemy, for through his wiles the incautious had been ruined. And God would have been unfaithful to this promise, if no fruit of the victory had returned unto Adam. For what could it have done but increase the man's pain to know that a deliverer was to come, but he was to have no part in him?

Adam understood, therefore, that this seed was to bring salvation not only to his posterity but to himself also; yet he did not know the particular time that it was to come. Both of these statements are proved by the following testimony: Gen. 4: 1, "She [Eve] bare Cain" (and gave him this name) "and said, I have gotten a man with [the help of] the Lord," or through the Lord. In these words are seen as in a mirror the desires of the woman. "I have gotten," she says, that is, I have found, obtained, or acquired (for that is the force of the Hebrew—"I have obtained," I say) "a man"—him, that is, whom God had promised under the name of "seed,"—"with God," or "through God," that is, by the goodness of God. Here you have the view they had of the promise of God. Here also the ignorance of the time, for they thought that he was already at hand who was hardly to come after the course of many years. In the same book, 5: 28 and 29, we see the same desires in Lamech. When Noah had been born to him, he said, "This same shall

---

*The Latin verse: "Ipse lignum tunc notavit, Damna ut ligni solveret," quoted by Zwingli, is taken from a hymn in honor of the sacred cross, by Venantius Honorius Clementianus Fortunatus, who lived in the sixth century. See his Miscellanea, Lib. II, cap. 2, in Migne, *Patrologia Latina*, Vol. LXXXVIII, col. 88; also Wackernagel, *Das deutsche Kirchenlied*, Vol. I, p. 61. For the life and work of Fortunatus, see Duffield, *Latin Hymnwriters and their Hymns*, (1889), chap. IX, pp. 88-96.

comfort us concerning our work and toil of our hands," thinking likewise that it was he who had been promised, because he was the tenth and a thousand years had now passed since the creation of the world. This pious man erred twice, but innocently, for the time was not yet at hand, nor was this he who was promised, but only a type of him, as Peter witnesseth [I Pet. 3: 20-21].

My object in all this is to show that the promise made to the first mortals was carefully kept in mind by them, even if expression was given to this in few words, and that the hope or confidence they had in this seed did not deceive them. On this matter I shall speak more distinctly in the third division. I have given a foretaste of it here as far as was necessary to justify me in myself pronouncing judgment when I was forbidding others to do so. For I do not deny that the damnation of all who had come from so contaminated a source would have followed, if the goodness of God had not counteracted the evil. Since it has done so, the problem must evidently be solved in this way—we must admit the great power for damnation that sin would have had, and we must likewise recognize how much of its strength has been taken from it by the remedy which God has provided.

To the second objection I answer that I never said without qualification that original sin cannot damn. For in the book upon Baptism I bore witness that I was speaking only of the children of Christians, saying that the original guilt could not damn them. The book itself plainly bears witness to this in two passages.* Hence I was not a little surprised at the theatrical cries, "Do ye see where Zwingli is going in the matter of original sin?" and "What is this but making Christ void?" This I have added simply because I am sure about the children of Christians, that they are not damned by original sin; as to those of others I am less sure, though, to confess frankly, the view that I have taught seems to me the more probable one, that we have no right to pronounce rashly about the children even of

---

*See ed. of Schuler and Schulthess, Vol. II, 1, p. 287: "For what we say here of the original sin of children, refers to the children of believers only." Also p. 288: "Hence it is clear, contrary to all theologians, that the children of believers cannot be damned because of original sin, for they do not know the law."

Gentiles and those who do the works of the law according to the law written in their hearts by the finger of God. This conclusion, then, that the children of Christians are not damned by the original disease, I establish in the following manner:

The condition of those who are born of Christian parents is on a par with that of those who were descended from Abraham. But the original disease did not destroy these; therefore, this disease will not destroy the others, I mean ours. The first proposition I prove thus: Those who are of the same Church are under the same condition, just as those who belong to the same commonwealth, share the same fortunes. Now the Church which is made up by joining Gentiles and Jews is one and the same. Therefore the condition is one and the same. Proof of this you will find all through the Scriptures and so richly that there is no need of tarrying long in setting it forth. Christ Himself testifies that he is the cornerstone which unites the two walls, Matt. 21: 42. Again He says there is one shepherd and one fold, again, that the vineyard is the same, and He fixes equal wages for the husbandmen, even though a large part of them had come late. Again, He says, "They shall come from the east and the west, and shall sit down with the God of Abraham, of Isaac, and of Jacob."* Therefore we are joined to them, not they to us. Again, He says that peace† came to the house of Zacchaeus, because he was a son of Abraham.

Paul, in the Epistle to the Romans, ch. 11 [: 17], says that they were cut off that we might be grafted in. In Gal. 3: 7, he says, "They which are of faith, the same are the children of Abraham," and in the same chapter, "So then they which be of faith are blessed with faithful Abraham." Peter teaches the same thing, I Peter 2: 10. If, then, Abraham's faith and ours are one (for he trusted in God just as much as we do, through the seed which had been promised him, rather than because he was now at hand in whom they trusted when only promised), it is clear that the Church of both is one. The lot and condition of this Church will, therefore, also be the same.

Now the second proposition, namely, that original sin has not consigned to everlasting damnation those who were born

---

*Matt. 8: 11. The words "God of" are not in Matthew.
†Luke 19: 9 speaks of "salvation," not "peace."

of Abraham according to the promise, I establish thus:—Jacob
was beloved by God before he was born; original sin, therefore,
cannot have damned him. So Jeremiah, John and others. If
you say that this has nothing to do with the case in hand, but
concerns election and predestination, you are altogether right.
Therefore, blessedness and grace are from election, so also is
rejection, not from the participation in signs or sacraments.
But let us hasten to plainer facts. In Gen. 17: 7, God thus
speaks unto Abraham, "I will establish my covenant between
me and thee and thy seed after thee in their generations, for
an everlasting covenant, to be a God unto thee and to thy seed
after thee." If, therefore, He promises that He will be a God
to Abraham's seed, that seed cannot have been damned because
of original guilt, and He is speaking of the seed born to him
according to the promise. For between those whose God He is
and Himself there is established a friendship; if there is established a friendship, no damnation because of the condition of
birth can intervene.

Now, whatever is said of the seed according to the promise,
is to be understood of us likewise who are born of Christian
parents. For we are sons of the promise as Isaac was, Gal. 4: 28.
From the initiation by the token it is clear that the children of
the Hebrews had not been damned because of original sin. For
the token of circumcision was the token of the covenant. For
so it is considered, Gen. 17: 10-12, "This is my covenant which
ye shall keep, between me and you and thy seed after thee;
every man child among you shall be circumcised. And ye shall
circumcise the flesh of your foreskin; and it shall be a token
of the covenant betwixt me and you. And he that is eight days
old shall be circumcised among you, every man child in your
generations, he that is born in the house, or bought with
money, etc." I have quoted this passage at length because there
are many profitable things contained in it, not only for the
present argument, but for the present day, all of which I will
briefly point out. First, we see the symbol of the testament,
circumcision, called here the "covenant" or "testament." Why,
then, do we wrangle so fiercely about the cup of the Supper of
thanksgiving, which is a testament, since Christ [Luke 22: 20]
called it a "testament" in exactly the same way in which circumcision is called the "testament" here, metaphorically

namely, for the name of the thing signified is transferred to the sign. So the bread is called "the body;" the wine, "the blood;" by metonymy, because they are symbols of these.

Now it is the Hebrew habit to use frequent figures of speech more than other nations. For their language, though of meagre vocabulary, is imposing through use of tropes. Indeed, scantiness of vocabulary forces one to turn to the use of tropes, as it were. Why do we devote study to language if we are to return to the point from which we have driven the pontifical party? They refused to accept tropes when you said there was a trope in, "He that eateth my flesh" [John 6: 54], and "My flesh is meat indeed" [John 6: 55], and they kept insisting, "The words are clear, are simple, are in harmony with the sacraments of the Church." If we ourselves now cry out in the same way about the words, "This bread is my body," "We won't have a trope; the words are simple, plain, inviolable, clear as glass," are we not like unto them? Nay, why do we object so mightily to their taking literally the much clearer words, "My flesh is meat indeed" (for they include the distinguishing mark "indeed"),* when in the passage, "This is my body," we do the same thing as the pontifical crowd themselves? But of this elsewhere. This is not the place to speak more at length than I have done before of this subject of Hebrew metonymy.

Second, we see the same token called "a token of the covenant," which had just been called the "covenant." Third, it is the token of that covenant which existed between God and Abraham. Therefore, the infants were included in the covenant, for the token was given to them, that it might be an indication that they were just as much in the covenant as Abraham. Therefore, also, our children are included in the covenant just as much as they were, for we are sons of the promise, as I showed from Galatians a little while ago. Fourth, even the slaves were circumcised, whether born in the house or bought, whence we see that the household was counted with its master or lord. And this is very hard upon the Catabaptists, but they do not look to the free election of God, but think salvation is

*This point becomes still more effective if we translate the Vulgate: "My flesh is truly meat." The Greek text reads literally: "My flesh is true meat."

bound up with symbols, as the pontifical party does.

Paul says, Gal. 4: 26, "But Jerusalem which is above is free, which is the mother of us all." This mother is nothing else than the liberation through Christ. For a little later [Gal. 5: 1] he says, "Stand fast therefore in the liberty wherewith Christ hath made you* free." If, therefore, we are not made free from original sin, being born of Christian parents, the condition of those who are in Christ after the coming of Christ is worse than that of the people of old, which is even more impious than it is foolish. For Paul is not speaking of carnal liberty, but liberty from the law. And if we have been freed from the law, original sin cannot damn us, for that would damn us through the power of the law that had been transgressed. Paul likewise alludes so plainly to this idea in Rom. 11: 16, that, though treating another topic, namely the election of Jews and Gentiles, he yet seems to have held this idea of mine most distinctly when he says, "If the first fruit be holy, the lump is also holy; and if the root be holy, so are the branches." And here I am not tying up the immunity of infants from original sin with the holiness of their parents but with that of God who elects, just as among the ancients children had immunity from it, not on account of the special holiness of the lump or dough, though they were partakers in the testament, but in consequence of the goodness of God who elects and calls.

He touches upon the same point Rom. 5: 19-21, and most plainly of all, when after many things that make for this view he says at length, "For as by one man's disobedience so many of us were made sinners, so by the obedience of one shall many of us be made righteous,"† (for "where sin abounded, grace did much more abound"), "that as sin hath reigned unto death, even so might grace reign through righteousness unto eternal life by Jesus Christ."

Here I ask, whether original sin proceeded from Adam or not? If not, why is Pelagius damned? But he is rightly damned in accordance with this testimony and the others of which mention has been made above. If so, then all the evil

*The Greek text has "us" instead of "you."

†Quoted by Zwingli in a slightly different form from that found in the Revised Version.

Adam did in sinning has been made good through the grace of Christ. For the first Adam was made a living soul, but the second a quickening spirit [I Cor. 15:45]. In a word, as Adam's sin so corrupted our birth that nothing is born but what is vitiated, so Christ's righteousness has renewed it so thoroughly that the corruption does not harm us unless when we have grown up we again become faithless and ruin ourselves by our own guilt, acting in contravention of the law. For they that trust in Christ are not damned even if they have transgressed the law. How much less are they damned who are in Christ and have done no wrong! Original and actual sin must be admitted to have been made good through Christ, just as we admit it to have come about through Adam. The words are in themselves so plain that they resist much elaboration.

And here it is proper to ask whether Christ restored the whole race or only the church of the faithful? Though I might have answered this question in a few words to the effect that Christ benefited by His healing power exactly as much as Adam injured by sinning; that, further, Adam infected the whole lump with original sin, therefore Christ restored the whole, I have preferred not to put forth this opinion, both because some things seem to contradict it, and because I do not know whether anybody has held it. But I have said this only, that original sin cannot damn the children of Christians, because although sin would, to be sure, damn according to the law, it cannot damn on account of the remedy provided by Christ, especially it cannot damn those who are included in the covenant which was concluded with Abraham. About these we have other strong and clear testimony; about the others, who are born outside of the Church, we have nothing but the present testimony, so far as I know, and things similar to this fifth chapter of Romans, by which it can be proved that those who are born outside of the Church are cleansed of original pollution.

But if any one shall say in regard to these also that it is more probable that the children of the heathen are saved through Christ than that they are damned, certainly he will diminish the work of Christ less than those who damn those born within the Church, if they die without the washing of baptism, and he will have more basis and authority for his view in the Scriptures than those who deny this. For he would be maintaining nothing more than that the children even of the heathen are not damned in tender years because of the original defect, and this through the blessing of Christ, while for grown persons there was no grace left because they did not trust in Christ. But if they show by their works that the law is written in their hearts, and that without hypocrisy, then it has already been shown plainly enough that they are to be reckoned among the circumcised. For where works worthy of God are done, there the fear of God existed before. This is proved by Jethro, whose heart was so imbued with the heavenly wisdom that he was of assistance in establishing the law even to Moses who talked with God face to face [Ex. 33]; and by Cornelius the centurion, whose alms and prayers God regarded before the Gospel had been explained to him [Acts 10:31]. Should one say, therefore, that their nature had been renewed through Christ, these things that I have said would follow. If, on the other hand, only the Church is restored, it will follow that salvation through Christ does not extend so widely as the ravages of the disease that began with Adam. For no one, I think, denies that the children of the heathen are just as much born with inclination to sin as our children. But however the case may be with the children of the heathen (for one might maintain, and perhaps rightly, that the words of Paul, "Where sin abounded, grace did much more abound," and "as sin hath reigned unto death, even so grace reigneth unto eternal life by Jesus Christ" [Rom. 5:20] and the like, were said by synecdoche and are not to be understood of others than the faithful and their children, and, therefore, I also attribute liberation from original sin to them only, leaving others to the judgment of God), so be it that we poor mortals in our boldness consign to everlasting death some about whom we have no clear word of God; are they on that account really damned?

This point also arises:—If a heathen shows by the works of the law that the law is written in his heart, and Paul really prefers him to the circumcised, then the office of faith is done away with and everything comes back to works. To this I answer, that Paul presupposes that he who does the works of the law, does them in consequence of faith, for he wrestles with the fact that many boasted the faith of Abraham on the ground that they had been circumcised. He is proving that they have not faith if they do not the works of faith, and so also is James to be understood. On the other hand, he argues that if the uncircumcised doeth, in consequence of faith to be sure (for who could approve what is done from hypocrisy?), the works which the law orders, he shows clearly that the fear of God is written in his heart [Rom. 2:29]. He demands, therefore, faith before all things. And he says this "is not of him that willeth, nor of him that runneth, but of God that sheweth mercy" [Rom. 9:16]. Therefore, the fear of God and piety,* as well as holiness, are not bound up with signs, although it is fitting that those who have been taught should not be without the signs, that they may give evidence to the rest as to whom they have given their allegiance, and be enrolled in the unity of the Church.

This point must not be passed over, either, that whether our children only or those of the heathen also, if that view should prevail, are altogether restored in nature through Christ as far as the original pollution is concerned, they are in the state of innocence as long as they are too young to know the law, as I have unhesitatingly maintained, relying for support upon the authority of Paul to the Romans, 4:15, "For where no law is, there is no transgression." And those of tender years who know not the law are just as much without the law as Paul was. Therefore, they do not transgress, and consequently are not damned. And Paul says, Rom. 7:9, that he was alive without the law once, but that is to be understood of no part of his life except infancy and boyhood. At that time, therefore, sin was dead to him. But when the law had come to life, he testifies that he died. In the same way, we ourselves do not sin, as long as we are ignorant of the law because of our age, but when the light of the law has shone upon us, we become liable to it. And if faith is in us we cease not to strive for what the law orders, and at the same time failing in all our efforts cry, "Forgive us our debts," and cling with sure confidence to the Lord, who pardoneth all things through His Son.

Now I will come to the last part of the discussion, in which I undertook to prove this thesis, that the original defect is removed only by the blood of Christ and cannot be removed

---

* εὐσέβεια.

by the washing of baptism. The first part I establish thus:—
The ancients thought of everything in symbols; especially was
this the case with the varied ritual of the animal sacrifices, the
mysterious symbol of the universal sacrifice which was to complete the old order in its consummation, as Daniel foretells
more clearly than the other prophets, chapters 9 and 12. [Dan.
9:27; 12:11]. But in these sacrifices soundness and cleanness
were the first requisites demanded. When, therefore, God says
plainly in various passages of the prophets that He is not pleased
with these offerings, it is clear that the cleanness of the animals
signified nothing else than that the sacrifice which was to cleanse
our consciences must be absolutely clean. But what created
thing is so clean that it can be made a sacrifice for the unclean in
the sight of the Supreme Good, or that it would not have become
unclean by the very fact of having been offered in sacrifice for
sinners? For the sacrifice had to be voluntary and free, as the
free offerings of old fore-shadowed, and Paul in the Letter to
the Hebrews, 10 [:1] teaches. Adam also had sinned volun-
tarily. Since, therefore, no created thing could without arrogance take this upon itself, it is manifest that the divine
righteousness could not have been reconciled by anything but
the Son of God who had created man, that he might be restored
through Him by whom he had been made.

The first essential for a physician is knowledge of the
disease he is to cure, as nobody denies. When, therefore, the
soul of man was sick, none could apply a remedy to it save one
who accurately understood the disease. And this none could do
but God. For He alone knoweth the heart of the sons of man,
III Kings* 8:39. The human heart, therefore, could be
restored to health through no other physician or medicine than
God.

When the divine Baptist says [John 1:29], "Behold the
lamb that taketh away the sins of the world," he shows plainly
that there is nothing else whatever that can atone for the world
but this lamb. For this is what he means.

Finally the Truth itself bears witness that He had to die.

*III Kings in Vulgate, but I Kings in English Version. In the
Septuagint and the Vulgate the books of Samuel are counted as I and II
Kings.

Since, therefore, He had to die, no other could in any way remedy the evil. Thus Matth. 26: 24 says, "The Son of man goeth as it is written of him." In the same chapter, "thus it must be." Luke 24: 26, "Ought not Christ to have suffered these things, and to enter into his glory?" Mark 8: 31, "The Son of man must suffer." John 3: 14 and 15, "The Son of man must be lifted up; that whosoever believeth in him should not perish, but have eternal life." Divine Providence, therefore, determined to reconcile the world to Himself through His own Son. Let it be, therefore, a sacrilege to inquire whether the thing could have been accomplished by other means or another author.

From this it is easily proved that absolutely no sin is taken away by the washing of baptism. For Christ the Lamb taketh away the sins of the world. And I John 2: 2, cries out thus: "He is the propitiation for our sins; and not for ours only, but also for the sins of the whole world." Also chapter 1: 7, "The blood of Jesus Christ his son cleanseth us from all sin." He who says, "from all," omits nothing. The blood, therefore, cleanseth from original sin also, not the washing of baptism. If we had not divine testimony to this, yet it would be witnessed to by the spirit, the water, and the blood, of which I John 5: 5-8 speaks thus: "Who is he that overcometh the world, but he that believeth that Jesus is the Son of God? This is he that came by water and blood, even Jesus Christ; not by water only, but by water and blood. And it is the Spirit that beareth witness, because the Spirit is truth. For there are three that bear witness —the spirit, and the water, and the blood; and these three are one." The water, therefore, that is, the heavenly teaching which the Spirit maketh to grow in our hearts that we may trust in the blood of Christ, shows well enough that these external things cannot cleanse the conscience. Otherwise the death of Christ were superfluous, if by corporeal things the incorporeal substance of the soul could be purified. And we have witness to this view in Paul's Letter to the Hebrews, 9: 9 and 10, "Which was a figure for the time then present, in which were offered both gifts and sacrifices, that could not make him that did the service perfect, as pertaining to the conscience; which stood only in meats and drinks, and divers washings, and carnal ordinances, imposed on them until the time of reformation." By these words of the apostle we see clearly that such externals have no efficacy towards perfecting the conscience.

Yet this must be noted at the same time, that baptism is sometimes used for the blood or passion of Christ. This, again, by metonymy, the name of the sign being transferred to the thing signified, for metonymy is a transposition of names. For instance, when I Peter 3: 20 and 21 teaches that we are saved through baptism in the same way that men were saved of old in the ark, we are not to understand, by heaven, the washing of baptism, but Christ Himself or His blood and death, for by these we have been redeemed, as the apostle himself immediately explains. We see here again incidentally the sign used for that of which it is the sign. How foolish, therefore, would any one seem, who because of these words should maintain that we were washed clean of our sins by the baptismal waters! Thus, consequently, what is said in Eph. 5: 26 of the washings of water by the word, and in Romans 6: 3 and 4, is not to be taken literally, but the force of these figurative expressions is to be judged by faith and our knowledge of heavenly things.

And this also we ought not to suffer to go unnoticed, that baptism is the sign of the Church of Christ, just as an army has its sign; not that this sign unites one to the Church, but that he who is already united to it receives the public badge, just as no one is enrolled in an army because he has the sign upon him (otherwise enemies and traitors, who sometimes exchange signs by stratagem, would belong to the army), but he who has been already enrolled in the army is thought worthy of a public sign that all men may see that he has promised allegiance to that leader under whom he has agreed to serve. We have fine proof of this view in Acts 2: 44 and 45, "And all that believed were together, and had all things common; and sold their possessions and goods, and parted them to all men, as every man had need," etc. But those who were together in this fashion, had already heard preaching and had been baptized. There is no doubt that their children also were with them. Otherwise those first fruits of the faithful would have been wilder than wild beasts. This gives me a two-fold argument, first, that these children were reckoned with the Church just as much as their parents; second, that they were baptized equally with their parents, of which more another time.

Furthermore, that by baptism nothing is achieved but the marking with a sign him who is counted a member of the Church, is effectively testified to by what Paul writes in I Cor. 10:1-4, "All our fathers were under the cloud, and all passed through the sea; and were all baptized unto Moses in the cloud and in the sea; and did all eat the same spiritual meat; and did all drink the same spiritual drink," etc. Now, it is an accepted fact that they were not initiated with the same rite of baptism which we use. When, therefore, he says that they were baptized by the cloud and the sea, it is manifest that baptism has no more power towards our justification than the sea and cloud had towards theirs. Those who had come out of Egypt and were in the congregation of the people of God were moistened by these waters; in like manner those who through Christ have come out of the bondage of the Devil are washed with the water of baptism. For St. Augustine proves* that they had different signs from ours but the same faith. Signs, therefore, are nothing but externals, by which nothing is effected in the conscience, but faith is the only thing through which we are blessed—that faith which clings truly and firmly to the promises of God. The external things, therefore, are symbols of spiritual things, but they are by no means themselves spiritual, nor do they perfect anything spiritual in us, but they are the badges, as it were, of those who are of the spirit.

I had purposed to put all this together more carefully than time allowed. The nearness of the market-time has forced me to hurry, and that habit of postponing things, by which countless occupations crowd all that I write into some brief moment, in which then I have to fulfil all of a sudden what I have promised.

I will, therefore, sum up in a few words by way of conclusion. This is my view in regard to original sin, that it is a defect and disease, which was inflicted upon our first parents as a penalty. Their progeny is so polluted by their transgression that whatever is born of them has inclination to sin, and, unless

---

*This thought is found in Augustine's Homilies on the Gospel of John, Tract 45, §9: "See then how that while the faith remained, the signs were varied. There the rock was Christ; to us that is Christ which is placed on the altar of God. . . . Under different signs there is the same faith." See Schaff, *Nicene Fathers*, First Series, VII, 252.

Divine Clemency had provided for an effective remedy at the right moment, all who have been born from that source would have perished. The goodness of God, therefore, met this catastrophe through the death of His own Son, so that, although the remnants of original sin, namely the disposition to self-love,* cling tenaciously to us, yet they cannot harm those who are in Christ Jesus. For original sin cannot damn in any other way than the law does, and that can damn no more, even if we sometimes sin, for "there is now no condemnation to them which are in Christ Jesus," Rom. 8: 1.

Our birth is, to be sure, contaminated by inclination to sin, but the contamination harmeth not, for its poison has been taken from it through Christ. And in Christ are not only the parents whom Divine Mercy has brought into the light and grace of faith, but also their children, no less than those who were born of Abraham according to the promise. For the faith is the same and the testament or covenant the same as far as the inner man is concerned. For those men of old leaned upon the mercy of God through the promise of Christ just as much as we do now that He has appeared. He, therefore, by His blood so thoroughly atoned for whatever could damn that there is nothing left that can exercise tyranny over us—not the flesh, nor the law, nor the Devil, the Prince of this World. So completely also did He obtain all things from the Father by His death that whatever we ask in His name is granted. Hence no created thing ought to be worshipped or held in such esteem as if it had any power for the cleansing of our consciences or the salvation of souls. And all this I hold in such a way that if any man shall convict me of manifest error by the testimony of the really Holy Scriptures, I am determined not only to let myself be torn from my error, but to be grateful to him who shall tear me from it.

This is what for some time, most learned Urbanus, I have been turning over in my mind about original sin. I have at times also looked into the ancient writers on this matter, but how dark and involved their utterances are, not to say, based upon human rather than celestial teaching, I think you also will remark when you go to them again. I have had no leisure to go back to them for several years. For on what testimony of

* φιλαυτία.

Scripture, pray, does it rest that by baptism original sin is taken away or grace conferred, unless under the symbol of baptism you understand Christ who is symbolized by it? For in Him are all things saved unto us. How much harsher is it that the children of Christians, if they have not been baptized, are irretrievably doomed to everlasting damnation, and that without any authority from Scripture! For how much I ask do the Scriptures which they twist differ from this their opinion!

Let us, then, I beg, preach Christian piety with solicitude and purity, and let us not be prematurely troubled as to the abolition of the mass or the casting out of the images, but let us labor to restore to their Creator the hearts that are given over to this world. The mass has fallen already; the images will, I think, disappear of their own motion. For we shall banish in vain one or the other unless public piety ratify the decree. And when that shall be done, all the princes of the world will try in vain to restore them. For they will get no spoil except to run against some wall like Balaam and hit their feet rather sharply. For he lieth not who said "him that falleth upon this stone it shall break, but upon whom it shall fall it shall grind him to powder" [Matth. 21: 44]. We must so live under God's protection secure and undaunted that if the world should break into fragments the ruins would strike us unafraid. How many of the heathen do we see honored and glorified by that death from which we all flee when life is prosperous, but for which all call when life is dark! For they have met nobly what in the belief of the crowd is the bitterest of all things. And shall we hesitate, we the soldiers of a commander so faithful and so devoted to us that He threw himself into the danger before us, especially when our hopes look not to the empty gain of winning a name but to the possession of an everlasting inheritance of no mean order, unless those things are trifles which God has given us in His only begotten Son? For we are co-heirs with Him.

Let us, therefore, fight vigorously and prudently on a fair field, for we are defending a most righteous cause, in which we feel sure there is no hidden wrong. Let them hurl upon us from the hostile camp those soldiers' insults—"traitors," "robbers," "weaklings." Let us care nothing for them, trusting completely to our cause. Things have come, alas, to such a pitch of boldness that we accuse others of that of which we are ourselves chiefly guilty, by a beautiful anthypophora,* *i. e.,* a reply made to a hypothetical objection, anticipating what can fairly be hurled at ourselves, that our enemy may be kept busy caring for his wounds and have no time to strike back. But though such weapons are sharp, they do not penetrate any more than the beards of grain, than which nothing is sharper and at the same time less effective.

Do you, dear Brother in the Lord, take all this in kind and good part. Let us pray the Lord for each other, that He finish His work which He has begun, and so strengthen our hearts that we shall nowhere lack His glory. Farewell, and greet Rana and Agricola,† whom I am so far from wishing any ill that I anxiously implore the Lord to make their ministry faithful in the Gospel and sustain them.

ZURICH, August 15th, 1526.

* ἀνθυποφορά, is lit. something put up against (ἀντί) an excuse or ob- jection (ὑποφορά).

†Both of them preachers at Nuremberg, along with Rhegius, and devoted to Luther. Rana's real name was John Frosch.

II.

An Account of the Faith of Huldreich Zwingli Submitted to the German Emperor Charles V, at the Diet of Augsburg.

(July 3, 1530)

[AD CAROLVM | ROMANORVM IMPERATO- | rem Germaniae comi- tia Augustae cele- | brantem, Fidei Huldrychi | Zwinglij ratio.| Then a woodcut of the Emperor Charles. Below: VENITE AD ME OMNES QVI LABORATIS | et onerati estis, et ego reficiam uos. | Anno M.D. XXX. Mense Julio. | Vincat ueritas. | At the end (p. 39) Tigvri apvd Chri- | stophorum Froschouer. | 40 unnumbered quarto pages. Signed, p. 39: Tiguri, tertio die Julij, M.D. XXX. A copy of this edition is in the library of Union Theological Seminary, New York. A second Latin edition of 72 octavo pages appeared in 1530, signed: Tiguri, XXVII. die Augusti. Anno M.D. XXX. Two German editions of 52 unnumbered octavo pages appeared also in 1530, the first entitled: *Zu Karoln Römischen Kei-* | *ser, jetzund vff dem Rychstag zu Augsburg,* | *Bekenntnuss des Gloubens, durch* | *Huldrich Zuinglium.* | Then a woodcut of Charles V. Below the verse: *Kummend zu mir alle die arbeitend vnd beladen sind, vñ* | *ich wil üch ruw geben. Christus Matth. XI.* | *Die Warheyt sol den sig haben.* | Signed at the end, p. 51: *Getrukt zu Zürich by Christoffel Froschouer.* Finsler, *Zwingli Bibliographie,* Nos. 92-93. A modern German translation appeared in R. Christoffel's, *Huldreich Zwingli,* (1857) Vol. II, pp. 237-262; an abbre- viated translation in modern German in *Ulrich Zwingli, Eine Auswahl aus seinen Schriften,* Zürich, 1917, pp. 739-757. An early English translation was published at Zurich in 1543. Its title is as follows: "The Rekening and de- | claracion of the faith and beleif of Huldrik | Zwingly, bischoppe of Züryk the cheif | town of Heluetia, sent to Charles V. that | nowe is Emprowr of Rome: holdinge a | Perlemente or Cownsaill at Aus- | brough with the cheif Lordis & | lerned men of Germanye. | The yere of our Lorde | M.D.XXX. In the | monethe of | Julye. | Come ye to me all that labour, & | ar laden: and I shall refres- | she you. Mathe. XI. | The verite will haue the victory : | Presse ye it down neuer so strongly. | Translated & Imprynted at | Züryk in Marche Anno | Do. M.D.XLIII. | 68 unnumbered small quarto pages, of which five are "The Preface of the

translatour, unto the reader." It concludes with five pages of "The com-
playninge Prayer of the pore persecuted maryed Preistis with their wyues
& Children chased owte of Englond into sondry places of Germanye : cry-
ing vnto God in their harde desolate exyle and greuouse affliccion." A
copy of this edition is in the library of Union Theological Seminary, New
York City. A later English rendering by Thomas Cotsford appeared in
Geneva in 1555.

The following English translation is based on that of Prof. Dr. H. E.
Jacobs, in his *Book of Concord*, Vol. II, pp. 159-179. It was revised
throughout by the editor.

When Charles V. had concluded peace with the king of France and the
Pope, he held, in the summer of 1530, the Diet of Augsburg, which was of
fundamental importance for the Reformation in Germany. At this Diet a
confession of faith, known as the "Augustana," which had been written by
Melanchthon and signed by the Protestant princes of Germany, was submitted to the emperor on June 25, 1530. The feeling against the adherents
of Reformed principles was so strong that neither the Catholics nor the
Lutherans would have anything to do with them. On June 23, Bucer wrote
to Zwingli: "Nothing more intolerant can be imagined than the hatred
which the Lutherans have against us." Hence the Reformed cities of South
Germany were compelled to hand in a separate confession of faith. In the
name of Strassburg, Constance, Memmingen and Lindau, Bucer and Capito
drew up a confession, known as the "Tetrapolitana," which was handed to
the emperor on July 11th. Jacob Sturm had sent Zwingli a copy of the
Augsburg Confession on May 31st, and he had expressed the hope that
Zwingli would also submit to the emperor a confession and defense, in
which he would "as piously as possible and without offending anybody
give an account of his faith." The harsh condemnation of the Reformed
faith by Melanchthon made such a statement seem even more necessary.
On June 28th, Sturm repeated his suggestion and added: "Who knows but
that in this way the emperor may be led to see the truth, which has been
wrongly represented thus far by the Papists" (Zwingli's *Werke*, VIII, 359,
469). As there was no time to assemble the Protestant Cantons of Switzerland and as silence might be open to misconstruction, Zwingli was compelled
to compose a confession in his own name, which he did in three days. He
sent it to Augsburg by special messenger. It was handed to the emperor
not by one of Zwingli's friends, but by a most violent opponent, the provost
of Waldkirch, who was then Bishop Designate of Constance (Zwingli's
Werke, VIII, 477). This was on July 8th, five days after it came from
the press. About this event Bucer and Capito wrote to Strassburg, on
July 12, 1530: "On the 8th day of July Zwingli's manly confession of
faith was handed to the emperor by a special messenger." The Diet paid
no attention to it, the emperor probably never read a line of it. The
Lutherans belittled it, while John Eck, the Catholic theologian made it
the occasion of a violent attack.]

[AN ACCOUNT OF THE FAITH OF HULDREICH ZWINGLI
SUBMITTED TO THE ROMAN EMPEROR CHARLES]

We who are preaching the Gospel in the cities of a Christian State,* were anxiously awaiting, O Charles, holy Emperor of justice, the time when an account of our faith, which we both have and confess, would be asked of us also.

While we are standing in readiness for this, there comes to us the report, more by rumor than by definite announcement, that many have already prepared an outline and summary of their religion and faith, which they are offering you. Here we are in a great dilemma† ; for, on the one hand, love of truth and desire for public peace urge us all the more to do ourselves what we see others doing; but, on the other hand, the shortness of the time deters us, not only because all things must be done very speedily and as it were superficially, on account of your haste, (for this also rumor announces) ; but also because we, who are acting as preachers of the Divine Word in the cities and country districts of the State already mentioned, are settled and separated too far apart to be able to assemble in so brief a time, and deliberate as to what is most fitting to write to your Highness. Moreover, as we have already seen the confession of the others and even their refutation by their opponents, which seem to have been prepared even before a demand was made for them, I believed that it would not be improper if I alone should forthwith submit an account of my faith, without anticipating the judgment of my people. For if in any business one must make haste slowly, here we must certainly make haste swiftly, since by handling this matter with careless neglect we run into the danger of being suspected because of silence or of being arrogant because of negligence.

To you then, O Emperor, I offer a summary of my faith, with this condition, that at the same time I declare solemnly, that I entrust and permit the judgment not only of these articles,

*Zwingli refers to Zurich, Berne and Basle, in whose name he writes.
†Literally: "Between the sacrifice and the stone of slaughter," a Latin idiom which means: "We are in a great dilemma." For the Latin adage, *inter sacrum et saxum stare*, used by Plautus and other Latin writers, see Desiderii Erasmi *Collectanea Adagiorum Veterum*, chil. I, cent. I, No. 15, in his *Opera*, Leyden 1703, Vol. II, p. 33.

but of all that I have ever written or, by the grace of God, shall yet write, not to one man only, nor to a few merely, but to the whole Church of God, as far as it speaks by the command and inspiration of the Word and Spirit of God.

First of all, I both believe and know that God is one and He alone is God, and that He is by nature good, true, powerful, just, wise, the Creator and Preserver of all things, visible and invisible; that Father, Son and Holy Spirit are indeed three persons, but that their essence is one and single. And I think altogether in accordance with the Creed, the Nicene and also the Athanasian, in all their details concerning the Godhead himself, the names or the three persons.

I believe and understand that the Son assumed flesh, the human nature, indeed the whole man, consisting of body and soul, which He truly assumed of the immaculate and perpetual virgin Mary; but this in such a manner, that the whole man was so assumed into the unity of the hypostasis or person of the Son of God, that the man did not constitute a separate person, but was assumed into the inseparable, indivisible and indissoluble person of the Son of God. And, although both natures, the divine and the human, have so preserved their character and peculiarity that both are truly and naturally found in Him, yet the distinct peculiarities and activities of the natures do not separate the unity of the person any more than in man soul and body constitute two persons. For as these are of the most diverse nature, so they function by diverse peculiarities and operations; nevertheless man, who consists of them, is not two persons, but one. So God and man is one in Christ,* the Son of God from eternity and the Son of Man from the time appointed†; one person, one Christ; perfect God and perfect man‡; not because one nature becomes the other, or because the natures are fused together, but because each remains its peculiar self; and yet, the unity of this person is not broken by this retention of the peculiarities.

Hence one and the same Christ, according to the character of the human nature, cries in infancy, grows, increases in wisdom

---

*Quoted from the Athanasian Creed, art. 37; see Schaff, *Creeds of Christendom*, II, 69.

†*I. e.*, from the time of his birth.

‡Quoted from the Athanasian Creed, art. 32.

[Luke 2:52], hungers, thirsts, eats, drinks, is warm, is cold, is scourged, sweats, is wounded, is cruelly slain, fears, is sad and endures what else pertains to the penalty and punishment of sin, though from sin itself He is most remote. But according to the peculiarity of the divine nature, with the Father He controls the highest and the lowest [*i. e.*, heaven and earth], he pervades, sustains and preserves all things, gives sight to the blind, restores the lame, calls to life the dead, prostrates His enemies with His word, when dead resumes life, ascends to heaven and sends from His home the Holy Spirit. All these things, however diverse in nature and character, the one and the same Christ does, remaining the one person of the Son of God, in such a way that even those things that pertain to His divine nature are sometimes ascribed, on account of the unity and perfection of the person, to the human nature, and those things that pertain to the human nature are sometimes attributed to the divine. He said that He was the Son of Man in heaven, [John 3:13], although He had not yet ascended into heaven with the body. Peter asserts that Christ suffered for us [I Peter 2:21], when the humanity alone could suffer. But on account of the unity of the person it is truly said both that: "The Son of God suffered" [Lk. 9:22], and that "the Son of Man forgives sins" [Mk. 2:10]. For He who is the Son of God and of man in one person suffered, according to the peculiar quality of His human nature; and He who is the Son of God and of man in one person forgives sins, according to the peculiar quality of the divine nature.

It is just as when we say that a man is wise, although he consists of body no less than soul, and the body has nothing to do with wisdom, nay rather is a poison and an impediment to knowledge and intelligence; and again we say that man is torn with wounds, when his body alone can receive wounds, but his soul in no way. Here no one says that two persons are made of the man, when to each part that is attributed which belongs to it; and vice versa no one says that the two natures are fused when that is predicated of the entire man which, because of the unity of the person, belongs indeed to the entire man, but because of the peculiar qualities of the parts to one only. Paul says: "When I am weak, then I am strong" [II Cor. 12:10]. But who is it that is weak? Paul. Who at the same time is truly strong? Paul. But is not this contradictory, inconsistent, intolerable? Not at all. For Paul is not one nature, although one person. When, therefore, he says, "I am weak," the person who speaks is undoubtedly Paul, but what he says is neither predicated nor understood of both natures, but of the weakness of the flesh only. And when he says, "I am strong and well," undoubtedly the person of Paul speaks, but only the soul is meant. So the Son of God dies, He who according to the unity and simplicity of His person, undoubtedly is both God and man; yet He dies only with respect to His humanity. Thus not I alone do believe, but all the orthodox, whether ancient or modern, did likewise so believe regarding the deity, the divine persons as well as the assumed human nature. So also believe those who today acknowledge the truth.

SECONDLY—I know that this supreme Deity, which is my God, freely determines all things, so that His counsel does not depend upon the contingency of any creature. For it is peculiar to defective human wisdom to reach a decision because of preceding discussion or example. God, however, who from eternity to eternity surveys the universe with a single, simple look, has no need of any reasoning process or waiting for events; but being equally wise, prudent, good, etc., He freely determines and disposes of all things, for whatever is, is His. Hence it is that, although having knowledge and wisdom, He in the beginning formed man who should fall, but at the same time determined to clothe in human nature His Son, who should restore him when fallen. For by this means His goodness was in every way manifested.

Since this goodness contained mercy and justice within it, He exercised justice when He expelled the transgressor from the happy home of Paradise, when He bound him to the mill of human misery and by fetters of disease, when He shackled him with the law, which, although it was holy, he was never able to fulfil. Here, twice miserable, man learned that not only his flesh had fallen into tribulation, but that his mind also was tortured by the dread of the law he had transgressed. For he saw that, according to its intent, the law is holy and just and a declaration of the divine mind, so that it enjoined nothing but what equity taught, yet he saw at the same time that by his deeds he could not satisfy the intent of the law. Being thus condemned by his own judgment, having abandoned all hope of attaining happiness, and departing in despair from God's sight, he had no prospect but that of enduring the pains of eternal punishment. All this was a manifestation of the justice of God.

Then, when the time came to reveal His goodness, which He had determined from eternity to display no less than His justice, God sent His Son to assume our nature in every part, except as far as it inclined to sin, in order that, being our brother and equal, He could be a mediator, to make a sacrifice for us to divine justice, which must remain holy and inviolate, no less than to His goodness. Thereby the world might be sure both of the appeasing of the justice and of the presence of the goodness of God. For since He has given His Son to us and for us, how will He not with Him and because of Him give us all things [Rom. 8: 32]? What is it that we ought not to promise ourselves from Him, who so far humbled himself as not only to be our equal but also to be altogether ours? Who can sufficiently marvel at the riches and grace of the divine goodness, whereby He so loved the world, *i. e.*, the human race, as to give up His Son for its life [John 3: 16].

This I regard as the heart and life of the Gospel; this is the only medicine for the fainting soul, whereby it is restored to God and itself. For none but God himself can give it the assurance of God's grace. But now God has liberally, abundantly and wisely lavished it upon us that nothing further remains which could be desired; unless someone would dare to seek something that is beyond the highest and beyond overflowing abundance.

THIRDLY—I know that there is no other victim for expiating sin than Christ (for not even was Paul crucified for us); no other pledge of divine goodness and mercy more certain and undisputable (for nothing is as certain as God); no other name under heaven whereby we must be saved than that of Jesus Christ [Acts 4: 12]. Hence there is left neither justification nor satisfaction based on our works, nor any expiation nor intercession of all saints, whether on earth or in heaven, who live by the goodness and mercy of God. For this is the one, sole Mediator between God and men, the God-man Christ Jesus. But the election of God remains firm and unchangeable. Those whom He elected before the foundation of the world He elected in such a manner as to make them His own through His Son; for as He is kind and merciful, so also is He holy and just. All His works, therefore, savor of mercy and justice. Hence His election also justly savors of both. It is goodness to elect whom He will; it is justice to make the elect His own and to unite them to Himself through His son, who for us has become the victim to satisfy divine justice.

FOURTHLY—I know that our primeval ancestor and first parent, through self-love, at the pernicious advice suggested to him by the malice of Satan, was induced to desire equality with God. When he had determined upon this crime, he took of the forbidden and fatal fruit, whereby he incurred the guilt of the sentence of death, having become an enemy and a foe of his God. Although He could therefore have destroyed him, as justice demanded, nevertheless, being better disposed, God so changed the penalty as to make a slave of him whom He could have punished with death. This condition neither Adam himself nor anyone born of him could remove, for a slave can beget nothing but a slave. Thus through his fatal tasting of the fruit he cast all of his posterity into slavery.

Hence I think of original sin as follows: An act is called sin when it is committed against the law; for where there is no law there is no transgression, and where there is no trangression there is no sin in the proper sense, since sin is plainly an offense, a crime, a misdeed or guilt. I confess, therefore, that our father [Adam] committed what was truly a sin, namely an atrocious deed, a crime, an impiety. But his descendants have not sinned in this manner, for who among us crushed with his teeth the forbidden apple in Paradise? Hence, willing or unwilling, we are forced to admit that original sin, as it is in the children of Adam, is not properly sin, as has been explained; for it is not a misdeed contrary to law. It is, therefore, properly a disease and condition— a disease, because just as he fell through self-love, so do we also; a condition, because just as he became a slave and liable to death, so also are we born slaves and children of wrath [Eph. 2: 3] and liable to death. However, I have no objection to this disease and condition being called, after the habit of Paul, a sin; indeed it is a sin inasmuch as those born therein are God's enemies and opponents, for they are drawn into it by the condition of birth, not by the perpetration of a definite crime, except as far as their first parent has committed one.

The true cause, therefore, of discord with God and of death is the crime and offense committed by Adam, and this is truly sin. But that sin which attaches to us is in reality a disease and condition, involving indeed the necessity of death. Nevertheless, this would never have taken place through birth alone, unless sin had vitiated birth; hence the cause of human misery is sin and not birth; birth only in as far as it follows from this source and cause. This opinion can be supported by authority and example. Paul in Romans 5: 6 [read 5: 17] says: "If by one man's sin* death reigned by one, much more," etc. Here we see that the word "sin" is properly used. For Adam is the one by whose fruit death hangs upon our shoulders. In chapter 3: 23 he says: "For all have sinned and come short of the glory of God," i. e., the goodness and liberality of God. Here sin is understood as a disease, condition and birth, so that we all are said to sin even before we come forth to the light, i. e., we are in the condition of sin and death, even before we sin in act. This opinion is irrefutably strengthened by the words of the same writer, Rom. 5: 14, "Death reigned from Adam to Moses, even over them that had not sinned after the similitude of Adam's transgression." See, death is our lot, even though we have not sinned as Adam. Why? Because he sinned. But why does death destroy us when we have not sinned in this way? Because he died on account of sin and, having died, i. e., being condemned to death, he begat us. Therefore we also die, by his guilt indeed, yet by our own condition and disease, or if you prefer, by our sin, improperly so called. The example [we spoke of] is as follows: A prisoner of war by his perfidy and hostile conduct has deserved to be held as a slave. His descendants become serfs or slaves of their master, not by their own fault, guilt or crime, but by their condition which was the result of guilt; for their parent of whom they were born had merited it by his crime. The children have no crime, but the punishment and requital of a crime—namely a condition, servitude and the workhouse.

If it please some one to call these a crime, because they are

---

*The Vulgate has "unius delicto," hence the Authorized Version "by one man's offence." The Greek text reads: τῷ τοῦ ἑνὸς παραπτώματι, hence the Revised Version translates: "By the trespass of one."

suffered for a crime, I do not object. I acknowledge that this original sin, through condition and contagion, belongs by birth to all who are born from the love of man and woman; and I know that we are by nature children of wrath, but I doubt not that we are received among the sons of God by grace, which through the second Adam, Christ, has repaired the fall. This takes place in the following manner:

FIFTHLY—It is evident, if in Christ, the second Adam, we are restored to life, as in the first Adam we were delivered to death, that in condemning children born of Christian parents, nay even the children of heathen, we act rashly. For if Adam by sinning could ruin the entire race, and Christ by His death did not quicken and redeem the entire race from the calamity inflicted by the former, then the salvation conferred by Christ is no longer a match for sin. Moreover (which God forbid) the word is not true: "As in Adam all die, even so in Christ shall all be made alive" [I Cor. 15: 22]. But, whatever must be the decision about the children of heathen, this we must certainly maintain that, in view of the efficacy of the salvation procured through Christ, those go astray who pronounce them subject to an eternal curse, not only on account of Christ's reparation already mentioned, but also on account of God's free election, which does not follow faith, but faith follows election, about which see the following article. For those who have been elected from eternity have undoubtedly been elected before faith. Therefore those who because of their age have not faith, should not be rashly condemned by us; for although they do not as yet have it, yet God's election is hidden from us. If before Him they are elect, we judge rashly about things unknown to us. However, regarding the children of Christians we judge differently —namely, that all children of Christians belong to the church of God's people and are parts and members of His Church. This we prove in the following way: It has been promised by the testimonies of almost all the prophets that the Church is to be gathered from the heathen into the Church of the people of God. Christ himself said: "They shall come from the east and west, and shall sit down with Abraham, Isaac and Jacob" [Matth. 8: 11], and, "Go ye into all the world," etc. [Matth. 28: 19]. But to the Church of the Jews their infants belonged as much as the Jews themselves. No less, therefore, belong our infants to the Church of Christ than did, in former times, those of the Jews; for if it were otherwise the promise would not be valid, as then we would not sit down with God on the same terms as Abraham. For he, with those who were born of him according to the flesh, was counted as in the Church. But if our infants were not thus counted with the parents, Christ would be sordid and envious towards us in denying us what He had given to the ancients, which it would be impious to say. If it were not so with our children, the entire prophecy regarding the call of the Gentiles would be void. Therefore, since the infants of Christians no less than the adults, are members of the visible Church of Christ, it is evident that they no less than the parents are of the number of those whom we judge elect. How godlessly and presumptuously do those judge who surrender to perdition the infants of Christians, when so many clear testimonies of Scripture contradict it, which promise not merely an equal but even a larger Church from the Gentiles compared with that of the Jews. All this will be plainer when we expound our faith concerning the Church.

SIXTHLY—Of the Church, therefore, we thus think, namely, that the word "Church" in the Scriptures is to be taken in various meanings. It is used for the elect, who have been predestined by God's will to eternal life. Of this church Paul speaks when he says that it has neither wrinkle or spot [Eph. 5: 27]. This is known to God alone, for according to the word of Solomon [Prov. 15: 11], He alone knows the hearts of the children of men. Nevertheless those who are members of this church, since they have faith, know that they themselves are elect and are members of this first church, but are ignorant about members other than themselves. For thus it is written in Acts [13: 48]: "And as many as were ordained to eternal life believed." Those, therefore, that believe are ordained to eternal life. But no one, save he who believes, knows who truly believe. He is already certain that he is elect of God. For, according to the apostle's word [II Cor. 1: 22], he has the seal of the Spirit, by which, pledged and sealed, he knows that he has become truly free, a son of the family, and not a slave. For the Spirit cannot deceive. If He tells us that God is our Father, and we confidently and fearlessly call Him Father, untroubled because we shall enter upon the eternal inheritance, then it is certain that God's Spirit has been shed abroad in our hearts. It is therefore settled that he is elect who has this security and certainty, for they who believe are ordained to eternal life. Yet many are elect who as yet have no faith. For the mother of God [Mary], John and Paul, did not believe while infants, and yet they were elect, even before the foundation of the world. But this they knew not, either through faith or revelation. Were not Matthew, Zacchaeus, the thief on the cross and Magdalene elect before the foundation of the world? Nevertheless, they were ignorant of this until they were illumined by the Spirit and drawn to Christ by the Father. From these facts it follows that this first church is known to God alone, and they only who have firm and unwavering faith know that they are members of this church.

Again, the "Church" is taken in a general sense for all who are rated as Christians, i. e., those who have enlisted under His name, a large number of whom acknowledge Christ publicly by confession or participation in the sacraments, and yet at heart shrink back from Him or are ignorant of Him. To this Church, we believe, belong all those who confess Christ's name. Thus Judas belonged to the Church of Christ and all those who turned away from Christ. For by the apostles Judas was regarded as belonging to the Church of Christ no less than Peter and John, although it was by no means the case. Christ knew who were His and who were the devil's. This church, therefore, is visible, albeit it does not assemble in this world. It consists of all who confess Christ, even though among them are many reprobates. Christ has depicted it in the charming allegory of the ten virgins, some of whom were wise and others foolish [Matth. 25]. This church is also sometimes called elect, although it is not like the first without spot. But as it is considered by men the Church of God, because of known confession, so for the same reason it is styled elect. For we judge that they who have enlisted under Christ are believers and elect. Thus Peter spoke to "the elect scattered abroad throughout Pontus," etc. [I Pet. 1: 1]. Here he means by "elect" all who belonged to the churches to which he is writing, and not those only who were properly elected of God; for as they were unknown to Peter, he could not have written to them.

Finally, the "Church" is taken for every particular congregation of this universal and visible Church, as the Church of Rome, of Augsburg, of Lyons. There are still other meanings of the word "church," which it is not necessary to enumerate at present. Hence I believe that there is one Church of those who have the same Spirit, through whom they are made certain that they are the true children of the family of God; and this is the first fruits of the Church. I believe that this Church does not err in regard to truth, namely in those fundamental matters of faith upon which everything depends. I believe also that the universal, visible Church is one, while it maintains that true confession, of which we have already spoken. I believe also that all belong to this Church who give their adherence to it according to the rule and promise of God's Word. I believe that to this Church belong Isaac, Jacob, Judah and all who were of the seed of Abraham, and also those infants whose parents in the first beginnings of the Christian Church, through the preaching of the apostles, were won to the cause of Christ. For if Isaac and the rest of the ancients had not belonged to the Church, they would not have received the Church's token, circumcision. Since these, then, were members of the Church, infants and children belonged to the primitive Church. Therefore I believe and know that they were sealed by the sacrament of baptism. For children also make a confession, when they are offered by their parents to the Church, especially since the promise offers them to God, which is made to our infants no less, but even far more amply and abundantly, than formerly to the children of the Hebrews.

These are the grounds for baptizing and commending infants to the Church, against which all the weapons and war engines of the Anabaptists avail nothing. For not only are they to be baptized who believe, but they who confess, and they who, according to the promise of God's Word, belong to the Church. For otherwise even the apostles would not have baptized anyone, since no apostle had absolute evidence regarding the faith of one confessing and calling himself a Christian. For Simon the impostor, Ananias, Judas, and no one knows who, were baptized when they declared their adherence to Christ, even though they did not have faith. On the other hand, Isaac was circumcised as an infant without declaring his adherence or believing, but the promise acted in his behalf. But since our infants are in the same position as those of the Hebrews, the promise also declares their adherence to our Church and makes confession. Hence, in reality baptism, like circumcision (I am speaking of the sacrament of baptism) pre-supposes nothing but one of two things, either confession, i.e., a declaration of allegiance or a covenant, i. e., a promise. All of which will become somewhat clearer from what follows.

SEVENTHLY—I believe, indeed I know, that all the sacraments are so far from conferring grace that they do not even convey or dispense it. In this matter, most powerful Emperor, I may seem to thee perhaps too bold. But my opinion is firm. For as grace comes from or is given by the Divine Spirit (when I speak of grace I use the Latin term for pardon, i. e., indulgence or spontaneous favor), so this gift pertains to the Spirit alone. Moreover, a channel or vehicle is not necessary to the Spirit, for He Himself is the virtue and energy whereby all things are borne, and has no need of being borne; neither do we read in the Holy Scriptures that visible things, as are the sacraments, carry certainly with them the Spirit, but if visible things have ever been borne with the Spirit, it has been the Spirit, not the visible things that have done the bearing.

Thus when the rushing of the mighty wind took place [Acts 2: 2] at the same time the tongues were conveyed by the power of the wind; the wind was not conveyed by the power of the tongues. Thus the wind brought the quails and carried away the locusts [Nu. 11: 31ff; Ex. 10: 4ff]; but no quails nor locusts were ever so fleet as to bring the wind. Likewise when a wind, strong enough to remove mountains, passed Elijah [I Ki. 19: 11] the Lord was not borne by the wind, etc. Briefly, the Spirit breathes wherever it wishes, i. e., just as the wind bloweth where it listeth, and thou hearest the sound thereof, and canst not tell whence it cometh and whither it goeth, so is everyone that is born of the Spirit [John 3: 8], i. e., invisibly and imperceptibly illumined and drawn.

Thus the Truth [Christ] spake. Therefore, the Spirit of grace is conveyed not by this immersion, not by this drinking, not by that anointing. For if it were thus, it would be known how, where, whence and whither the Spirit is borne. If the presence and efficacy of grace are bound to the sacraments, they work whithersoever they are carried; and where they are not

used, everything becomes feeble. Nor can theologians plead
that the proper disposition of the subject is demanded as a pre-
requisite [for the right use of the sacraments]. For example,
the grace of baptism or of the Eucharist (so they say) is conferred upon him who is first prepared for it. For he who
according to their opinion receives grace through the sacraments, either prepares himself for it or is prepared by the Spirit.
If he prepares himself, we can do something of ourselves and
prevenient grace is nothing. If he is prepared by the Spirit for
the reception of grace, I ask whether this be done through the
sacraments as a channel or independent of the sacraments? If
the sacraments mediate, man is prepared by the sacrament for
the sacrament, and thus there will be a process ad infinitum; for
a sacrament will be required as a preparation for a sacrament.
But if we be prepared without the sacrament for the reception
of sacramental grace, the Spirit is present in His goodness before the sacrament, and hence grace has been shown and is
present before the sacrament is administered.

From this it follows (as I willingly and gladly admit in
regard to the subject of the sacraments) that the sacraments are
given as a public testimony of that grace which is previously
present to every individual. Thus baptism is administered in
the presence of the Church to one who before receiving it either
confessed the religion of Christ or has the word of promise,
whereby he is known to belong to the Church. Hence it is
that when we baptize an adult we ask him whether he believes.
And only when he answers "yes," then he receives baptism.
Faith therefore, has been present before he receives baptism, and
is not given by baptism. But when an infant is offered, the
question is asked whether its parents offer it for baptism. When
they have answered through witnesses that they wish it baptized,
then the infant is baptized. Here the promise of God precedes,
that He regards our infants, no less than those of the Hebrews,
as belonging to the Church. For when members of the Church
offer it, the infant is baptized under the law that, since it has
been born of Christians, it is regarded by the divine promise
among the members of the Church. By baptism, therefore, the
Church publicly receives one who has previously been received
through grace. Hence baptism does not convey grace but the
Church certifies that grace has been given to him to whom it is

administered.

I believe, therefore, O Emperor, that a sacrament is a sign of a sacred thing, i. e., of grace that has been given. I believe that it is a visible figure or form of the invisible grace, provided and bestowed by God's bounty; i.e., a visible example which presents an analogy to something done by the Spirit. I believe that it is a public testimony. Thus when we are baptized the body is washed with the purest element; by this it is signified that by the grace of divine goodness we have been gathered into the assembly of the Church and of God's people, wherein we should live upright and pure. Thus Paul explains the mystery in Romans VI. The recipient of baptism testifies, therefore, that he belongs to the Church of God, which worships its Lord in soundness of faith and purity of life. For this reason the sacraments, which are sacred ceremonies (for the Word is added to the element and it becomes a sacrament*) should be religiously cherished, i. e., highly valued and treated with honor. For though they are unable to bestow grace, they nevertheless associate visibly with the Church us who have previously been received into it invisibly; and this should be regarded with the highest veneration, since with their administration the words of the divine promise are declared and pronounced.

For if we think otherwise of the sacraments, namely that their external use cleanses internally, it would be but a return to Judaism, which believed that, by various anointings, oblations, offerings, sacrifices and feasts, sins could be atoned and grace could be purchased and secured. Nevertheless, the prophets, especially Isaiah and Jeremiah, always most steadfastly urged in their teaching that the promises and benefits of God are given by God's free goodness, and not with respect to merits or external ceremonies.

I believe also that the Anabaptists in denying baptism to infants are entirely wrong; and not here only, but also in many other points, of which this is not the place to speak. That men might avoid their folly and malice, I have been the first to teach and write against them,† not without danger, but relying

---

*A quotation from Augustine's Commentary on the Gospel of John, Tract LXXX, §3; cf. Migne, *Patrologia Latina*, XXXV, col. 1840.

†The first tracts of Zwingli against the Anabaptists were published in

on God's help, with the result that now, by God's goodness, this plague among us has greatly abated. So far am I from receiving, teaching or defending anything of this seditious faction.

EIGHTHLY—I believe that in the holy Eucharist, *i. e.*, the supper of thanksgiving, the true body of Christ is present by the contemplation of faith. This means that they who thank the Lord for the benefits bestowed on us in His Son acknowledge that He assumed true flesh, in it truly suffered, truly washed away our sins by His blood; and thus everything done by Christ becomes as it were present to them by the contemplation of faith. But that the body of Christ in essence and really, *i. e.*, the natural body itself, is either present in the supper or masticated with our mouth and teeth, as the Papists or some* who look back to the fleshpots of Egypt assert, we not only deny, but constantly maintain to be an error, contrary to the Word of God. This, with the divine assistance, I will in a few words, make as clear as the sun to your majesty, O Emperor. First, by citing the divine oracles; secondly, by attacking the opponents with arguments derived therefrom, as with military engines; lastly, by showing that the ancient theologians held our opinion. Meanwhile, thou Creator, thou Spirit, be present, enlighten the minds of thy people, and fill with grace and light the hearts that thou hast created!

Christ Himself, the mouth and wisdom of God, saith: "The poor ye have always with you; but me ye have not always" [John 12:8]. Here the presence of the body alone is denied, for according to His divinity He is always present, because He is always everywhere, according to His other word: "Lo, I am with you always, even unto the end of the world" [Matth. 28:20], viz., according to divinity, power and goodness. Augustine agrees with us.† Neither is there any foundation for the assertion of the opponents that the humanity of Christ is wherever the divinity is, otherwise the person is divided; for this

1525, see Zwingli's *Werke*, ed. of Schuler and Schulthess, Vol. II, pt. I, pp. 230-303 and pp. 337-369.

*The Lutherans.

†See Augustine's Homilies on the Gospel of John, Tract L, §13, where he writes: "In respect of His divine presence we always have Christ; in respect of His presence in the flesh it was rightly said to the disciples, 'Me ye will not have always.'"

would destroy Christ's true humanity. Only the deity can be everywhere. That humanity is in one place, but divinity everywhere, divides the person just as little as the Son's assumption of humanity divides the unity of the divine essence. Indeed, it would be easier to effect a separation in the unity of essence if one person of the divine being would assume the form of a creature but the others not at all, than to separate the person if the humanity be at one place but the divinity everywhere; since we see even in creation that bodies are confined to one place, but their power and influence extend very far. An example is the sun, whose body is in one place, while his power pervades all things. The human mind also surmounts the stars and penetrates the underworld, but the body is nevertheless in one place.

Christ says also: "Again I leave the world and go to the Father" [John 16: 28]. Here the word "to leave" is used, just as "to have" before, so that the opponents cannot say: "We do not have Him visibly." For when He speaks of the visible withdrawal of His body, He says: "A little while and ye shall not see me," etc. [John 16: 16]. Neither would we maintain anything but a delusion if we were to contend that His natural body were present, but invisible. For why should He evade sight, when He nevertheless would be here, who so often manifested himself to the disciples after the resurrection? "But, it is expedient for you," He says, "that I go away" [John 16: 7]. But if He were here, it would be expedient that we should see Him. For as often as the disciples thought about seeing Him, He manifested Himself openly, so that neither sense nor thought might suffer in aught. "Handle me," He says; and "Be not afraid, it is I," and "Mary, touch me not," etc. [Lk. 24: 39; John 6: 20; 20: 17].

When in departing He commended His disciples to His Father, He said: "I am no more in the world" [John 17: 11]. Here we have a substantive verb ("I *am* no more in the world"),* no less than in the words: "This *is* my body;" so that the opponents cannot say that there is a trope here, since they deny that substantives admit of the trope. But the case has no need of such arguments, for there follows: "But these are in the world." This antithesis clearly teaches that He was not, according to His human nature, in the world at a time when His disciples were.

* καὶ οὐκ εἰμὶ ἐν τῷ κόσμῳ.

And that we may know when He took His departure—not, as they invent rather than explain, when He made Himself invisible—Luke says: "While he blessed them he was parted from them, and carried up into heaven" [Lk. 24: 51]. He does not say: "He vanished," or "rendered himself invisible." About this Mark says: "After the Lord had spoken to them he was received up into heaven, and sat at the right hand of God" [Mk. 16: 19]. He does not say: "He remained here, but rendered his body invisible." Again Luke says in Acts: "When he had said these things, as they were looking, he was taken up; and a cloud received him out of their sight" [Acts 1: 9]. A cloud covered Him, of which there would have been no need if He had only removed His appearance but otherwise had continued to be present. Nor would there have been any need of removal and elevation. Again: "This same Jesus, who was taken up from you into heaven, shall so come in like manner as ye beheld him going into heaven" [Acts 1: 11]. What is clearer than this? "From you," he says, "he was taken up;" therefore, He was not with them visibly or invisibly, according to His human nature. When, then, we shall see Him return as He departed, we shall know that He is present. Otherwise He sits, according to His human nature, at the right hand of His Father until He will return to judge the quick and the dead.

But since there are some who deprive the body of Christ of restriction to a place and say that He is not in a place, let them see how clearly, and with closed eyes, they oppose the truth. He was in the manger, on the cross, at Jerusalem when his parents were on their journey home; in the sepulchre and out of the sepulchre; for the angel says: "He is risen, he is not here: behold the place where they laid him" [Mk. 16: 6]. And that they may not be able to say that His body is everywhere, let them hear: "When the doors were shut, Jesus came and stood in their midst" [John 20: 19]. What need had He of coming if His body was everywhere, but invisible? It would have been enough to come, but merely as one who was present to manifest Himself. But let such sophistical trifles be gone, which rob us of the truth both of Christ's humanity and of the Holy Scriptures.

These testimonies deny the presence of Christ's body anywhere but in heaven, scripturally speaking, i. e., as far as Scripture tells us about the nature and properties of the body assumed by Christ. And however far the contradictions, which are involved in our propositions regarding the power of God, drive us, we ought not to wrest it to such a point that we believe that God acts contrary to His Word. That would be a sign of impotence, not of power. Moreover, that the natural body of Christ is not eaten with our mouth, He Himself showed us when He said to the Jews, disputing about the corporeal eating of His flesh: "The flesh profiteth nothing" [John 6: 63], namely, eaten naturally, but eaten spiritually it profits much, for it gives life.

"That which is born of the flesh is flesh; and that which is born of the Spirit is spirit" [John 3: 6]. If, therefore, the natural body of Christ is eaten with our mouth, what else than flesh can come out of flesh, eaten naturally? And lest anyone think lightly of this argument, let him hear the second part: "That which is born of the Spirit is spirit." Therefore, that which is spirit, is born of the Spirit. If then the flesh is salutary to the soul, it should be eaten spiritually, not carnally. This applies also to the sacraments, that spirit is born of Spirit, and not of any corporeal matter, as we have already indicated.

Paul announces that if he once knew Christ according to the flesh, henceforth he would know Him no more after the flesh [II Cor. 5: 16].

In view of these passages we are compelled to confess that the words: "This is my body," should not be understood naturally, but figuratively, just as the words: "This is Jehovah's passover" [Ex. 12: 11]. For the lamb that was eaten every year with the celebration of the festival was not the passing over of the Lord, but it signified that such a passing over had formerly taken place. Besides there is the temporal succession, in that the Lord's Supper followed the eating of the lamb; which reminds us that Christ used words similar to those employed at the passover, for succession leads to imitation. Moreover, the arrangement of the words is the same. The time affords an additional argument, since in the same evening meal the passover was discontinued and the new act of thanksgiving was instituted. A further consideration is the characteristic of memorials, in that they take the name from the thing which they commemorate.

Thus the Athenians named σεισάχθεια, [removal of debts]

not as though the debts were remitted every year, but because what Solon once did* they continually celebrate; and this their celebration they dignify with the name of the thing itself. Thus those things are called the body and blood of Christ which are the symbols of the true body. Now follow the proofs:

As the body cannot be nourished by a spiritual substance, so the soul cannot be nourished by a corporeal substance. But if the natural body of Christ is eaten, I ask whether it feeds the body or the soul? Not the body, hence the soul. If the soul, then the soul eats flesh, and it would not be true that spirit is only born of Spirit.

In the second place, I ask: What does the body of Christ, eaten naturally, bring about? If it be the forgiveness of sins, as one party claims, then the disciples obtained forgiveness of sins in the Lord's Supper, and therefore, Christ died in vain. If that which is eaten imparts the virtue of Christ's passion, as the same party claims, then the virtue of the passion and re-demption was dispensed before it had taken place. If the body is fed for the resurrection, as another [Luther] very ignorantly asserts, much more would the sacrament heal our body and deliver it from sickness. But Irenaeus† wants to be understood differently, when he says that our body is nourished by Christ's body for the resurrection. For he desires to show that the hope of our resurrection is strengthened by Christ's resurrection. Behold, what an appropriate figure of speech!

Thirdly—If the natural body of Christ was given to the disciples in the Supper, it necessarily follows that they ate it

---

*Through seisachtheia, or removal of debts, Solon in 594 B. C. rescued the peasants of Attica. The debts, with which the farms were encumbered, were cancelled. Servitude for debt was annulled and Attic citizens who had been held in slavery were set free by the State purchasing their freedom. σεισάχθεια is literally a shaking off (σεισμός) of a burden (ἄχθος).

†Luther had quoted him for his view. See Irenaeus, "Against Heresies," Bk. IV, c. 18, 5, where he writes: "Then again, how can they say that the flesh, which is nourished with the body of the Lord and with His blood goes to corruption, and does not partake of life? . . . For as the bread, which is produced from the earth, when it receives the invocation of God, is no longer common bread, but the Eucharist, consisting of two realities, earthly and heavenly; so also our bodies, when they receive the Eucharist, are no longer corruptible, having the hope of resurrection to eternity." Roberts, *Ante-Nicene Fathers*, Vol. I, p. 486.

as it then was. But it was then capable of suffering; hence they ate a vulnerable body, for it was not yet glorified. For if they say: They ate the same body, yet not as it was capable of suffering, but the same as it was after the resurrection, I reply: Either He had two bodies, one not yet glorified and another glorified, or one and the same body was at the same time capable of suffering and incapable. And so, since He dreaded death so much He was doubtless unwilling to suffer, but wanted to make use of that bodily endowment, by virtue of which He was free from pain. Therefore He did not truly suffer, but only by appearance; in this way Marcion* is again brought back by these blindfolded gladiators. Six hundred arguments could be adduced, O Emperor, but we shall be content with these.

Moreover, that the ancients agree with us on the last part of this article I shall now establish by two witnesses, both of the first rank, viz.:

By Ambrose, who in the [Commentary on the] First Epistle to the Corinthians says concerning the words: "Ye do show forth the Lord's death," etc.: "Mindful that by the Lord's death we have been freed, we signify in our eating and drinking the flesh and the blood which were offered for us,"† etc. Now Ambrose is speaking of the food and drink of the Supper, and asserts that we signify those things which were offered for us.

By Augustine also, who in this thirtieth discourse on John‡ affirms that the body of Christ which rose from the dead must be in one place. Here the printed copies have "can be" instead of "must be," but incorrectly, for in the Master of the "Sentences [Peter Lombard] and the Canonical Decrees [of Gratian], in which this opinion of Augustine is quoted,** the reading is

*Marcion, a Gnostic of about 150 A. D. appears to Zwingli as a type of docetism, i.e., the view that Christ had only an apparent body.

†See Migne, *Patrologia Latina*, XVII, 256.

‡See Migne, op. cit., XXXV, 1632.

**Augustine writes: "The body of the Lord, in which he rose again from the dead can only be in one place *(uno loco esse potest)*; but his truth is everywhere diffused." Commentary on John, Tract XXX, §1 (Migne, *Patrol. Lat.*, XXXV, 1632). But instead of the words: "can only be in one place," a number of later Fathers express the meaning of Augustine more forcibly when, in quoting these words, they substitute "must only be in one place." Thus even the Benedictine editors remark: "All editions and Mss., which we had the privilege of consulting, agree in reading: *uno loco* "must." By this we plainly see that whatever the ancients said so excellently concerning the Supper, they thought not of the natural but of the spiritual eating of Christ's body. For since they knew that the body of Christ must be in one place, and that it is at the right hand of God, they did not withdraw it thence to submit it for mastication to the foul teeth of men.

Augustine likewise teaches in the twelfth chapter "Against Adimantus"* that the three expressions: "The blood is the life," and "This is my body" and "The rock was Christ," were spoken symbolically, i. e., as he himself says, in a figure and figuratively. And among many other things he at length comes to these words: "I can interpret that command as given for a sign. For the Lord did not hesitate to say: 'This is my body,' when He was giving a sign of His body." Thus far Augustine. Lo, a key for us whereby we can unlock all the declarations of the ancients concerning the Eucharist! That which is only a sign of the body, he says, is called the body.

Let them who wish go now and condemn us for heresy, only let them know that by the same process they are condemning the opinions of the theologians, contrary to the decrees of the Pontiffs. For from these facts it becomes very evident that the ancients always spoke figuratively when they attributed so much to the eating of the body of Christ in the Supper; meaning, not that sacramental eating could cleanse the soul but faith in God through Jesus Christ, which is spiritual eating, whereof this external eating is but symbol and shadow. And as bread sustains the body and wine enlivens and exhilarates, thus it strengthens the soul and assures it of God's mercy that He has given us His Son; thus it renews the mind by the confidence that, by His blood, the sins with which it was being consumed were destroyed. With these passages we shall now rest content, although any one could compile whole volumes in expounding and confirming the fact that the ancients are of our opinion.

esse potest. However, Ivonis Decreta, pars. II, c. 8 (Migne, CLXI, 151f), Gratianus, De Consecratione, Dist. II, c. 44 (Migne, CLXXXVII, 1752), the Master of Sentences, Bk. IV, Dist. 10, 1 (Migne, CXCII, 860) and after them Thomas Aquinas, Summa, pars 3, quaest. 75, art. 1, quote these words, *uno loco esse oportet.*"

*See Migne, op. cit., XLII, 144.

Neither let the pamphlet recently published* concerning the opinions of the ancients, which it expressly promised to defend, move any one. For in a very short time we shall see the refutation of our very learned brother Oecolampadius, the object of whose exordium it was to defend the opinion of the ancients. But what things should be required in this matter for its clearer exposition and the refutation of the opponents we who hold this opinion have shown, I believe, abundantly, in many books, written to different persons.

NINTHLY—I believe that ceremonies which are not through superstitious use contrary either to faith or to God's word (although I do not know whether such be found) can be tolerated by charity until the light of day shines clearer and clearer. But at the same time I believe that by virtue of the same charity the ceremonies mentioned should be abolished when it can be done without great offense, however much the evilminded may clamor. For Christ did not forbid Mary Magdalene to pour out the ointment, although the dishonest and evilminded Judas made an ugly disturbance. Images, however, which are misused for worship, I do not count among ceremonies, but among the number of those things which are diametrically opposed to the Word of God. But those which do not serve for worship and in whose cases there exists no danger of future worship, I am so far from condemning that I acknowledge both painting and statuary as God's gifts.

TENTHLY—I believe that the work of prophesying or preaching is most sacred, so that it is a work most necessary, above all others. For to speak scripturally or strictly, we see that among all nations the outward preaching of apostles, evangelists and bishops preceded faith, which nevertheless we attribute to the Spirit alone. For alas! We see very many who hear indeed the outward preaching of the Gospel, but believe not, because there is a lack of the Spirit. Whithersoever, then, prophets or preachers of the Word are sent, it is a sign of God's grace, that He wishes to manifest a knowledge of Himself to His elect; and to whom they [the preachers] are denied, it is a

---

*Its title was: *Quid de Eucharistia veteres et Graeci et Latini senserint dialogus, auctore Jo. Oecolampadio; in quo etiam epistolae Phil. Melanchthonis et Jo. Oecolampadii insertae.* 8vo. Tigurae 1526. It is also found in the Letters of Oecolampadius, fol. 130a-168b.

sign of His impending wrath. This can be inferred from the prophets and the example of Paul, who was sometimes forbidden to go to some, and again called to others.

But also the laws themselves and the magistrates can be assisted in maintaining public justice by no other means more effectually than by preaching. For in vain is that which is just taught unless they upon whom it is enjoined have a regard for what is just and love equity. But for this prophets prepare minds as ministers, and the Spirit as leader both of teachers and hearers. This kind of ministers, namely those who teach, comfort, alarm, care for and faithfully watch, we acknowledge among Christ's people. That also we recognize, that they baptize, and in the Lord's Supper administer the body and blood of Christ (for thus we also call figuratively the holy bread and wine of the Supper), visit the sick, feed the poor from the resources and in the name of the Church; finally this that they read the Scriptures, interpret them and make a public profession, by which either they or others are prepared for presiding at some time over the churches. But that kind of ministers, with bishop's mitre and staff, who are mere numbers and born bread eaters, we regard as a useless burden on the earth and illegitimate. They are in the body ecclesiastical what goiters and hunchbacks are in the human body.

ELEVENTH—I know that the magistrate when lawfully installed, holds God's place no less than the prophet. For as the prophet is a minister of heavenly wisdom and goodness, as one who teaches faithfully and brings errors to light, so the magistrate is the minister of goodness and justice. Of goodness, in that with fidelity and moderation, like God, he both hears and determines concerning the affairs of his people; of justice, in that he breaks the audacity of the wicked and protects the innocent. If a prince have these endowments, I believe that no fear need be entertained for his conscience. If he lack these, though he make himself an object of fear and terror, his conscience can in no way be cleared, upon the ground that he has been lawfully installed. Yet, at the same time I believe, that a Christian should obey such a tyrant, until that time comes whereof Paul says: "If thou canst become free, use it rather" [I Cor. 7: 21]. Nevertheless, I believe that this time is indicated by God alone, and not by man; and this is done not obscurely but as openly as when Saul was rejected and David became his successor. Regarding tribute and taxes, to be paid for protection, I am of the same opinion as Paul, Romans 13.

TWELFTHLY—I believe that the figment of purgatorial fire is as much an affront to the redemption of Christ freely granted to us as it has been a lucrative business to its authors. For if it be necessary by punishments and tortures to expiate the guilt of our crimes, Christ will have died in vain and grace will have lost its meaning. Can anything more wicked be imagined in Christianity? Or what sort of a Christ do they have who wish to be called Christians and yet dread this fire, which is no longer fire, but smoke? But that there is a hell, where the unbelievers, disobedient and public enemies are forever punished with Ixion and Tantalus,* I not only believe, but know. For when the Truth [Christ] speaks of the universal judgment, He asserts that after this judgment some will go into everlasting fire. [Matth. 25:41]. After the universal judgment, therefore, there will be everlasting fire. Hence the Anabaptists cannot cover up with His [Christ's] word their error, that 'ôlam, or "for ever" does not extend beyond the general judgment. For in this passage Christ is speaking of everlasting fire that will burn after the judgment and will torment the Devil and his angels, and the ungodly who despise God, and the savage men who suppress the truth with falsehood and do not mercifully and faithfully aid the necessities of their neighbor.

The above [twelve points] I firmly believe, teach and maintain, not by my own utterances, but by those of the Word of God; and, God willing, I promise to do this as long as the mind controls these members, unless some one from the declarations of Holy Scripture, properly understood, explain and establish the reverse as clearly and plainly as we have established the above. For it is no less agreeable and delightful than fair and just for us to submit our judgment to the Holy Scriptures, and the Church, deciding in harmony with these by virtue of the Spirit. We could have explained everything more amply and exhaus-

---

*Ixion, king of the Lapithae in Thessaly, who, according to Greek mythology, boasted of having been intimate with Juno, was hurled by Jupiter into Tartarus, where he was bound to an ever revolving fiery wheel. Tantalus, who disclosed the secrets of the gods, was sent to the infernal regions, where he was tormented with unquenchable hunger and thirst.

tively, but since opportunity is lacking, we are content with these points, which we consider such that, while some one may readily pick flaws, which today is so common and easy, none will be able to pick it to pieces. If nevertheless anyone will attempt it, he will not do it unpunished. Then we shall perhaps draw forth what ammunition we have in reserve. Now we have presented enough testimony for the present.

Wherefore, most excellent Emperor, and ye other princes, rulers, nobles, deputies and heads of States, I beseech and implore you, by Jesus Christ, our Lord and Brother, by His goodness and justice, by His judgment, which He will pronounce on all according to their merits, whom no plan escapes, who brings to confusion the designs of princes that counsel and rule wickedly, who exalts the humble and overthrows the proud, in the first place, not to despise the lowliness of the petitioner. For even the foolish have often spoken opportunely, and the Truth itself [Christ] chose for the proclamation of its message the weak and men of low estate. Again, remember that you also are men, who yourselves can err and can also be misled by others. For every man is a liar [Rom. 3: 4]. And unless he be taught something else by the inspiration of the Spirit than what he himself knows and desires, nothing can be expected of him than that he be overthrown by his own arts and plans. For the prophet Jeremiah says only too truly: "Lo, they have rejected the word of Jehovah; and what manner of wisdom is in them?" [Jer. 8: 9].

Moreover, since you are the overseers of justice, none should know the will of God more thoroughly than you. But where else can this be sought than in His oracles? Do not shrink back, therefore, from the opinions of those who rely on God's Word. For we see it happen every day that the more adversaries oppose it, so much the more does the Word of God shine forth and falsehood is banished. But if, as does not escape me, there are those with you who zealously defame us as ignorant and, if possible also as malicious, consider in the first place, whether we who adopt this view of the Gospel and the Eucharist, have ever so conducted our lives that any good man can ever doubt as to whether we can be regarded as good men? Furthermore, have we from infancy been so far removed from culture and literature that all hope of our being learned must be given up? Certainly we boast of neither of these, since even Paul was what he was by the grace of God [I Cor. 15:10]. But even if a rather cheerful life has been our lot, it has never degenerated into luxury and shamelessness, nor, on the other hand, turned into cruelty, arrogance or obstinacy; so that the designs of our enemies, often confounded by the good report of our life, have been forced to sound a retreat. Our learning, although greater than our enemies can bear or in the face of their consciences can despise, is notwithstanding far less than our followers think we possess.

However, to come to what we are aiming at, we have for many years made such studies in sacred and likewise in profane letters, that what we teach is not done thoughtlessly. May we also be permitted to praise the grace and bountifulness of God, so liberally bestowed upon our churches! Truly, the churches that hear the Lord God through us have so received the Word of God that falsehood and dishonesty are diminished, pride and luxury subdued, and violence and wrangling have departed. If these are not truly fruits of the divine Spirit, what are they then? Consider indeed, most excellent Emperor, and all ye princes and nobles, what good fruit the so-called "human doctrine" has produced for us! The masses that were bought increased the lust and the impudence of both princes and people. Likewise they introduced and increased the luxury of the pontiffs and the excesses of the ministrants of the mass. Yea, what wicked deeds have they not kindled? For who can distribute the wealth accumulated through the mass, unless we tie up the veins, so to speak, and stop them flowing?*

May God, therefore, who is far better than all of you— whom we both gladly call and believe to be most excellent men —grant that you may undertake to cut the roots of this and all other errors in the Church, and to leave and desert Rome with her rubbish which she has thrust upon the Christian world, and especially on your Germany. Moreover, whatever force you have exerted against the purity of the Gospel may you direct against the criminal attempts of ungodly Papists, that justice, which has been banished by your indifference and our innocence, which has been obscured by artful misrepresentations,

---

*Zwingli seems to compare the Catholic Church to a robber, who will not release his ill gotten spoils, unless he is choked and rendered unconscious.

may again be restored to us. There has been enough cruelty, unless it be not savage and cruel to issue unjust commands, to condemn, yea to slaughter, kill, rob and outlaw. Since this way has not been successful, we must certainly go another way. If this counsel is from the Lord, do not fight against God; but if from elsewhere, it will fall to the ground by its own rashness. For this reason permit the Word of God to be freely disseminated and to sprout, O children of men, whoever ye be, who cannot forbid even a grain from growing. You see that this seed is abundantly watered by the rain from heaven, neither can it be checked by any heat from men so as to become parched. Consider not what you most of all desire, but what the world requires in regard to the Gospel. Take this counsel, such as it is, in good part, and by your earnestness show that you are children of God.

Most devoted to your Majesty and all believers,

HULDREICH ZWINGLI.

Zurich, the 3rd of July, 1530.

III.

REFUTATION OF THE ARTICLES OF ZWINGLI, PRESENTED TO
HIS IMPERIAL MAJESTY, BY JOHN ECK, UNDER THE
PATRONAGE OF THE MOST REVEREND FATHER AND MOST
HONORABLE PRINCE, LORD ERHARD, S. R. E., CARDINAL
BISHOP OF LIÈGE, July 1530.

(July 17, 1530)

[REPVLSIO AR- | TICVLORVM ZVVINGLII | Caes. Maiestati obla-
torum. | Johanne Eckio authore | 1530 | in Julio | Sub Reuerendissimi
patris & amplissimi prin- | cipis D. Erhardi S.R.E. Cardinalis ac | Leo-
diensis Episcopi Patrocinio. | (Coat of Arms). No date, place or printer.
72 unnumbered quarto pages, the last of which is blank. A copy of this
tract is in the library of Union Theological Seminary, New York. The following English translation is based on one by Mr. Henry Preble, but it was
revised throughout by the editor.

John Eck, more correctly Johann Maier, was born at Eck (now Egg,
near Memmingen, south of Augsburg) in Swabia, November 13, 1486.
When twelve years of age he began his studies at Heidelberg and continued
them at Tuebingen, Cologne and Freiburg. When fourteen years of age he
became Magister Artium, when nineteen bachelor of theology, when twenty-
two priest at Strassburg, and in 1510, when twenty-four years, doctor and
professor of theology in the University of Ingolstadt.

Having studied under humanistic teachers he advocated at first liberal
views in theology and philosophy and as early as 1517 entered into friendly
relations with Luther. But his unbounded ambition to be regarded as the
leading theologian of Germany caused him to become the defender of the
papacy and of Catholic doctrine. In 1519, he began his fight against
Luther. In 1520, he visited Rome at the invitation of the Pope, when he
presented to him his work on the *Primacy of Peter against Luther*, Ingolstadt 1520, for which he was awarded with the appointment as papal
prothonotary. When on June 16, 1520, the papal bull, *Exsurge Domine*,
appeared, in which forty-one propositions of Luther were condemned, Eck
was entrusted with its execution in Germany.

At the Diet of Augsburg, Eck took a leading part as defender of the

Roman Catholic position. He extracted 404 articles from the works of the reformers and with seventy other theologians collaborated in the *Confutatio pontificia*, in which the Catholic refutation of Protestantism was embodied.

Against Zwingli and his party, Eck first appeared at the public disputation at Baden, in Catholic territory, twelve miles northwest of Zurich, on May 21-June 18, 1526. The affair ended in favor of Eck, who induced the authorities to suppress the reformation at Baden. The dispution of Berne, which was conducted in the absence of Eck in January 1528, was won for the reformation.

When Zwingli's account of his faith had been submitted to the emperor in July 1530, it was turned over to Eck for answer. He sat down at once and within three days, as he boasts, he produced what he intended to be a crushing reply. It was completed on July 17, 1530, dedicated to the Cardinal of Liege and printed most likely in the same month at Augsburg.

Eck was more highly esteemed as the champion of the true faith in Rome than in Germany, where he had many enemies. He was accused of drunkenness, immorality, unbounded greed for money and passionate desire for honor and preferment. When Rome did not gratify all his ambitions, he made overtures for peace to the Protestants, but they failed through hatred and contempt by which he was generally regarded.

But through his scholarly attainments, and controversial ability, he made himself the most prominent, and also the most violent opponent of the reformation. He died at Ingolstadt on February 10, 1543. Numerous works in Latin and German testify both to his ability and to his violent temper.]

To The

Right Reverend Father in Christ and Most Estimable Prince Lord Erhard von Arnberg,* S. R. E., Cardinal Bishop of Liège, His Most Gracious Lord, John Eck Sends Greetings and Presents His Ready Allegiance.

The ancients tell us, Most Worshipful Father, that the Greeks made offerings to the most eminent physician Hippocrates, as to a present divinity, because his help and labors drove away the contagious plague, and the grievous pestilence that was creeping in from Illyricum. Hercules also merited divine honors because he overcame monsters dangerous to mankind. Yet far more estimable will be our august and imperial ruler,

---

*Erhard de la Marck, bishop of Liège and Cardinal, born at Sedan in the year 1472, was descended from a very wealthy family in the Ardennes. Elected as bishop of Liège in 1506, he beautified the city with a number of magnificent buildings, among them the Episcopal palace. When the efforts of Francis I of France to secure for him the cardinal's hat miscarried, through the intrigues of the Duchess of Angoulême, Erhard became a violent enemy of France. It was mainly through his efforts that the attempts of Francis to become emperor of Germany, after the death of Maximilian, failed. He supported the claims of Charles V, and when he became emperor, the latter showed his gratitude by securing for Erhard the dignity of Cardinal. The administration of his diocese was marked by cruelty and fanaticism, for he persecuted the Protestants relentlessly. He died at Liège, February 16, 1538.

Charles V, Roman Emperor, and he will win undying glory for his name, if, following the example of the great Constantine, he shall by his power and piety suppress and do away with the destructive commotions in the Church, more serious and more widespread than we have ever read of. For this all Catholics are offering up most devout prayers, that dissension and discord may be done away, and peace, quiet and harmony return to Germany, especially in our sacred religion, for there is small reason to hope that God will be gracious to us, since He is the author of peace not of dissension, unless returning to grace we come into unity of faith, and all think the words of Paul applicable to us Germans also, "Now I beseech you, brethren, by the name of our Lord Jesus Christ, that you all speak the same thing, and that there be no schisms among you" [I Cor. 1: 10]. For in consequence of our sin so many schisms have arisen in the faith, that a Christian cannot even think of them without great distress. What Catholic would not bewail the breaking of his vows by Luther, the destruction of the mass and eucharist by Zwingli, the bringing back of Catabaptism by Balthasar [Huebmaier], the casting away of the Old and the New Testaments by Ambrosius Pneumaticus? If God give us not a godlike emperor as a Hercules for these monsters, an Hippocrates for this pestilence, alas for poor torn Germany!

I have refuted Zwingli's pamphlet which he had caused to be presented to the Emperor as a confession of his faith, and if I seem pretty harsh to any one I beg him by those above not to judge that I had bitter feelings towards the followers of Zwingli, but with a Christian heart and brotherly love most deeply grieve for them because so many thousand souls are thereby brought to peril, I will not say, destruction, and nothing is more truly my desire than that they may return to the unity of the faith and the primitive religion. Though I despair of the chief heretic, for not in vain does St. Paul admonish us that such a one, after the first and second admonition, is to be rejected, yet I trust in God the Father of Mercies and in the Lord Jesus Christ our Saviour that many now wandering in the bypaths of error will be turned wholeheartedly to seek the Lord God again and confess Him in the great Church and praise Him in the mighty people [Ps. 35: 18]. And this refutation of mine, a labor of three days, I wanted to dedicate to Your Worship, Right Reverend Father and glory of the Court, not only that I might show my zeal and devotion to you, but because, through the favor with our high Emperor Charles which your faith, power and wisdom give you, you of all primates are the wisest to whom to commend a matter of the faith. May you continue unceasingly, as you do, to appeal to, admonish, exhort, urge His Majesty to come to the assistance of Germany in her trouble and danger. I know how much His Majesty values your counsels and regards you as his Nestor. May God Almighty long preserve Your Gracious Worship in safety. Farewell, Ornament of Bishops.

Augsburg, July 17, 1530.

IN THY NAME, SWEET JESUS

When I read Zwingli's confession of faith, most sacred Emperor, I do not clearly know whether to wonder the more at the man's ungodliness or his impudence, for he excels so in both that one cannot easily decide upon which he has spent more labor, trying with marked viciousness to outdo himself in them more each day. He has been for ten years constantly at the task of extinguishing all the piety of the Christian faith among the Swiss, of abolishing divine worship, of ruining, destroying, banishing beyond Sarmatia and the Caspian mountains all the rites, usages and customs of Church ceremonies and the entire Christian religion. First he championed the errors of Luther, and spread them among the people. Soon, scorning Luther, he withdrew from him in numerous tenets, and reintroduced various sects, such as a new sect of Capernaites, a sect of the Berengarians, of the Pelagians, and others. He thereby brought it about among his people of Zurich that they blotted out the ancient Christian religion and refused to listen to the Right Reverend Bishop of Constance, when he more than once gave them fatherly admonition, and, shaking off his regular jurisdiction, did and disposed everything according to their own sweet will independently of right and wrong, and are to this day so doing and disposing.

They have turned just as deaf an ear to the pious admonitions of the Federated Cantons, by whose aid, not to say blood, they reached such a high rank of dominion and grew to such power, so that they not only disregard the other Swiss, but scorn them, and try to offer them violence and to turn them away by threats and force from the true Christian faith. My spirit shudders, my heart shrinks back, my limbs tremble, mighty Emperor, when I would relate Zwingli's impious acts. Their number overwhelms me when I try to count them on my fingers. But do you, while I do this a little, put yourself into the frame of mind that you seem to hear me recounting to Your Majesty the deeds not of a Christian but of some Turk, or wild Tartar, or savage Hun, or ancient Nebuchadnezzar, or Antiochus, or Heliodorus. First he altered many ceremonies with the apparent purpose of reforming the Church; presently he abolished them altogether. He invited the people to the Communion in both forms contrary to the ordinance of the Church, then immediately cast away both forms and took away the whole consolation of the sacrament of the Eucharist, exhibiting in his churches, instead of the most sacred body and blood of Jesus our Saviour, nothing but baker's bread. And when he had brought the men of his nation over to this view of denying the reality of Christ's body in the sacrament, there was no sin too monstrous, no crime too impious and execrable for them to be driven headlong into by Zwingli.

Therefore, the administration of all the sacraments except baptism has lapsed; all the ceremonies of the Church have been abolished, the canonical hours, the offices of the Mass, both public and private, have lapsed in all the churches, colleges, and monasteries, and he who first spent so much toil in frequent changes of the Mass into now one shape now another has finally destroyed and abolished all masses. The invocation of the saints, the praises of God by night and day have ceased among them, no honor is shown to the Virgin Mary and the rest of the saints, the once well-filled church of Maria Einsiedeln is deserted. The anniversary foundations and other divine offices have lapsed, the altars are destroyed and overthrown, the images of the saints and the paintings are burned or broken up or defaced. All the ornaments of the churches are taken away, especially the chalices and monstrances and all the gold and silver and silk there was in the churches. The revenues and incomes of the churches and monasteries have been diverted to profane uses, all the monks and nuns, spurning their vows, have returned to the world and given themselves over to incontinence. Hence the most holy foundations of the pious dukes of Austria, of the counts of Haspurg, Kiburg, Nellenburg, Tockenburg, and especially of Charlemagne, Your Majesty's predecessors, have been utterly destroyed and overthrown, and everything has been profaned and ruined, so that they no longer have churches but rather stables, and the monasteries seem not places in which perennial service is offered to God, but temples of Venus or Bacchus.

After all these impieties, sacrileges, plunderings and blasphemous doings, after all the errors he has spread abroad and all the heresies he has introduced, he ventures to address a confession of his faithlessness to the imperial head of the world, ventures to put forth before the most Christian Emperor of the Roman Empire articles far from Christian. This mad recklessness of his ventures, after he has dragged the men of Berne, Basle and Schaffhausen over to his view, after he has infected with his own errors the cities of the Holy Empire, Constance, and Mülhausen, and the town of St. Gall, and has alienated them from the faith of the House of Austria, after he has torn and defiled the noble commonwealth of Strassburg with his errors under the leadership of Capito and Bucer, after he has stirred up insurrection in the realms of His Serene Highness, the King of Hungary and Bohemia and Archduke of Austria, has done many wrongs to the nobles, faithful to the Holy Empire and the House of Austria, and robbed them of their goods, after he has so often and in such mean fashion expressed scorn, derision, indifference for your absent Majesty and your sacred person,* this minister of sin, this leader of ungodliness and sacrilege, this scorner of gods and men, ventures, I say, in addition to all this, to present to Your Majesty a pamphlet of his faithlessness, and to give an explanation of his heresies, so that not without reason a vast wonder has taken possession of my mind whether Zwingli is more proficient in impiety or in impudence. A most stupid busybody surely, who thinks he can impose upon Your Sacred Majesty with his deceits, and deceive your distinguished watchfulness with his crafty wiles. Although, therefore, your most wise Imperial Majesty will easily understand the craftiness of the man, shudder at his impiety, and scorn his pride and arrogance, yet, in accordance with the allegiance and obedient service I owe and with the Christian office I fill, I will examine the faithless confession of the faith-destroying heretic, and put it to the test, trusting to the righteousness of your most Christian mind as a faithful servant of God and patron of the Church to take wise measures to suppress and exterminate at length this heresy that threatens so many souls with damnation, and to restore to

*There is, of course, no proof whatever for all these wild assertions.

Christian liberty the Catholics oppressed under the dominion of these people. But now let Zwingli's Confession come in for a castigation!

In his preface he admits that the companions of his faithlessness had waited anxiously for the time when an account of their faith should be demanded of them. They are anxious, I imagine, because they fear to "come to the light, lest their deeds should be reproved," as Christ says, John, 3 [: 20].* They are anxious, lest they experience the rigor of imperial righteousness according to their works, for they are not ignorant of Paul's words, "But if thou do that which is evil, fear: for he beareth not the sword in vain. For he is God's minister: an avenger to execute wrath upon him that doeth evil," Rom. 13 [: 4].† They are anxious because, while there was no limit to their wrong-doings, they thought they could do anything they would with impunity since Your Imperial Highness was in Spain, in the uttermost parts of the west, separated from the Empire by so many lands, and was distracted by so many vast and difficult affairs that it would never happen that you would come back to the Empire.

But now that God Almighty, caring for His holy Church and Empire, has caused you, beyond all human conjecture and though not contrary to hope, absolutely contrary to expectation, so quickly to triumph most happily over all obstacles and difficulties, and has caused you to be most gloriously crowned with the imperial diadem, anointing and consecration having gone before; now that He has restored peace to the powers of Italy and has brought Your Imperial, Sublime Highness back to Germany, the heretics are anxious, yea, terrified at your imperial presence, because now every avenue is closed to the lies by which they were imposing upon the simple-minded people, saying that the divine Emperor Charles was not in Italy, and had not been crowned, and that these things were made up by the Catholics to frighten the people. Therefore are the preachers of the heretics in very truth anxious, saying with the wicked in Isaiah, "We have conceived, and uttered from the heart, words of falsehood. And judgment is turned away backward, and justice hath stood afar off: for our wicked doings are with us; and we have known our iniquities, in sinning and lying against the Lord," etc. Isa. 59 [: 12-14].‡ Yet in the midst of such anxiety, they still flatter themselves that they stand erect when they really lie sunk in such deep pits and ditches of error and heresy, "Woe to you that are deep of heart, to hide your counsel from the Lord: and their works are in the dark," Isa. 29 [: 15].

We must believe Zwingli, therefore, in this place, when he admits that they are between the devil and the deep sea, but presently he returns to his usual lies, saying that he and his associates were spurred on by love of the truth and desire for peace to put forth the pamphlet of their confes-

*As the verse division was not introduced into the Greek New Testament till 1551, and into the Vulgate till 1555, Eck quotes the Bible by chapter only. We add the verses in square brackets.
†The translations of the Scripture quotations are throughout *this tract* those of the Douay Version, the authorized English version of the Catholic Church.
‡In the King James version the construction of the beginning is different and the order of the parts different.

sion, for everything applies to them which Jeremiah uttered about lying prophets in chapter 23. How have they dared to boast of love of the truth before our most pious Emperor? For it is in their very character that Isaiah says, "We have placed our hope in lies and by falsehood we are protected," 28 [: 15]. With equal falsehood they arrogate to themselves a desire for peace, though they seem to have been born to overthrow the peace and quiet of the commonwealth and country, and are verily men seditious and sanguinary, as Zwingli and his crowd showed in the uprisings at Ittingen,* at Rothweil† and elsewhere. And the desire for peace shone forth most brightly when, on account of the burning of one Lutheran priest at Schwyz,‡ he called the men of Zurich, Berne and Thurgau to arms against the five ancient Cantons of the Swiss who were most firm in the Catholic faith, and marched out into the field not far from the town of Rapperswyl, where much human blood would have been shed if Zwingli's followers had listened to him, as this herald of the Gospel strenuously urged them to join battle.** Most applicable to him and his associates are the words of Jeremiah, "They healed the breach of the daughter of my people disgracefully, saying: Peace, peace: when there is no peace," 8 [: 11]. For Zwingli is of the number of those of whom David says, "Who speak peace with their neighbor, but evils are in their heart," Ps. 27 [: 3].††

As to Zwingli's putting forth the pamphlet of his confession very hastily, he had first assigned as the reason of its appearance a love of the truth and a desire for peace, but presently, forgetting this (for liars are apt to be forgetful) he gives a different reason, and Your Sacred Majesty will easily understand that he was rather goaded by the sting of envy and stirred by contentiousness. Being filled with undying hatred against Luther and attacking him with many insulting words, for the peace patched up at Marburg was a flimsy affair, when he saw that illustrious princes and wise councillors, accepting the doctrine of Luther, had presented to Your Majesty and the princes of the Empire the articles of their faith, in which the ungodly Capernaitic dogmas of Zwingli and Oecolampadius are frequently condemned and repudiated, he plunged into this fray also, and through an unknown messenger,‡‡ as I hear, got the pamphlet of his confession into Your Majesty's hands by stealth. Thus relying upon the truth of the Gospel, this new preacher and bishop of Zurich did not dare to present this document openly and publicly to your Imperial Majesty,

---

*This uprising arose because the prefect of Thurgau had seized by night at Burg, near Stein on the Rhine, a Reformed preacher named Oechsli and carried him off to Frauenfeld. See Zwingli's *Werke,* Vol. III, 1914, pp. 511-538.

†The Catholics had driven the reformers from the country and these sought refuge at Zurich and other places.

‡Jacob Schlosser, who had the cognomen Caesar.

**This refers to the First Cappel War, 1529-30, see Jackson, *Huldreich Zwingli,* pp. 299-306.

††So in the Vulgate, but 28: 3, according to Hebrew text and the Authorized Version; because in the Septuagint and Vulgate, Ps. 9 and 10 are counted as one Psalm.

‡‡Zwingli's Confession was presented to the Emperor through the Bishop Designate of Constance. See Jackson, *Huldreich Zwingli,* 332.

either by his own hand or by that of any respectable man acting for him.

But how reverently Zwingli looks up to this imperial head of the whole world, the tenor of his preface reveals clearly enough, for he seems to be offering a pamphlet of confession of his humility, obedience and subjection to the Emperor, as well as of his faith, and to recognize him as Roman Emperor, but if we examine its words more thoroughly we find nothing in it but a sort of arrogance and empty conceit and vain boastfulness, for the judgment of all his writings he submits not to any one man nor to any few men, but to the whole Church, and even this he does not grant unconditionally, as they say, but is willing to listen to the judgment of the Church only in so far as she judges in accordance with the precepts of the Word of God and the Spirit. Lo, the fierce Philistine, the great and savage giant, who bows not to the judgment of the Emperor alone nor to that of a few assembled in holy synod nor even to that of the whole Church, if God should cause all Christians to come together some time! He demands the inspiration of the Spirit in her, as if it could ever happen that Christ should desert His Church to which He has promised that He will be with her alway even to the end of the world, Matth. 28 [: 20], as if one did not have to stand by the decision and judgment of the priest, as even the old law proclaims, Deut. 17 [: 12], as if the power of the Church, in which even St. Paul boasts, I Cor. 10* and testifies more than once that it has been given to him, did not exist, as if for the sake of one or another rash assailant of the faith the whole Church must be assembled, whose judgment one could still evade when so impelled by frivolous suspicions at his own sweet will, and thus in Zwingli's judgment the saying of Paul would fall to the ground, "The Church of the living God, the pillar and ground of the truth," I Tim. 3 [:15]. Let none, therefore, of discreet judgment take it hard that this faith-destroying leader of heretics is not willing to defer to the most Sacred Emperor, since he even scorns and rejects the judgment of the Church Universal. And this mighty Nimrod writes to the Swiss that he will triumph over all the doctors of the whole world (Ad Helvetios, An. 1526),† and in his book on baptism he declares that it is certain that his opinion will prevail and endure even if the whole world oppose him (Folio 26).‡ How much better Zwingli would have done if he had listened to the advice of the sage when he says, "Extol not thyself in the thoughts of thy soul like a bull; lest thy strength be quashed by folly, and it eat up thy leaves, and destroy thy fruit, and thou be left as a dry tree in the wilderness," Ecclesiasticus 6 [: 2-3].**

*I Cor. 10 should be II Cor. 10: 8.

†In his letter to the twelve confederated cities of Switzerland. Zwingli declared, that if they would hold a conference at Zurich, Berne or St. Gall, he was willing to meet not only Eck and Faber, but all the doctors who opposed the Word of God. See "Ein freundliche Geschrift an gemein Eidgenossen," ed. Schuler and Schulthess, Vol. II, pt. 2, p. 428.

‡In his work on Baptism (ed. Schuler and Schulthess, Vol. II, pt. I. p. 258), Zwingli actually wrote: "In short, it is certain, though the whole world should undertake to fight against me, that no outward element or application can purify the soul."

**Thus in Vulgate; somewhat differently in Greek and hence also in the so-called "Variorum Apocrypha," printed at Oxford.

But let us examine Zwingli's Confession.

ARTICLE I.

In the beginning Zwingli wishes to seem a Christian, though he is very far removed from Christianity, for he adopts a profession of faith in general after the pattern of both the Nicene and the Athanasian Creed. Now this confession of the holy Council of Nice the whole Orthodox Church Universal adopted twelve hundred and six years ago and has held to firmly, so that there was no need of Zwingli's taking up the time of His Imperial Majesty, already overwhelmed with other most serious matters, by rehearsing this confession as if it were new. But there are many things in this article which, though true and undoubted among us Catholics, yet are wondrously at variance with Zwingli's dogmas. For what does he mean by using the Nicene and Athanasian Councils to support the first and chief article of his Confession, when he is otherwise so hostile to the Councils and the Fathers that whatever is determined by them he regards as inventions of man? Likewise, why does he admit three persons in the Godhead when this word "person" in this meaning is not found in the sacred Scriptures, and it is a principle of Zwingli that nothing must be accepted in the faith which is not asserted in clear and plain passages of Scripture? This principle was also used by the men of Berne* in their disputation in January of the year 1528, held in spite of the prohibition of the Imperial Government.†

Furthermore, when he says the Son put on humanity, he finds this nowhere in the sacred writings,‡ nor is the humanity of Christ man. That was the pernicious error of the heretic Nestorius. Zwingli is right when he admits that Mary is perpetually a virgin, but he has this, contrary to his own principle, solely from the tradition of the Church, as also Bucer of Strassburg admitted at Berne (Folio 27), and it will not serve as a proof for Zwingli that he somewhere quotes Isaiah, "Behold, a virgin shall conceive, and bear a son," 7 [: 14] for by these words of the Prophet the virginal birth is indeed proved, which also the heretic Helvidius believed, but that she remained virgin after the birth of her son we learn from the authority of the Church. In like manner Zwingli truly admits (Damasce, fol. 119)** the indissoluble union of natures in Christ, contrary to his own principle, for he cannot prove by the sacred Scriptures that Christ did not lay down what He had once taken up. So he does well

---

*Haller said at Berne (see Zwingli's *Werke*, Schuler and Schulthess edition, II, 1, p. 109): "The Church of Christ has never accepted anything which is not founded upon the Word of God; the Church which is not of Christ, has accepted much that is outside of the Word of God."

†This was the Disputation at Berne, January 5-26, 1528.

‡But see Phil. 2: 7-8.

**The marginal references of Eck are given in the body of the text, to distinguish them from the notes of the editor at the foot of the page. Some of the marginal references are obscure and enigmatical. We reproduce them verbatim, without attempting to explain all of them. In the above quotation, Eck seems to have reference to John of Damascus, who in his "Exposition of the Orthodox Faith," Bk. III. chaps. 3-7, discusses the union of the two natures of Christ. See Schaff, *Nicene and Post-Nicene Fathers*, 2nd Series, Vol. IX, pp. 46-52.

contrary to his own principle in not confusing the natures in Christ, yet in the disputation of Berne they admitted the mixture of the natures with the heretic Eutyches. But it is an innovation on Zwingli's part, contrary to all Scripture, contrary to the Fathers, and contrary to the usage of the Church, when he says "ingenium" instead of "idioma, individual quality" or "genuina natura seu proprietate, inherent nature or characteristic." For he says, "Christ in virtue of the 'native bent' of His human nature, cried as a babe and grew."

But Zwingli consents to explicit heresy when he says here of our Lord Jesus Christ that He increased in wisdom, for which he has given elsewhere (Berne, Folio 125) as the reason that Christ is subject to limitation and measure in His human nature. But this is the heresy of Nestorius that arose from a misunderstanding of Luke's words, "And Jesus advanced in wisdom and age," 2 [: 52]. But the Church has learned from St. John, who with John the Baptist, recognized that Christ is full of grace and truth, John 1 [: 17], and that to Him was given the spirit not by measure, John 3 [: 34]. St. Paul testifies that in Christ "are hid all the treasures of wisdom and knowledge," Col. 2 [: 3]. Therefore Isaiah foresaw in the spirit how the spirit of wisdom and understanding should rest upon Him, Isa. 11 [: 2]. Hence this part of the Confession is to be absolutely rejected, since the whole Church admits that Christ even according to His human nature is omniscient. Therefore, as far as this part is concerned, Zwingli wrongly attributes to the orthodox a view with which they are altogether at variance.

ARTICLE II.

In the second section Zwingli confesses the providence of God, since it determines freely about all things and His designs wait not on the exigencies of created things. Then he takes off the point of this by adding, Thus free will falls to the ground. But although all of us orthodox attribute to God providence over all things—"for so much then as thou art just, thou orderest all things justly," as the Sage says, Wisdom 12 [: 15]—yet to deny free will on that account is the heresy of Manichaeus, or to say that all things take place according to absolute necessity is the heresy of Wycliffe, condemned at the Council of Constance. For the Sage testifies to both the providence of God and free will at once: "God of my fathers, . . . who hast made all things with Thy word, and by Thy wisdom hast appointed man, that he should have dominion over the creature that was made by Thee, that he should order the world according to . . . justice, and with an upright heart," etc. Wisdom 9 [: 1-3].

Only how could he order, how show uprighteousness of heart, if he had no free will, as this new Manichaeus declares? And since Zwingli himself does so many things according to his own depraved free will, one must assuredly wonder why he so shamelessly denies free will, since to him and to Oecolampadius are most truly applicable the words of Isaiah, "Thou hast done evil things, because thou has been able," Isaiah 56.* Verily

*The reference ought to have been to Jer. 3: 5.

Zwingli is a blockhead, a dolt, a dunce, who denies free will. Let him hear even God saying by the mouth of Isaiah, "If you be willing, and will hearken to me, you shall eat the good things of the land. But if you will not, and will provoke me to wrath, the sword shall devour you," Isa. 1 [: 19-20].* And lest our opponent grumble, I will quote even Christ's words against him, "Jerusalem, . . . how often would I have gathered together thy children, as the hen doth gather her chickens under her wings, and thou wouldest not," Matth. 33 [: 37].† Do you hear, Manichaeus, when God would gather them, men would not? And how are all of us Christians to take the statement with composure that thus free will falls to the ground when we are sure from the words of St. Paul, who framed his course firmly in his own heart, not being bound but having power to follow his own will, Rom. 7.‡ Granting, therefore, divine providence which all of us Christians frankly confess, it was not on that account necessary to reject and deny free will with the heretic Manichaeus and the stupid philosophers Empedocles, Critolaus, Diodorus and the rest, who were hissed and driven out even by the heathen.

Nor is Zwingli free from guilt when he charges the fathers of the Old Testament with the most serious sins, that they saw themselves damned in their own judgment, that they cast off all hope of attaining felicity, and that they went in despair from the sight of God because their only thought was that they were going to suffer the pain of everlasting torture, when really the fathers of the Old Testament relied on the greatest of hopes and awaited with incomparable faith the mediator between God and man. In this faith St. Paul says, the elders had witness borne to them [Hebr. 11: 2]. St. Paul brings forward Abel, Enoch, Noah, Abraham, Sara: "All these died according to faith, not having received the promises, but behold-ing them afar off, and saluting them, and confessing that they are pil-grims and strangers on the earth. For they that say these things, do signify that they seek a country." Hebr. 11 [: 13-14]. He bears witness of Moses that "he looked unto the reward," and having enumerated several fathers St. Paul sums up with the words, "by faith conquered kingdoms, wrought justice, obtained promises," [11: 33]. Since, therefore, the chosen vessel attributes so much faith and such good works to the fathers, who is going to believe Zwingli when he attributes to them a sort of despair and other execrable sins? The assertions of Zwingli in the rest of this article are rather obscure and put in very general terms, and I will therefore postpone routing their mists until the cataracts of his errors shall be let loose.

ARTICLE III.

Zwingli here brings forward Christ as the one and only victim for our sins, and reasons cunningly from this that there is no justification by works, no atonement. Though it does not escape me what impieties and heaps of errors Zwingli founds upon this article, yet, since they are all

*This is the reading of the Vulgate. The King James Version differs somewhat.
†A misprint for 23.
‡Where did Paul make such a statement in Romans, chap. 7?

wrongly deduced, I want, for the present, only to defend that which Zwingli repudiates here, for as to the justification by works, that not only takes nothing from the excellence of the victim, that is Christ, but makes it especially necessary, and since I have brought forward elsewhere much to support this, let it suffice now to quote the testimony of St. Peter when he says, "Wherefore, brethren, labor the more that by good works you may make sure of your calling and election" II Pet. 1 [: 10].* So also I have proved atonement from the Scriptures, for that holy soul John in the Apocalypse says to the Church at Ephesus, "Be mindful therefore from whence thou art fallen, and do penance, and do the first works," Rev. 2 [: 5]. John does not say, "There is one victim for expiating sin, namely Christ, and there is no need of making atonement," but he bids us repent and do works.

So also St. Paul well knew how grateful and acceptable the offering of Christ was, yet he does not fail to note that justification by works is necessary, saying of the coming of our Saviour, "who gave himself for us, that he might redeem us from all iniquity, and might cleanse to himself a people acceptable, a pursuer of good works," Titus 2 [: 14]. Christ did not, therefore, wish to make us idle by His holy offering, but, as St. John the Baptist preached, he wishes us to "bring forth fruits worthy of repentance," Matth. 3 [: 8]. This it seems to me David indicated beautifully in the Psalms, especially when he said, "Blessed are they whose transgressions are forgiven, and whose sins are covered," Ps. 31 [: 1],† signifying that it is not enough that sins be forgiven. They must also be covered by atonement. For thus St. Ambrose skilfully explains this passage. Zwingli is too near the Novatian heretics who deny the value of repentance, for he rejects atonement which is no mean part of it. Hence the complaint fits him which St. Cyprian addressed to Pope Cornelius in the matter of the Novatians:—"They labor to prevent divine clemency from healing the wounded in His Church, they corrupt the repentance of the wretched men by the deceitfulness of their lies, that it may not satisfy an offended God, that one who has been ashamed or afraid to be a Christian may not afterwards seek Christ his Lord, nor he that had withdrawn from the Church return to her. They put forth efforts that sins may not be atoned for with just satisfaction and lamentations, that the wounds may not be washed away with tears." (Book I, Epist.).‡ I might bring forward other most certain proofs had I not determined carefully to shun and avoid overdoing things. I have treated briefly of this testimony in another answer, and if by the one mediator Zwingli meant to repudiate the invocation of the saints, I have refuted his view in the same answer.

ARTICLE IV.

Zwingli brings out his view on original sin in such uncertain words

---

*The best Greek Mss. omit the words "good works."
†Psalm 32: 1 in the Authorized Version.
‡Migne, *Patrologia Latina*, Vol. III, 839*f*; 12th epistle, §13. See also *Cypriani Opera*, Oxford edition, Letter LIX, §13; Vol. I, 839; *Ante-Nicene Christian Library*, Edinburgh, 1868, VIII, 171.

that in one breath he asserts it, in the next denies it. In his little book on baptism* he altogether denied that the original blemish was a sin, it was just a natural defect like stammering. Here he both admits and denies original sin. But before we examine this article, the Catholic doctrine must be set forth, namely that all the descendants of Adam contracted original sin except those who by special privilege were preserved guiltless, for to say the contrary was the heresy of the Pelagians, condemned first in the Council of Mileve,† afterwards in the Roman Council. The Holy Scriptures also plainly prove this. David cries out, "Behold, I was conceived in iniquities; and in sins did my mother conceive me," Psalm 50 [: 7].‡ Paul, the apostle, cries out, "we were by nature the children of wrath, even as others," Eph. 2 [: 3]. He also writes to the Romans, "For all have sinned, and do need the glory of God," Rom. 3 [: 23], and again, "As by one man sin entered into this world, and by sin death; and so death passed upon all men, in whom all have sinned," Rom. 5 [: 12], and below, "As by the disobedience of one man many were made sinners," etc., Rom. 5 [: 19]. This heresy was destroyed by those two hammerers of heretics, St. Augustine and St. Jerome. Let us now hear how Zwingli raves. "Sin," he says, "properly taken, is guilt, a crime, offense, or wrongdoing," and in this way he denies that original sin is sin, and straightway forgetting himself he admits that we are born into slavery, as sons of wrath, and subject to death. But now I challenge Zwingli and all Zwinglians to say whether to be subject to wrath and death does not mean wrong-doing, and since they will not venture to deny this if they have any brains, it follows that original sin is properly speaking sin, which Zwingli distinctly repudiated in the beginning.

Moreover, what he adds about the necessity of death being original sin is wide of the truth. Otherwise, since in the case of the baptized the necessity of death remains, original sin would also remain, but to say that would be to invalidate the truth of the faith and the efficacy of the sacraments, as Luther does, for St. Peter declares that we have been "regenerated unto a lively hope, by the resurrection of Jesus Christ, unto an inheritance incorruptible," I Pet. 1 [: 3-4], whence St. Paul calls baptism the washing of regeneration and renovation of the Holy Spirit.** Therefore Zwingli belabors St. Paul, twisting his above quoted utterances, as is plainly evident from Augustine, "On the Merits and Remission of Sin."†† Hence Zwingli's view is impious, that we die in consequence of another's guilt but through our own condition, nor will he get any support from the Theologians (Li. 2. def. 32),‡‡ who hold that original sin is the habitual sin of Adam, for they are far from explaining it as Zwingli does, as can be easily seen in the Theological Commentaries, (in the articles at the end).

*See ed. Schuler and Schulthess, II, 1, p. 287f.
†The Synod of Mileve, Numidia, was held in 416 A. D.
‡Ps. 50: 7 in Vulgate, but 51: 5 in King James Version.
**Titus 3: 5.
††See Migne, 1. c., XLIV, 110-199; Schaff, *Nicene Fathers,* 1st Series, V, 15-78.
‡‡Eck has here reference to Peter Lombard's Sentences, Bk. II, Dist. 32, in which the Master of the Sentences discusses the question of original sin and how it is removed through baptism.

Let us, therefore, admit that children have not only the penalty of sin but also its guilt.

But one point Zwingli passes over in silence, namely, what he heralded forth so loudly at Zurich, that the young children of Christians are saved without baptism.* Thus, contrary to Christ's decree, one not "born of water and of the Spirit," John 3 [: 5], could enter into the kingdom of heaven. He should have added where in the sacred writings he found his distinction between the young children of Christians and those of infidels. Finally let him show how he is in harmony with the Church of Strassburg, where Bucer writes that original sin is a stain upon mankind, such that unless it be cleansed by the blood of Christ one cannot attain salvation. For how can he be saved whom deadly disease holds in its grasp? Thus shall the kingdom divided against itself be made desolate, Matth. 12 [: 25]. All the points he makes therefore in his fifth article fall to the ground. In it he not only openly champions the Pelagian heresy, but draws the unwarranted inference from the Apostle's words that young children of the class that die without baptism are saved, because St. Paul writes, "As in Adam all die, so also in Christ shall all be made alive," I Cor. 15 [: 22], by which he means that even young children are restored to life in Christ. But here it becomes clear to everybody in what spirit Zwingli handles the sacred Scriptures, nay distorts and mangles them, for while St. Paul is speaking in this passage of the resurrection from the dead after the manner of Christ, this perverter of the sacred writings has the effrontery to twist it into meaning the resurrection from sin through grace. But if he wanted to do this at all, why did he not make a statement about the young children of infidels, since St. Paul puts their case and life on the same footing— "as in Adam all die." This certainly is proclaimed to unbelievers also. Why, then, does only what follows, "so also in Christ shall all be made alive," not apply to the same individuals? With the like lack of knowledge he argues from the children of the Jews. For I want the Scripture passage for his assumption that the uncircumcised infants of the Jews belonged to the Church of God, since according to the view of Augustine as it was said of the Church—"Unless a man be born again," etc., John 3 [: 3],—so also to the ancients it was said, "The male, whose flesh of his foreskin shall not be circumcised, that soul shall be destroyed out of his people; because he hath broken my covenant," Gen. 17 [: 14]. This pamphlet of confession is therefore to be rejected, being, as it is, so often at variance with the Church, with the Catholic faith and with the sacred Scriptures. I might also reproach him with contradicting wholly Luther and the Lutherans who declare that original sin is properly speaking sin.

ARTICLE VI.

Zwingli tries to explain here what the Church is, but after the manner of Anaxagoras confuses the whole thing and makes it more involved. And not this only. He mixes in errors and heresies all through it, for his articles are strewn with flowers and gems of the kind. Let us run through

*Zwingli discusses this point in his tract "On Original Sin," see above p. 18f.

them cursorily and mark with a dagger the things not to be believed.

In the first place, I wonder that he says "Church" is used in different senses in the Scriptures, since otherwise he scorns and jeers at the distinctions of the theologians. But let us see how he classifies the varieties. First he says "Church" is used for those elect who have been destined by the will of God to eternal life, the Church of which Paul speaks when he says it has neither spot nor wrinkle, Eph. 5 [: 27]. In this statement there are about as many errors as there are words. For it is a damnable error that the Church consists only of the predestined,* an error condemned in both the Roman Council and the Council of Constance, and I have refuted it elsewhere, nor can he ever prove his assertion from the sacred writings, as I shall show presently by laying bare the perversion by which he has distorted St. Paul's words. I admit, therefore, that to the perfect Church belong by number and right the righteous only, for the Sage says, "The sons of wisdom are the church of the just : and their generation, obedience and love," Ecclesiasticus 3 [: 1].†

Secondly, he did not quote St. Paul appropriately whom he mangled so badly. For St. Paul says, "Christ loved the Church, and delivered himself up for it, that he might sanctify it, cleansing it by the laver of water in the word of life, that he might present it to himself a glorious church, not having spot, or wrinkle, or any such thing; but that it might be holy and without blemish," Eph. 5 [: 25-27]. If one pays attention, he notices that Paul does not declare that the Church is without wrinkle or spot. But he teaches at least for the time being, that it is undergoing sanctification and cleansing by Christ, that he may present it to himself a holy and glorious church. For, if it had been holy and without spot before, there would be no need of cleansing, but the heavenly husbandman, as Christ says, will purge every branch that beareth fruit, that it may bring forth more fruit, John 15 [: 2]. These words St. Augustine well explains of purification in this life. The Church is not, therefore, at present without wrinkle or spot but it is daily undergoing purification and purging by Christ, that he may be able to present it to himself a glorious church,—at the time, namely, "When he shall deliver up the kingdom to God, even the father," I Cor. 15 [: 24].

Let me add also that Zwingli in this article contradicts both the Catholics and the Lutherans. I say the Lutherans (Luther in *Assert. Art.* 31),‡ because though they maintain (albeit wrongly) that the righteous man sins in all his works, and that all the works of men, however praiseworthy in appearance, are works absolutely vicious and sins worthy of death, (Melanchthon in *Locis Communibus*), Zwingli, on the other hand, has the effrontery to set up a church without wrinkle or spot made up out of his saintlets. Moreover, the orthodox and Zwingli do not agree, for

*Eck refuses to make the distinction between visible and invisible Church.

†This passage, found in the Vulgate, is missing in the Septuagint and the English version based on the latter. It goes back to a secondary Hebrew text. See Charles, *Apocrypha.*

‡The reference is to Luther's "Assertio omnium articulorum M. Lutheri per bullam Leonis X," 1520. See Luther's *Werke,* Weimar edition, Vol. VII, p. 37.

though they deny that the righteous man sins in all his works, yet sin creepeth daily upon the righteous, "for there is not a just man upon earth, that . . . sinneth not," Eccles. 7 [: 20]; and all, however saintly, pray daily, "And forgive us our debts," Matth. 6 [: 12], so that the Council of Mileve, according to the rule of the faith, rightly condemned the Pelagians in this, to whom and to Zwingli St. John also is opposed when he says, "If we say that we have no sin, we deceive ourselves, and the truth is not in us," I John 1 [: 8]. Let Zwingli be off, then, with his righteous mannikins that have no wrinkle nor spot.

We, on the contrary, in the Church know our Mother, and as lawful offspring recognize her when she says, "I am black, but comely," (she calls herself black because of sin) "as the tents of Kedar," Song of Solomon 1 [: 5] (which belong to Ishmael, who did not inherit with the son of the free woman, as Paul says, Gal. 4 [: 23]); she calls herself black "as the curtains of Solomon," sprinkled with daily spots, but since many in her shine brilliantly in Christian love, she also ventures to call herself comely. It is clear, therefore, in how many things Zwingli is blind here, though he wishes to seem so clearsighted to the Emperor. It is as if we heard the monster himself belching forth his harangues to the ignorant and mad populace. But let me proceed to the rest of his errors.

Zwingli lays it down besides that this Church is known only to God, for according to Solomon's words He only knoweth the hearts of the children of men, III Kings 8 [: 39].* I shall show later that this view also is without truth, but Zwingli himself, I may say in passing, contradicts and destroys his own statements here, for having said that the church of the predestined was known to God alone, he yet forgets himself and says further that those who are members of the church when they have faith, know that they are elect and are members of this first Church. Forsooth, what do I hear? This holy church of Zwingli is known only to God, and yet it is at the same time known to the Zwingli saintlets. They that have faith know according to Zwingli that they are elect, but according to Scripture and the Church they do not know it, for the Preacher says, "Man knoweth not whether he be worthy of love or hatred,"† Eccles. 9 [: 1], and St. Paul says, "Wherefore he that thinketh himself to stand, let him take heed lest he fall," [I Cor. 10: 12].

Now this godlessness Zwingli owes to his teachers, Luther and Melanchthon, although in his pride he disdains to acknowledge them, for one writes, (Melanchthon, in Locis Communibus) "It is a perfectly certain proposition that we are always perfectly certain of the forgiveness of sin. The holy know that they are in favor, and that their sins have been pardoned," and the other says, (Luther on Gal. 5 and Psal. 5): "Let the Christian beware of ever feeling any uncertainty as to whether he is in God's favor, or whether his works are pleasing to God. For he that doubts thus sins, and loses all his works." From this sink Zwingli drew a cup of error, and is sure of his salvation, but the devout sons of the Church, even though

---

*I Kings in Authorized Version.
†Thus in Vulgate. Slightly different in Authorized Version.

they "have confidence, hope being set before them," as Job says, 11 [: 18], are yet not without fear, because "he that is without fear cannot be justified," says the Sage, Ecclesiasticus 1 [: 28],* and on this account all the days of their lives are they in the fear of the Lord because they shall have hope on the last day.

It is a very small point but it shows the marked ignorance of Zwingli that quoting the passage from the Acts of the Apostles, "and as many as were ordained to life everlasting believed," Acts 13 [: 48], he turns it about and says, "Therefore those that believe are ordained to eternal life,"† which is a most pernicious error, arising here from the fallacy of the consequent. For though it is true that all those ordained believe, yet we may not turn this into the statement that all believers are thus ordained, although Bucer sticks tenaciously to this heresy, and at Berne burst out (Folio 43) into the impiety that he who has once believed that Christ Jesus has redeemed him has the seal of the Holy Ghost and never can commit deadly sin. Luther, driven by the same madness, raves that there are no works of a believer in Christ so bad that they can accuse and condemn him (De votis et in ser. Sic deus dilexit, etc.), while St. Paul contradicts them in the words, "And if I should have all faith, so that I could remove mountains, and have not charity, I am nothing," I Cor. 13 [: 2].

Then Zwingli comes down to the other two uses of the word "Church." For secondly, "church" is used universally for all who have given allegiance to Christ, and thirdly "church" is understood of any particular company of any individual church, as the Roman Church, the Augsburg Church, etc. But here I challenge Zwingli, since we Christians ought to speak according to a fixed rule in the opinion of Augustine, and it is clear from Scripture that this second use of the word "Church" is the really proper one,—I challenge him to show why he abandons this and goes over to his own visions and concoctions about his new church of saintlets, when otherwise he is so hard upon the heavenly saints as to declare that they are not members of Christ (Berne, 146),‡ whence it follows that in his opinion they are not members of the Church, which the orthodox would shudder to admit. And that this is the true and proper meaning of the word "church" is clearly seen from Christ's words, for a guest came to the wedding "who had not on a wedding garment," Matth. 22 [: 11], and the kingdom of heaven is "like unto ten virgins, who taking their lamps, went out to meet the bridegroom and the bride,** and five of them were foolish," Matth. 25 [1-2],†† and in the Lord's field there grow both good grain and cockle, Matth. 13 [: 26], and in the net of the Church both good fish and bad are taken. St. John the Baptist bears witness that Christ will find both chaff and wheat upon His threshing floor, Matth. 3 [: 12].

*Thus in Vulgate; but 1: 22 in "Variorum Apocrypha."
†The text has "fidem, faith," but that must be a slip for "vitam, life."
‡What Zwingli actually said was, that Paul's reference to one body, which has many members, in I. Cor. 12: 12, did not include the saints in heaven, but only those in this world. See Zwingli's *Werke*, ed. Schuler and Schulthess, II, 1, p. 169.
**The words, "and the bride," omitted in the King James Version, appear in the Vulgate, as well as in several Greek Mss.
††The text has Matth. 20, a misprint for 25.

Since, therefore, Christ has so often taught us how we ought to speak of the Church, why does Zwingli depart, along with Luther, from the Gospel form of speech, and in order to bring a new error into the Church, make use of a new method of speaking also, at variance with the Church? For as in the natural body there are good and bad humors, so in the body of Christ, which is the Church, are there good and bad, and as in hell there are only bad, in heaven only good, so in the middle sphere, namely the Church, there are both good and bad. That there is this mixture in the Church all Scripture testifies, all the faithful admit, save only these new teachers of churches who take to themselves more than the Apostles, the pillars of the Church, fancying that they can separate the tares from the wheat even before the time of the harvest, Matth. 13 [: 30].

Having, therefore, destroyed the foundations of this article, it is easy to demolish what the foolish man Zwingli thus builds upon the sand, Matth. 7 [: 26]. For as to his including the Roman Church among his examples as a particular church, that, I think, not even the Pontiff will deny him, who when he goes out of the confines of the diocese of Rome dates his letters from the individual churches where he happens to be tarrying. But if, with his usual viciousness, Zwingli means by this to assert that "Roman Church" is never to be understood of that which is universal, I do not allow that for it is not in accordance with the truth, as I have abundantly shown in my three books on the Primacy of Peter. For the Christian world of Europe, as it now exists, belongs properly to the Roman Church, not only because the Chief Pontiff presides over that, but also because he is the real Patriarch, nay the Roman patriarchate was once far larger than Christianity is now, since there were under it all the bishops of Africa, Numidia, Mauretania, also of Greece, for whom he had as vicar the Bishop of Thessalonica. But a great portion of the earth has now, for our sins, been taken away from the Roman patriarchate, nay from Christianity, and serves a wretched slavery under the Mohammedan yoke or the cruel Turks or the barbarous kings of Tunis, Fez, Morocco and others.

Thus Zwingli narrows too much the church which cannot err, by confining it to that which is without spot, but of this further on. Let Zwingli himself consider how far he has wandered with the Lutherans from the one visible Church, since the pamphlets of their confessions, though not at all agreeing with the Catholic Church, differ very greatly from each other, as in the Appendix he controverts the confession of the Anabaptists on the subject of the baptism of the infants of Christians. Yet Zwingli forgets that elsewhere (In Articul. & de Baptismo*) he expressed the opinion that it is far better that infants be not baptized until they grow up, and Balthasar,† the father of the Anabaptists, bears witness that he had a writing of Zwingli in which he urged him to this heresy.‡

*In his book on Baptism, Schuler and Schulthess edition, Vol. II, p. 1, p. 245. But Zwingli confesses that he had been misled into this error.
†Balthasar Huebmaier, born 1480, burned at the stake 1528.
‡Huebmaier related (as quoted by Schuler and Schulthess, l. c., 1, p. 245 note a)

But let us press Zwingli a little closer here. Since he mentions a triple use of the word "Church," why does he pass by with ears stopped up, so to speak, the "church representative," which is recognized in the General and the Oecumenical Councils?* But I know what obstacle prevented him. He denied once that the congregation of the Pontiff, Cardinals, Bishops, Prelates and Doctors was the Church, for he was afraid of being crowded by the authority of the Councils, and he thought that in this way he could break the authority of the Synods, and not be pressed too hard. This is plain in his Zurich articles. This error of his was tenaciously held by Haller, the corrupter of Berne, by Bucer and others. (Art. 8 Fol. 3, etc.) But after the fashion of heretics Zwingli is at variance not only with the Church but with himself, for in his Subsidium de Eucharistia, written to the Maii, those Capernaites, he says among other things,† "Certain people slander us in regard to the usage of the Two Hundred (that is the two hundred senators), saying that we allow things which ought to belong to the whole Church to be managed by two hundred, when the Church in the whole city and neighborhood numbers seven thousand, more or less." Afterwards he makes further statements about The Two Hundred, that they act in the name of the Church, and concludes with the words, "Thus we use at Zurich the Senate of Two Hundred, which is the supreme authority, in place of the Church." Since, then, Zwingli asserts the church representive at Zurich, why does he deny it in other places, in provinces and kingdoms, and even in the whole Roman Empire? Why does he not mention among the meanings of "church," this meaning also of church representative? Since this use also of "church" is based upon the sacred writings, it is wrongfully passed over by Zwingli here.

I want, therefore, to prove the church representative at this point. We read in the Book of Kings in regard to Solomon, "The king turned his face, and blessed all the assembly of Israel : for all the assembly of Israel stood," etc., III Kings [I Kings] 8 [: 14]. We have heard the Holy Spirit speaking of the Church; what it spoke of the Church Representative, is plain from the beginning of the same chapter, where we read, "Then all the ancients of Israel, with the princes of the tribes, and the heads of the families of the children of Israel were assembled to King Solomon," [8: 1].‡ Not, therefore, all the people of the Jews assembled unto King Solomon, but the princes, the heads, and the ancients, who represented all Israel.

ARTICLE VII.

Presently he adorns the seventh article with the boldness of a Hercules—"I believe, nay, know that all the sacraments are so far from

that Zwingli confessed to him personally, when they took a walk along the moat one day, that infant baptism was not right, before the children were instructed in the faith.
    *Zwingli refers to this "representative church," in his book "De canone epicheiresis," see *Werke*, ed. Egli and Finsler, II, 571, where he discusses the different meanings of the Church; see also his "De vera et falsa religione," in Zwingli's *Werke*, ed. Egli and Finsler, III, 747-751.
    †See ed. of Schuler and Schulthess, Vol. III, p. 339.
    ‡Thus in the Douay Version; slightly different in the Authorized Version.

bestowing grace," etc. While Zwingli, not only believing but also knowing (perhaps he had been carried off with St. Paul into the third heaven) that the sacraments do not bestow grace, has involved himself in the greatest impiety—for a heretic was excommunicated for holding a view about the sacraments other than that taught by the Roman Catholic Church (C. Ad abolendam de heret.)—this article has been condemned by Pope Leo X, of blessed memory, against Luther. For this article denies the virtue of the passion of Christ, from which all the sacraments derive their force and efficacy. It takes all comfort from the faithful, whose consciences, otherwise troubled, are refreshed by the mystery of the sacraments, and, what is most abhorrent to the feelings of the faithful, to say that the sacraments do not bestow grace is just the same as if one said a sacrament was not a sacrament.

The expounding of this article involves Zwingli in so many errors that he depicts himself plainly, what ignorance and lack of knowledge he brings to the treatment of the sacred Scriptures. He uses the word "gratia" [grace] in Latin, in place of "pardon" and "indulgence." This, because some one from the school of Priscian and Perotus ventures to usurp the chair of St. Paul. This Rhadamanthus* among theologians, Zwingli, refuses to accept anything unless it agrees with the sacred Scriptures, yet here he is diametrically opposed to Holy Scripture, because the little grammatical pettifogger does not yet know in what sense the Holy Spirit used this word "gratia," etc.,—full of grace and truth," John 1 [: 14]. Yet Christ by no means needed indulgence and forgiveness of sins. So often does Paul testify of grace given to him and to others, I Cor. 3 [: 10]; 15 [: 10], as we see upon almost every page, and he writes to the Corinthians, "Now there are diversities of gifts, but the same spirit."† Therefore the holy Fathers understand by "gratia" a gift given by God, which either is given "gratis, freely," or makes one "gratum, acceptable," to God. I know what deceived our grammarian-theologian Zwingli. He happened to hear from the theologians that sins were remitted by the grace of God, and being unskilled in things theological he did not know that sin was not remitted by a general law without the bestowal of an exceptional gift which is called grace. It is from this that Zwingli's error arose.

When, furthermore, he says that the sacrament is not a vehicle of the Spirit, if I mistake not, he is looking to the followers of Luther, who in the pamphlet of their confession, presented by their most illustrious princes, conceded that the Spirit is given by the sacraments and by the Word as by an instrument. (Article 5).‡

Zwingli is here trying to upset this article, on the ground that the Spirit does not need a vehicle. Certainly Zwingli is a most stupid seer who in the bluntness of his perceptions does not yet understand how the Fathers

*Rhadamanthus was a judge in the infernal regions.
†I Cor. 12: 4.
‡Article 5 of the Augsburg Confession, reads: "For by the Word and Sacraments. as by instruments, the Holy Spirit is given." See Schaff, *Creeds of Christendom*, Vol. III, p. 10.

say that the Spirit is given by the sacraments. The Spirit does not drive in on a chariot, but God alone, by His almighty power, infuses grace into the human soul by visible signs made efficacious by Him. The water is not in itself effective unto grace in the soul of the child except as an indispensable accompaniment, but God Himself creates grace in the soul of the child. But I speak to deaf ears, for the thing is above Zwingli's comprehension, as is evident from his inappropriate raillery about preparation for the sacrament. For he says like a parrot, since there is not a uniform method of preparing for the different sacraments, "And it is necessary for the Holy Spirit to precede the reception of the sacrament by grace given freely, making him acceptable before he receives grace, yet in the case of a child nothing of this kind is demanded, if he makes no objection."*

It remains to show how wrongly he maintains that the sacraments are given as a testimony only. How near is Zwingli now to the Anabaptists, whom nevertheless, like a new Phalaris,† he torments to death in the Wellenburg‡ and tortures limb by limb! For they too deny all the sacraments and admit them only as signs and witnesses without efficacy, and, taught by the impious Carlstadt, father of the Capernaites, dare to call the holy mysteries of the Church "Sekerment," and, copying the faithlessness of the Jews, say a sacrament is a lie and vanity and deception. How far, therefore, from the Anabaptists is Zwingli when he recklessly proclaims here, "The Church by baptism publicly receives him who has been previously received through grace?" Why then did Christ say, "Unless a man be born again of water and of the Holy Ghost," etc., John 3 [: 5]? If he has previously been washed by grace and by the Holy Spirit, he would not have to be born again. Not, therefore, of past grace is the sacrament the sign, but of present grace, bestowed upon the baptized through the Holy Spirit present in the sacrament.

It is therefore, empty jeering when Zwingli says here in his sleep that a boy has already been baptized when he is brought up for baptism, because the divine promise has preceded, but let this profaner of all sacraments come forward and make us believe that that promise has been made that the boy should receive faith before baptism has been submitted to. Let him show clear Scripture for that promise, and not spit out in a demoniacal spirit** whatever his own mad brain suggests to him. He quotes the Apostle to the Romans, but in both cautious and Zwinglian fashion suppresses some of his words, for if he brought them forth, his view would suffer great loss. Paul says, "All we who are baptized in Christ Jesus, are baptized in his death," Rom. 6 [: 3], which words are so far from supporting Zwingli that they utterly confute him. For to be baptized in the death of Christ means that through the virtue of His passion we attain the grace of God in baptism. Otherwise,—if baptism bestowed no grace and the grace of God were given previously, how could St. Paul have said

*This is a perversion rather than a quotation of Zwingli's confession.
†A tyrant of Agrigentum, Sicily, 570-554 B. C.
‡That Catabaptists were tortured in the Wellenburg, the prison at Zurich, at Zwingli's demand, cannot be proved, though he was an onlooker.
**For "phytonico" we read "pythonico," from pytho, "demon."

that we are baptized in the death of Christ, all we who are baptized? And all this St. Augustine confirms most strongly by the testimony of the sacred Scriptures, but for brevity's sake I will not quote his words.

Let Zwingli, therefore, go to perdition with Oecolampadius, Bucer, Zwick, and Haller,* who with reckless impiety calls the Christian view of the sacraments Judaism, as if the holy mysteries of our faith were no more efficacious than the shadowy and figurative ceremonies of the Jews. I laugh at the empty boasting of Zwingli that he was the first to teach and write against the Anabaptists, since I am aware that it was Zwingli who by his counsel and advice really founded this lost sect, and was goaded more by jealousy than love of the truth in his pursuit of Balthasar the Catabaptist, as all his neighbors testify. Wherefore let no good man believe Zwingli even under oath when he says that he has not accepted nor taught any of the doctrines of this seditious party, for his published books convict him of lying. For we read in his articles (Art. 18, Fol. 71),† "Although I know, as the ancients tell us, that in old times infants were sometimes baptized, yet this was not so very frequent as in our day. They were taught together publicly after they were old enough to use their reason,—and on that account they were called catechumens,—and when they confessed with their lips that faith was firmly implanted in their hearts, then they were admitted to baptism, and this fashion of teaching I want to see revived in these days of ours." Similarly in the book De vera et falsa Religione, he writes (Fol. 159)‡ "Because even the ancients baptized only those who were in the death struggle, and did not always baptize infants." Balthasar the Catabaptist also, in a pamphlet published at Nikolsburg in Moravia had words of Zwingli's printed which advised against the baptism of infants, and said in a note that he had a writing to that effect. Since, therefore Zwingli has been so prominent in the harm done by this sect, how does he dare before our sacred Emperor to say so wantonly that he is guiltless of this sin? Now let us hasten on to other points.

ARTICLE VIII.

This article forms the head and front of Zwingli's impiety; in it he denies the real presence of the body and blood of our Lord Jesus Christ in the venerable sacrament of the Eucharist. Before going on to examine this blasphemous article, I establish the Catholic opinion upon a solid basis from the beginning. In Matthew, Luke and Paul where the institution of this most venerable sacrament is described and where Christ is reported to have made the simple statement: "And taking bread, he gave thanks, and brake, and gave to them, saying: This is my body, which is given for you. Do this in commemoration of me," Matth. 26 [: 26], Mark 14 [: 22], Luke 22 [: 19], I Cor. 11: [: 23-24]. Since, therefore, the Evangelists have shown such close agreement in describing the institution of the sacrament,

---

*John Zwick was preacher and reformer in Constance, Berchtold Haller was the reformer of Berne.

†See Zwingli's *Werke*, Vol. II, 1908, p. 123.

‡See Zwingli's *Werke*, Vol. III, 1914, p. 823. Not a literal quotation.

without any suggestion of a trope or metaphor anywhere, it is a reckless thing to overturn by means of tropes the pure and simple statement of Christ out of one's own brain and in opposition to the understanding and agreement of the whole Church Universal. Besides Christ promised in John, "And the bread that I will give is my flesh, for the life of the world," John 6 [: 52].* He promises that He will give the bread which he did give at the Supper, and He tells what this bread is, namely that it is "my flesh."† And lest some falsifier should twist the word "flesh" into some other meaning, He added clearly "for the life of the world," as much as to say, "the bread that I will give is that same flesh that I shall give on the altar of the cross for the salvation of the whole world." This is also manifest from St. Paul, for he wrote to the Corinthians among other things, "The chalice of benediction, which we bless, is it not the communion of the blood of Christ?" I Cor. 10 [: 16]. He does not say "the communion of wine," but when we take the sacrament of the cup, we take part in the communion of the blood of Christ. And below, "For we, being many, are one bread, one body : all that partake of one bread" and one cup,‡ I Cor. 10 [: 17]. Now it is evident that we are not all partakers of one baker's bread, but the one bread is the body of Christ which is at once in heaven and in all churches. This view of the orthodox Paul confirms to the same Corinthians when he says, "But let a man prove himself, and so let him eat of that bread, and drink of that chalice. For he that eateth and drinketh unworthily, eateth and drinketh judgment to himself, not discerning the body of the Lord," I Cor. 11 [: 29]. He sins in partaking of Christ's body unworthily because of the presence of Christ's body. For how could he be "guilty of the body" of Christ, if he did not eat that, and all opportunity to get away from this is removed by what St. Paul adds, "not discerning the Lord's body"—not distinguishing the sacrament of the Eucharist from baker's bread or ordinary food.

Thus all the councils, all the holy Fathers, the whole Church Universal have always regarded it. And Zwingli himself held it as absolutely established even at the time when he left the Church and gave adherence to Lutheranism. For he says in putting forth his articles, (Fol. 75)** "Let the simple-minded know that it is not brought into controversy here whether the body of Christ and His blood are eaten and drunk, for on that point no Christian has any doubt." And below, (Folios 76, 78 and 97) "Christ has by His own words taught that we are to eat His body and drink His blood. For this it means in both the Greek and the Latin."††

*So in the Vulgate, but John 6: 51, in Authorized Version.
†Augustine may be quoted to explain these words: "Except ye eat the flesh of the son of man," says Christ, "and drink His blood, ye have no life in you." This seems to enjoin a crime or a vice; it is therefore a *figure*, enjoining that we should have share in the sufferings of our Lord, and that we should retain a sweet and profitable memory of the fact that His flesh was wounded and crucified for us. Augustine, Christian Doctrine, III, 16, §24; in Schaff, *Nicene Fathers,* 1st Series, II, 563.
‡The last three words "and one cup," are neither in the Vulgate, nor in any Greek text.
**Zwingli's *Werke,* Voll. II, 1908, p. 128.
††Zwingli's *Werke,* Vol. II, 1908, p. 132. How these words are to be understood

And he adds how God might have spoken more briefly or more literally or clearly, and these clear words he testifies are known to all Christians. Thus more than a score of times is repeated in his books the assertion of the truth of the presence of the body of Christ, even at the time when he had sent back the messenger of the Church. But certainly the words of John are most true, "he that is filthy, let him be filthy still," Rev. 22 [: 11]. Having, therefore, become dirty and filthy with Luther's mud, Zwingli afterwards remained filthy with the mud also of Berengarius, deacon of Angers, whose heresy has been very frequently condemned—in the Council of Turin, in the Council of Worms, and finally in the Council of Rome under Pope Nicholas. Therefore he does wrong to the most reverend Synod who persists in bringing up again and publicly disputing what has been once decided and duly settled, says the Emperor Martian. (L.nemini c. de sum.tri. & fid. Cathol.) Let the sacred Emperor, Charles V, execute the law of this Catholic Emperor in regard to this and other errors, and everlasting renown will be his. Now let us hear Zwingli himself sounding the charge of the forces of impiety.

Stoutly vaunting his heresy and shamelessly condemning the Catholic doctrine, this great Goliath with vast arrogance sings a paean of triumph before victory, and promises the sacred Emperor that he will in a few words make the matter as clear as the sun. How religiously he follows in the footsteps of his grandfathers and great grandfathers! For "all heretics are in the habit," says Gregory, "of promising the truth at the very moment that they teach error." Then he arms himself from the Gospel wrongly understood, draws therefrom captious and clearly illogical arguments, vitiates and mangles the opinions of the doctors of old. Although this impious mockery has already been answered by the learned Bishop John of Rochester,* in most scholarly and complete fashion, yet I will in a very few words demolish his ill-taken points.

In the first place he quotes Christ's remark, "The poor you have always with you : but me you have not always," Matth. 26 [: 11], and "here," says Zwingli, "the presence of the body is denied, for as far as His divine nature is concerned He is always present. Augustine agrees with me, and there is no reason why my opponents should plead that the human part of Christ is everywhere where His divine part is." But who does not understand in what spirit Zwingli handles the sacred Scriptures? It is true that Christ spoke of the presence of the body, but not of every kind of its presence. For He does not deny mysterious presence, but the visible pres-

is clear from a later passage (p. 143): "Behold then, O pious Christian, the body and blood of Christ differs in nothing from the word of faith, that is, His body, slain for us, and His blood, shed for us, has redeemed us and reconciled God to us. If we firmly believe this, our soul has eaten and drunk the flesh and blood of Christ. Moreover, in order that He might make the essence of the testament more easily comprehensible to the simple-minded, Christ gave to His body an eatable form, namely for His body the bread and for His blood the cup or the drink, that they might be confirmed in faith by a visible action, just as in baptism the dipping into water does not wash away sin. unless the one baptized believes in the salvation of the Gospel."

*John Fisher, bishop of Rochester (1459-1535). The book to which Eck refers is entitled "Assertionis Lutheranae Confutatio," 1523.

ence of human intercourse in a body endowed with feeling. The man who does not understand this is blind. But let us put the matter plainly before us. Hilary says, "The meaning of a remark or speech should be found in the reason for making it." If then we look more sharply at the reason for making the remark here, there is no difficulty about the meaning. Mary poured ointment on our Saviour's head; Judas asks indignantly why it was not given to the poor; Christ defends her with the words, "the poor you have always with you;" Luke adds, "and whensoever you will you may do them good," Luke 22.* Therefore we have not Christ with us as Mary anointed Him, and as we do good to the poor who dwell among us in want, for He does not dwell among us to sense, nor is His body henceforth capable of kindly care of this sort. This and nothing else is what Christ meant. And in citing Augustine he acts after his usual fashion. For Augustine puts forth absolutely nothing on Zwingli's side.† He makes two statements. The first applies to Judas and the wicked, that they have not Christ, just as Zwingli has not. The second statement is that though as far as the presence of His Majesty is concerned we have Christ always, as far as the presence of His flesh is concerned, it was right to say to the disciples; "but me you have not always." Thus Augustine. But that Augustine does not deny sacramental presence but only the presence of sense is shown by what follows,—"he only grasps by faith, he does not see with his eyes."‡ And certainly it is great perverseness on Zwingli's part to drag Saint Augustine over to his view, when he avowedly holds and embraces most unequivocally the Catholic view,** that the body of Christ is in the Eucharist as a real presence. But of this more below. It is marked ignorance combined with malice when he foists upon the orthodox the assertion that the human part of Christ is everywhere, just like His divine part. For this is a dream of Zwingli, not of any Catholics. For to be everywhere belongs exclusively to God. But the body of Christ is in many places by repetition through the divine will, which can effect this, "for with God nothing is impossible," Luke I [: 37].

Zwingli quotes further the words of Christ in John, "Again I leave the world, and I go to the Father," John 16 [: 28]. But this bears the same meaning as the former quotation, and this is not impugned by Zwingli's impious rejoinder, "And we should only promote a juggler's trick if we maintained that His natural body was present but invisible." This impiety is a suggestion of Lucifer, who ventures to call the highest mystery of our faith a juggler's trick. For without reason and without Scripture, he babbles out this in sheer recklessness. And that Christ is speaking solely

*The quotation should be Mark 14: 7.

†See Augustine, "On the Gospel of John," Tract L, §13.

‡Augustine's words are: "In respect of His presence in the flesh it was rightly said to the disciples, 'Me ye will not have always.' In this respect the Church enjoyed His presence only for a few days; Now it possesses Him by *faith,* without seeing Him with the eyes." These words certainly favor Zwingli's view.

**Impartial modern historians admit that Augustine does not hold the Catholic view of transubstantiation. Thus Harnack says: "Augustine deals with the elements symbolically." See Harnack, *History of Dogma,* Engl. Trans., Boston, 1903, Vol. V, p. 159.

of visible leaving of the world and human intercourse, He Himself openly
declares when He says, "A little while, and you shall not see me," John
16 [: 16]. And His showing Himself in visible and palpable shape later,
after the resurrection, contributed to strengthening faith in the resurrection, as Luke bears witness "To whom also He shewed Himself alive after
His passion by many proofs, for forty days appearing to them, and speaking of the kingdom of God," etc., Acts 1 [: 3]. This same point St. Paul
treats at length to the Corinthians, "For if Christ be not risen again, our*
faith is vain," 1 Cor. 15 [: 17]. Therefore the truth in the matter of the
resurrection of Christ had to be well established, and after it was established it was expedient for Him not to appear visibly any more but to be
veiled in mysteries. "For human faith has no merit when human reason
furnishes experimental proof," says Gregory.

Thirdly Zwingli quotes Christ's words thus : Ego post hac non ero in
mundo : hi sunt in mundo, i. e., "Henceforth I shall not be in the world, but
these are in the world," John 17 [: 11]. "This antithesis plainly shows that
He was not in the world in a human sense at the time when the disciples
still lived," says Zwingli. But Christ is here also speaking of bodily
presence, as to which He was going to leave the world and human intercourse. Why does he not bring up Augustine† here? He says: "Thus He
speaks, like a man to men, according to the custom and usage of human
speech." But it is a fair and beautiful spectacle to see Zwingli, the famous
boaster, talking Greek in the presence of the sacred Emperor. . He quotes
John in Greek, "καὶ οὐκ ἔτι εἰμὶ ἐν τῷ κόσμῳ, and now I *am* no more in
the world," but as he plainly alters the text, he is easily seen to be
a falsifier and subverter. For while Christ says, "οὐκ εἰμί. i. e., I am
not," Zwingli vitiates it and reads, "non ero, i. e., I shall not be,"
and while Christ says, " ἔτι, " which points to present time, Zwingli
mangles it into the future "henceforth." Hence the translator whom the
Church employs‡ is more correct in his reading, "Et iam non sum in
mundo," i. e., "and now I am not in the world." This is the reading of
Augustine, of Chrysostom, of Theophylactus, but Zwingli, in order to shut
out future presence in the Sacrament, has dared to change the writing of
the Holy Spirit—evident impostor and worthless deceiver that he is!

Furthermore he brings in Mark and Luke in both the Gospel and the
Acts to testify that Christ was received up into heaven, was taken up and
carried into heaven, and would return, Mark 16 [: 19], Luke 24 [: 51], Acts
I [: 9]. But who denies this? Such a one would be to us as a pagan and
a publican. For Christ is no longer with us in visible bodily presence and
human intercourse, having left the world, but He will return in the same
visible form to judge the quick and the dead. But as to this crafty de-
stroyer of the vineyard of the Lord pretending there are some who say
that the human part of Christ is everywhere or nowhere, that is trifling

---

*The King James version has "your," as has also the Vulgate.
†Augustine, "On the Gospel of John," Tract CVII, §4. In this paragraph
Augustine says also: "He declared that He was no longer in the world, that is to
say, in His bodily presence."
‡Jerome in the Vulgate.

and nonsense. Neither is asserted by the Catholics. Perhaps, though, Zwingli, being wholly ignorant of all theology, has failed to get at the meaning of some doctor.

We have seen how far from accomplishing anything Zwingli was against the reality of the body of Christ in the sacrament, however much he vaunted the passages quoted. Let us examine what follows, in which he tries to discredit the communion of the Eucharist, on the ground that when the Jews disputed about bodily eating of the flesh of Christ He said, "The flesh profiteth nothing," John 6 [: 63], namely, as far as physical eating is concerned. But Zwingli plainly shows himself here to be a new Capernaite. For when Christ had spoken to them of eating His body, they murmured and said, "This saying is hard, and who can hear it?" John 6 [: 60]. "They looked upon flesh," says Augustine (August. tract 57),* "as it is torn asunder in the case of a carcass or sold in the market place." No one may eat the body of Christ in this Turkish fashion. Hence it is a blasphemous idea of Zwingli that when the body of Christ is eaten by our mouths, nothing comes of the flesh save flesh. For the flesh of Christ is not eaten physically, so as to pass into the stomach, be changed by the natural heat, assimilated by the liver and sent out to nourish the members. What ugly and ill-omened notion is this, to have any such idea about the glorious body of Christ that can experience no sensation? The body of Christ is taken in mystically in its real and true essence veiled under the sacramental forms—without any breaking, any separation, any change, any suffering. When, therefore, Christ says, "The flesh profiteth nothing," who will say that the flesh of Christ, in which He wrought the salvation of the whole world, is valueless? For if the flesh profiteth nothing, the word would not have been made flesh (says Augustine), to dwell among us. For if the flesh of the Apostles, from which the sound of their voice has come into all the earth to us, has profited us, how should not the flesh of Christ have profited us?

Therefore we must extract a deeper meaning from Christ's words than their grammatical form would suggest. But heaven-taught Zwingli fills out Christ's words—The flesh profiteth nothing, "namely, as far as physical eating is concerned." Lo, the man who scorns and rejects all glosses, now thrusts upon us a gloss of his own, which, if he understands it in St. Augustine's sense, I do not reject. But this one-eyed, half-blind fellow in the matter of the Sacred Scriptures knows only two ways of eating, the physical and the spiritual; he cannot see the genuine and special way of eating the Eucharist, which is sacramental and mystical.† But I will ask him whether he does not believe that the flesh even as eaten is of value? For Christ said, "Whoso eateth my flesh, and drinketh my blood, hath

---

*It ought to be Augustine, "On the Gospel of John," Tract XXVII, §5.

†It is interesting to compare with Eck's explanation that of Augustine on John 6: 54: "Understand spiritually what I have said; ye are not to eat this body which ye see; not to drink that blood which they who will crucify me shall pour forth. I have commended unto you a certain mystery, spiritually understood it will quicken. Although it is needful that this be visibly celebrated, yet it must be spiritually understood." Schaff, *Nicene Fathers*, 1st Series, VIII, 486.

eternal life," John 6 [: 54]—certainly a thing of the greatest value, to have eternal life. Vain and vicious, therefore, is all that Zwingli has brought up, and I most amply refuted Zwingli's wrong understanding of the subject in the disputation at Baden against Oecolampadius.

He next brings in St. Paul,—"and if we have known Christ according to the flesh, but now we know Him so no longer," II Cor. 5 [: 16]. This passage Zwingli also vaunted prodigiously in the disputation at Berne, but who does not see his ignorance and carelessness in thinking that "to know according to the flesh" is to know in bodily shape? Therefore, when St. Paul says, "Henceforth we know no man according to the flesh," that means according to Zwingli's interpretation of it that he did not know in the body Peter, Titus, Timothy, Luke, Aquila, Gaius and other dear friends. But who can be so stupid? Therefore a higher meaning must be extracted, and this the holy Fathers have handed down to us. St. Paul means by knowing after the flesh to know with fleshly longing, "for even the Apostles were too eager for the bodily presence of Christ, and took His going away greatly to heart," says Augustine against the Manichaeans, and this was to know after the flesh. But Christ, wishing to turn them away from this eagerness and raise them to higher things, says, "But I tell you the truth: It is expedient to you that I go," John 16 [: 7]. They, therefore, had known Christ after the flesh who wanted so much the intercourse of His bodily presence, but when they had seen the glory of His resurrection and ascension, they ceased to be so keen for intercourse of His bodily presence. This meaning is hinted at in St. Paul's previous words, "that they who live, may not now live to themselves, but unto him who died for them, and rose again," II Cor. 5 [: 15]. I omit the explanation of certain persons who understand "knowing after the flesh" of observance of the Law.

At length our counterfeit theologian, stuffed with jeerings and sophistries, comes forward and maintains that "est, is," has the force of "significat, it signifies." He tries to prove it by its being so used in Exodus 12 [: 11], "hoc est paessa," that is "it signifies paessa, which is the passage of the Lord." For since the Supper took the place of the Paschal lamb, the fact suggests that Christ used similar words. Then he supports the view from the quality of memorials that they take the name of the things they commemorate. But these things do not at all support Zwingli's impious contention, for in the first place the braggart wishing to seem, in our sacred Emperor's eyes, conversant even with the Hebrew tongue, gives a fine example of this, reading פסח, paessa, contrary to all Hebrew usage, since it does not have a dagesh in the samech,* and has the aspirate "h" at the end, whence it would have been more correct to read "Pesach," which we call "Pascha." Now Pesah signifies both the Paschal lamb and the feast of the Paschal lamb. It is used often for the lamb, especially when it is called a victim, but is used oftener for the feast in the book of Chronicles —"Josias kept a passover, phase, to the Lord in Jerusalem," II Chron. 35 [: 1], and below: "The children of Israel that were found there kept the phase, passover, at that time, and the feast of unleavened bread seven

---

*The edition of Schuler and Schulthess, IV, 13, reads Paesa.

days. There was no phase like to this in Israel from the days of Samuel the prophet," II Chron. 35 [: 17-18]. Here it is clear that "pesah" is used for the feast. When, therefore, Zwingli brings forward, "This is Paessa," I answer, "Pasah" is used here for the feast not for the lamb, and with what the interpreter added about the Lord's passage, he wished to indicate that from which the name was given, but primary school boys know that the thing from which and the thing for which a name is given are different. We do not, therefore, want Zwingli to spoil the text for us and interpret "est, is" as "significat, signifies," as the Sophists do in official documents. It is used in the simple demonstrative sense, and that this is true I prove from the fact that in the Hebrew this verb "is" in which Zwingli works up his trope does not occur, but only the pronoun הן ,* which has the force of "ipsum, self," so that the meaning is, "a passover itself unto the Lord," or "to the Lord." The Chaldaic Targum reads "before the Lord,"† and that is in accordance with my explanation that it is used for the feast, for the feast is kept unto the Lord or before the Lord. As to his adding furthermore that the form of speech is similar in the case of the type and that of the reality, first, it never was established in the case of the typical lamb that "is" was used for "signifies;" second, even if we grant him this, he will not make out that the same form of speech was observed in the case of the Eucharist. For who does not know that baptism took the place of circumcision? Yet in the proclamation of circumcision [Gen. 17: 10-14], the words are to be understood of the actual foreskin and of actual and literal circumcision, while in the case of baptism the expressions are not used in like manner. For when Christ said, "Unless a man be born again, he cannot see the kingdom of God," Nicodemus understood the words literally of actual rebirth and said, "How can a man be born when he is old?" Now it is as clear as the sun how Zwingli's reasoning falls utterly flat. But in mentioning a memorial Zwingli destroys Zwingli here. It is an old saying that a liar hath need of a good memory. For this sternest of iconoclasts once wrote to Valentine Compar of Uri, (Fol. 33)‡ wildly forbidding that images or statues or memorials be called by the names of the things they commemorated, but now he imposes upon us as a law what he previously forbade—this new Vertumnus** asserting everything at will, when it seems to champion his own side. What sort of a memorial, however, the Eucharist is in the Church Zwingli no longer knows,—renegade from the faith as he is. It is the sign of the present body of Christ and a memorial of the passion of Christ and of redemption and all the benefits of God.--such a memorial, I say, as David exulting in spirit foresaw when

---

*It should be הוא. The correct rendering is, of course, "A passover it is to Jehovah." In a nominal sentence the subject and predicate are expressed by a noun or pronoun. See Gesenius, Hebrew Grammar, §141, 2d.

†Eck means the Targum of Onkelos, see Etheridge, *The Targum of Onkelos and Jonathan Ben Uzziel on the Pentateuch,* Vol. 1, p. 370.

‡See Schuler and Schulthess edition, II, 1, p. 34. Zwingli objects to calling "impotent blocks of willows," by the name of saint so and so, because it indicates higher veneration than the wood deserves and suggests the thought that saints can help men, and that men should, therefore, have saints.

**An Etruscan deity, the god of the changing year.

he sang "He hath made a remembrance of his wonderful works, being a merciful and gracious Lord." Ps. 110 [: 4].* And what were these wonderful works to be remembered? That "He hath given food to them that fear Him," not, therefore, baker's bread, but the living bread which was given upon the cross for the world, John 6 [: 51].

THERE FOLLOW NOW THE ARGUMENTS OF THAT GREAT DEBATER, ZWINGLI.

First he asks whether when the Eucharist is partaken of the body is fed or the soul. If the soul, then the soul feeds upon flesh, which is absurd. But who would not laugh at this doughty fighter? If he has such confidence in these arguments, why did he not come to the disputation at Baden according to the request of the twelve Cantons, accompanied by a safe-conduct? I should surely have beaten him and stripped him of all his arms, and now I will break his bow and the arms in which he puts his trust. For I will reply to his dilemma that the soul is fed by the Eucharist. If he thinks that absurd, I should like to have him bring forward his Scripture proofs. Furthermore, is not also the spirit of Christ in Christ's body, unless one is infected, like Luther, with the Nestorian heresy? Has he not read Chrysostom, Ambrose, Cyril on the partaking of the body of Christ, or at least St. Augustine's description of the efficacy of the food in question—"I shall be changed into thee, not thou into me," etc. A farmer's reasoning, therefore, is this of Zwingli—"The sensual man perceiveth not the things that are of the Spirit of God," I Cor. 2: [: 14]; therefore the soul is fed by the sacramental partaking of the flesh of Christ.

So also the second argument with which he tries to floor us, is empty— as to the effect of the Communion, that it will either effect the remission of sins or dispense the virtue of the passion of Christ; therefore the virtue of the passion was dispensed before it took place. Who would not be astonished at such ignorance of Holy Writ in a man who claims for himself a new sect in religion? As to his contention about the effect of the Communion, I admit that the blood was shed, the body was offered for the remission of sins. For Christ bears witness to this of the blood in Matthew 26 [: 28]. But the Sacrament of the Eucharist was not ordained in the first place to wash out mortal sin, since the Sacrament of Penance was instituted to that end, as Baptism was in the case of original sin. It is partaken of in atonement for sin, for the increase of grace, for the acquiring of blessings and merits, and is offered in order to appease God in individual emergencies.

Having denied, therefore, the first part of the dilemma, it is clear that I admit the second. For beyond a doubt God gave increase of grace at the Supper to the disciples who worthily partook of it. It is a defect, therefore, in so great a master in Israel not to have known to what end the sacraments were instituted by Christ. But as to Zwingli's considering it absurd that the power of the passion was poured out upon men before it

*Ps. 110 in the Vulgate, but 111 in the Hebrew and in King James Version.

took place, our great theologian is not aware that all who have been saved, all who have been made just, all who have gone down into the limbo of the fathers, were justified through having foreseen the passion of Christ, just as we are through His passion having been manifested. Hence the fathers are said by St. Paul to "have the same spirit of faith, as it is written, I believed, for which cause I have spoken," Ps. 115 [: 10]* and II Cor. 4 [: 13]. Therefore he says, they "did all eat the same spiritual food, and all drank the same spiritual drink," I Cor. 10 [: 3-4]. For from whom had circumcision the efficacy of its meaning if not from Christ, as also baptism has now? And all the just men in the Old Testament had it from the virtue of the passion of Christ, although they had not received the promises, says St. Paul, Hebr. 11 [: 13], for the price had not yet been paid. They could not fly forth, because the gates of heaven had not yet been opened unto them. As to what Zwingli finally says about the food of the body, I leave it out as a dream unworthy of notice.

Zwingli's third sophistry is, what sort of a body did the disciples eat at the Supper, one capable of sensation or one incapable of sensation? If one incapable of sensation, then Christ had two bodies. This sophistry shows up Zwingli as unskilled in dialectics also, and I will play him with the like quibble. If one of my hands moves, while the other is at rest, I ask him whether my soul moves in my hand which is shown to be at rest or not. If not, then there are two souls, one which moves in the right hand, and one which is motionless in the hand at rest. This is the cradle stage of dialectics. Let Zwingli answer if he can, and he will see that this quibble has no substance; it is a pure and absurd sophism. I answer Zwingli, therefore, that the disciples partook of the same body which Christ had, and he had one capable of sensation and of being hurt. Therefore it is a dream on Zwingli's part that the disciples partook of such a body as Christ had after the Resurrection. And I would say this to Zwingli, which is beyond his comprehension, that the apostles partook of Christ's body, capable of sensation, in a manner not involving sensation, because they did it sacramentally; for although this body was capable of sensation, yet it was now without sensation under the form of the Eucharist. For the capability of sensation demands limitation in space on the part of the thing feeling the sensation. The body of Christ is not now limited in space in the sense that a portion of place corresponds to a portion of the thing placed, but in this I talk to a deaf man, as far as Zwingli is concerned, for a pig cares nothing for perfume.† Now all these things follow from Scripture, and having laid as the foundation what Christ said—"This is my body," Matth. 26: 26—I have shown how that is not impossible with God, as Zwingli in his folly imagines.

*Ps. 116: 10 in Authorized Version.

†Eck quotes here a part of a Latin proverb which is found in full in Aulus Gellius, *Noctium Atticarum Libri XX,* pref. 19. It reads: "For a jay cares nothing for music nor a pig for perfume." It has the same sense as the N. T. proverb "to cast pearls before swine." Eck means that such fine theological distinctions as he is making, between spiritual and sacramental presence, are beyond Zwingli's comprehension.

As a reserve line Zwingli leads out, not without injustice to the Fathers to be sure, Ambrose and Augustine as champions of his impious views. He quotes from Ambrose on the First Epistle to the Corinthians [I Cor. 11], in which he says, "For since we have been set free by the Lord's death, being mindful of this, we signify in our eating and drinking the flesh and blood which were offered up for us."* But if Zwingli were not blind and bereft of reason he would surely never have quoted these words of Ambrose, which invalidate his own view by their plain testimony that we are mindful of this thing (the Lord's death, namely) in eating and drinking the flesh and blood. But Zwingli refers "the flesh and blood" to the last word "significamus, we signify."† But this is to twist and do violence to the words of Ambrose, since St. Paul spoke of showing the death, about which Ambrose also speaks. Therefore the meaning of Ambrose's words is, "because we have been set free by the Lord's death, mindful of that death when we eat in the Eucharist the flesh and blood which were offered up for us, we plainly signify or show the same death of the Lord," I Cor. 11 [: 26].

And that our opponent may not mutter here, it is incontrovertibly true from other places that this was the purport of Ambrose's words. Just before the words already quoted he had said, "The celebrating of the mystery of the Eucharist while suffering shows that it is not a supper; it is a spiritual medicine which taken with reverence purifies the faithful." Zwingli's followers have nothing but a supper; their baker's bread is not a spiritual medicine, and does not purify the faithful. Furthermore in his Book on the Mysteries (last chapter), Ambrose says, "This sacrament which you receive is made what it is by the words of Christ. If the words of Elijah had power to bring down fire from heaven, shall not the words of Christ have power to change the nature of the elements?"‡ And below, "Why do you seek here the order of nature in Christ's body, when contrary to the course of nature He was born of a virgin?" And again, "The words of Christ which were able to make out of nothing that which was not, can they not change things which already are into what they were not?" Here he asserts the body of Christ and transubstantiation. Further, in his book on the Sacrament of the Lord's Incarnation Ambrose says, "For if you believe that flesh was taken up by Christ, you will also offer the body to be transfigured upon the altar."** And on Psalm 118, "Now am I admitted to the honor of the heavenly table. For my feast the rain does not pour down

---

*Migne, *Patrologia Latina*, XVII, 256.

†Zwingli's interpretation is perfectly correct. This is shown by the sentence that follows the passage quoted from Ambrose, "The Covenant was established by blood, inasmuch as blood is a witness of the Divine mercy. For a *type* of which we take the *mystic cup of the blood* for the protection of our body and soul."

‡Migne, *Patrologia Latina*, Vol. XVI, Col. 424; and Schaff, *Nicene Fathers*, Second Series, Vol. X, p. 324.

**Migne, *Patrologia Latina*, Vol. XVI, col. 859, Chap. IV. Eck overlooks the fact the both the tract on the "Mysteries," as well as the tract on the "Sacrament of the Lord's Incarnation" are probably not by Ambrose. See Wm. Goode, *The Nature of Christ's Presence in the Eucharist*, London, 1856, Vol. I, p. 493f; also Hugh Watt, on "Eucharist," in Hastings, *Encyclopaedia of Ethics and Religion*, V, 551.

nor do the beasts of the earth, nor the fruits of the trees toil, nor are rivers or springs to be sought for to supply me with drink. Christ is my food, Christ is my drink. The flesh of God is my food, and the blood of God is my drink."* What more do we ask of Ambrose? And this villainous Zwingli has the effrontery to fasten falsely upon so holy a man this impious view of a Berengarius. Credence is given to all that I have quoted by the fact that Ambrose speaks of the thing again, confirming it by a miracle, in his book about his brother's death.† His brother Satyrus, having the Eucharist tied up in his neckerchief, was once saved from shipwreck."

Furthermore Zwingli quotes Augustine (Tract. 30) with no less injustice than Ambrose. First, commenting on John, he asserts that the body of Christ which rose from the dead must be in a particular place, and because in the copies examined "potest, can," is read instead of "oportere, must," he quotes from the Master of the Sentences and from a decree of Gratian that "oportet, must," is what should be read. But if Zwingli saw how Peter the Lombard and Gratian read the word, why did he not also see their explanation? Why does he correct the manuscript of Augustine in accordance with theological "Sentences" and a decree, when otherwise he attributes no authority whatever to them? Why does he venture to quote Augustine in support of his view, when he did not blush to write to the King of France to this effect:—"Augustine, who was keen and prudent beyond other men, did not venture to state the truth plainly about the Sacrament in his time." (Commen., Folio 282).‡ If he did not dare to state it, since the opinion of the bodily presence in the Sacrament had become firmly established, why does he venture to claim that Augustine's statement is on his side? I say, therefore, to Augustine, with the Master of the Sentences, (Dist. 10, quarti.):** The body of Christ must be understood to be in a particular place in so far as it is anywhere visibly in human form, but His truth, that is, His divinity, is everywhere. His truth also, that is, His true body, is on every altar where the Mass is celebrated, though, as far as I am concerned, Augustine may have been speaking of the truth of the Gospel spread through the world by the Apostles. While quoting Gratian, Zwingli might have glanced at Bernard's statement on this point:—"The body of Christ must be in a particular place in so far as it has a form and manifestation in which it can be submitted to the bodily human senses; for though it is on every altar in its true form which it took from the Virgin, yet it is not there submitted to the bodily

---

*See Ambrose on Psalm CXVIII, Sermon XVIII, §26, in Migne, *Patrologia Latina*, XV, 1537. Over against these passages we read in these same tracts, ascribed to Ambrose, that the elements in the Supper are "a *figure* of the body and blood of our Lord Jesus Christ," (De Sacr. IV, 5) and again, "we *signify* in our eating and drinking the flesh and blood that were offered for us," (Com. on I. Cor. XI, 26) and also, "before the blessing of the heavenly words another nature (species) is spoken of, after consecration the Body is *signified*," (On the Mysteries, IX, 54).

†See "De Excessu Fratris Sui Libri Duo," Bk. 1, §43; printed in Migne. *Patrologia Latina*, XVI, 1361.

‡See Zwingli's *Werke*, Vol. III, 1914, p. 811.

**Peter Lombard, "Sententiarum Libri Quatuor." Lib. IV, Dist. 10; in Migne, *Patrologia Latina*, Vol. CXCII, col. 860.

senses." So in quoting Augustine against Adimantus, (Cap. 12.) he is carrying coals to Newcastle, for all of us Catholics to this day agree with Augustine: "The Lord did not hesitate to say, 'This is my body,' when He gave a symbol of His body." For the Catholic Church teaches and has always taught that the forms of bread and wine are sense symbols of the most sacred body and blood of the Lord. For how could the Eucharist be a sacrament if it were not a symbol of a sacred thing? And by reason of the symbol the holy Fathers sometimes mention the sign or symbol, meanwhile always confessing the thing itself in the sacrament, that is, the reality of the body and blood of Christ. Therefore it is absolutely false that we condemn Augustine, and it is equally false when this slanderer says in conclusion that the ancients always spoke symbolically when they mentioned the body and blood in the Lord's Supper. And to make our opponent blush, I set Augustine over against him speaking of the Lord's words (Aug. Ser. 28) :—"When I was treating of the sacraments I said to you that before Christ's words that which is offered is called bread; when Christ's words have been uttered, it is no longer called bread but is named the body. Why, therefore, in the Lord's Prayer, which comes afterwards, does He say, 'Our daily bread'? He said 'bread,' to be sure, but $\epsilon\pi\iota o\upsilon\sigma\iota o\nu$, that is, supersubstantial.* This is not the bread that goes into our bodies, but that bread of eternal life which supports the substance of our souls." Here Augustine plainly shuts out Zwingli's tropes and symbols. So also he says to Count Julian, "Let the piety of our Lord Jesus Christ free us from these and may He give Himself to us to eat, who said, 'I am the living bread which came down from heaven. Whoso eateth my flesh, and drinketh my blood, hath eternal life.' But before any one receives the body and blood of our Lord Jesus Christ, let him examine himself," etc. Augustine says moreover in another place (On Psalm 33), "And He was borne in His own hands,† but who can understand, brethren, how this could be in the case of a man? For who is carried in his own hands? A man can be carried by the hands of others, no one is carried by his own hands. We do not see how this can be understood literally in the case of David himself, but do see in the case of Christ. For Christ was borne in His own hands when commending His body He said, 'This is my body.' For He bore that body in His own hands."‡ Through these perfectly clear words** it is manifest

*So the word "daily" is translated in the Vulgate, Matth. 6: 11.

†In illustration of the historical situation calling forth Ps. 33, Augustine quotes here I Sam. 21: 13, where he reads: "He was carried in His hands," instead of the Hebrew, "He feigned himself mad in their hands."

‡Migne, *Patrologia Latina*, XXXVI, 306. Augustine qualifies his words by what follows: "How was He borne in His own hands? Because when He delivered His own body and blood, He took into His hands what the faithful know, and He Himself *in a certain manner carried* Himself, when He said: 'This is my body.'"

**The words of Augustine are made clear by another passage: "How many even now in the Supper itself, although they have not seen that table which then was [*i. e.*, the table at which the Lord presided], nor seen with their eyes, or tasted with their jaws *the bread which the Lord carried in His hands,* yet inasmuch as that which is now prepared is the same, how many even now, in the Supper itself, eat and drink damnation to themselves." Sermon, 112, §4. Hence there is no transubstantiation, the bread remains bread.

to any Catholic that the impostor Zwingli does injustice to this holy Father
in twisting his words and distorting them into the error of the Capernaites, and still less ought Oecolampadius, the apostate, to do this, for he
once swore allegiance to the rule of Augustine in the order of St. Brigitta.
Zwingli vaunts the books of Oecolampadius here. I oppose to all their
writings the Bishop of Rochester to whom they have not made answer by
a syllable these three years and more.

ARTICLE IX.

Zwingli here casts out two things from the Church which have always
been a great bulwark to the feeble and unlearned, raising their hearts
more towards God, church ceremonies, namely, and images. He decrees
that ceremonies are to be tolerated if they are not through their superstitious character opposed to the faith and the word of God. Although I
grant that the ceremonies of the Church are of this character, being based
upon the sacred writings, or designed to rouse the hearts of the faithful to
faith through piety and to draw their emotions thither, as it would not be
difficult for me to show of them individually, as Thomas of Walden did
two centuries ago against the followers of Wycliffe, yet as Zwingli does
not tell us which he tolerates and which he casts out, I pass them by also.
But as to the images, in regard to which he is at variance with Luther, the
Capernaites have started up here the ancient heresy of the Iconoclasts (In
imaginum fractores) which was condemned in the Second Council of
Nicaea, in that of Constantinople under Irene, and in three councils of
Rome, under Gregory II and III, and Stephen II. This heresy got into
Germany through a certain presbyter named Felix, whence it was called
the Felician heresy, but the Emperor Charles the Great (who founded
Zurich) presently called together the Synod of Frankfurt and crushed it
out, and now the Zurichers, forgetful of their founder, restore it with
great impiety. The Emperor Charles had written four books against this
heresy. Serenus, Bishop of Marseilles spread it in Provence, but Gregory
the Great (In regist.), promptly suppressed it. It is, therefore, a heresy
many times condemned that Zwingli is now reviving, so that the Lord may
truly complain of him and his companions by the mouth of the prophet,
"My people have done two evils. They have forsaken me, the foundation
of living water, and have digged to themselves cisterns, broken cisterns, that
can hold no water," Jer. 2 [: 13]. For what else does Zwingli do but hew
out the fetid pools of ancient heretics, and bring up their old rubbish? If
the use of images were new, he might perhaps have an excuse and something
to take hold of, but since it is very old, Zwingli shows that he is one of the
false prophets who are to rise up in the last days, Matth. 24 [: 24]. For
John of Damascus declares that we have the use of images from the tradition of the Apostles. St. Athanasius tells of a miracle certainly worthy of
respect which happened with an image of the Crucified at Beirut in Syria,
and testifies that this cross belonged to Nicodemus, who went to Jesus by
night, John 3 [: 2], and showed himself so devoted to Him in the burial.
Athanasius (after having told what insults the Jews had heaped upon

the image of the Crucified, and how one had smitten his right side with a spear), says, "And when this great outrage had been perpetrated, a strange and exceedingly marvellous thing, never heard of at any other time, suddenly took place. The place of the wound immediately began to flow with water and blood, and just as once at the passion of the Son of God, the Saviour of the world, it happened that the heavens trembled, so now the same thing occurred afresh by the ordinance of God. For verily at this act not only the elements of the world might have been shaken but the powers above shuddered at such a deed." Eusebius of Caesarea tells of miracles which were wrought in Caesarea by an image of Christ, which the woman mentioned in the Gospel, Luke 8 [: 43-44], as having been healed by touching the hem of His garment, had set up in that city. Since, therefore, images edify the simple, serve as reminders to the educated, and have an effect upon all, the Catholics are right to use them, and all risk of idolatry is easily avoided, if according to the teaching of the great Basil all worship is directed to their originals.

ARTICLE X.

In this article Zwingli testifies to the office of preaching, which was instituted by Christ and first entrusted to the Apostles in Judaea. After the Resurrection He appointed them to go out into the whole world, and entrusted to them the office of baptizing and preaching. (Matth. 10 & 28, Mark 16, Luke 9.) But Zwingli has in many places before this done the opposite, making the ministry of the word and preaching of small account. For he has often borne witness that he did not wish to be taught by men, but by God alone, as in the book published against the Canon, [of the Mass] (Fol. 23),* and in the Second Acts of Zurich (Fol. 59),† and he rolls up this stone all through the book "On the Clearness of the Word of God."‡ And finally Zwingli pours forth venom in jeering at the Bishops—that they are legion and born to devour the harvest, are a useless weight upon the earth, are in the Church what goiters and hunchbacks are in the human body. This is the way this evangelical gentleman is in the habit of raining abuse and vomiting forth heaps and mountains of insult, in accordance with long suffering, with love of one's neighbor, with a gentle Christian heart. But the whole Church has a far different opinion. It was the heresy of the Arians not to distinguish a bishop from a plain priest, as Augustine is a witness. Christ by no means appointed disciples only but also apostles, Luke 10 [: 1]. Bishops succeeded the apostles, priests the disciples, as Bede explains, and this the whole Church has always observed

*While criticising Zwingli for every slight deviation from the authorities which he quotes, Eck himself is very careless in quoting Zwingli. Thus, in this case, the actual words of Zwingli were: "After I perceived that there is nothing more wily and deceitful than human reason, I learned to assert those things only that we have learned out of the mouth of God." See Zwingli's "De canone missae epicheiresis," in his *Werke,* ed. Egli and Finsler, II, 594. At the second disputation at Zurich, Zwingli said: "For all things which God has not taught but come from men, are never good." See *Werke,* ed. Egli and Finsler, II, 739.

†The Acts of the Second Disputation at Zurich, October 26-28, 1523.

‡It is the book: "Von Klarheit und Gewissheit des Wortes Gottes," 1522.

from the very times of the Apostles. For St. Dionysius, the disciple of the
Apostle St. Paul, wrote of the consecration of a bishop, and a priest, and a
deacon, and that the title of the Civil Law also indicates this—Of the
Bishops and Clergy, in the Code. The High Priest as well as the Priest also
figured under the old law; why should the Church, the bride of Christ, have
less honor? Why should there be a smaller number of ministrants in her?
But Zwingli covets the title of Bishop, and rejoices when he is called
Bishop and Antistes of Zurich by his companions in error.

ARTICE XI.

In defining the civil magistrate as deputy of God Zwingli does rightly.
For Holy Writ teaches this in various passages, and Paul enjoins it upon
the Romans, Rom. 13 [: 1]. But I fear he says this more from a desire to
flatter than from love of the truth, for if he were not afraid of their power,
he would inveigh against them as violently as he does against the
ecclesiastics, whose jurisdiction is just as much founded upon divine right
as that of the secular authorities. Otherwise perhaps he would even cry
out with Luther: "The secular government lies as thoroughly prostrate as
does that of the tyrants of the Church," (De potestate saeculari, Folio 25).
How long till one worthless wretch shall perish with the other?

ARTICLE XII.

Zwingli repudiates the fire of purgatory as a myth and a thing insulting to the redemption given through Christ. It will be well first to
prove a purgatory and then to answer objections. For purgatory is
expressly asserted by St. Paul when he writes to the Corinthians on building upon a foundation, and adds, "If any man's work burn, he shall suffer
loss; but he himself shall be saved, yet so as by fire," I Cor. 3 [: 15]. For
this passage was understood of purgatory by Ambrose, Jerome, Augustine,
Gregory. Thus also St. Gregory reasons from the words of Christ, "He
that shall speak against the Holy Ghost, it shall not be forgiven him,
neither in this world, nor in the world to come," Matth. 12 [: 32].* From
this it is clear that even in the world to come some sins are forgiven, and
this can only happen in purgatory. This also Judas Maccabaeus believed
before the birth of Christ. For we read in the Church, "That brave leader
Judas Maccabaeus, having made a collection, sent twelve thousand drachms
of silver to Jerusalem for sacrifice to be offered for the sins of the dead,"†
II Macc. 12 [: 43], and below, "It is, therefore, a holy and wholesome
thought to pray for the dead, that they may be loosed from sins," II. Macc.

---

*Gregory the Great, who has been called "the real inventor of the doctrine of
purgatory," (Hagenbach, *History of Christian Doctrine*, II, 97) infers from Matth.
12: 32, that, while "some sins are forgiven in this life, others can be forgiven in the
future life," but he limits these latter to "light sins," the hay, straw and stubble of
I. Cor. 3. These can be purged away on condition that good works have been done
in this life. Gregory, Dialogorum Libri IV, §39, in Migne, *Patrologia Latina*,
LXXVII, 396.
†Thus in the Douay Version; somewhat differently in the so-called "Variorum
Apocrypha," and the sum is stated there as 2,000, not 12,000 dr.

12 [: 45]. If the book is canonical in the Church, and the Church has admitted it into the canon, as St. Augustine testifies, this custom of having a care for the dead has obtained in the whole Church, and upon this usage of the Church St. Augustine based his argument in a book especially devoted to this matter eleven hundred years ago.* John of Damascus testifies that this custom of praying emanated from the traditions of the Apostles. Tertullian mentions the anniversary,† Ambrose the first, seventh and thirteenth, though the usage of all the Churches was not the same. Some took eight, others forty days. Monica, the mother of St. Augustine, asked that prayers be made after death,‡ and the opposite was condemned as the heresy of the Waldenses and Picards. Recently also this article of Luther's has been condemned by Pope Leo X,** of blessed memory, simply because he maintained that purgatory could not be proved from Scripture. Also I attack Zwingli in an argument ad hominem. He wrote in the declaration of his articles (Fol. 93), "No one can subvert the teaching of that powerful and brave servant of Christ, Luther."†† This I say he taught and promulgated in print in the year of our Lord 1523, and yet before this Luther had said in public disputation at Leipzig in the year of grace 1519 on the 8th day of July, "I who firmly believe, nay, I will venture to say, know that there is a purgatory, am easily persuaded that mention of it is made in the Scriptures." He had also said then that the Book of Maccabees was an authority for the faithful. If, therefore, he praised Luther so heartily, why does he not believe him when he declares that he knows there is a purgatory? Why does he not accept the Book of Maccabees, which is authoritative for the faithful, unless he prefers to be considered unfaithful himself and a deserter from the Church?

But now let us hear how he tries to invalidate the doctrine of the Church in regard to purgatory. "If," he says, "it is necessary to wash away the effects of sin by punishment, Christ died in vain, and grace is void." In this trap most of those are caught who are unwilling to make reparation for the faults they have committed, thinking the passion of Christ sufficient for them. But they are very much mistaken. For although Christ made reparation for sin, so far as to remove its guilt, so far as to change its eternal punishment into temporal punishment, it does not therefore follow that He broke the force of all punishment. For in the first place He did not remove punishment and guilt in such fashion that they

---

*The tract of Augustine referred to is entitled, *"De Cura pro mortuis gerenda,"* cf. Migne, *Patrologia Latina*, XL, 591 ff.

†Tertullian traces the custom to pray for the dead to a command of Christ (mandatum a Domino) and says, "we bring offerings for the dead on the anniversary day," see Tertullian, *De Corona militis*, Cap. 3, in Migne, *Patrologia Latina*, II, 99.

‡In his Confessions, Bk. IX, chap. XI, Augustine reports his mother to have said to him, shortly before her death: "Lay this body anywhere, let not the care for that any way disquiet you; this only I ask of you, to remember me at the Lord's altar, wherever you be."

**In the bull of Leo X, *Exsurge Domine*, §37.

††In the 57th article of the First Disputation at Zurich, Zwingli had declared (*Werke, II*, 414): "The truly Sacred Scriptures know nothing of purgatory after this life." When Zwingli spoke of Luther as a powerful and brave servant of God (*Werke II*, 149) he had no reference to purgatory.

did not still remain in the case of Judas and of Pilate. Therefore, the mere reparation of Christ, though absolutely sufficient in itself for sin, "not for ours only but for the sins of the whole world," I John 2 [: 2], yet is not efficacious unless one becomes a partaker in it, namely through the sacraments, through fervid devotion, and through good works. And that the reparation of Christ did not remove all punishment is clear from the death that we all suffer, is clear from all our infirmities and hard condition, is clear from the sin of David, the sin of which was destroyed by repentance, though the punishment due the sin remained, for the prophet said to him, "The Lord hath put away thy sin," II Samuel 12 [: 13]. This putting away cannot be understood of the guilt, since "the son shall not bear the iniquity of the father," Ezek. 18 [: 20]. The putting away must, therefore, be understood of the punishment. Why, therefore, do our opponents and enemies of the Church venture to deny that after the guilt has been done away in the case of a penitent a certain amount of temporary punishment due to sin generally remains? There follows in the same place, "Nevertheless, because thou hast given occasion to the enemies of the Lord to blaspheme, for this thing the child that is born to thee shall surely die," II Samuel 12[: 14]. Let this be enough for the present.

Zwingli finally adds an appendix on the everlasting fire of hell, with which I have no fault to find except that with regard to his boastful assertion that he not only believes but also knows that the fire of hell exists, I would ask him, how he knows. I am satisfied with the simple faith that it is so, and I thereby even believe that unless Zwingli makes recantation of his errors, he will learn by experience the violence of that fire which he is feeding and nourishing at so great a loss to so many thousands of wretched souls.

He ends his confession without mentioning various errors and heresies of his. For he does not touch at all on penance, on the vows and celibacy of the clergy, on fasts and Lent, on the ordination of priests, on the ritual of the Mass, and many other things. If he had I should have liked not only to puncture his utterances but to slash them utterly asunder with "the sword of the Spirit, which is the word of God," Eph. 6 [: 17]. Even though that savage giant threatens still more wildly, if any one should try this he would come off badly, if he is so recklessly eager for revenge instead of showing the patience taught by the Gospel, why did he not take vengeance for our disputation at Baden, as he has so often promised? Why does he not avenge the injury done to the disputation of Berne by our powerful refutation? Why does he not give vent to his wrath in answering the Bishop of Rochester or the Parisian theologian Clithoveus?* He is trying to catch the popular breeze, and does everything by uproar and violence. He babbles much stupidity without wit, without learning, and destroys innocent paper, so that as often as I read what he writes I am reminded of Aesop's, "What a head and no brain!" and of what the fox said about the

---

*This is Jodocus Clichtovaeus, who in 1523 wrote a book entitled: "De veneratione sanctorum libri duo Judoci Clichtovei Neoportuensis," Paris, 1523, to which Zwingli refers in his "De vera et falsa religione," see note of Finsler in Zwingli's *Werke*, III (1914), 839.

captured nightingale—" a voice and nothing more."

At last Zwingli winds up his address to our most Sacred Emperor and the princes of the Empire by asking them first not to disregard his humble person. It would be a bad thing for the Empire if such an important man were disregarded. Then because the princes have perhaps forgotten that they are men, he recalls it to their memory that they must remember that they are men and may be deceived because all men are liars. Verily Zwingli is the biggest liar of all, having the effrontery to deny before the cantons of the Swiss what he had put before the whole world to read in print, and falsely declaring that it was made up by me to make him unpopular in high places. And this was the nature of the thing. He had written (Fol. 25), Against the Canon of the Mass, "The frequent making of the sign of the cross has a terrifying effect upon the mind, as the signs used by necromancers terrify the ignorant when used."* Therefore he thinks we should refrain from so many crosses in the celebration of the Mass. Afterwards in writing to the Swiss he says that he did not write anything of this kind, but that I made it up. I have been the more willing to bring this up again here because he vaunts again here as the inspiration of the Deity what is certainly entirely foreign to the revelations of God and rather inspired by a lying spirit.†

He asks the princes of the Empire not to shrink away from the views of those who rely upon the word of God. The princes will be right to obey him in this even without being asked, as is in accordance with their Christian and Catholic ideas and sympathies, but the more they rely upon the word of God, the more they will shrink away from the false interpretations, distorted views, and corruptions of Holy Writ which Zwingli, Oecolampadius, Bucer, Zwick, Haller and men of that type, having made shipwreck of faith, are thrusting upon the untaught people as the real and true interpretation of the word of God. But to make this faithless confession of his seem more probable, he would make himself out such a saint that no good man ever had any doubt about his goodness. But I make no

---

*The exact title of this tract of Zwingli is, "De Canone missae epicheiresis." For the passage quoted above see Zwingli's *Werke*, Egli and Finsler edition, II, 597.

†As Eck accuses Zwingli here of lying, it is but fair to Zwingli to give his side of this incident. In his reply to "some untrue and unchristian answers which Eck made at Baden" (Zwingli's *Werke*, ed. Schuler and Schulthess, II, 2, 498), Zwingli writes: "After this Eck has invented many articles and has called them 'Pseudologiam Zwingli,' but they should properly be called, 'The book of lies regarding Zwingli.' For, in the first place, he does not give the passages where I have used such words, so that his lies can't be quickly detected. Then he tears some passages out of their proper places, falsifies their meaning, detracts from some, adds to others, still others he perverts entirely, in some he criticises me, when they express the true Christian faith. In one instance he says, that I stated, 'when man makes the sign of the cross on himself, he was terror stricken.' This is an invention." The actual remarks of Zwingli, in his book, "De canone missae epicheiresis," which called forth this statement of Eck, were: "The frequent making of the sign of the cross terrifies the mind, as the signs of the magicians terrify the ignorant people, if they are at any time admitted to them, wherefore they should stay away." But Zwingli adds: "We do not despise the making of the sign of the cross, but I would have the disciples of the Lord inclined oftener to meditate upon what took place on the cross than to make crosses in the air." See Zwingli's *Werke*, ed. Egli and Finsler, II, 597.

attack upon his life, although many people declare it is not so altogether guileless. In this "to his own lord he standeth or falleth," says the Apostle, Rom. 14 [: 4]. Therefore far be it from me to pass any unfavorable judgment. I will only say that he might better have left this praise of the innocence of his life to his neighbors. For the Sage says, "Let another praise thee, and not thine own mouth; a stranger, and not thine own lips," Prov. 27 [: 2].

In his satisfaction with his own learning he exhibits conduct worthy of a heretic. "For they are in the habit of boasting of their knowledge of the Scriptures, and associating it with secular learning," says St. Jerome, (On Isaiah 19)* and again "they are generally strong in oratory, and thus seduce poor souls, for they are swollen and puffed up with high-sounding words ." (On Hosea 10).† Does not St. Jerome paint Zwingli in his proper colors? Does not Zwingli swell up, claiming for himself an amount of learning that his enemies cannot withstand, though his equipment in knowledge is so scanty that he did not dare to come out into the field when his opponents were there? This is shown by the fact that when the twelve Cantons summoned him to the town of Baden to meet me in a discussion upon the articles of faith, and sent him a safe-conduct for that purpose, which would be enough even for a prince,‡ he, a native, refused to come three miles, when I, a stranger, had come thirty-three miles to get there. (1526 A. D.) Which, therefore, could not withstand the learning of the other? If he continues in his pride and arrogance, I am ready to try again before His Imperial Majesty and the princes of the realm whether Catholic truth is not mightier than the heresy of a Zwingli.

At length with his accustomed arrogance, Titus 1 [: 10], he boasts of the fruits of his Gospel, that it makes men so true, so holy, so free from all stain, that one might think them saints in life. St. Jerome bears witness that this is a special characteristic of heretics, saying, "But because their belly is their God, for the sake of base gain they desire to win disciples of their own, that they may be supported like teachers by their followers." But we can also understand this expression "for the sake of base gain" otherwise, and regard the common saying that all heretics while teaching error are in the habit of declaring themselves gainers of men, though it is no gain but ruin to kill the souls of their dupes. This is what Zwingli is doing now. The fruits of his Gospel I have described in such a way in my introductory remarks to His Imperial Majesty that no right-minded man will judge the tree of much value from its fruits, Matth. 7 [: 16].

Oh, is not Zwingli ashamed to ask the princes who will scatter the wealth which has been heaped up by means of the Mass? As if you and your associates did not know—you who under the guise of some public chest seize the gifts of kings and princes, the benefactions of counts and nobles, the alms of the citizens, and heap them all up for yourselves,

---

*See Migne, *Patrologia Latina*, XXIV, 261.
†See Migne, *Patrologia Latina*, XXV, 958.
‡Such safe-conduct might be absolutely worthless, for many Catholics taught that a safe-conduct given to a heretic could be broken.

neglecting meanwhile the servants of Christ, neglecting the poor! Luxuriously live these false prophets, these apostates, these breakers of vows, and all their ilk. All the ceremonies of the Church have perished among you, but tithes meanwhile are rigorously exacted. All the dues and revenue are paid to the last penny to the colleges, the monasteries, the foundations—these institutions, I say, are not abolished. And where before many of the neighbors were supported by the monasteries—peasants, artisans, poor people—now some bloated prefect consumes it all, takes all for himself alone, and marches into Zurich, fat, obese, bloated and stuffed with the wealth of the Church. When they have drunk generously and are filled with wine, they treat the sacred chalices as cups and the platters as plates in their banquets, if facts agree with the report, and boastingly vaunt, like new Belshazzars, the profanation of the sacred vessels, Dan. 5. Does the perjured Zwingli still venture to ask who will scatter the wealth which has been heaped up by means of the Mass? I may seem rather too bitter because my words have such a sting here, but Zwingli looked for it and has found it. Zwingli, made Councillor of the Emperor and the whole Empire, comes to the Council, contrary to Cato's principle, even when not asked, and advises that all the errors in the Church be cut out from their roots. Therefore, in his own judgment Zwingli must be cut out, Oecolampadius, Capito, Zwick, Bucer, Simpert, and their associates must be cut out, and, like withered branches, be cast into the fire at the Lord's command. Luke 3 [: 9]; John 15 [: 6]. He bids us abandon Rome—like Jeroboam who bade the people not to go up to Jerusalem, I Kings, 12 [: 28], but the eloquent Zwingli does not know that Lactantius Firmianus, the Christian Cicero, wrote that the desolation of Rome was the sign of the coming desolation of the whole world.* But how finely and fittingly he praises our august Emperor and the other princes of the Empire because they have used their powers against the purity of the Gospel, because through their sluggishness justice is banished and innocence is smeared with the paint of imposture, bestowing upon the princes the savage cruelty of giving orders and condemnation contrary to truth, nay of killing and slaying, plundering and proscribing!

Who will say now that Zwingli is not the most learned of orators whom his enemies cannot withstand, when he winds up his speech of confession so skilfully and kindly, and adds an epilogue so neatly as to soften the hearts of all his hearers and judges, turn their minds and win their favor, especially as he judges the princes rebels against God if they do not accede to his wishes? But what lover of the Christian faith, nay, of virtue, would not be disgusted at such a monster of sycophancy and condemn it? Our holy Emperor, most serene King and the other princes of the Empire cannot do anything more acceptable to God, more adapted to enhance their own fame, more conducive to the peace and quiet of their

*Firmianus Lactantius in his "Divine Institutes," Bk. VII, chap. 25, writes: "When the capital of the world shall have fallen . . . who can doubt that the end has now arrived to the affairs of men and the whole world." See Migne, *Patrologia Latina*, VI, 812-13; translated in Roberts and Donaldson, *Ante-Nicene Fathers*, VII, 220.

subjects than to crush, destroy, and banish as far as possible from the Holy Empire these sects of perdition and their lying teachers. God Almighty deign in His mercy to grant unto His Imperial Majesty and the other princes of the Empire this purpose and a peaceful means of carrying it out.

Let it be done, good Jesus,
Let it be done.

Accept, holy Emperor, this short refutation of Zwingli's Confession. It might fairly have been attacked more at length and repudiated more vigorously, but I have taken special pains to be brief, and have excluded much that presented itself spontaneously, lest the refutation should be overlong. I have followed the thread of his articles, but have suppressed much and passed over much in silence that I might properly have said in objection to him. For his books teem with errors which I have frequently refuted in previous years. But since Zwingli does not confine himself to his own province but constantly plots to take away and despoil the flocks of others—for the word of heretics "spreadeth like a canker," says St. Paul, II Tim. 2 [: 17]—this seducer has invaded several cities of the Holy Empire already, as I mentioned in my introduction, and this pestilence has extended even to my neighbors of Memmingen. And it will spread further if it is not restrained by your holy Imperial Majesty. "Arius was a little flame at Alexandria," says the blessed Jerome, but because it was not quickly quenched, it devastated the whole world. Perform the function of an excellent prince, therefore, august and invincible Emperor, and save thy holy empire from this godlessness, that those who are faithful to thee and to the Empire may serve God worthily in peace and quiet, may follow thee bravely through Greece and Asia, to recover the tomb of our Saviour, and shake off the Turkish yoke. May the Lord God be the guide, protector and director of Your Majesty, to the glory of His holy name and the peace and safety of the whole Empire.

AMEN.

To the cities that accept the teachings of Zwingli.

I adjure you, magistrates and people of the cities, not to take in bitterness the sharp things I have put forth against the arch-heretic Zwingli. Reflect that unless your salvation were dear to me, unless I wished you very well, unless the happiness of your souls goaded me on, I never should have wielded so sharp a pen against Zwingli. For, taught by Paul, I have little hope left of his salvation, but I have a large hope of converting you. And let not the abuses which exist in the Church be a stumbling block to you. The faults in things should be removed, not the things themselves, and the true ancient Christian religion should endure. God Almighty bring you back as speedily as possible into the fold of the Church.

AMEN.

IV.

Letter of Huldreich Zwingli to the Most Illustrious Princes of Germany Assembled at Augsburg, Regarding the Insults of Eck.

(August 27, 1530)

[AD ILLUSTRIS- | SIMOS GERMANICAE PRIN- | cipes Augustae congregatos, De Conui- | tiis Eccij, epistola Huldr. Zwinglij. | TIGVRI APVD CHRISTOPHORUM | FROSCHOVER, ANNO M.D. XXX. | 32 unnumbered quarto pages, signed on p. 31, Tiguri XXVII. die Augusti. Anno M.D. XXX, *i. e.,* "Zurich, on the 27th of August 1530." Printed in *Opera Zwinglii,* Tom. II. fol. 545a-550a; Schuler and Schulthess ed., Vol. IV. pp. 19-41. Finsler, *Zwingli Bibliographie,* Nos. 96-97. At the same time a German edition appeared entitled: *"An die durchlüchtigen | Fürsten Tütscher nation zu Oug- | sburg versammlot ein sendbrieff | Huldrych Zwinglis, die schelck- | wort Eggens so er wider die | warheyt vssgossen- | betreffendt, | i. e.,* "A Letter of Huldreich Zwingli to the illustrious Princes of the German nation, assembled at Augsburg, regarding the calumnies of Eck, which he poured out against the truth." 40 unnumbered quarto pages. A copy of this edition is in the library of Union Theological Seminary, New York City. The following English translation, based on one by Henry Preble, was revised throughout by the editor.

While Zwingli refused to dignify the scurrillous attack of Eck with an answer, he felt that he owed it to his position to defend more at length the two principal points to which Eck had taken exception, that no grace was conferred by the sacraments and that Christ was not bodily present at the Lord's Supper. These two points he elaborated in a letter addressed to the princes of Germany. Vadian, who was at Augsburg during the sessions of the Diet, and who was in continual correspondence with Zwingli, notified Zwingli of the appearance of Eck's answer of the 16th of August. Shortly afterwards Zwingli wrote his reply, which was signed on August 27, 1530.]

UPON the Most Illustrious Princes of Germany, assembled at the Diet of Augsburg, Huldreich Zwingli implores grace and peace from God the Father and His Son, our Redeemer

Jesus Christ. As far as I am concerned, Most Illustrious
Princes, I might have passed by Eck's insults without any sor-
row, both because our Saviour comforts us with the words
"Blessed are ye when men revile you," and because wise men
teach that no insult exists except where the recipient so takes it.
For if he so strengthens his soul as to make himself invulnerable
from such missiles, they will have no more effect upon him than
upon a rock. But since Eck sets to work to overturn piety with
impunity by lies and to strike down the ancient city of Zurich,
I should fail in piety itself if I did not use sling and stone to
attack that alien in his proud trampling upon the truth.
Furthermore he is certainly either cracked or hide-bound. For
whether he brought all those loud insults out of his own mind
(a mind stretched so violently to such a monstrous spouting of
abuse must be bursting or breaking up mentally) or whether he
did not of himself indulge in the debauch, so that no danger
threatens him from such an uncommon birth of revilings, each
reason is sufficient for my not writing anything to him. For if
he is mad, he would tear up and not read the letter, and if he is
not mad, but thundering so mightily from hypocrisy, he would,
after his fashion, not weigh what I say, but distort my sane
words with insane slanders and accusations.

Hence it is that I let him go and address myself to Your
Highnesses, depending on nothing else than my confidence in
your wise fair-mindedness, through which I hope that with true
German steadfastness and faithfulness you will lend your ears
just as attentively to one setting forth his view and case in sincerity as to the slanderers, however they try to overwhelm you
with their din or insinuate themselves into your good graces.
For though in themselves, perhaps, the matters in question do
not present so very much difficulty, yet through eagerness of
contention, they have grown to such proportions that unless you
show yourselves to the contentious as unapproachable and just
judges who do not pronounce an opinion until the whole case
has been examined on all sides, some uproar is likely to be
caused by a disagreement of no small extent, though it sprang
from small beginnings. And since among all the things in the
exposition of my faith which Eck not so much criticises as
tramples under foot, running amuck like a wild boar, nothing,
please the gods, is so obnoxious to the Romanists as these two:

"That the sacraments do not bestow or dispense grace," and, "That in the holy supper of our Lord Christ's natural body is not eaten"—nay, not only to the Romanists but also to some of those who seem to be upon the side of the Gospel—it has seemed to me worth while to send forth a few words upon these points as a sort of reinforcement, in the hope that if anything seems to any one to have been said somewhat obscurely it may become more transparent. I will, therefore, do this, with God's help, on the understanding that I am not to make answer to the adversary's raving nor add a spur to it, but to show my view in these matters more and more clearly to Your Highnesses. Thus:—

In sacraments two factors in general are to be considered, the thing and the sacrament or sign of the thing. The thing is that for the sake of which the sign is instituted which we call a sacrament. In circumcision the thing is belonging to the people of God, the sign of this sacred thing is the cutting of the fore-skin. In the feast of the passover the thing is giving thanks for liberation from the Egyptian bondage, the sign of this sacred thing is the roasted lamb with the other things that were customary in that thanksgiving. So in baptism the thing is belonging to the Church of Christ, the sacrament is dipping into water with holy words. In the eucharist the thing is giving thanks in accordance with faith for Christ delivered to us by God and crucified for our sins, the sacrament is the giving of bread and wine with the holy words of the Lord.

Since then all sacraments agree in this respect, it happens that the names of the things of which they are the signs are given to the sacraments. Hence circumcision is called a cov-enant, when the covenant was that the nation, born of Abraham, should be the peculiar people of God, and circumcision was the sign and, as it were, external seal of this covenant. The lamb is called the passover, since the passing was the passing over by which the smiting angel passed over Israel when he slew the Egyptians, and the lamb was the external sign of that passing over. And the names of the things are rightly given to the signs on account of analogy of meaning. For when the sign of circumcision was given to those who were of the people of God, that sign signified the thing, namely, that he who had been circumcised was of the people of Israel. For this is common to all rites and ceremonies that the signs and ceremonies receive the names of the things of which they are signs. The written instrument is called a testament, but the thing itself which is bequeathed and assigned by the testament, namely, money, gold, silver, raiment, furniture, houses, lands, the whole inheritance, whether undivided or in parts, that, I say, is the thing of the testament. The writing is the sign and assurance of these things. For the bequeathing preceded and was completed in the mind of the testator when he declared and solemnized his purpose to bequeath the things. And the sign of this solemn declaration by which the wish of the testator is disclosed to others is the writing, in which the things bequeathed are contained in name but not in fact. Yet the writing is called the testament though this is really the thing bequeathed according to the wish of the testator. When the keys are presented to a prince or emperor upon his ascending the throne, they are the sign of delivering into his power, though the delivering itself is the offering and handing over of the things. But though the keys are not the things, when it is said, "Such and such a city or fortress presented the keys to the prince," we understand that a surrender to or a reception of the monarch is made, which was determined upon before the sign of the surrender or reception was given.

In contracts and agreements the terms are the things of the contract or agreement. The sign of these terms is the clasping of hands, whence we say that a thing has been agreed upon by clasping hands to show that it cannot be repudiated after that sign. When, therefore, we call the clasping of hands a contract or agreement we give the name of the thing to the sign. For the clasping of hands cannot be a contract, but a contract is a thing in accordance with certain terms previously made. The clasping of hands is only the sign of the contract. But this sign, though it is not the thing, yet strengthens the thing when added as a sort of witness and confession that it may not be invalidated. For the rest, if breach of faith did not have to be feared, the mere settlement of the terms of the contract between two parties would be enough.

In this way also we ought to regard the sacraments. In baptism the thing is belonging to the church and the people of Christ. Baptism is a sacrament, indicating this thing, namely that the recipient belongs to the Church. Not that baptism bestows the thing, but that it bears witness to the multitude of the previous bestowal of the thing. In the Eucharist the thing is giving thanks according to faith to the Lord for the benefits that He has bestowed in redeeming us through His Son. The partaking of bread and wine, sacred symbols sanctified by God's word, is the sacrament of this thing. Neither, therefore, the giving of thanks nor the remission of sins, nor the bread and wine is the natural body of Christ, but they only symbolize the thing and as it were bring it into actual presence by representing it and offering it to the contemplation of faith. For if they bestowed the thing or were the thing, they would be things and not a sacrament or sign. But every sacrament is a sign, as also the Master of the Sentences [Peter Lombard]* has it. If they are only the sign of a thing, they are not the thing itself. Nor, when we give signs, do the names of the things thereby pass over into things nor things into signs. But the use of signs or sacraments for the things themselves is combined with much grace in speech. And in this figurative use the apostles also followed after Christ. How often does Paul call his nation "the circumcision," because that nation was God's nation! How often by the same right does he call the unbelievers "the foreskin," though the retention of the foreskin was no sacrament! But since circumcision was a sacrament, which is taken sometimes in the sense of the circumcised, sometimes in that of the covenant itself, and retention of the foreskin is the opposite of circumcision, the power of using words freely with grace is so great that "foreskin" is put for the uncircumcised, though the retention of it is not a sacrament. Not that circumcision is the same thing as circumcised or foreskin the same as uncircumcised, but it is correct to use the names of the sacraments for the names of the things.

Paul likewise speaks thus to Titus, "But after that the kindness and love of God our Saviour toward man appeared, not by works of righteousness which we have done, but according to his mercy he saved us, by the washing of regeneration, and renewing of the Holy Ghost; which he shed on us abundantly through Jesus Christ our Saviour" [Titus 3: 4-6]. Who does

*See Sentences Bk. IV, dist. 1, 2: "A sacrament is the sign of a sacred thing."

not see that there is attributed here to the washing of regeneration that which really and truly belongs only to the divine Spirit? For though Paul said first that we were renewed by the washing of regeneration, yet, that he might be the more clearly understood, he immediately added an explanatory "and," meaning "and by the washing of the renewing of the Holy Ghost." Or does not the regeneration belong really and truly to the Holy Ghost? When, therefore, baptism is called the washing of regeneration, does not the sacrament receive truly the name of the regeneration of the Spirit? But how graceful it is when not the symbol is called the washing, but the internal working and renewing of the divine Spirit which is indicated by the sacrament is called the washing! Thus the names of the things and their symbols are in turn borrowed from each other.

Paul brought out the same meaning in the epistle to the Ephesians but in a less transparent and more involved figure, "That he might sanctify and cleanse it with the washing of water by the word" [Eph. 5 : 26]. Not to mention here that the Hebrews use "word" for "thing" and put "in" for "with,"* is the Church washed with anything but the blood of Christ? What, then, is the baptismal washing but the sacrament of this original and real washing? But besides this, who can imitate this grace of speech by which he put the sacrament for the thing itself of which it is the sacred sign? Nay, who would not embrace the sacraments as sacred, joyful and venerable things, since they not only indicate such high things to us, but even in a sense present them to our eyes and senses? For when a child or a catechumen is taught or asked to confess belief in these divine things, are not the divine mysteries proclaimed and represented even through the words? When he is dipped, are not the death and burial of Christ placed before his eyes? When he comes out, the resurrection? When in the Lord's Supper His death is proclaimed not only by the words of the officiating priest but in the glad thanksgiving of the faithful soul, is not the divine bounty set forth and brought to mind with the giving of thanks? And when the bread and wine, consecrated by the very words of the Lord, are distributed among the brethren, is not the whole Christ presented as it were in visible

*The Hebrew for *cum verbo* is bidebharo, but this cannot mean in this connection "with the thing," as Zwingli seems to think.

form to the senses? (I say more, if words are demanded, than is commonly said). But how? Is the natural body itself to be handled and masticated? Certainly not. It is presented to the mind for contemplation, and the sacrament is the part that appeals in visible form to the senses. For the mind works most freely and quickly when it is not distracted by the senses. When, therefore, the senses have presented to them what is most like that on which the mind is working, the assistance of the senses is by no means slight.

And besides, a point of no small importance, these signs were so instituted by Christ Himself, that by their very analogy they might be especially effective for bringing one to the consciousness of the actual thing through faith and contemplation. Hence, since the sacraments were instituted to give teaching, suggestion, delight through the senses just as much as the external word, it happens that, when given the names of the things of which they are the signs and which are themselves the real refreshment of the mind, they kindle the mind more effectively than any one can do by contemplating the divine goodness, however faithfully it may be, without the signs. And since this is so, the most learned and holy men have rightly made frequent use of the sacraments for the things of which they are the sacraments and signs, being well aware how much must be attributed to each.

This is evident from the example above from Paul about cleansing with the washing of water by the word. For it is the blood of Christ alone, which, offered on the altar of the cross and sprinkled upon the four quarters of the globe and poured out upon the foundations of the whole earth, purified the world. But when these things are contemplated the sacraments not only set them before our eyes, but even enable them to penetrate to the mind. But what leads the way? The Spirit. For when we baptize a catechumen, unless faith shall have previously taken possession of his heart, so viewing the things that it has them actually present before it as it were, neither external declaration nor visible representation is of any avail.

In the baptism of infants the faith of the parents is enough, or, if that fails, the faith of the Church. But I do not believe that this contemplation by faith is great enough unless it grasps the thing itself as surely and undoubtingly as if it were shown to the natural eye. Hence the ancient writers said that Christ's body was really present in the Supper, and this in view of two things, first, because of this clear contemplation by faith I have spoken of, which sees Christ dying for us on the cross as vividly as Stephen with his fleshly eye saw Him reigning at the right hand of the Father. (And I dare assert that this revelation to the senses was made to Stephen as an illustration to us that He would ever be thus present to the faithful who suffered for Him, not indeed to the eye of sense, but in the contemplation and consolation of faith. For are there not many endowed with such unshaken faith that, when dragged to punishment, they see the presence of Christ so vividly, that, though no visible manifestation appears to them from above, they have no need of any such?).

Secondly, in view of the human nature truly assumed by the Son of God.* For Marcion worried the ancients on this point, since the general mass of Christians did not know how to distinguish clearly between the attributes and works of the two natures in Christ, and yet could see there were some things among these that did not at all harmonize with a real body. These, Marcion either could not or would not refer to the divine nature. Therefore he found it easier to argue among the ignorant that Christ's body was not real and natural but spiritual and imaginary. To meet this error successfully the Fathers offered the supper in which Christ had instituted the sacrament of His body—His real and natural body—to represent not a spiritual or imaginary body, but a real one. For this reason, therefore, they said that Christ's body was really present in the Supper, but only sacramentally. And I have never denied that Christ's body is present in the Supper sacramentally and mysteriously, both with a view to the contemplation of faith and to the whole working of the symbol, as I have said. And this assertion and exposition of mine can be found in Tertullian†

*Zwingli stated above that the ancient writers said that Christ's body was present in the Supper for two reasons. He has given the first reason in the preceding paragraph. He adds the second reason now.

†Zwingli was probably thinking of the following passages in Tertullian's treatise "Against Marcion." In Book I, chap. 14, he writes: "Indeed up to the present time, he has not disdained the water which the Creator made wherewith He washes His people; nor the oil wherewith He anoints them;

without trouble.

Since, therefore, this presence amounts to nothing without the contemplation of faith, it belongs to faith that the things are or become present, and not to the sacraments. For, however much they lay hold on the senses and lead to reverence for the things that are done, these handmaidens can yet effect nothing unless their mistress, faith, first rules and commands on the throne of the heart. Hence it is apparent that the sacraments cannot justify nor give grace, for we know no other justification than that of faith. It follows also that grace is not bound up with the sacraments. This, in fact, needs no proof. For if it were bound up with the sacraments, they would profit and renew wherever they were celebrated. Since, however, that is at variance with the truth (for there are those who in consequence of lack of faith eat and drink judgment upon themselves), it is apparent that grace is not bound up with the sacraments, and consequently they do not justify or dispense justification, but, acting as a sort of a stimulant, call into action the faith or promise which is already there and bear witness to the other members of the Church. All this will become clearer when we have heard two confirmatory passages from St. Augustine.

Augustine on the Trinity, Book 15, Chap. 26: "Nor did any one of His disciples give the Holy Ghost, since they prayed that it might come upon those upon whom they laid their hands, they did not give it themselves. And the Church preserves this custom even now in the case of her rulers. Finally, when Simon the Sorcerer offered money to the apostles, he does not say, "Give me also this power that I may give the Holy Ghost," but that "Upon whomsoever I lay hands, he may receive the Holy Ghost" [Acts 8:19]. For the Scripture had not said before, "And when Simon saw that the apostles gave the Holy Ghost," but it had said, "And when Simon saw that through laying on of the apostles' hands the Holy Ghost was given" [v. 18]. Therefore also the Lord Jesus Himself not

nor that union of honey and milk wherewithal He gives them the nourishment of children; nor the bread by which He *represents* His own proper body, thus requiring in his very sacraments the 'beggarly elements' of the Creator." Again he writes in Bk. IV, chap. 40: "He made the bread, which He took and distributed to His disciples, His own body, by saying, 'This is my body,' that is, a *figure* of my body."

only gave the Holy Ghost as God, but also received it as man, and was therefore said to be full of grace [John 1:14]. And it is written even more plainly of this in the Acts of the Apostles: "Since God anointed Him with the Holy Ghost" [Acts 10:38]. Certainly not with visible oil, but with the gift of grace, which is symbolized by the visible ointment with which the Church anoints the baptized. Nor was Christ anointed with the Holy Ghost at the time when He descended upon Him as a dove, after He had been baptized. For at that time He deigned to prefigure His body, that is, His church, in which pre-eminently the baptized receive the Holy Ghost," etc.*

In this passage of Augustine we have to consider three things. First, since he says that the Holy Ghost was not given by the disciples, that they only prayed for it, much less is it true that the bestowal of the Holy Ghost is bound up with the sacraments administered by the clergy. Secondly, that the bestowal of the Holy Ghost was not bound up with the laying on of hands, which I do not deny is a sacrament. For since they only prayed that the Holy Ghost might be given to those upon whom they laid hands, they had no power to promise this by laying on of hands. Finally, when Augustine says, "In which pre-eminently the baptized receive the Holy Ghost," he is speaking symbolically (for he does not use the word "preeminently" to indicate a certainty that they who receive baptism necessarily also receive the Holy Ghost, but in a sense like that of "to wit," "namely," etc.,—in the sense, "the church, namely the one in which the baptized receive the Holy Ghost"). Thus receiving the Holy Ghost is not the effect of baptism, but baptism is the effect of having received the Holy Ghost. And Francis Marot† was looking to this in his annotations to the arguments when he said, "The second argument is that if the sacraments themselves by their own efficiency produced grace, then the ministers who administer them would give the Holy Ghost." Hence it is plain that under whatever scheme or figure of speech any working of the Holy Ghost is attributed to the symbols or sacraments, a metonymy appears, by which the name of the original thing is transferred to the symbol. For Augustine's remark that Christ

*See Schaff, *Nicene Fathers*, First Series, Vol. III, p. 224.

†A scholar of the order of Friars Minor writing about 1320. A large collection of his theological works was published at Basel in 1498.

received the Holy Ghost before His baptism,* and that the apostles do not give the Holy Ghost, shows that there is no intimate connection of the Holy Ghost with the minister or the sacrament. From this it follows at once that the language is used symbolically and not in its simple sense when that which belongs to the Spirit is attributed to the sacraments. And this will be made plainer by the second quotation.

Augustine in the third book of the Questions, Quest. 84, says†, "We must notice how often He says, 'I, the Lord, who sanctify him,' speaking of the priest, and having also said to Moses, 'And thou shalt sanctify him' [Ex. 29:24]. How then does Moses sanctify and the Lord? For Moses does not act instead of the Lord, but he sanctifies with the visible sacraments through his ministry, while the Lord sanctifies with invisible grace through the Holy Ghost, in which is all the efficacy of the visible sacraments. For what do the visible sacraments profit without this sanctification of invisible grace? And it is also fair to ask whether this invisible sanctification without the visible sacraments with which a man is visibly sanctified, is equally ineffectual? This is absolutely absurd. For it would be more sensible to say that the sanctification does not exist without the sacraments than to say that though existing it profits nothing, for all the efficacy of the sacraments depends on this sanctification. But we must also consider whether there is any ground for saying that it cannot exist without the sacraments. Certainly visible baptism profited Simon the Sorcerer nothing, since he lacked the invisible sanctification.

"But those whom the invisible sanctification, being present, profited, had received also the visible sacraments and had been similarly baptized. Nor is it shown where Moses, who visibly

*Augustine, "On the Trinity," Bk. XV, chap. 26, §46, writes: "And Christ was certainly not then anointed with the Holy Spirit, when He as a dove descended upon Him at His Baptism. . . . But He is understood to have been then anointed with the mystical and invisible unction, when the Word of God was made flesh. . . . For it is most absurd to believe Him to have received the Holy Spirit when He was near thirty years old; for at that time He was baptized by John; but that He came to baptism as without sin at all, so not without the Holy Spirit." See Schaff, *Nicene Fathers*, First Series, Vol. III, p. 224.

†Augustine, "Questions on Leviticus," Bk. III, Question 84, cf. Migne, *Patrologia Latina*, XXXIV, 712.

sanctified the priests, was himself sanctified through sacrifices or oil. Yet who would venture to deny that he was invisibly sanctified whose grace excelled all others. The same can be said of John the Baptist. For he appeared as a baptizer before being baptized [Matth. 3: 11-14]. Hence we cannot possibly deny that he was sanctified. Yet we do not find that done visibly to him before he came to the ministry of baptizing. Also of the thief to whom, when crucified with Him, the Lord said, "Today shalt thou be with me in paradise" [Lk. 23: 43]. For he was not given this great blessing without invisible sanctification. Accordingly it is argued that invisible sanctification has been bestowed upon certain men and profited them without the visible sacraments, which are changed to suit the varying conditions of different ages and were different in the olden days from what they are now, but the visible sanctification which is conferred by visible sacraments can be present without the invisible, but cannot profit. Not, however, is the visible sacrament to be despised on that account. For he who despises that cannot possibly be invisibly sanctified. Hence Cornelius and his people, though evidently already sanctified by the Holy Ghost, were yet baptized [Acts 10: 44-48], and the visible sanctification was not considered superfluous, though the invisible had preceded it." Thus Augustine.

To what purpose should we now treat in detail this opinion of Augustine, clearer than light as it is? It must be clear to every one that Augustine in the early days held the same view that I hold today, namely that the sanctification of the Spirit is the real sanctification, which is by itself sufficient for justification without the external, provided this be not despised, as may be seen in the case of the thief, and indeed that the external is nothing without the internal. Furthermore, that no one ought to despise and neglect the external justification of the sacraments. Nay, he who has faith cannot neglect or despise the external when occasion offers. For who can disdain the things of love? And is not the love of God and of one's neighbor eager to call to mind the goodness of God and to praise and magnify Him with thanksgiving? Is it not eager to be united to its neighbor by the bond of the Spirit, and to bear witness thereto openly? Does it not desire to have its faith propped up and restored, when it sees it wavering? And where in the world can he hope to find that better than in the celebration of the sacraments, as far as visible things are concerned? For grant that all created things invite us to the contemplation of the deity, yet this invitation is an altogether dumb one. In the sacraments we have a living and speaking invitation. For the Lord Himself speaks, the elements speak, and they speak and suggest to the senses the same thing that speech and the Spirit do to the mind. But all these visible things are nothing unless the invisible sanctification of the Spirit go before them.

Thus, not to be too lengthy, I will suffer myself to be thrown back with all my opponents upon Augustine as umpire and mediator in this controversy over the sacraments and their efficacy. For nothing can be said about the sacraments so grandly eloquent as to offend me, provided we take as symbolical what is said symbolically and give the glory to God, and not to the holiness of the ministers nor to the efficacy of the elements or sacraments. For since, as is incontrovertible in baptism and the eucharist, that which is symbolized by the sacraments is at hand before we use the sacraments, what in the world is the reason why we should attribute to the sacraments what we had before, when the sacraments simply make confession of, bear witness to, and call into use what we have before? How far shall we tempt the Spirit of God in so evident a matter? Or is not he at length admitted to baptism who through faith or promise of it has been previously counted in the Church? Is not the man who has not proved his faith before offering himself at the table of the Lord's Supper refused by the apostle?

Are the sacraments, then, in vain? By no means, as has been said. For they proclaim salvation from God, turn the senses to it and thus exercise the faith which they also promise to the neighbor, drawing us to brotherly love. And one and the same Spirit worketh all these things, sometimes without, sometimes with, the external instrument, inspiring whom it will and drawing him whither and as it will.

I spoke above of the sanctified and consecrated bread, and this I do not wish in any way understood in the sense of the Papists, as if the bread were converted into the real and natural body of Christ. It is converted into His sacramental body. Grant that daily bread is blessed by the word and by prayer, then much more is that bread which before was common bread but now is changed so as to be the sacramental body of Christ, made divine and sacred by blessing and consecration, exactly as the ancients said it was changed and blessed, not so that the susbstance of bread passed over into the substance of Christ's body, but so that the bread became Christ's sacramental body. And what Christ's sacramental body is, there is no need for me to tell you who know. Only let us not impose upon the ignorant in the very name of the sacrament, but let signs be signs. But if any one says to me, "If you subscribe to the opinion of Augustine in regard to the efficacy of the sacraments, what reason is there why you should not return to harmony with the Papists?" I answer, "The bulk of the controversy remains." For they attribute to the sacraments the power of working wherever they are administered, as if divine efficacy were bound up with them. For this increases their wealth, as they have all the gifts of God for sale, nay they sell God Himself at a far higher price than Judas did. I, however, say that the sacraments do not bestow grace, but call it into activity and testify to it when already bestowed—these sacraments which are bought for a price in proportion to the grace possessed. But that which is already possessed is not bought, and the active manifestation of it cannot be acquired from any body except as an external thing which without the internal grace of faith is without value. "Let a man prove himself," says Paul [I Cor. 11: 28], not, "Let every one prove somebody else," or, "let one sanctify another." So much for the efficacy of the sacraments.

Now I will treat of the Eucharist in shorter compass. For these are the two pillars, as it were, upon which the greed of Rome rests.

The strife about the Eucharist Eck himself would have brought to an end, if one could trust what he said when he spoke of the body of Christ being eaten in the Supper mysteriously. For I say the same thing. And then he said that the body is eaten indeed in the Supper but not physically. I again say the same thing. But when he says "mysteriously," he lays a snare with this word "mysteriously;" he does the same with the word "physically." He does not understand that a mystery was to the Greeks about the same thing as a sacrament to the

Romans.* Thus when the people of old said that the body of Christ was eaten they understood this in the same way as if one said "mysteriously" or "sacramentally." If Eck understood it so, harmony would have been completely established between us. All controversy would have been equally brought to an end, if he took "physically" in the sense of "materially" or "substantially." But since they have invented some third thing between the real and material body of Christ and His sacramental body, not that spiritual body which we eat, but a kind of thing that does not exist, being neither material nor sacramental, that is symbolical and significative,—I see clearly enough what stand they would take if one should meet them a hundred times. They have two retreats into which to flee. One is that the man who does not understand that body they have invented is a blockhead. The other is that words are able to effect the thing they say. To this last I simply oppose (for I will attack their first retreat afterwards), "Let Eck, then, say to me or to that devil by whom he maintains I am possessed, 'Be still and come out of him,' " and he will see how still I become while he lies so shamelessly and rends the truth so godlessly. For there is no reason why he should refuse me this request. I am among the living, I am still awaiting the bridegroom, my hope of pardon is still secure, hence this is due me in charity. He cannot plead inability, for words are able to effect the thing they say, and these are Christ's words. But let us put this aside and come to the examination of the body of Christ, with suppliant prayer to Him that He will disclose himself to us.

I have no quarrel with any man as to the words of the Supper, as if I would have them changed as some falsely charge, or absolutely done away with, as others slanderously assert. For when the words are, "This is my body," they give the sacrament a more impressive character than if we said, "This symbolizes my body." So I would not have them changed at all. And how can I want words utterly done away with, which I do not even wish changed? My opponents have these words, therefore, and I have them. Let the words stay unaltered with them, for they shall stay unchanged with me:—"This is my

*So Tertullian uses sacrament in the sense of the Greek word "mystery." See Rogers, *Peter Lombard and the Sacramental System*, New York, 1917, p. 10.

body which is given for you," and "this is my blood" and so forth. My opponents say that the body of Christ is offered here. I also say the same thing. Where then is the difference? It is here. My opponents say the material and substantial body of Christ is offered, I say the sacramental. Hence the strife. Let them answer, therefore, whether they desire to understand physically or spiritually the words, "This is my body," that is, whether He offered His body to be eaten physically or spiritually. For between material or physical and spiritual there is no middle term. Though you put together everything there is, both creator and created things, you will have either spirit or body. To this combat, therefore, I challenge them, Did Christ offer His body to be eaten materially and physically or spiritually? If they say, "spiritually," they withdraw from their opinion and come over to mine. If they say, "physically," they deny their own postulates. For they say body is eaten but not physically, which is a difference of words and not of things. For if Christ's body is physically and materially body and they eat His material body, they eat it physically. To talk about eating it otherwise is mere trifling. For I have no use for that notion (of which Eck declares me ignorant) of a real and true body that does not exist physically, definitely and distinctly in some place, and that sort of nonsense got up by word triflers.

I go to the root of things when I say, "If the body of Christ is finite,—indeed, if it is a clarified body, such as ours shall also be, it exists physically and truly after the manner of clarified bodies. It is, therefore, eaten, as it exists, if it is eaten in a material sense. For the manner or quality cannot be taken away from a material body. If you take it away, the body is no longer material but spiritual." And again we conquer. You can in the mind abstract the quality from the thing, but in actual fact it cannot be separated from it. For everything that is has the qualities peculiar to its kind and inseparable therefrom, and without them the thing never does exist or can exist as long as the kind endures, whatever our minds take away or add, put together or put asunder. This, perhaps, Eck, led astray by sophistry, fails to understand. But I understand and know that I say what is true and sound, for I am supported both by the testimony of Holy Scripture and by the opinion of St.

Augustine,* who assigns the body of Christ to some particular place in heaven according to the fashion of real body. If the real body of Christ has the character of body so that it occupies some particular place in heaven, Augustine attributes to it its appropriate and inseparable characteristic. I shall, therefore, compel those who wish to eat the material, substantial, or real body of Christ, materially, substantially and really, to eat it also physically in accordance with all the necessary properties of body. For without those properties it would not be real body, as I am constantly proclaiming and constantly in vain.

The passion of hatred, ignorance, and vainglory, having overpowered a man, holds his eyes fast as the tyrant does the free man. As he dares not speak out what is true, so the eye bewitched by such passions fails to see what is true and sound, so that you should not trust, most wise princes of Germany, any of the scholars who in this day have fallen into this controversy. But we must pray the Lord to make firm the wavering. For you see clearly what trivial explanations, what distortions of language they concoct, appealing now from the sacred Scriptures to the Fathers, and again from the Fathers to the naked Word, as they say, in their efforts not to seem beaten. Question your faith and your mind and your heart and they will tell you that what satisfies here is simply the spiritual. If you admit this, what quarrel have we? I, too, believe and confess the same.

Furthermore, that the sacrament not only should be called body, but be its representative and symbol to the senses, to suggest to our senses and hold them bound, gives me no offense,

*Augustine refers to this thought repeatedly. Thus he says in Sermon 361, §7: "According to the presence of His glory and divinity He is always with the Father; according to His bodily presence, He is now above the heavens at the right hand of the Father; but according to the presence of faith, He is in all Christians." Again in his Letter 187, to Dardanus, he writes: "Doubt not that Christ is wholly present everywhere as God, and is in the same temple of God as indwelling God, and in some one place of heaven on account of the measure (or limit) of a true body." (c. XIII, or §41). In the same letter, c. III, or §10, he writes: "As respects this form He is not supposed to be spread abroad everywhere. For we must take heed, that we do not so maintain the divinity of the man as to take away the truth of the body . . . For God and man is one person, and both make one Christ Jesus; He is everywhere by that which is God, but He is in heaven by that which is man." See also his Commentary on John, Tract XXX, 1, quoted p. 54, note **.

nor shall I be angry even if all that the Spirit works be attributed to the external sacrament, provided we understand such language symbolically, as the Fathers used it. It is silly to wrangle about words when we do not differ about the thing. I have long been saying that the body of Christ is in the Supper to the eye of faith. Now whichever way my adversaries turn they will find no way of dragging it into the Supper otherwise. What unfairness it is, to be dragged into side issues by noisy contentious fellows! But to end this complaint I will give a short illustration in which my view about the Eucharist shall be outlined as it were.

The master of the house on the point of starting upon a long journey and handing to his wife a splendid ring with his image cut upon it, and saying, "Here am I, your husband, for you to keep and delight in my absence," typifies our Lord Jesus Christ. For He, when going away, left to His spouse, the Church, His own image in the sacrament of the Supper. As He is the strong foundation of our hope, so does the bread strengthen mankind, and as wine refreshes the heart of man, so does He raise up the despairing soul. He gave us His image with the words, "This is my body," sacramentally and symbolically, like the ring of the master of the house. "Do this in remembrance of me, giving thanks and offerings and pouring out prayer and praise because I, the spouse of your souls, have redeemed you." In saying "Here am I myself," the master of the house gave much more than if he had said, "Here is my ring," even though he did not actually and physically give himself, being now on the point of going away. By these words, he gave himself wholly—all that he represented of conjugal faithfulness and love—as though he would say, "I want you to be sure not only of my faithfulness and love towards you, but that I am wholly yours, and for this I give you this ring, the one chief thing I own, as a sign and symbol, that as often as you look upon it you may have me as it were present before you and call to mind my face and faithfulness." So in the Eucharist that noble man, when going away to a distant country, gave Himself to us in the bread and wine far more vividly and intimately when He said, "This is my body," than if He had said, "This is a symbol of my body," though He was going to take away His material body and place it in heaven. Yet by these words He gave Himself just as entirely, as far as faith and grace are concerned, as if He had said, "Now I am going to death for you, and a little later I shall go away from here again, but I do not want you to doubt of my love and care for you. I am wholly yours in all that I am. In witness of this I entrust to you a symbol of this my surrender and testament, to awaken in you the remembrance of me and of my goodness to you, that when you see this bread and this cup, held forth in this memorial Supper, you may remember me as delivered up for you, just as if you saw me before you as you see me now, eating with you and presently to be taken away from you to suffer for you," etc.

Thus, I say, we have the Lord's Supper distinguished by the presence of Christ. But in all this is not the presence of the body of Christ sacramentally to the eye of faith, as I have always said, the gist of the whole matter? For as her husband's ring is no common gold to the wife but more than all the gems of the Indies, so to us is this sacrament, the food and drink of the Lord's Supper, sweeter than the flavor of the finest viands. And as the ring, though not itself the husband, has a touch of the husband's value because it was given by him as a sign of undying love, and because it recalls his form whenever it is looked upon, so the repast of the Supper, though not Christ's material body, rises to high value because it was given and instituted as an everlasting sign of the love of Christ, and because as often as it is celebrated it brings Him who so loves us before us so vividly that we gaze upon Him with the eye of the mind and adore and worship Him. And as this contemplation by faith is far more precious than even the touch of that body (for many touched it in the flesh to their own destruction, while none ever contemplated it thus by faith, as I have said, without salvation), so is this contemplation or partaking the one thing needful in the Supper. Paul bids us prove our faith, not our credulity or opinion, to see whether we doubt about physical eating.

This, too, should be by no means passed by here, that the wife will value her husband's ring in proportion to her love for him. So in the Supper the body of Christ is the more vividly present to the eye of faith, the greater is one's faith and love towards Christ. Hence arise such expressions as, "He was taken up by their hands," just as the husband offered himself to his wife—"He was at once fellow banqueter and banquet," for He presented himself to them sacramentally, and also sat and ate with them in the flesh. Thus, I say, do I understand the highly figurative and hyperbolic language regarding the Eucharist. And, as I have often borne witness, I can easily put up with all expressions of this kind, provided we do not go on to understand physically the thing said of spiritual partaking, and understand symbolically what is said symbolically in the way that Augustine also was in the habit of speaking.

Furthermore as to Eck himself, his refutation is so weak and feeble that my confession of faith needs no defense against it. And where his followers had a right to expect something, he is utterly dull, namely, where he tries to draw out from me ancient and exploded arguments. Who is not minded to laugh when he gives to Augustine's words, "For the Lord did not hesitate to say, 'This is my body,' when He offered a symbol of His body," the explanation, "The properties without the substance are the symbol of Christ's body." I say, "Then the properties are the sacrament," for symbol is used here for sacrament. Therefore Augustine said that Christ gave His disciples properties, for he adds, "when He offered a symbol." Then when they say, "Christ's body is in the sacrament of the altar," they really say, "Christ is in the properties." Therefore it is false what they teach, that Christ's body is identical with the sacrament and is the substance of the sacrament, since the properties are the sacrament, or else Christ's body is to them only a property. But who could count the silly and ridiculous things that would follow from Eck's utterances and explanations? This, too, is charming, when he brings forward about two hands ruled by one soul,—and he a philosopher, please the gods! As if he would admit that Christ had two bodies at once, just as there are two hands. For as to the soul of Christ and the number of members it rules at once, we have never had any dispute. Or as if, when he will have it that Christ's soul ruled two bodies at once, which is irreverent, Eck would allow that these two bodies were equal and like unto each other, as one's two hands are alike, when I had said that if Christ had two bodies at once, they must have been unlike, and one subject to death, the other immortal! But I will not discuss these absurdities further.

Furthermore as to his slanders and lies, I say they are so

many and so extensive that if you take them out of the book there will not be enough left to throw into the fire, where alone the book belongs, even if there were any truth in it, that such wholesale madness may not go unpunished and sometime become a precedent.

Examples are, that I alienated certain cities from allegiance to the House of Austria; that I roused seditions at Rottweil, a place I never visited, and at Ittingen, for whose sake I have suffered and borne many hardships; that I drew Balthasar the Catabaptist into heresy by a letter,* when I never wrote to the man except once, when I took him sharply to task for the heresy he had taken up, for both his character and his company were always suspicious to me. The first time he met me he told me how closely he was associated with Eck.† I had no doubt then that the viciousness of the man, who was overweening enough in himself, had quickly been increased by that companionship. Hence I never admitted him into close relationship, so that he finally expostulated with me and upbraided me for wrongfully snubbing such a man as himself.

*Huebmaier relates the following *conversation* with Zwingli about baptism: "In 1523 . . . I conferred with you in Graben street upon the Scriptures relating baptism; then and there you said I was right in saying that children should not be baptized before they were instructed in the faith; this had been the custom previously, therefore such were called catechumens. You promised to bring this out in your 'Exposition' of the Articles, as you did in Article XVIII, on Confirmation [See Zwingli's *Werke*, ed. of Egli and Finsler, II, 123]. Any one who reads it will find therein your opinion clearly expressed . . . So you confessed in your book on the "Unruly Spirits," that those who baptize infants could quote no clear word of Scripture ordering them to baptize them [See Zwingli's *Werke*, ed. of Egli and Finsler, III, 409]. From this learn, friend Zwingli, how your conversation, writing, and preaching agree." Quoted by Prof. Vedder, in his *Balthasar Hübmaier*, p. 126f. In the latter passage Zwingli adds that, as there was no *clear* command to baptize children in the New Testament, it was necessary to go back to the Old Testament custom of circumcision, of which baptism was the N. T. counterpart.

†Balthasar Huebmaier was a pupil of Eck, who studied under him at Freiburg, taking the master's degree there probably in 1511, at which occasion Eck delivered an oration. When Eck was called to Ingolstadt, Huebmaier followed him and took the doctor's degree there on September 29, 1512, when Eck again delivered an oration, in which he gave a sketch of the candidate's scholastic life. See H. C. Vedder, *Balthasar Hübmaier*, pp. 32-34.

Moreover, that I was ever averse to infant baptism or was tinged with Catabaptism, no lover of the truth and right ever said of me. For I can bring forward witnesses of no ordinary sort who know how I suppressed the foolish gossip which some persons had started about not baptizing infants, two years after the Catabaptists came on the scene, doing it in a not unfriendly way and reminding them that the meaning of Scripture in this matter was at variance with their contention. If Balthasar had that writing of mine, no doubt his executioners found it upon him, or he left it to the Catabaptists. Let, therefore, those who have it show it, and convict me of treachery or high treason.

Of the same character is his statement that I thrust something into the mouths of the ancient orthodox writers, as if they had written that Christ's body is everywhere. What I said as an absurdity in regard to the crosses in the mass, by way of refutation and with a view to dissuasion, he declares I said in sober argument. This I deny with the utmost possible emphasis. But who would be a greater fool than I, if I should continue to review all the lies of this lying person? So much for what pertains to teaching, for his other carpings of this sort show not a scholar but a purblind creature, and the leeches will protect us from harm from that source.

The most ancient city of the Zurichers (early history and especially the Roman consul, Lucius Cassius, whom they slew, have borne witness to their character for all these ages) he not only refers to Charles the Great as founder, uninformed in history as he is, but attacks with such lying statements before the whole world that he could not be more shameless towards a city he had reason to hate utterly. And this though it is acknowledged that no city in these times or in ancient times ever devoted itself to the Roman Empire so faithfully—none, I say—and through the services of none has greater profit come to the House of Austria and to the Empire itself. Therefore, I call to witness next to the ancient historical records the annals of the emperors and of the dukes of Austria. I tell the truth when I say that this city has drained its treasury in the service of the Gospel, but has not diverted one of the monasteries to the uses of its own treasury. They all either remain for the support of those who had been destined for the monasteries or appointed to teach there, or are turned into funds for the poor. We have no chest and have not learned to steal.

Therefore, Your Highnesses, notice what this champion of the Pope is aiming at. He shows with perfect clearness that the Romanists under the guise of a synod—general synod, doubtless—are going to control your assembly, he calls the Emperor openly to arms. How all this will turn out is for Your Highnesses to consider. Dangers threaten on all sides, but the Lord will dissipate them all, if you lay hold upon truth and righteousness. To take a stand against truth is destruction, to yield to her is the first essential of safety. God Almighty grant that we may reverence her and see her through a glass in this world, but see her face to face and embrace her in the world to come! Amen.

Zurich, August 27th, 1530.

V.

Reproduction from Memory of a Sermon on the Providence of God, Dedicated to His Highness, Philip of Hesse.

(August 20, 1530)

[AD ILLV- | STRISSIMVM CATTORVM PRIN- | cipem Philippum, sermonis De providentia | Dei Anamnema. VENITE AD ME OMNES QUI LA- | boratis et onerati estis, et ego reficiam vos. Matth. XI. Tigvri apvd Christophorvm | Froschouer, Anno M.D. XXX. | 160 octavo pages, numbered by leaves (2-80). Signed on p. 159 : Tiguri XX. Augusti M.D. XXX. *Opera Zwinglii*, Tom. I, fol. 352a-379b; Schuler and Schulthess ed. Vol. IV, pp. 79-144. A German edition, translated by Leo Juda and printed by Froschouer in 1531, has the following title:

An den Durchlüchtigesten Fürsten vnd Herren, Herrn Philippen, Landgraff in Hessen, Von der Fürsichtigkeyt Gottes, ein büchlin inn Latin beschribenn durch Meister Huldrich Zwinglin. Vertütschet durch Leo Jud. Matth. XI. At the end, on p. 221: *Getruckt zu Zürich by Christoffel Froschouer.* M. D. XXXI. 224 unnumbered octavo pages. Finsler, *Zwingli Bibliographie*, Nos. 94 and 95. The following English translation is based on one by Mr. Henry Preble. It was revised throughout by the editor.

The work of Zwingli "On the Providence of God" is a free reproduction from memory of a sermon, delivered by Zwingli at Marburg during the Marburg Colloquy, October 1-4, 1529. As rewritten by Zwingli the sermon has become a philosophical treatise. In his philosophy he follows principally Aristotle and the Stoics. The doctrine of God, starting from the conception of the Highest Being, is developed into a cosmological argument for the Being of God. Upon this basis the discussion of the Divine Providence proceeds, culminating in the question of Divine Predestination. It is the most abstruse as well as the most penetrating Latin work of Zwingli.]

Huldreich Zwingli to His Highness Philip of Hesse

GRACE and peace from our Lord and Saviour Jesus Christ. You ask a thing, most pious Prince, which you might fairly have claimed or demanded—the sermon that I delivered in your castle at Marburg. I would be as quick to give it as you to ask it, if my memory listened to my inclination. For why should not the abilities of all, who try to advance our religion by preaching or teaching, spontaneously put themselves at the service of Your Highness? For you alone strive frankly to have the infancy of religion nourished conscientiously and allowed to develop peacefully. You alone have duly considered that save God alone none duly knoweth all things; that, therefore, all things are not wisely ordered according to the dictum of one man. You alone, seeing among the servants of the Christian religion the power of rivalry and jealousy, nay, to speak with full frankness and openness, the power of error and lust of glory, take anxious care to prevent that band of followers, emulating the defects of their master, from breaking forth in their zeal into some discord or disturbance. You alone understand that if we truly hold fast to the chief point of religion, difference of opinion upon other points is not of such moment as to justify us in breaking for their sake that cord of charity which, like the red cord of the Athenian assembly, brings us together in one spirit and one mind. You alone, though fully convinced,* and sure in regard to a matter as to which others still dispute somewhat unmannerly and ignorantly, by a sort of holy hypocrisy pretend to waver and be in doubt, that as a companion of the erring ones you may tear them from their error through your friendship and gentle kindness, through the protection of your name and the hope of security, when they see you steadfastly embracing the truth that has dawned, and that you may free them from fear when they behold in you a haven to which they may hasten if any danger threatens from a change of their opinion. This is indeed to be a peacemaker†, this is rightly and really to know the ways of Christian peace, this is to show one's self a pious prince.

Moreover you make yourself an example not only to the learned but to all, both peoples and princes, to be looked up to and imitated, because you alone rule your subjects with such moderation and gentleness that you alone seem to point out to ·

---

* πληροφορηθείς. The Greek words which Zwingli inserts into the text we add in the notes.

† εἰρηνοποιεῖσθαι.

the rest the way by which rulers may learn to command willing subjects, and subjects to obey just commands. This courage, fidelity and wisdom of yours, I say, young though you are,* show that those who do not reverence you either have not yet seen the radiance of your glory, or, having seen, maliciously envy it. If you go on as you have begun, God who giveth the increase will make you grow, contrary to their hopes, to be a noble example of constancy and piety to the present generation and to posterity.

But now I come back to myself. If, I say, my memory could recall all that I said in word and order of arrangement, nothing would delight me more than this opportunity of complying with your wishes. Since, however, the faithful retentiveness of memory, through which perhaps a Cato or a Seneca might recover it all, has been denied me, I will do this: I will write a short, but I think substantial, summary regarding Providence, dividing it into not more than seven chapters. When you examine them I think you will admit that you have received, if not the sermon itself, at least the same material and line of argument—all in homely and plain workmanship. Do then, brave hero, meantime so cultivate goodness and the knowledge of holy things that we shall all rejoice that the Prince of Hesse† is, according to the precept of Christ, our Saviour, as wise as a serpent and as harmless as a dove. May He long preserve you to His cause! Amen.‡
Zürich, 1530.

FIRST CHAPTER

Providence must exist, because the supreme good necessarily cares for and regulates all things.

*Philip of Hesse was born in 1504.

†The play upon words involved in "Cattorum principem" and "catum serpentem" seems impossible of reproduction.

‡Bucer wrote to Zwingli of this preface, "You slashed them [the Lutherans] more than offensively in the preface to the Prince of Hesse. You ought not by this ill-omened preface to have exposed to odium a work so fine and worthy of immortality." For Bucer was already treating with Luther and his associates with regard to certain formulas that might satisfy them and yet leave a loop-hole for the understandings of those who thought differently. Zwingli was opposed to this scheme of clever compromise. See Letter of Bucer to Zwingli, Sept. 18, 1530, ed. Schuler and Schulthess, Vol. VIII, pt. 2, p. 516.

The supreme good is not so called because it is above all goods, as if there were some goods that were good in their own nature but were surpassed by this good, just as gold surpasses the value of silver though both are valuable. It is called the supreme good because it is the only thing good by nature, and every good that can be imagined is itself really this supreme good. This Christ set forth by the words: "Why callest thou me good? There is none good but God" [Matth. 19: 17]. In these words we see that God alone is good in the sense of being an absolutely and perfectly good being, and that consequently there can be nothing good which is not He, and, in short, that the things which are called good, as "all that he had made was very good," and "every creation of God's is good," are good not by nature but by sharing His goodness, or rather, by derivation. That is, they are good in so far as they are from that supremely good being and in that good being and to the glory of that good being.

Now, to go to the root of the matter, it follows necessarily that what is good by nature and good in the highest degree, and whatever is good in itself, must also be true. And this the philosophers knew when they attributed at the same time the quality of truth to the good and only one.* For, of course, the One must be good, they said, but cannot be good unless it is likewise true, that is, pure, genuine, clear, complete, simple and unchangeable. For all these belong to the conception of the true. For that which changes is not simple, nor complete, clear, genuine and pure. For however much we conceive the elements as simple in our imagination, they are in fact mixed. For fire could not travel unless it were set aflame by the air, and whither would water run without the air? How could it draw in and pour out again its whirlpools? How through drink fill us? Without the air the earth could not emit its vapor nor bring forth fruit, nor, finally, absorb the salt sea like a sponge, and sifting it through its internal arteries, as it were, make it come out fresh and sweet. And the air itself which is the guide and author of all motion and movement, how could it come warm and hot from the south or colder than ice from the north

*Thus e. g., Plato in his "Republic," Bk. VI, 507, "That which imparts truth to the object and knowledge to the subject is what I would have you term the idea of good."

unless it were mixed with fire or water? Since, therefore, these things which we believe or assume to be simple in order to refer the origin and beginning of things to some primary cause, are in reality not simple, and are consequently subject to change, it follows that only the one supreme good is true that is, simple, pure and unalloyed, since that alone is unchangeable. And, conversely, since only that one supreme good is unchangeable, it follows that it alone is true, that is, pure, genuine and so forth.

Now that which is supreme and true, simple, pure and complete, must first of all know and understand all things. For in whatever quarter it failed in understanding anything, it would not be clear and lucid, nor complete and pure, which qualities belong to the nature of the true. Secondly, that which is supreme and true, must also have power over all things. For as to the supreme, it is easy to see that it cannot be supreme unless it is first and supreme in might and power. But it will perhaps be a task to prove that what is true is also powerful over all things, except that I have already said that we are speaking of the supreme good which is by nature as true as it is good, and it is the supreme good, because whatever belongs to the nature of the good is itself that Divinity of which we are speaking and that to a supreme degree. That is, if power and strength are good, our Divinity is supremely powerful, if truth is good, it is supremely true, and so on. Thus the supreme good is supreme and indeed unlimited power, is supremely true, that is, is truth in its essence, so that there is not anywhere power and strength, no truth, simplicity, genuineness, purity, which is not from this foundation of truth, nay, is not this very truth itself.

Hence I conclude, if the Supreme Divinity is the supreme good, and truth belongs to the nature of the good, so that the supreme good cannot be such unless it is true and indeed truth itself, I conclude, I say, that the supremely true is also supreme might and power. Let us now join these three and with the understanding of faith weld together the Supreme Divinity, that is, supreme power and might, secondly the supreme good, that is, the whole sum and essence of the good, finally essential truth, that is, simplicity, purity, light, genuineness and unchangeableness.

As a result we shall see both that Providence must exist and that it cares for and regulates all things. For since it is of the nature of supreme truth to see through all things clearly, inasmuch as that which is divinity must see all things, and since it is of the nature of supreme might to be able to do what it sees, nay, to do all things, and, finally, since it is of the nature of the supreme good, to will by its goodness to do what it clearly sees and can do, it follows that he who can do all things, must provide for all things. For, suppose that being able to do all things he should allow some things to go at random. Then either the things that go this way escape his notice, or, if nothing can be hidden from him, he abandons or turns away from the care of them out of disinclination. If anything escapes his notice, he would fail to fulfill the nature of the true and would not be the supreme good, supreme truth or truth itself, but rather, inasmuch as he did not notice this or that, would be obscurity, darkness, and ignorance. If, on the other hand, he neglects anything from disinclination, he is not the supreme good, because he turns away from the care of things created by himself, while brutes, to say nothing of man, care for their young. For it cannot be that God should create or cause to come into existence anything which before it was born He should think would be good, but which afterwards, when born, should deceive the expectation of its Maker, so that He would have to say, "I had not thought so." For this is the mark of the foolish, not of Him who is truth and whom nothing can escape or evade, who is the light that shines upon and illumines all things, who is a limpid fountain, or a mirror overhanging all things so that everything that was or is or shall be is reflected in Him.

Suppose, in the second place, that being the supreme good, he inclines with favor towards the things he has made but is not able to regulate or help them. Then he is no longer the supreme, nor that might which has power over all things. Therefore, he is not God. And if he is not God, he is not the supreme good nor the very truth. Suppose, finally, that he is indeed the truth which sees thoroughly into all things, but that he either cannot or will not care for the things which are objects to his knowledge. Could any one imagine such a poverty-stricken and envious yet wise being, who foreseeing the needs of his creatures yet from lack of power and means could not establish nor help them, or, if he could, would not because of jealousy? You make God powerless, weak, infirm, as well as jealous, gloomy and cruel.

Such a being is so far from being God that under such a definition we include the evil spirit or even that blind reckless spirit
the Greeks called "Aτη *.

I think it is now established that Providence exists and
must exist, since it has been proved that the Supreme Divinity
is light, sincerity, purity, simplicity, completeness, that is,
truth. For since He sees all things, unless He also regulates all
things, it is because of lack of power or of good intention. But
since this same Divinity is both all power and in all respects good
and kind, it is clear that He not only knows all things, but
regulates, orders and disposes all things. Of this more at length
by and by. Meantime I can easily show that the things we
attribute to the Father, Son and Holy Ghost, who are yet one
God and Divinity, derive their origin from this source. For in
the sacred Scriptures omnipotence is attributed to the Father,
grace and goodness to the Son, truth to the Holy Ghost. Yet all
these we know belong to one and the same divine being,† just
as here I have shown that power, goodness, and truth, though
distinguished in conception and definition, are yet to be considered as one and the same supreme good.

As the Father is almighty, the Son gracious and the earnest
of mercy, the Holy Ghost the spirit of truth, and all three by
nature are one God, so is the Divine Being omnipotent, good and
true by nature.

SECOND CHAPTER

What Providence is and how it differs from Wisdom.

Having shown, in order to make the philosophers better
disposed towards us, that Providence not only exists but must
exist, I have next to show what It is. For those men say that the
natural and true order with problems is first to establish whether
a given thing exists, then to establish the nature of the thing we
have already discovered to exist. We know, then, that even in
the sacred Scriptures "wisdom" and "discretion" are used inter-
changeably, although there is no little difference between them
when the proper significance of each is carefully considered.

*Ate was the goddess of mischief and of all blind actions.
† ούσία.

For "wisdom" is the kind of thing the philosophers call δύναμις, that is, a power or ability; "discretion" is what they call πρᾶξις ἢ ἐνέργεια, that is, an action or performance.* This will be clearer from an example.

The sense of hearing, for instance, is a power or an ability. So also is sight. But seeing and listening are actions. The sleeper possesses sight and the sense of hearing, but the act of seeing and of hearing cannot be predicated of him, for these exist only when we see or hear something. So wisdom is the energy and power of the Supreme Intelligence (which is truth, light, and purity) by which It knows all things; discretion is the effective skill in managing and regulating what It knows and sees. Thus discretion connotes rather an activity, wisdom an energy and power. But, as I have said, "discretion" is used for "wisdom" and vice versa, on account of their resemblance in meaning. And that no one may think what I say frivolous, I will adduce the authority of Scripture.

In Genesis 41: 33, we have: "Now therefore let Pharaoh look out a man discreet and wise" and so forth, where the Hebrews have נבון and חכם, nabon and hacham, and our translators, as if by agreement, render by "intelligentes" and "sapientes," "understanding" and "wise," except Jerome, who used "sapientem" and "industrium," "wise" and "diligent," and we easily see that this keen judge of words put "industrium, diligent" here for "prudentem, discreet." The Septuagint rendered the words by φρόνιμον καὶ σύνετον, that is, "discreet and sagacious" or "wise." I do not wish to thrust upon this passage a sense different from the one that belongs to it and has been accepted by the translators, but, as far as the words are concerned, I would rather say "virum sapientem et prudentem, a man wise and discreet." For there are people who have, to be sure, clearsightedness in abundance, but who are absolutely helpless in respect to forming, perfecting and carrying out any plan of action. A discreet man, then, if we wish to speak properly, is a wise man who is skilled and sagacious in deliberately carrying out what he sees is going to be expedient. And such a man was needed for the work of which Joseph was

*The term "energy" is taken from Aristotle, see his "Metaphysics," Bk. VII, chap. 2.

speaking before the king. Diogenes was wise, as was also Heraclitus. I am inclined to doubt whether they ought to be called discreet, since they took no care to urge the things which they saw were best for mankind. But Joseph, Moses, Josiah, were discreet, for they devoted themselves with all their might to the accomplishment of what through their wisdom they saw was likely to be of service to their countrymen and religion. Thus wisdom signifies clear-sightedness especially, discretion adds to wisdom activity in carrying out a purpose. Yet although we sometimes use "discreet" for "wise," we are hardly accustomed to use "providence" for "knowledge" or "wisdom," especially when speaking of the Deity. When we hear the word "Providence," we understand that wisdom which foresees, and having foreseen, regulates all things.

Hence, I define Providence thus, "Providence is the enduring and unchangeable rule over and direction of all things in the universe." By rule I mean the power, authority and dignity of the Deity, of which I said enough before in showing how the supreme good must have power over all things. But since this power is not one of violence, troublesomeness and tyranny, and therefore hateful and unbearable, I added dignity and authority in defining "rule," for I would show the rule of the Deity to be so conscientious, holy, acceptable, and delightful that everybody willingly obeys it, who has gotten even the merest taste of a knowledge of it. And I appended the word "direction," both on account of the character of the sway, that none might, as I have said, suppose it to be monstrous, and on account of the abundance of things in the universe. For God does not command as men command, who, having acquired power over things, demand that all things be supplied them necessary for their care and attention to the affairs of state. He, however, freely supplies all with all things, asking nothing in return except that we shall take with gladness and gratefulness the gifts of His bounty. For since He is in need of nothing, is rich in all things, and is good and kind, nay, is the father of the things He has made, it follows that He cannot be wearied or exhausted through giving, that He rejoices in giving, that He cannot help giving. For the more and the oftener He gives, the better known His kindness becomes.

Then I said this rule and direction were enduring. Not

that I took "enduring" in the sense in which some people use it to make a distinction between "eternal," as that which never had a beginning and never has an end, and "enduring," as that which once had a beginning but never has an end. I took "enduring" in the sense of "eternal." Thus this sway is eternal as far as power is concerned. For the Deity can have no beginning. And after created things have come into being, the government and regulation of all things becomes also enduring.

Moreover, I called the direction and regulation unchangeable for this reason, that I might show that the opinion of those who declare that man's will is free is not altogether well grounded, and that the wisdom of the Supreme Deity is too unerring to allow the possibility that anything can happen without its notice and force it afterwards to reverse or change its design. Providence, is therefore, immovable, because the Deity is infallible and unerring, because His power is unwearying, because His goodness is uninterrupted.

Finally, I defined Providence as the rule over and direction of all things in the universe. For if anything were guided by its own power or insight, just so far would the wisdom and power of our Deity be deficient. And if this happened, the wisdom of the Deity would not be supreme, because it would not include and comprehend all things. Nor would His might be all powerful, because there would be a might independent of its power and therefore different from it. Thus there would be a force which was not the force of the Deity, and light and intelligence which were not the wisdom of that Supreme Deity. And then, if that second light and power were said to have been created, it could not have been created except by the Deity, and if it is from the Deity, power and wisdom of its own cannot rightly be attributed to it. For it would have these by derivation from the Deity, like all created things, nay the light and power would belong to the Deity Himself. If, on the other hand, that light and power were said not to have been created, then they would be a God, and we have a multiplication of gods brought in again. For all power is either created or uncreated. If uncreated, it is Deity and God. If created, it must be the creation of that Deity. Yet this so-called created power, since all power is the power of the Deity,—for there is nothing which is not from that, in that and through that Deity, nay is not a part of

Himself,—this power is said to have been created, I say, because it is a manifestation of the general, all-embracing power in a new individual form. Moses, Paul, Plato, Seneca are witnesses.

There is then, nothing which is not ruled by the Deity, nothing so high or powerful that it can avoid the sway of our Deity, nothing so lowly or humble that it is abhorrent to His care. All this will be set forth more at length and clearly in the sequel. It is enough in the present chapter to have shown that wisdom, goodness, and might, that is, to use the original terms, truth, goodness, and power, are what necessarily constitute Providence, and that Providence is the eternal and unchangeable government and direction of all things in the universe.

THIRD CHAPTER

Secondary causes are not properly called causes. This is of fundamental importance for the understanding of Providence.

But that the matter may be the plainer, I will trace the origin, existence, and working of all things from the beginning. Not one of the things exposed to our senses has its origin in itself. This I will prove by the highest and the lowest, that is, by the stars and the earth. Of man I will treat separately. To come, therefore, as quickly as possible to an understanding of the truth, how could the earth, that dull thing without feeling or intelligence, create itself or from what seed could it produce itself? If it produced itself from nothing, it existed before it did exist—as that which called itself forth from nothing. But if it comes from something else, it comes from it either as cause or as material. If as material, the material of the earth is different and this is either of the same kind as the present or of a different kind. If it is of the same kind, then the parent earth next to ours must also have a mother of its own, the grandmother, to wit, of ours. Then the grandmother must needs have a great grandmother, the great grandmother a great great grandmother, she a great great great grandmother and so on, until we come to that crowd of earths and worlds of which the so-called Great Alexander indignantly, if the thing be true, lamented that he had not yet conquered one.*

This view was brought to light and exploded by the philosophers at an early date. For we should thus assent to infinite and eternal worlds. But the one which we ourselves occupy is not yet ended; how much less those which are its authors! Moreover, if they grow up in this fashion, each earth and world being born out of another one, then, as with all processes of generation, the decrepit worlds, now ready for the grave, must die, and young ones step into their places. For if they do not die, there would long ago have been infinite worlds. But I will leave this nonsense. If, on the other hand, the material from which the earth is born is of a different kind from its daughter—the so-called equivocal generation of the more recent philosophers and theologians—we are driven into the same corner as before. For there will be a different material for this material, and still another for that one, and so on till we are plunged into infinity. Nor can the earth maintain its place among the elements. For that other material takes its place which is the mother of our mother earth, nay the mother of this also, nay the great grandmother and so forth, finally no material, for there is really no material than the one.

Now I come back to the principal division. If the earth comes from another cause, it must have been created. For we have just seen that it does not come from a material cause. Therefore it must come from nothing. For what is put together from nothing so as to exist is created. For this is the definition of creation, "to be out of nothing" or "to be, not having been before, but not coming from something else as material." Therefore, not to hurry so much as to pass by this point, the philosophers failed in circumspection when they raised the question whether the universe was created or uncreated.† For, see-

---

*This is an allusion to the story found in Plutarch's tract, "On the Tranquility of the Mind," which is as follows: "Alexander wept when he heard from Anaxarchus that there was an infinite number of worlds, and his friends asking him if any accident had befallen him, he returns this answer: Do you not think it a matter worthy of lamentation, that, when there is such a vast multitude of them, we have not yet conquered one?" See *Plutarch's Morals*, translated by Wm. W. Goodwin, Boston, 1871, Vol. I, p. 140.

†Aristotle (*Physics*, I. 10, 8) teaches that matter is eternal or "unproduced." Plato held the same view.

ing that those two vast subdivisions of the universe, the earth and the heavens, were without sensation and intelligence and yet maintained positions and motions of their own, they set over them an outside mover and guardian, and said that he was endowed with a mind and soul, but they did not at the same time duly consider that this mind must be either prior to the universe or contemporary with it. If it was prior to the universe, then the universe has a beginning and was created. For the argument I made above about the creation of the earth always holds good. But if the mind is contemporary with the universe, who gave the mind dominion over the universe? For the universe would be just as everlasting as the mind, and we cannot conceive a thing as being subordinate unless marked by inferiority or posteriority, and so the co-eternal cannot be the lesser. For the eternal is infinite, and things which are co-eternal are beyond a doubt equally infinite. But if this mind of which we are speaking is eternal and the universe is contemporary with it, as the mind is infinite so will the universe be infinite; and how absurd this is, even sense, to say nothing of the mind, can see. But since there can be only one single thing that is infinite, and the universe cannot be infinite, since its parts all have to be infinite, (for however great anything is, if it consists of parts, it must be finite unless the parts also are infinite, which is again perfectly absurd—for if one part is infinite whither can another stretch its own infinity or immensity?), since the universe, I say, consisting of parts, must be finite, it is proved that that mind which the philosophers call the original mover is the infinite we are after. And this is our Deity and God.

Having learned, therefore, that to have had a beginning is of the nature of the finite, and never to have had a beginning is of the nature of the infinite, that, accordingly there is only one single being that is infinite and, properly speaking, eternal, and having seen that the universe and all its parts are finite and, therefore, temporal and not eternal, the philosophers should open their eyes and see that the universe is finite and created, and not eternal. Whether it be enduring, this is not the place to discuss, because we are seeking for the beginnings, not the endings, of things, and because the divine Scriptures satisfy the faithful upon this point, namely that the world shall pass away.* Since

*See Matth. 24: 35.

then, to come back from the philosophers to myself, the universe had a beginning, it is evident that our mother earth is not of eternal existence nor lasting by nature, unless by autonomasia you understand nature to be the Deity of which we have been speaking, which is being and power unto all things. Nor does the earth come from itself. It must have come into being and have been produced out of nothing.

Now I ascend to the stars to investigate whether they come from themselves. The human mind, which is slower and duller in understanding things than it thinks it is, might fancy that the earth could be admitted to have been created, both because of its grossness and darkness and because of its inertness and sluggishness. For gross and impenetrable to light, dark in its depths and conscious of nothing, as it is, it simply lies there and suffers itself to be cleft and manipulated and dug and turned up. It is so inert and sluggish and incapable of moving that if air gets into its caverns and is stirred up in any way so that it has to burst forth, by which the earth is disturbed and shaken, ·it is regarded as a sign that the earth has moved. Every one is so thoroughly persuaded of its inertia, that its motion seems a miracle. Hence it may well seem unendurable that any one should deny that it had been produced or created. But the stars, whose bodies are so vast and, therefore, of such unusual force, so rapid that their motion surpasses all speed, so bright that, though so far away from us, they yet penetrate to us and blind our gaze —the stars, I say, may be imagined not to have been created, on the ground that by their movements and power things endowed with sensation suffer increase or diminution, and they seem in general of more divine and noble quality than the earth and its inhabitants.

To this reasoning we may first answer, as was done in the case of the earth and its parts, that the stars, however vast, rapid and bright their bodies are, either come from themselves or from something else. If from themselves, they either took beginning from themselves or have existed by themselves from eternity. If they took beginning from themselves, they existed before they did exist, for they brought themselves into existence. Nothing cannot beget anything. If they have existed from eternity, they are infinite, for only the infinite is eternal, infinite and eternal are convertible terms, that is, are equal or rather actually identical. But since the stars are not infinite (for what an army of them that little organ, the eye, can take in at a glance!), it follows that they come from some one else and that some one else, the mover and author of all things, is their God and father. For though we listen to the philosophers discussing about their heavens, about spheres and circles and their powers, yet we must at last come to one only and original mover*, as our starting point. This is the Deity.

Secondly, I answer the argument that appeals to the simple: that the stars have bodies quite the opposite of the earth's, to wit, that they are rapid in motion, while it is sluggish and dull, that they are very bright while it is dark and black, no more proves that their original generation is of themselves than if one should maintain that plants are of original self-generation, because they increase and grow, bloom, bear fruit, wither and die, while the earth does none of these, basing this argument on the ground of their superiority of endowment over the earth in power and action. For they spring from the earth and are nourished and supported by her, as nearest cause. So untrue is it that greater perfection of activity can remove the fact of creation, though the more perfect a thing is, the more it proclaims and bears witness to the perfection of its maker.

Since, then, it must be admitted that the earth and stars were produced or created, and that they and all things emanate equally from one and the same source, the next thing is to show by virtue of what power all things exist. As it is futile to believe that there are many creators of the universe, so it shows an unskilled and inexperienced mind to hold that anything can be or exist, except it have its being and existence in that and from that which alone *is*. For since the first essential of things is that they exist (what and how they are comes later), existence is in the first place given them by Him who is the source and origin of all things that are. But this existence which is given to things by Him, did He get it from Himself or borrow it from some one else to give them? If He borrowed it, we meet two difficulties, one, that created beings would then be more justly set down to the credit of that creditor from whom their existence was borrowed, that is, created being should properly be accredited to Him from whom they had really received exist-

* κινητής.

ence, the second, that the Deity which is the origin of all things would not be the original and supreme good, and therefore would not be God. For that good from which things received their existence would be richer and more powerful, and, therefore, would also be the Deity, and this God of ours would be only by derivation or by metonymy, and not really, the Deity. And what a foolish thing to say this is, even a fool can see.

If, on the contrary, He took from Himself this existence which he gave to His works and creatures, everything that is, is in Him and through Him and a part of Him. For since there must be some one original existence, everything which has come into existence, came into it from this original. Not as though the existence of created beings were so utterly different from that of the Deity, but of the same kind, from the same source and parent. This I want understood in this way: If any one should reject our disjunction that the existence given to things must be either borrowed from something else than the Supreme Deity or derived from this Deity Himself, maintaining that this disjunction was not exhaustive because a new kind of existence might have been given to things by the Deity which He did not take from His own nor borrow from another, which new existence of the creature was different from the existence of the Deity, he shall have this answer, that there is only one thing infinite by nature. For if two different essences were declared to be infinite, no less difficulty would follow than if one maintained that light was darkness. For in whatever direction one of the infinites was stretched out and extended, there the other would have to be curtailed or removed. Now since the infinite, as a fact, is so-called just because it is infinite in essence and existence, it is clear that outside of this infinite there can be no existence. For whatever such you grant, where this outside existence is, there the infinite will not be, and, therefore, it will not be infinite. Since, therefore, there is but one infinite, nothing can exist outside of it. And from this it follows that whatever is, is in it, nay, what is and exists comes from it, and since it does not come from it in the sense that its being and existence is different from its own, it is certain that as far as being and existence are concerned, there is nothing which is not of the Deity. For it is the being of all things.

This opinion, treated rather philosophically,* as it has been (although why call that philosophical which is sacred and according to religion, except that some people do not hesitate to make the truth odious, attributing it to the philosophers and not noting that the truth, wherever found and by whomever brought out is from the Holy Spirit), this opinion, I say, I will support first by an example and then by Scripture.

The example is this. Take the earth, a plant, an animal, anything you will, except man (for of him I will treat separately, as I said), and consider the thing you have taken as regards its essence and existence, not as regards its particular substance or kind, but, as has been said, as regards its essence and existence alone; you will see that each of these exists forever. For though the animal breathe out its life, it returns into the air and as it were pays back what it had received; when it lays aside its body, it presently ceases to be an animal, but it does not cease to be. For it suffers the body which it has returned to the earth to be with her, nay to be earth until some new form is brought forth from it, which, afterwards, also loses its form, returns to the earth, and again produces something new, and this continues as long as the earth keeps the character with which it is now endowed. The earth, having once begun its existence, never loses it, for though it shall put on sometime another form, yet it will never cease to be.

Hence I believe that palingenesis,† or the doctrine of rebirth, of the Pythagoreans, was unjustly made the object of so much ridicule. They recognized its necessity, since they saw that everything that is, is from that which is existence, and must therefore always have some existence. But the others, who either philosophized rather badly or wished, by unfair distortion of their teachings, to seem to offer something new, held them up maliciously to derision, as if they had maintained that the same species endured and at the same time was constantly passing over into another. Hence that immoderate laughter‡ at the

---

* φιλοσοφικοτέρως.

†According to Porphyry, *Life of Pythagoras*, §19, the only teachings that can with certainty be attributed to Pythagoras himself were palingenesis (or metempsychosis), the periodic cycle and the kinship of all living creatures.

‡ συγκρούσιος.

notion of Pythagoras that he had been Euphorbus and a cock and so forth, which thing he probably did not say himself. It was more likely put maliciously into his mouth by the scoffers.*

So, too, their metempsychosis, migration of souls, which they did not maintain in the sense that the soul of Euphorbus passed into the soul of a cock, for that would be to change one species into another, but they meant that the ὕλη, or matter, over which the soul of Euphorbus had once ruled, after its return to the earth and after losing its previous form, might furnish material for fashioning body and infusing life into a cock, in spite of the difference in form both as far as body and as far as spirit are concerned. And this is really metempsychosis, that is, an exchange of spirit, not a transformation, a succession, not a continuance. For while he who was Euphorbus had been endowed with a soul which understood, drew inferences, and remembered, and with a body that represented the human form, it came about that after this body had crumbled in the earth, a new form of body, namely that of a cock, came forth from it after many changes. Here you have palingenesis. And this form presently received the spirit which belongs to a cock, not the soul of Euphorbus with which he had fought so heroically at Troy. Here you have metempsychosis, that is, an exchange of spirits, and a succession, not a transmutation or transformation of one form of spirit into another form while still remaining the same spirit.

Finally [they deride unjustly] Gaius Pliny who said that that which we call God was the power of nature.† For being a most learned man he revolted at a multiplicity of gods and accordingly at the nomenclature involved. Hence he denied

*According to Diogenes Laertes, in his life of Pythagoras (ed. H. Stephanus, 1570, p. 310) Pythagoras claimed that he was first Aethalides, secondly Euphorbus, who was slain by Menelaus before Troy (Iliad, 17, 59), which Pythagoras proved by recognizing the shield of Euphorbus, hung up in the temple of Apollo; next Hermotimus; then Pyrrhus and lastly Pythagoras. Ovid in his Metamorphoses (XV, 160ff.) represents Pythagoras as making the same claim. The story of Euphorbus changing into a cock is found in Lucian's satire on transmigration, as given in his Gallus, §18f; see Works of Lucian, tr. by Thomas Franklin, London, 1781, Vol. III, 318ff.

†See Pliny's Natural History, Bk. II, ch. 5: "By these considerations the power of Nature is clearly proved, and is shown to be what we call God."

that there were gods, but he did not really deny, indeed he asserted, the existence of the Deity. For what he called nature we call the Deity. For where is that nature whose power he proclaims as so vast? Are we to suppose that, according to the habit of the atheistic philosophers, he was speaking of that nature which belongs to each thing individually? Who then could establish peace and harmony in the vast discord of things? Who prevent a chaotic confusion of all things? Especially when we see that not only men but the elements are so mutually antagonistic that, unless you harmonize them by means of some neutral mediator, you will never succeed in making fire and water, for instance, work together. If, then, any one believes that Pliny means by nature the natural characteristic of individual things, we shall find everything in chaos. For everything is so antagonistic to its opposite that without some outside force nothing can exist. For what Prometheus has brought fire to the cuttle fish in the depths of the sea and to the other fishes to warm their blood? It must have some kind of warmth, since it is red and flows.

Even the original elements, therefore, are by their nature ἀσπόνδια, that is, incapable of leaguing and uniting themselves together. Thus it is not this that Pliny means when he calls the power of nature what we call God. For thus no two things could unite together so that a third would result from their union, since the natures of things are so antagonistic that no one will receive a second unto it, unless compelled by some stronger outside force. He seems, therefore, to understand by nature that power which moves and unites or separates all things. And what is that but God? This most learned man saw that dull mortals are as far as possible from the truth, each one making a god of whatever he desired or hated. Hence he became disgusted with gods as a shameless and senseless invention. But he saw that there must be some power, by whose might and intelligence the universe was formed and maintained, and this power he preferred to call nature rather than the gods of whom he saw there could not be a plurality.

The earth, the stars, plants and animals, therefore, exist because they are from that and in that which always and alone exists, and this is such that if you should happen to fancy it non-existent (which is impossible), as soon as that Deity did not exist, nothing at all would exist. All substances, all bodies, stars, earth and seas, in short, the whole structure of the universe would collapse in an instant, and be reduced to nothing.

Now I will bring in the testimony in support of this view, as I promised, having first called attention in passing to the fact that from them is proved the immortality of the thinking soul. For since things never cease to be, after they have begun to be, how could it happen that that mind should perish which is so lively, unwearying and active a substance that, following its author, it has a right to the name ἐντελέχεια, complete reality.* For not even an ox or a pig perishes so completely as absolutely to cease to be. But I will come to the testimony.

When Moses asked the name of God, the answer came from heaven, "I AM THAT I AM," and God added, "Thus shalt thou say unto the children of Israel, 'I AM hath sent me unto you.'" These words are to be understood in the sense that the second "am" of the expression I AM THAT I AM shall have its force heightened κατ' ἔμφασιν, by special emphasis. If this is not done, you have the most lifeless and empty form of speech possible, as when you say, "A man is a man," "an animal is an animal," and the like. For what light do they convey to the human understanding? What do they tell? The second "am" then, has this emphasis "that really am," or, "that am the very being of all things," as the fathers divinely inspired, have explained it before me. And this very thing is also shown by the fact that presently He calls Himself "The I exist" as it were, as the one who not only Himself exists, but who bestows existence upon all things that exist. For if anything existed by its own powers, God would have said nothing more than if one declared himself to be the lieutenant of one who existed. He calls Himself "The I exist," then for this reason that He both exists of Himself, and furnishes unto others the foundation and basis of being and existence, so that nothing is or exists which does not have its being and existence of Him and in Him. I should certainly shrink from coining an unheard of word, unless I saw that he really says more who calls

*Rudolf Eucken, in his *Geschichte der philosophischen Terminologie*, p. 25, defines *entelecheia* as a condition of completion, a real existence and activity, as over against a mere capability and potentiality. The term itself is derived from Aristotle, see the latter's *Metaphysics*, Bk. X, chap. 9.

God, "Existonem," "The I exist," than "existentem, "the Existing," and unless this form approached more nearly the spirit of the Hebrew word אהיה , "I am." Since then "to be" and "to exist" are prior to "to live" or "to act," nay are the basis of these, it follows that all that lives and acts, has its life and activity from Him and in Him, from whom and in whom it has its being and existence. Of which more clearly later.

When the apostle Paul, in writing to the Romans, had fallen into this line of reasoning, he expressed his view in the words "For of him, and through him, and in him, are all things" [Rom. 11: 36]. I know that this last phrase "in him" is given in the Greek as εἰς αὐτὸν, that is "in ipsum, to him" rather than "in ipso, in him," but the divine heart of the apostle tried to proclaim thus vigorously by the more active form of speech the truth of the existence of all things in God, and not so much to say that all things were ordered unto God as in Him and with Him, that is, existed according to His power personally present and in His very might. Thus εἰς αὐτὸν, was used for ἐν αὐτῷ καὶ ἀντὶ ἐπ' αὐτῷ, that is "in ipsum" for "in ipso" and "apud ipsum." And this the old translator, who was by no means always asleep, saw, when he rendered the phrase by "in ipso, in him."* From God, therefore, as from a fountain source and (if one may speak so) substance matter, all things come forth into existence. Through God's power all things exist, live, and act, nay all things are in Him, who is everywhere present, and of Him, who is the being, existence, and life of all things.

Also when beginning to preach the gospel at Athens, he says of the Deity, "God that made the world and all things therein, seeing that he is Lord of heaven and earth, dwelleth not in temples made with hands; neither is worshipped with men's hands, as though he needed anything, seeing he giveth to all life, and breath and all things;

"And hath made of one blood all nations of men for to dwell on all the face of the earth, and hath determined the times before appointed, and the bounds of their habitation;

"That they should seek the Lord, if haply they might feel after him, and find him, though he be not far from every

*The Authorized Version has "to him."

one of us;

"For in him we have our being, and live, and move; as certain also of your own poets have said, For we are also his offspring.

"For as much then as we are the offspring of God, we ought not to think that the Godhead is like unto," etc. [Acts 17: 24-28].

By these words Paul fortifies and strengthens what was said above, so that it is superfluous to say more, except that I would not omit to state that in the sentence, "For in him we have our being, and live, and move," the order of the words in the Acts is not as I give it. It is a Hebrew hysteron proteron,* and the word for being, which naturally belongs first, is there put last.

Since Jerome and others (as I have shown in my *Isaiah*) often correct inconveniences of this kind by restoring the natural order, I have allowed myself to think it proper to do as the case demands. Nor does man alone have his being, and live, and move in God; all the things that are, have their being, and live and move in Him. Nor of man alone did Paul speak when he said: "In him we have our being, and live, and move;" he spoke by synecdoche of all created things. For since man alone among the creatures that have sensation is endowed with intellect and speech, he alone of all speaks as a sort of patron and champion.

But man is not alone the offspring of God; all creatures are so, though one differs from another in nobility and freedom. They are by birth of God and in God, and the nobler any one is, the more it proclaims the divine glory and power. Do not the creatures of the species of rodents proclaim the wisdom and providence of the Godhead? The hedgehog when with its spines he most cleverly carries a large quantity of fruit to its dwelling place, by rolling over the fruit and planting its spines in it. Alpine rats or marmots, which we now call the mountain rats, station one of their number upon an elevation, that, as they run about intent upon their work, no sudden danger may fall upon them without his timely cry of warning, while meantime the rest of the band carry off the softest hay from all around. And since they have no wagons, they turn themselves into wagons by turns, one lying upon his back and holding

*It inverts the natural order of words.

fast with all his feet the hay loaded upon his stomach and chest, while another seizes by the tail his comrade thus transformed into a wagon, and drags him with the plunder to their dwelling place to enable them to sleep through the inclemency of the harsh winter season. The squirrel, dragging a broad bit of wood to the shore by its mouth, uses it as a boat to cross the water, hoisting its bushy tail, and being thus driven by the favoring breeze,* needs no other sail.

What word, what speech, pray can proclaim the divine wisdom as well as these creatures which are among almost the humblest of living things? And do not things without sensation† bear witness that the might, goodness and lifegiving power of the Godhead are ever present with them? The earth that nourishes all things forgets the wounds inflicted by hoe and plow, and refuses not to furnish rich provision; the dew and rain so rouse and fill and replenish all the streams which by their increase stay the ravages of drought that, by the wondrous growth of all vegetation, they bear witness to the presence of the divine power and life. The mountains, dull, clumsy, lifeless mass that they are, hold fast and strengthen the earth as bones do the flesh; they bar the way to passage or make it difficult; though heavier than the surface of the earth, they rest upon it and sink not in; do they not proclaim the invincible power of the Godhead, and the solidity and vastness of His grandeur?

In all these things, then, not less than that of man, we discover the presence of the divine power by which they have their being, and live, and move. Christ Himself declares that the hairs of our head are numbered, nay that not even sparrows, two of which are sold for a farthing, fall to the ground without the knowledge of the Deity [Mt. 10: 29, 30]. By this we learn that even the things which we call fortuitous or accidental are not fortuitous or random happenings, but are all effected by the order and regulation of the Deity. His mind is not degraded by attention to lowly things, but His goodness and perfection are made plain by His scorning nothing that He has made, and by the absolute wisdom and power with which He works, seeing all things, watching over all things, loving all things, and that without toil and reasoning.

* οὖρος.
† ἀναίσθητα.

If I bring in testimony from outside the Scriptures, I shall not be utterly dismayed at carping criticism on the part of any one who has not yet learned that writings are properly called sacred when they proclaim the thought of the holy, pure, eternal and infallible mind. If, then, you find in Plato or Pythagoras what you scent as flowing from the fountain of the divine mind, this is not to be disregarded because a mortal embraced it in his records, but all the more must we press on to communion with the Deity, that we may see the light of truth more and more clearly, as we find that men who did not venture to profess the religion of the one God, yet had it in them. This is from the Deity wherever one is, even though one dwells among the beasts.

I am, therefore, especially glad to place here Seneca's words about Plato's views, because all that I have said and all that I am going to say in this book is derived from one source, namely from the nature and character of the Supreme Deity. This source Plato also tasted, and Seneca drank from it. These are his words on ideas in the sixty-sixth* letter to Lucilius: "God has within Himself these patterns of all things and comprehends in His mind the harmonies and measures of the totality of things that are to be carried out. He is filled with these forms which Plato calls "ideas"—imperishable, unchangeable, not subject to decay and therefore, though men die, humanity itself (or the idea of man) according to which man is moulded, lasts on, and though men toil and perish it suffers no changes.

Accordingly there are, as Plato says, five kinds of causes,† that of which, that by which, that in which, that according to which, and that on account of which, finally we have the result of all these. Thus, in the case of a statue (since we were speaking of this), that of which [it is made] is bronze, that by which is the sculptor, that in which is the form which is adapted to the material, the model is the pattern, imitated by the artist, that on account of which is the purpose of the maker, and finally,

---

*The 65th letter in the edition of Otto Hense, Leipzig, 1914, p. 205. See English translation in Loeb's Classical Library: Seneca, *Ad Lucilium Epistolae Morales*, Vol. I, p. 449.

†The four categories as established by Aristotle, plus the "idea" of Plato. The five causes are the material, the artist, the form, the model and the purpose.

the result of all these is the statue itself. The universe also as Plato says, possesses all these elements. The maker here is God, that from which is matter, the form is the shape and arrangement of the visible universe, the model that according to which God made this great and beautiful work, and the purpose that on account of which He made it. Do you ask what God's purpose is? It is goodness. So at all events Plato says. What was God's reason for making the universe? He is good, what He has made is good, and no good person is ever grudging of anything that is good."

And a little later, referring all things to one cause, he says: "But we are now searching for the original and general cause. This must be simple, inasmuch as matter is simple. We ask, what is the cause? It is surely creative reason, that is, God. For indeed, those to which you referred are not several independent causes; they all hinge on one alone and that will be the creative cause. Do you maintain that form is a cause? This is only what the artist stamps upon his work; it is part of a cause, but not the cause. Neither is model a cause, but a necessary tool of the cause. A model is as necessary to the artist as the chisel and the file; without these art can make no progress. But for all that, these things are neither parts of art nor the cause of it. "Then," perhaps you will say, "the purpose of the artist, that on account of which he undertakes to create something, is the cause. True it is a cause, but not the efficient cause. It is an accessory cause. Of such there are a vast number, but we are discussing the general cause. In making that other statement, that the whole universe, the completed work is a cause, they [Plato and Aristotle] did not display their usual penetration. For there is a great difference between a work and the cause of a work."

And somewhat further on he justifies and recommends in the following fashion the consideration both of the original and only real cause and of the condition and order of the universe. "Do you forbid me to contemplate the universe? Do you compel me to withdraw from the whole, and restrict me to a part? May I not ask what are the beginnings of things, who fashioned things, who separated the general mass wrapped up in dull matter? May I not inquire who is the Master-Builder of this universe, how its vast bulk was brought under law and order, who gathered together the scattered atoms, who separated the disordered elements and assigned an outward form to elements that lay in one vast shapelessness. Or, whence all this light was shed? And whether it be fire or something brighter than fire? Am I not to ask these questions? Must I not know the heights whence I descended? Whether I am to see this world but once or to be born many times? Whither I am to go hence? What abode awaits my soul, when freed from the laws of human slavery?

"Do you forbid me to have a share in the heaven, that is, do you bid me live with my head bent down? I am greater [above such existence] and born for greater destiny than to be the bondman of my body, and I look upon this body as a chain which shackles my freedom. Therefore, I present it as a shield against the blows of fortune, and shall suffer no wound to penetrate to my soul. For my body is the only part that can suffer injury in me. In this vulnerable dwelling, exposed to peril, my soul lives free. Never shall this flesh drive me into fear nor into any pretence unworthy of a good man. Never shall I lie in order to honor this poor body. When it seems proper I shall sever my connection with it. At present, while we are bound together, our alliance shall not be one of equality. The soul shall bring all quarrels before its own tribunal. Contempt of the body is sure freedom.

"To return to our subject; this freedom will be greatly helped by the contemplation of which we were just speaking. Verily all things are of matter and of God. God controls matter, which encompasses Him, and follows Him as its guide and leader. That which creates, in other words, God, is more powerful and precious than matter which is acted upon by God. The soul occupies in man the place that God occupies in this universe. What matter is there, the body is in us. Let, therefore, the inferior serve the higher," etc.

Thus speaks Seneca, that unparalleled cultivator of the soul among the Gentiles, not only eloquently but religiously, in regard to the condition and government of the universe. And here we must note that he does not assign matter to God like clay to a sculptor, as if matter existed or had its being through itself, and God then applied a moulding hand to it as a thing already existing. For this divine soul [Seneca] had no difficulty in mounting to the height of understanding that the matter of the universe, that is, the visible world (for even the sacred writers often use the term "visible" instead of "sensible" or "natural") must have been made in order to be matter.

He does not, therefore, deny that matter was created out of nothing, matter which the mouth of God calls תהו [tohû] and בהו [bohû], and the poets of the heathen* call chaos, before form was given to things made of.it, but that after the world began to be, and the matter of the universe was first made and became visible, the hand of God was laid upon His creation in activity and skill, and thence forward is constantly laid upon it, creating all things and governing them when created. Thus he declares that the Deity manipulates, performs, sets in motion, keeps in operation all that takes place with the matter of the universe rather than makes matter, as a thing originating of itself, equally with God the cause of the Universe.

And, secondly, we must also note that man also was created from matter and is a type of the whole universe, so that as that is ruled and regulated by God, so is he by the soul, not by a soul that is different from God or exists of itself, but one which is subject to and dependent upon God, is inspired, fostered, ruled, and fed by God, consisting of the Spirit of God. Of this later.

Supported, then, by divine oracles on all sides (for whatever is true, holy, and infallible is divine. God alone is true. Hence he who speaks the truth, speaks from God, and he who in this way climbs with his understanding from the things visible to the contemplation of the unseen God, does a thing, according to the testimony of Paul [Acts 17: 24ff.], worthy of God and himself, useful and not without divine illumination. I venture, therefore, to call a thing borrowed from the heathen divine, if only it is holy, religious, and irrefutable. For it must come from God, whatever the quarter from which it comes directly to us) —supported thus, I say, by divine oracles, we must admit that there is only one true cause of all things. Other things are not truly causes any more than the representative of a potentate is truly the potentate, or than the chisel or hammer of the artificer is the cause of a drinking cup, the beast of burden of husbandry. Who would attribute to the representative the name of his prince, to the chisel the making of the cup, to the ox the plowing

*See e. g., Ovid in his *Metamorphoses*, Bk. I, 3.

of the field? Although we are in the habit of saying, "The king's legate demanded satisfaction," yet the action is not the legate's but the king's. And though the silversmith himself sometimes attributes the work of a platter to the hammer, saying, "This platter is the work of this hammer," yet the hammer is not truly and properly the cause, but the silversmith. So the farmer calls his ox the tiller of many acres, when he says, "That ox plowed this great field, however much the plowing was done by the plow." Yet the farmer himself is the author of the whole business of husbandry, for he reared the ox for it, trained him and guided him, and bought the plow to which equally with the ox is attributed what does not rightly belong to it. The plow breaks up the earth, we say. If it did, husbandry would go back to the blacksmith, nay to the anvil itself as its source.

It is established, therefore, that secondary causes are not properly called causes, though I have always determined not to fight obstinately about words, provided agreement as to the truth of the matter is attained. For we often use words in a somewhat varied sense on different occasions and from different considerations. Thus we even speak of a man who has conferred some great benefit as a god, not because we wish to designate him by the name of God, but though God is the only effective force, and He alone can do and does do all things, yet when we have received a blessing from a man, we speak of him by hyperbole* as a god, either from a feeling that God has blessed us through him or because he has benefited us as God is wont to do.

Whatever means and instruments, therefore, are called causes, are not properly so called, but by metonymy, that is, derivatively from that one first cause of all that is. It is the same thing as when what is attributed to an angel does not belong to the angel, but to God who sent the angel. Hence the constant assertion in Exodus that Moses saw God in person and face to face, while in the same place the sight of God is declared impossible to mortal eye.† What then? Did he see God or did he not? As far as form goes, he saw the angel, not God, except so far as He is in the angel and in every created thing.

* καθ' ὑπερβολήν.
†Compare Ex. 33: 11 with 33: 20.

But as far as authority and real cause are concerned, he saw God. Hence Paul says [Gal. 3: 19] that the law was given into the hand of the mediator Moses by the angels, that is, the angels were the deputies and officers in charge, while in Exodus the law is said to have been given to Moses by God in person talking in a friendly way with Moses after human fashion. It is for the same reason that we assign to the sun and the stars things that belong to God alone. For He is in the stars themselves, nay, the stars, being of Him and in Him, have not their own essence, power, and activity, but God's.

They are, therefore, instruments by which the power of the Godhead shows its active presence. For it was for this that He created things, that He might use them for the mutual benefit of each other, so that that wonderful example of the divine wisdom, man, might everywhere contemplate the Deity, and in all things and in himself still more closely perceive God existing, living and working, as he gazed upon His power and activity and nature in all the things that are or take place.

Thence it comes that to man is ascribed what belongs only to God alone. Thus remission of sins is credited to the apostles, though God alone remits sins, and the apostles themselves preach that pardon for sins is given only through Christ. For the Godhead was present in them, and illumined their minds so that they could clearly see the truth. He gave courage to their hearts, so that they boldly proclaimed the truth they had seen, and so kindled the souls of the hearers that they absorbed straightway by the Spirit and fed upon the teaching of the Spirit.

Do we not see here that the apostle and the word which he uses for the setting forth of the truth are instruments, not causes, and that the one cause, by which even the apostle exists and preaches, is the Deity? And to put it briefly, the ground does not bring forth, nor the water nourish, nor the air fructify, nor the fire warm,* nor the sun itself, but rather that power which is the origin of all things, their life and strength, uses the earth as the instrument wherewith to produce and create. And since created things are preserved by food, that power feeds and gives them to drink by water, quickens, fills and increases them by air, purifies, beautifies, refines and perfects them by fire

* οὐ θάλπει τὸ πῦρ.

and sun. For unless that power had appointed these instruments for this purpose, that is, had made and fashioned them in order to use them for this work, what would they be but useless and the refuse of other things?

Furthermore, since they are lifeless by nature, and yet through them and from them the divine bounty supplies nourishment unto all living things, it is clear that they are more properly called instruments than causes. For there can be but one cause. For, as the origin of all things is one, so must the cause be one. And because things minister unto each other, and all unto man, although the power of God could by its very life and presence, without the aid of the aforesaid means, support and nourish man and all his dominion (for he was set over all the things that are on the earth or in the sea or the air, to govern them), as indeed it did support Moses forty days without food,* it is clear that all these things by which we are nourished and supported are instruments of the divine working, not causes. For even some philosophers have been reluctant to admit matter into the realm of causes, as a thing that does nothing active, but suffers itself to be manipulated, and receives upon itself the blows of the worker. And we, knowing that matter and all power flow from one source, see that it is an unassailable fact that all working, fashioning, and preserving are from that source, and that the things which are nearer and accordingly better known to us, cannot really be causes, though we call them so, but are instruments of the one actual cause.

Thus when we look upon the fostering earth pouring forth her grain, the tree its fruit, the sun its light and warmth, we see the hand of God at work just as when a kind father puts a cherry into his little boy's palm. It is the kindly power of the Deity that giveth all things; the earth, the tree, the sun, and the rest are the stalk and branches which hold that bounty and supply it to us.

But it is now time to summarize and then continue. In this entire chapter I have been aiming to prove that since all things have their being, existence, life, movement and activity from One and in One, that One is the only real cause of all things, and those nearer things which we call causes, are not properly causes, but the agents and instruments with which the

* ἄσιτον.

eternal mind works, and in which it manifests itself to be enjoyed.

From this conclusion we learn in brief that nothing happens by chance or at random, however much philosophers and theologians dispute that point, for that chief Intelligence has numbered the hairs of our heads. Nay, even though we pass by the authority of Scripture, it yet must be that that Intelligence which is the beginning and the origin of all light and all knowledge and is Itself wisdom and light, knows all things. For, otherwise, however insignificant the thing which It did not know, It would not be chief and supreme, since It would not know all things.

And we also learn that that Intelligence must regulate, care for, and manage all things. For if It did not care for what It saw, this would happen either from jealousy or from lack of power. But, since It is good and almighty, It cannot help caring for, regulating, and ordering all things. Nothing, therefore, can happen by chance. This conclusion is so certain and secure that whoever denies Providence in all things, by the same statement denies the existence of God. For if there is a God (as there is; I am only arguing against atheists, that is, those who do not believe in a God), it is He who sees all things, cares for and regulates all things, puts and keeps all things in operation.

On the other hand, if anything takes place by chance and at random, if anything exists of its own right and independently of the direction of the Deity, then everything is at random and drifts along by chance, and accordingly all the wisdom, thought and reason of all intelligent beings is empty and vain. For if anything exists, lives, and moves beyond the jurisdiction of the Deity, man can with equal right be said to be beyond God's jurisdiction. Therefore, intelligence, reason, thought will count for nothing. All things will be at their own sweet will, so that everything will obey chance and fortune, and nothing intelligence, reason and thought. Thus there will simply be no Deity. And how godless and wicked it is even to imagine this, is sufficiently shown by the contemplation of the universe, where whatever you gaze upon is so incomplete and small and feeble that it cannot come from itself. Thus, since the universe must come from something else, we are brought, whether we will or no, to the one and only source of all things, from which everything runs forth as if from the starting place of a race course. But now I come to man.

FOURTH CHAPTER

Regarding man and why the law was given to him when all things are directed by Divine Providence.

Abdallah, the Mohammedan,* said that man is the most wonderful of all the things seen upon the stage of the world. If any one should ask me, I should answer that he is the most peculiar and most wonderful of creatures, and more wonderful than the beauty of the angels. Just as if you compare a cock and a steer, though you will find the steer more imposing, yet you will never be tired of wondering at the royal adornment of the cock, his splendid courage, his proud gait, his indefatigable watchfulness, his eminent characteristics of leader and commander, ruling as he does over a vast brood of hens. So the angel is of noble substance, to wit, a pure spirit, but if you consider man beside him how will you not be struck at this being both heavenly and earthly? In all the hosts of spirits you will not find one clothed with an earthly and visible body, (unless it happens to be put on for a little while and laid aside), and in all the vast multitude of animals of all sorts you will find none in which an intelligent mind acts as ruler and director.

Thus we easily infer that God, the creator of the universe, made man not only that there might be an image and copy of Himself, but that from among the creatures made from the earth there might be one to enjoy God through fellowship and friend-

*This quotation is taken most likely from the opening sentence of Giovanni Pico della Mirandola's remarkable oration on the dignity of man, with which he planned to open the great disputation at Rome, to which he had challenged all scholars: "Legi, patres colendissimi, in Arabum monumentis interrogatum Abdalam Sarracenum; quod in hac quasi mundana scaena admirandum maxime spectaretur, nihil spectari homine admirabilius respondisse;" i. e., "I have read, Most Reverend Fathers, in the monuments of the Arabs, that Abdalla, the Sarracen, having been asked what could be seen on this earthly stage that was most to be wondered at, answered that nothing could be seen more wonderful than man." Prof. George L. Burr, of Cornell University located this quotation. For the passage quoted see *Pici Mirandulae opera novissime revisa*, Argentorati, 1504, fol. 84b; also in *Opera omnia Pici Mirandulae Concordiaeque comitis*, Basileae [1572], p. 313.

ship here, through possession and most intimate contact in the hereafter. Also that He might foreshadow in a sense that intercourse with the world into which He was going to enter through His Son. For how could we have been more clearly brought to the understanding of the incarnation of the Son of God than through seeing from the beginning an intelligent spirit planted in a dull body? And His wisdom was to shine forth in this creation like that of the artificer (I cannot recall his name)* in the shield of Achilles. He made the strength of that wonderful work so depend upon a little bolt, displaying his own image, that he who loosened that scattered the whole shield apart. So he who should take man out of the world, would bereave, debase and defile all the visible universe. For take man away; will there be any one of all the creatures of sense to enjoy God, to know Him, to have intercourse with Him?

Man is, therefore, to the world what God is to man. God is the lord and director of the human mind; man is the lord of the world. All that we see was made for him and his good. Take him away from them, and have you not left all things bereft like the widow and orphan? Whom will the sun warm, for whom the fructifying zephyrs and breezes blow? For the brutes? Whose advantage will the brutes serve? For whom has the earth spread out its broad expanse? There will be no one who understands how he ought to make use of things.

It was necessary, then, that this lord and master of such a vast realm should have in him something from that realm over which he was to be set, and it was also necessary that he should be endowed with some surpassing endowment, by which he could conquer and break the rebellious spirit of things. He was, therefore, given a body as he was marked out to be the chief of all bodily beings, and he was also given a soul, as he alone of all bodily creatures was to have kinship and fellowship with God and all other spiritual beings—a body and a soul, two most widely different things. For what differs more widely from the clearness and light of the mind and intelligence than the dull inactivity of the earth and the body? But when the great Master Workman was going to insert a soul into this clay, see how He softened and shaped it in order not to dishonor a worthy guest through an unworthy dwelling. The lion had come forth

*He had Hephaistos in mind, see *Iliad*, XVIII, 478-608.

with hairy breast and terrible teeth and claws, the bear had crept forth shaggy in all his body and powerful of paw, the stag had leaped forth with branching horns, with shaggy hair, and having his foot fortified with an invincible hoof, and all the rest had their own peculiar armaments of spikes, spears and shields. But how remote from all roughness, O Lord, does the human body appear!

Some regard this as a misfortune; I think it a mark and omen of happiness. For since he was born to enjoy God and all created things, it was fitting that he should be adapted to gentleness, peace and friendship. Hence this coarse earth of which man is made had to be softened rather carefully in order not to produce sharp claws and fierce teeth, and scales or iron-like hide to lead to stubbornness and force. Therefore this abode of the celestial soul was made pliant and smooth and clean on all sides. Other creatures drop down on four feet, this body of ours stands upon two, that man's gaze might be fastened more directly upon that heaven of which he aims to become heir. But why go on? The beauty and loveliness of the human body is indescribable if you compare it with other living beings.

Nevertheless, though the human body has been created in such form and a heavenly mind has been entrusted to it, yet each part preserves its own nature and character. The mind loves the truth and, therefore, worships the Deity, from whose substance it derives its kinship. It aims for justice and integrity. The body inclines to its native clay, and follows the nature of the flesh. Thus if you wish to compare man with something, he would seem like nothing so much as a lump of muddy earth plunged into a very clear, pure brook. The stream which had flowed with limpid waters now becomes clouded and we cannot even hope for the former clearness as long as the lump of earth stays immersed in it.

So it is with man. His mind is a clear, limpid stream, flowing forth from the Godhead itself. Hence it is so eager for truth and right and so devoted to them that if you could consider it apart from the dull mass of the body, as the angels are, you would detect nothing base, disturbing, or defiling in it. The body is clay, taken from the earth, and when you attach this to the soul it is like letting a wild boar into a liquid spring. Thus what the soul by itself would see clearly and would follow readily and without hesitation, it now sees dimly, on account of the grossness of the clay being like a mist upon it, and is held bound by the weight of that clay as by fetters, so that it can no more pursue the perfect course than Tantalus could seize his fruit. Hence that sort of internal war in which the mind and the body are engaged against each other. When the mind begins to contemplate God, to talk and commune with Him about the things it has in common with Him, suddenly the flesh, fashioned from clay, draws it back. "Fool," it cries, "Where are you going? There is no Deity; much less one that cares for our affairs." Thus each part of man constantly looks back upon its origin. The mind yearns for light, purity and goodness, inasmuch as its nature is light, its substance pure and devoted to the right, seeing that it derives its origin from the Godhead; the body inclines to idleness, laziness, darkness and dullness, as it is lazy and indolent by nature, and without reason and intelligence, seeing that it consists of earth.

Hence it is that neither part ever carries off so fortunate a victory that the conquered part does not constantly rebel. For if the spirit gains the upper hand, does not the flesh rebel, however sternly it sees its king and commander hold destruction over its head? For who distributes his goods among the poor for God's sake, without the flesh sometimes repeating: "So you will come out distinguished, so you will make for yourself a name, so you will be able to aim at the presidency or some other office?" And though it is fair to suppose from the skill and watchfulness of some people that they forthwith overcome and throw down the enemy stealing in by this sort of scaling ladder, yet the flesh does not lay down its boldness, but struggles none the less obstinately and mixes some disturbing element in with good beginnings, so that its persistency is like a woman's obstinacy. But however much the flesh refuses to listen to any counsel but what the belly dictates, whenever it succeeds in getting the ascendency over the spirit, yet the nobler and kindlier spirit never ceases to warn, advise or dissuade as occasion offers. For it is certain that that phenomenal drunkard Torquatus did not so drown himself in drink, nor Heliogabalus bury himself in ostrich's brains, nor Nero so shamelessly indulge himself with harlots, matrons, and lewd men, nor Dionysius or Phalaris so savagely drink human blood, nor dread Hannibal so ruthlessly lay waste cities and fields and districts, provinces and kingdoms, without each one of them and their likes, worn out at last with indulgence, saying to himself, "But who art thou? What now? Where wilt thou stop? Are not these men? Why art thou now sad? How bloodless and feeble thou art! What will happen if each man goes on doing to others according to his own caprice?"

The soul is never so kept under that it forgets itself forever, it is never so down-trodden by the arrogant tyranny of the flesh as not to give warning however late. On the contrary the spirit is like a gentle father following his children with the utmost faithfulness and indulgence. Hence also, to come back to the subject, the flesh not only growls at the spirit, but in a spirit of pretence and mockery copies its works. By uprightness and purity of life, the soul admonishes us, the favor of the Deity is to be won; by white raiment, says the flesh. The spirit gives up its dwelling place, the blood namely, for the sake of its lord, the flesh declares that the purple mantle in which it wraps itself is sufficient. The mind sighs for God and expects all things from His bounty, not from its own deserts; the flesh, even though it thunders and roars, announces that all things are due to itself. Hence, to reach the conclusion more quickly, there arises so much superstition, hypocrisy, and deceit. For the flesh imitates the spirit like an ape.

Here arise for us two very great questions. First, why, then, did God create man so unhappy a being, who is never at peace with himself? Second, why is the spirit given over to everlasting torment when it is overcome and kept under by the flesh, though the flesh is just as much a part of man as the spirit, and he received both from God the Creator Himself?

To the first question Paul would answer, may not the potter make different kinds of vessels from the same lump [Rom. 9: 21]? Has God not the right to join spirit and clay? Man can mould clay into varied forms, but he cannot give them breath and make them live. Unless God could make a living being from the dull, senseless matter, He would be no way superior to any artisan. But as it is, when He makes earth not only living but also intelligent and attentive to the divine (let both body and soul ever keep their peculiar characteristics, provided the nature of each is treated separately), He shows how

He is above the skill and wisdom of all. Oh, the depth of the wisdom and bounty of God! Oh, on the other hand, how ignorant and inexperienced in things we poor mortals are, who, asking why God created man in his present condition, have not yet learned that this question is suggested by the flesh, which does not only demand an account of the spirit, which is bound by a certain weight and check, but ventures to demand even of God the reason of His actions! Why madest Thou me so? Yet no mortal knows the sources of any art or science so well as not to be ignorant of some things that belong to it, and nothing that we see is so gross and coarse and big that we can give a reason for its formation in detail.

The elephant is an immense creature. Though you see its trunk and tusks and consider their use, yet you do not know why God fashioned them thus for those uses. The wild boar has tusks projecting on both sides and a snout, and uses these. God might, then, have made an elephant like a boar, you say. He might, I answer, but the boar was not destined to be an elephant. And He was pleased to show variety in making many creatures, that man also might be pleased. The boar plunges either tusk without distinction into any kind of food; the elephant uses only one of his tusks to dig up the roots which he feeds upon, and keeps the point of the other intact for battle. Why did the Deity bestow this care upon him? What is the object, when not only men kill each other with steel, but even elephants go about with their sharp pointed instrument with which to extinguish the life both of each other and of men? Here surely we must call a halt. It so pleased Him to whom whatever pleases Him is lawful and whom nothing pleases which is not good and holy and just. Man, therefore, was made after the fashion that pleased God, and that will please all who are endowed with power of reason and intelligence. All things have their own order and class. Here the spotted leopard, there the savage tiger, here the helpful ox, there the intelligent horse. Here the rapacious eagle threatens, there the crafty vulture hangs over its prey. Here the merry nightingale, there the tuneful blackbird sings. Here the one-eyed tunny-fish swims, there the happy dolphin leaps. Here the idle mussel opens its mouth, there the band of polypi lay their fangs and cleverly tear off the mussel's flesh. But who could enumerate all the species of creatures, when there come forth daily new ones not seen before or at least forgotten, so that man has not had time from the creation of the world to acquire a knowledge of all of them? Man, therefore, stands first in the company and circle of all creation, having in common with the immortal existences reason and a soul, in common with mortals, earthly life and a body. The Deity willed to make him so, and for Him to have so willed it is enough. So much for the first question.

To the second, why, when sin is due to the allurements or the impetuous nature of the flesh, is the soul damned? I answer briefly, because the law is sinned against. For the law is enacted that transgression be not committed, and where there is no law, there is no transgression. They cannot offend against the law, to whom no law is given. This is shown by experience. Dogs tear each other to pieces, but they are not brought to trial for assault. Wolves plunder, but no one demands restitution of them. Storks and eagles cast off the inefficient among their young, but no one charges them with cruelty of treatment. The stallion openly covers all the mares of a neighborhood, but no one brings him up for adultery. And all this is simply because they have no law. But since a law has been given unto man, and he offends against the law, he is properly punished as the law orders. Man, therefore, is damned, because he has resisted the law and rashly stirred up rebellion against it.

But now a more serious question arises, namely, why then did God give man a law against which he can offend? Why did He not rather suffer him to live without the law, like the other living creatures, especially when all things are ordered by Divine Providence and accomplished by the power of the same? Before I answer this question, I want to consider what a law is. Some define it sometimes, starting from its form, as when Paul says, "The law is spiritual" [Rom. 7: 14], sometimes from its purpose, as when Paul says, "By the law comes knowledge of sin" [Rom. 3: 20], that is, the law is the indicator of sin, and when Chrysippus* in "De legibus et senatus consultis et longa

*Zwingli's quotation is from the *Corpus Juris Civilis*, the Code of Justinian, see Digest, lib. I, cap. 3, entitled: "De legibus senatusque consultis et longa consuetudine." It reads as follows: "Marcianus, in his first book of the Institutions, also Demosthenes, and also the philosopher of the highest Stoic wisdom, Chrysippus, thus began his book, which he wrote

consuetudine," *i. e.,* "On the Laws and the Decrees of the Senate
and Ancient Custom," defines law thus, "Law is the knowledge
of things divine and human," *i. e.,* "Law leads us to learn things
divine and human," yet no one has defined it from the point of
view of its material substance—what the law really and in
essence is.

This fountainhead of law (with your permission) I will
open up, and define the divine law thus:—The law is the divine
order, expressing His nature and will. If one wishes to put it
more concisely he may say, the law is the constant will of God,
though I want to set forth the former that the latter also may be
made plain. Thus I touch first upon the source, in referring
the law to the Deity, and secondly upon its nature, in calling it
an order. I wish order, however, to be taken in a wide sense,
so that it shall include what is forbidden as well as what is prescribed. Finally we see what the law is in essence, namely the
will and nature of the Deity, so that when we hear the law, we
know what God wills and that He is Himself of the nature of
that which he shows us. And this is so true that even in those
crudest laws, Thou shalt not kill, Thou shalt not steal, Thou
shalt not commit adultery, we learn that God's nature is such
that He hates violence, injustice and wrong. For unless His
nature were such, He would expose Himself to the charge of
duplicity in ordering one thing and wishing another. Therefore it is evident that since the law is the order of God, it is the
expression of His will, and since it is His will, He also gives His
approval to that which He enjoins upon us, and this is what the
second definition has in view. Hence it is clear that at our time
some persons of the first importance*, as they think, have spoken
without sufficient circumspection about the law in saying that
the law is only to terrify, damn, and deliver over to torments.
In reality, the law does not do that at all, but, on the contrary,
sets forth the will and nature of the Deity. And what can be

'Regarding the Law': 'The law is the king of all things divine and human.
He must of necessity be the patron of the good and bad, as well as their
ruler and leader.' " In Mommsen's edition of the *Corpus*, Digest, p. 5. It
is possible that Zwingli had another reading in his edition of the *Corpus*,
in place of the word "king," on which his word "notitia," or "knowledge,"
is based. The editor owes the identification of this quotation to the kindness of Prof. George L. Burr, of Cornell University.

*He means Luther.

compared with that? If a king or emperor entrusts his views, plans, and nature to a councillor or commander, how that official leaps and exults for joy! When God by the promulgation of the law discloses His will and nature to us, do we venture to make light of it?

Paul used such commonplace sayings more clearly and more discreetly. In Romans he carefully avoids using such strong commonplace sayings as "the law damns," "the law sentences to hell." In general his effort is to preach the sanctity of the law, calling it now "spiritual" and again "good," as when he says, "Was then that which is good made death unto me?" "God forbid," he says. "But sin, that it might appear sin," that is, that it might be recognized as sin, "worketh death in me by that which is good" (that is, by the law which he calls that which is good here), "that (thus) sin" (which of course was not yet recognized since the law was not known), "by commandment might become exceeding sinful," (that is, that the magnitude and monstrousness of sin might be made plain) [Rom. 7 : 12]. See how well he guards against making the law detested, as he would do if he assigned damnation and death to it. I do not mean by this that I consider it irreverent to use commonplace sayings of that kind on occasion. But since there are some persons who claim for themselves alone the right to explain divine Scripture, although one sees them both in the passage quoted and in many other passages stumble like children from sheer ignorance of rhetoric, which nevertheless they avowedly arrogate to themselves, I would like to direct their attention to modesty and to themselves—to modesty, that they may cease to seem to despise the law, which is the everlasting will of God, to themselves, that they may learn that they are men, whose characteristic it is to err, be ignorant, stumble, be deceived and deluded. For these things happen to them as well as to others.

There are, moreover, in the argument of Paul above mentioned most charming figures of speech and personifications, as when sin is made a geometer and measurer, the law a plumb-line, or again when sin is made exceeding sinful or a sinner, like a thief caught in the very act, or as when we are said to be delivered from the law, when the law can no more be abolished or cease to be (I am speaking of the spiritual law, not the law of ceremonials) than can God Himself,—when we are delivered not from the law but from damnation, which is rightly due to us for our contempt of the law. And when he presently calls the law "spiritual," he shows clearly that the law cannot in any way be abolished. These figures, being either not recognized or neglected, force those great men either to leap over things that they have undertaken to expound, or to babble out something obscure, ambiguous, and high sounding, to hide their ignorance, so that you may not understand that they do not themselves understand what they are talking about. Forms of expression like, "the law damns," "the law convicts of sin," are true only in the same way that one may say it is true, if any one should bring a light into an assembly of deformed people and they should cry, "Do not bring a lamp. It will make us all deformed." A light certainly cannot make them deformed, but it makes their deformity visible. So the law does not damn, but human vileness is brought forth by the agency of the law. The law, therefore, is light. If it is light, it is the mind, intelligence, and will of God. Thus, then, to come back to my purpose, I think I have sufficiently expounded and supported my definition of the law.

Now I will add a few illustrations and exceptions as an exposition of the above statement. "Thou shalt love the Lord thy God with all thy heart, and with all thy soul, and with all thy mind, and with all thy strength" [Deut. 6:15]. These words directed to man are a law by which he first learns that our God and Lord is to be loved above all things, and that because of His natural goodness peculiar to Him. What knowledge can be nobler or more useful to the mind of man than this? What more welcome message than that God announces Himself as that which is to be cherished and loved above all things? When, therefore, He presents Himself to be loved, it is certain that He Himself also loves. For unless He loved us, why, pray, should He disclose Himself to us?

We learn, therefore, from this law in the second place, not only that it is God whom we ought to love above all things, but also that He by His nature loves not only man but all His creatures. For unless He loved them, He would not create them, sustain them, live and work in them. Only there is this distinction that what God loves He loves as a father. For He has no one above Him to look up to with wonder and reverence. But we love Him as our Creator and Father. Hence it follows—and that belongs to the exception—that what is law to us is not law to God. For who should make a law for Him who is the Highest, or who should enlighten Him who is the Light? What is law to us is, therefore, nature and character to Him. When He commands, "Thou shalt love me only," we learn first that He loves not in consequence of the law, which none can impose upon Him, but by His nature and character. Secondly we learn that we also ought duly to love Him. Thus He is above the law, we are under the law; He *is* the love which is commanded of us.

Now I will add another illustration by which the above will be more clearly explained, and this exception that God is not under the law will become more evident. When it is commanded, "Thou shalt not kill" (the killing of men, not of beasts, is forbidden thereby), we learn first that God loves justice and abhors violence, we learn secondly that it is right for us to refrain from violence, following His example. Then, when He slays according to His will, He is no murderer, because He is not under the law, and not being under the law He does not sin. "But what is law to us," some one says, "you said was nature to Him. If, therefore, by nature He killeth not, He is on the same footing as they who kill not because of the prohibition of the law. If He does kill, though He does not offend against the law, He yet seems to act inconsistently with His nature. For if what is law to us is nature to Him, you will have to admit either that He contradicts Himself when He kills or that murder is not contrary to His will, or if He is not inconsistent with Himself nor in contravention of the law and yet kills, then killing does not infringe upon the law."

This objection I easily overcome by saying that God is not a murderer, because when a judge has heard a case and passed sentence he is not a murderer. He only is a murderer who kills a man under the influence of some wrong personal emotion, as anger, hate and greed. If a judge yields to influences of this sort, he also is a murderer however imposingly he sits upon his seat. On the other hand, when such motives are absent, even a private person is absolved from the charge of murder, as when one restrains force by force or slays a wicked and godless foe in open war. And since God cannot be exposed to influences of that kind, He cannot commit murder. The law and the divine nature are again reconcilable in this way. To kill in accordance

with law is not forbidden to man. Therefore to kill is not contrary to the nature of God. For if the law may kill, the Deity
also may kill. When a judge, the guardian of justice and right,
sentences one to death with judicial impartiality, he is free
from any stain of guilt, and can God, who is the essence of
justice and whose are all things in the universe, commit murder
when He slays a man? He can do naught but what is just and
holy. It is true, then, that the law, when we look at it closely,
is in essence God's character, will, and nature.

Therefore, whenever the law of God is proclaimed it has a
wonderfully quickening effect upon whatever possesses the
knowledge of God. Hence it follows that those creatures who
have not the knowledge of God derive no satisfaction or advantage from the hearing of the law. When, therefore, God communicates His will to man by the law, by this communication
He assures us of two things, one, that we are born to attain to a
knowledge of God, the other, that we are destined to enjoy Him.
These things are manifest, because if we were not born to attain
to a knowledge of God, He would not present and manifest
Himself to us, and when He discloses Himself to us, He gives
proof enough that we ought to lay hold on Him. This part of
the matter is readily comprehended by anybody.

The other, though thus far not expounded, is yet easily
deduced from the first, namely :—If man had not been created
to enjoy God, it would be superfluous to have a knowledge of
Him. For the same end would await man and beast. Man would
get nothing from the knowledge of God more than the mere fact
of having lived, if after this life he did not live and enjoy God,
and that is the lot even of the brute. But since God manifests
Himself unto us, and presents Himself for a more intimate
comprehension, this is done not vainly, but to the end that we
shall possess Him, and fully comprehend Him with whom we
have begun fellowship here. And if a good part of mankind
are bound over to everlasting imprisonment and chains, and
though they deserve that for their rebelliousness, yet they were
born by Divine Providence to the end that, being made examples
of, they might proclaim His justice. For even the Evil Spirit,
damned because of his pride, does he not commend to us the
justice of God, as soon as we consider him? Equally so, therefore, do the rest who are damned by the same judgment.

That man was born, then, to know and enjoy God follows of necessity, from the fact that God by the law communicates His will and character to man. No other living creature has such knowledge and understanding of Him, and yet they all exist and live and manifest their activity in Him. And since, as I hinted a little while ago, that which has no knowledge of God, revolts from His law and will, and the flesh is the property of those that have not the knowledge of God, it follows that the spirit is receptive for holy things, but the flesh resists, as I have said. For the maker reserved intact unto each part its own character, that man might be a wonderful work. For if the flesh laid aside its dullness and rebelliousness at the coming of the spirit, or if the spirit upon union with the flesh sank to its level, man would be either an angel or a brute. In order that man remain a special kind of creature, each part of him must retain its special characteristics. Hence, while we are willing to embrace the law according to the desire of the mind, another law which has been written upon our members, that is, the flesh, resists, so that through the wickedness of the flesh we perform not what in the integrity of the spirit we really desire. And since the strength of each is not its own but God's in it, who is the being, existence and power of all things, it comes to pass that of His will and knowledge the flesh growls at the spirit, just as the spirit desires to obey His commands. Thus the law seems to be given in vain, since the ever rebellious flesh rejects it and can never be so tamed and subdued as not to revolt again, and the spirit seems wrongfully damned for the wantonness of the flesh, since whatever the flesh does, it does of and through God.

After having thus set forth many statements I would make answer to this objection, which is the real gist of this chapter, or, rather, I would sum up the answer already given more at length, and say, "So difficult a problem must be approached with a reverent and religious spirit." Even Paul, the chosen instrument of God, coming to consider the problem closely, exclaimed in view of its vastness, "Oh the depth of the riches both of the wisdom and knowledge of God!" [Rom. 11: 33]. How much more is it to be treated with fear and trembling by the average preacher, such as I do not yet call myself! But having learned that to the believer nothing is impossible and that the truth maketh the believer free, I am set free by the truth from fear though not from religious awe, and shall venture reverently to try to answer the question.

Enough and more has been said to show how each part of man retains the character of its own class. The mind, therefore, has to be inspired from above in order to be maintained in its appropriate life, that is, in light and the knowledge of God, just as much as the body has to be supplied by the power of the same deity with its being, existence and life. In order, therefore, that man should be man and not beast, he must be illumined by the divine Spirit just as the pure dew drops from above in pearls. Hence it is clear that the law and the setting forth of the divine will are not superfluous simply because the flesh refuses to receive them. Rather the more the flesh resists, the more necessary is a reinforcement of the spirit which is brought in unknown to the flesh. For unless the spirit, thus fortified by this aid, held out against or frustrated the attacks of the flesh, man would not be man but a brute, even though he retained his human form. Take from man the knowledge and care of divine things, and his skill and care in human things will not take him out of the ranks of the brutes. For the brutes all have a care for themselves and their kind, and, as Cicero says, protect themselves, their bodies and lives.* If, therefore, man sees, cares and hopes for nothing more, the care of human things is not a whit different from that of the brutes. In order to be man, then, and not a brute, man must have a care for and knowledge of things nobler and better, and only when that is given him from above does he become man. For that creature which is to be neither simply angel nor simple brute must have a spirit and a body. But that God supports and maintains the obstinate flesh, though it war constantly against the soul, happens for the same reason the soul is inspired from above. For man must be a wonderful creature by just this fact that he aspires to the divine and makes use of the body.

*The passage of Cicero Zwingli refers to is probably the following, *De Officiis, Bk.* 1, §4, "Nature hath implanted in animals of every kind, a disposition to preserve life and health to avoid injury, and to pursue and procure the means necessary to any prolongation of their being." But the idea that animals tend to *perseverare in esse suo*, appears in all of Cicero's philosophical writings.

Hence it is, to touch the point in passing, that, save the one Son of God, no one is so perfectly learned, wise and just that he does not in something betray that he is man. We wonder that some men err, when not to err is the wonderful thing. We wonder when they show ignorance of anything who, with their little bit of learning, we foolishly imagined knew all things, when not only no one man but not even the whole company of men and angels knows all things; for that belongs to God alone. We wonder that some men fall from righteousness, when it is impossible to live with this flesh without defilement. You might as well expect a person whom you had ordered to sit down in dirty mire to come out with garments bright and clean as to demand spotless righteousness of man. The flesh is mire; hence whatever comes from man is stained. The Cumaean lion shows his ears somewhere.*

Today there is a dispute as to whether the body of Christ is eaten in the Eucharist essentially or physically and actually. There are men† who distinctly declare this, whom the Lord knows so well that unless He gave them life and strength for this and other things, they would not even be alive, much less indulge in discussions. But by such errors He shows us that those are but men, whom we are beginning to regard as something more than human, that we may see that unchangeableness‡ and infallibility are His alone.

Since then, God shows Himself as a friend to man, by revealing His will and character to him through the law, when man in his boldness disobeys either from the negligence of the spirit or the violence of the body, he is rightly condemned. To live exempt from the law has in no wise been permitted to man. For he who is exempt from law knoweth not the will of God, and

*This is an allusion to the well-known fable of the ass in the lion's skin. It is given at length by Erasmus, in his *Adagia*, chil. I, cent. III, prov. 66; cf. also the proverb, *Asinus apud Cumanos*, Erasmus, *Adagia*, chil. I, cent. VII, prov. 12. Zwingli alludes to this fable elsewhere, see his *Werke*, ed. Egli and Finsler, Vol. II, 1908, p. 156. One form of this fable is found in the *Fables of Avianus*, written in the 4th century A. D., see the edition by Robinson Ellis, Oxford, 1887, No. 5, p. 7; the town Cuma is added in Lucian's Piscatores, see the *Works of Lucian*, ed. London, 1781, Vol. II, p. 30.

†The Lutherans.

‡The text reads ἀνάλητον, a misprint for ἀνάλωτον.

that which knoweth not the will of God was not created for His friendship and companionship. Man, therefore, would be counted among the host of the beasts, if he were not through the law and the knowledge of God placed in the company of the angels and the blessed.

Herewith I think it has been shown that the law also is the gift of Divine Providence, though that Providence cares for all things and orders even those upon whom no law is imposed. For It determined by means of the law to indicate Its will to man, and to guide and educate him by means of it as by means of a teacher, in such a way that the law is the knowledge of God itself, by which He is known to be the Lord and Moderator of all things. Nor are governing by providence and educating by the law two processes. Providence gives the law in order rightly to regulate that most remarkable of creatures, the race of man. This will be made clearer in what follows.

FIFTH CHAPTER

Divine Wisdom was not making a mistake, either in creating man or in teaching him by the law when it knew he would fall.

Now one might grant the admission that the law was not superfluous after man had been thus created out of mind and body, but he might hold that the very wisdom of God had made an error in creating such a being. For if He knew that man was going to fall, His divine goodness comes under suspicion. Why did He not guard against the fall? If He did not know it, man must suffer because of his ignorance, like a person who is lame because his broken leg was not properly set through carelessness or ignorance on the part of the surgeon. This point must not be passed over, although it seems to belong rather to the subjects of wisdom and goodness than that of Providence. For, having in the beginning shown that Providence is necessarily implied in truth, wisdom, goodness and omnipotence, it will not be irrelevant to settle a question in which the goodness and wisdom, which go to make up Providence, are involved. For if they fall, Providence collapses.

As to goodness, therefore, I will say that the divine goodness did not cease to act when it did not guard against the fall of man, but manifested itself in a two-fold manner, in creating man and restoring him when created. In creating, because, since God's natural and inmost cause for creating is goodness (since, influenced by this, He made the universe and was favorable towards it that it might enjoy Him), goodness must have had its share in the creation of man as well as of other things. This, with the aid of that goodness, I will show a little more clearly.

The whole vast creation is divided into two classes of creatures, those endowed with intellect, and those without intellect. Those endowed with intellect again comprise two classes, those destined to live without a body and those destined to live with a body. The first class consists of the angels, the second of men. Both of these, angels as well as men, were endowed with intellect, that they might know first the supreme good and secondly the things created by it. But since the goodness of God, of which mention has been made above, contains in itself justice and righteousness as well as kindness and mercy, it was necessary that when the intellects of both angels and men were to be created they should be so made as to recognize God's righteousness just as much as His kindness. But how can righteousness be recognized if there be not also unrighteousness? So kindness and gentleness cannot be known unless there be violence and fierceness. For what good is cannot be known unless there be evil, by comparing and judging which one gets the notion of the good. No one would ever have sought the sweet so eagerly, unless astonished by the taste of the bitter, he had learned that the one was preferable to the other. This the philosophers knew when they taught that virtue would have amounted to nothing if vice and wickedness had not shown how pleasant and profitable virtue was, and the philosopher Demetrius, according to the testimony of Seneca, wisely called a life without care and free from the inroads of fortune a "dead sea."* And since the Deity could not posssibly show us unrighteousness in His own person, inasmuch as He is by

*Seneca, in his "Epistolae Morales," Letter 67, §14, writes: "In this connection I think of our friend Demetrius, who calls an easy existence, untroubled by the attacks of Fortune, a 'Dead Sea.'" See the edition of Otto Hense, Leipzig, 1898, Vol. III, p. 215.

nature perfectly true, holy and good, He produced an example of unrighteousness by means of a created being, not as if the created being produced it of itself, since it has neither being, life, nor activity without the Deity, but the Deity is Himself the author of that which to us is unrighteousness, though not in the least so to Him.

Since, therefore, both angel and man were to know righteousness, and this without its opposite, unrighteousness, would be obscure and unintelligible, He prescribed unto both what is right and holy and forbad, on the other hand, what was wicked and wrong. There was no unrighteousness yet, because no one had yet transgressed the law. Both, therefore, transgressed, because both had to know what righteousness and integrity were, and as soon as they transgressed they saw the face of righteousness. One [the angel] was driven from the abode of the blessed and given over to everlasting fire; the other [man] was deprived of his happy home, but yet was saved through mercy, just as one who might be killed by the law of war is yet saved and made a slave. God wrought both of these things, but by means of an instigator as instrument, in the case of the angel, his ambitious spirit, in the case of man, the flesh and the devil. Yet He is not Himself unrighteous, nor is what He did unrighteousness as far as He is concerned, for He is not under the law. When He commanded the angel, "Thou shalt obey me, Thou shalt worship me," and commanded man, "Thou shalt abstain from this fruit and worship me," it is easy to see that the Deity is not bound by these laws. When, therefore, He makes the angel and man transgressors, He still does not stand forth as a transgressor Himself, since the law is not applicable to Him. Therefore what God did is not sin, but to man and the angel it is, for the law pursues and accuses them. God may deal freely with His creatures, as a householder may with his property or a potter with his clay. Though, therefore, He instigate the creature to this, or drive him to that, so far is it from His sinning that He does not do these things without some distinct good, though meantime man, to whom the law has been given, sins, even when he is instigated thereto, for he acts in contravention of the law.

This will become clearer through two illustrations. The head of the family has given certain domestic laws to keep his children from dainties and laziness. He who touches a jar of honey, shall be whipped. He who does not put on his shoes as he should or who, having put them on, takes them off without suitable occasion or loses them, shall go barefoot. And the like. Now if the good wife or the grown up children not only touch the honey but use it, they are not straightway whipped. For they are not bound by the law. But the children are whipped if they touch. For the law has been given to them. If a steer covers and impregnates a whole herd it is accounted a merit in him. If the owner of the steer knows a single woman besides his wife, he is accused of adultery. The reason is that upon him has been imposed the law, "Thou shall not commit adultery." No law restrains the other. So Paul expressed the fundamental thought of this argument briefly and truly, as he does all things, when he says, "Where there is no law, there is no transgression" [Rom. 4: 15]. Upon God, as upon the head of the family, no law has been imposed. Therefore He sinneth not when He does in man that which is sin to man but not to Himself.

When, therefore, to return to the question, angel and man were to be created to contemplate His truth and righteousness, it was necessary for them that there should be falsehood and unrighteousness. For the good, therefore, of angels and men both were so fashioned that they could fall. For by the fall of the angel faithlessness and falsehood made their appearance, by the fall of man, unrighteousness and sin. And these show their faces to both classes as a sort of guide to truth and faithfulness, integrity and righteousness. Thus by creating man so that he could fall, God manifested His goodness. For by the fall the splendor of the divine righteousness was made apparent. Thus it appears again incidentally that the wretched proclaim the glory of God, for, being illustrations of His righteousness, what more could they render unto Him?

We have as witnesses to this truth not only men and angels of whom I have already spoken, but all other living creatures also. For they are all either gentle and kind or savage and cruel. The tiger and the crocodile proclaim the majesty of God just as much as do the ox and the sheep. For as the one pair exhibits His goodness so the other shows His righteousness, not as if their dispositions aimed at anything in harmony with righteousness or like unto it, but because all they do smacks of violence and injury. They cruelly tear to pieces, and live not by honest toil, but by plunder, nor do they commit their depredations in fair and open battle, but circumvent their victims with stealth and treachery as it were. And do not the most wicked of men abominate their ways? Why? On account of their cruelty, violence, and unrighteousness, to be sure. The most unrighteous, therefore, bear witness to righteousness, in thus condemning in the wild beast that was created to live by plunder the bloodshed, robbery, depredations, plundering, burning, pillaging, plots and treachery which they allow to themselves. For thus even the most worthless of men are warned to correct in themselves that which they abhor in the brutes.

When, therefore, these brutes by their natures bring unrighteousness before our eyes, in picturing unrighteousness, without which the face of righteousness cannot be recognized, they manifest the righteousness of God just as much as the domestic cattle that proclaim His goodness. Thus all creatures, reduced to two classes—those which profit and those which injure man—equally extol the righteousness and kindness of God. It is clear, therefore, that the goodness of God shone forth and did not lie dormant when He so created man that he could fall. For in this way he came to the knowledge of the divine righteousness.

In the second place, His goodness displayed itself in the restoration of man. For when He might have restored the fallen in any way He pleased, He preferred to adopt none other than that by which He who had been man's Creator became his Redeemer, that there might be no less goodness and righteousness in the redemption than in the creation. This goodness appears in the creation, in that man, created to enjoy God, falls into unrighteousness in order to recognize righteousness. This goodness also appears in the redemption, in that He who had freely created man out of kindness frees him, and frees him in order that, when freed, he may enjoy God. When the Righteous redeems the unrighteous, so that redeemed he recognizes that God only and alone is righteous, and sees how great a thing sin and unrighteousness are, so great, namely, as to have needed an atonement,—and when our unrighteousness has been expiated by the Son of God, it is plain that nothing is so repugnant to God as sin, and on the other hand nothing is so pleasing to Him as devotion to righteousness and integrity. This much to show that the divine goodness was not jeopardized when He created man, knowing that he was going to fall.

Now we must show that His wisdom did not make a mistake either, as if man had come out otherwise than it had determined. I say, then, that what has been said before applies to this part of the subject also. For it is the part of wisdom to find a way by which to bring a thing out into clear light. Hence it belongs to wisdom to prepare a way for man to the knowledge of righteousness. Then also that wisdom was not deceived is clear from the fact that man's redemption was not determined upon as an afterthought to his creation. For whatever the Deity has must be everlasting. But He has wisdom. Hence it is everlasting. Hence, the redemption was determined upon from eternity just as much as the creation. But the redemption could not have been determined upon, unless wisdom had seen that man was going to fall. For who appoints a remedy for a disease he knows not of? Divine wisdom, therefore, could not fail to know that man was going to fall, for it provided a remedy therefor. And since the Deity cannot do anything new as an afterthought, it is evident that the redemption was determined upon from eternity and that wisdom had an insight into the disease which needed the remedy of the redemption. Man is, therefore, not, if we consider anything carefully, a work of ignorance but of the wisdom which knoweth all things and knoweth the course of all things from the beginning to the end.

Therefore, we ought not to put to this wisdom the question why it made man so, or any other thing whatever, but we ought to reflect that since man has been made so, he must have been so made with perfect wisdom, just as we do not ask of the stars why they were so made or why they keep their particular course, but when by long observation we have discovered their limits and power we bear witness that they were wisely made. So to take God to task on account of the creation of man is arrogant, impudent and rebellious, but to be moved by the study of man to wondering appreciation of the divine wisdom is pious and holy. For who could imagine the reasons of man's creation and redemption, to say nothing of understanding them before these took place? When we see him created and redeemed, we

contemplate the fact with reverence and cannot praise enough
the wisdom, goodness, power, and providence of the Creator in
all things. The Deity is to be reverenced by us, not taken to
task nor asked the reason of His acts. His work is to be studied
and His wisdom and power in it to be admired with gratitude,
not found fault with, improved, or set aside. For nothing can
come from that Good Being which is not absolutely and perfectly adapted to the use for which it was made. He sees all
things even before they take place. He orders all things as
they ought to be done and accomplished. He considers and
decides nothing that is not sure and enduring. This will become
clearer, when I treat of election from the words of the Apostle
which will bring testimony in support of all that has been said.

SIXTH CHAPTER

On Election, which the Theologians call Predestination;
that it is sure and unchangeable, and that its source is goodness
and wisdom.

That I treat this part of the subject at length is not accidental. I do it to make clear that not only justice, as the theologians have generally held, is the source of predestination, but
also goodness, and that recognizing Providence thus is not to
shield the wicked, as Chrysostom complains, but to damn them.
Thus, to make a brief recapitulation of the preceding serve as
an introduction to what is to follow, God is all-knowing, all-
powerful, and good. Hence nothing escapes His notice, nothing
evades His orders and His sway, nothing which He does is
anything but good. When He was upon the point of creating
man, an animal with intellect, that he might know and enjoy
Him, He saw how he must be taught the knowledge of His
righteousness. He saw how he was going to fall, He saw how
that fall was going to open his eyes, so that at one glance as it
were he would recognize both the righteousness of God and his
own unrighteousness. For as soon as he had run counter to the
command of the law, he feared the voice of God calling to him
as that of the righteous person whom he had offended. And
when God foresaw this and did not guard against it, this was
from goodness, not from malignity or ignorance. For not to
have learned the righteousness in Him would be to remain in

ignorance of His highest endowment and the most excellent part of His character. And since what this righteousness is could not be shown except for its opposite, unrighteousness, man fell for his own good, namely in order to come to the knowledge of righteousness. For man had to be such that, consisting of soul and body, he might contemplate the divine and heavenly with his soul, and live with the brutes with his body. And that the spirit might not go over to the brutes and sink to their level, if the rebellious flesh should rush into continual resistance unrestrained by fear of the law, the law was given as a guard which the spirit ever listens to and follows, but which the flesh ever resists and seeks to evade.

All these things were so ordered for man's good. For he among all creatures had to be of the nature of a heavenly creature such as there is none beside him. From this we clearly gather that goodness is the source of these things, as a sort of genus comprehending justice and kindness or mercy, not justice alone, so far as it is a species of goodness. But if we make justice a sort of genus, like goodness, so that justice shall contain in itself mercy and kindness, as the holy Scriptures often use it, as in "In thy justice deliver me" [Ps. 31:1], then I have no objection to the doctrine that justice is the origin of election and predestination. For justice and goodness will then be the same. And if this seems to anybody rather overdone or too subtle, he ought to reflect that I am only trying to show that all of God's doings in regard to man savor of goodness no less than of justice. For since man was made the kind of creature he is, he must have been well and wisely made by Him who can do nothing but what is good, so that the things that we consider to be evils are really done for our good. Of this I shall speak later by examples.

In the second place, I treat this matter at such length in order that no one may be influenced by the complaint of Chrysostom. As if I were wrong to put punishment upon the wicked, while attributing all things to Divine Providence, and the rest of the numerous complaints he makes so rhetorically. For inasmuch as the law has been given to man, he always sins when he runs counter to the law, however true it is that man neither exists nor lives nor displays activity except in God, of God, and through God. But what God brings about through man's agency is imputed a crime to man, but not also to God. For the one is under the law, the other is the free spirit and mind of the law. And when we say that Divine Providence did this or that wrong which one man or another has perpetrated, we speak improperly. For in so far as God does it, it is not sin, because it is not against the law. The law has certainly not been imposed upon Him as the Righteous One. For "the law is not made for a righteous man," according to the view of Paul [I. Tim. 1:9]. One and the same deed, therefore, adultery, namely, or murder, as far as it concerns God as author, mover and instigator, is an act, not a crime, as far as it concerns man, is a crime and wickedness. For the one is not bound by the law, the other is even damned by the law.

What God does, He does freely, uninfluenced by any evil emotion, therefore, also, without sin. David's adultery, so far as concerns God as the author of it, is no more a sin to God, than when a steer covers and impregnates a whole herd. And even when He slays a man whom He kills by the hand of a robber or of an unjust judge, He sins no more than when He kills a wolf by means of a wolf or an elephant by means of a dragon. For all things are His, and He has no wrong feeling towards anything. Therefore He is not under the law, because he who cannot be influenced by any evil emotions has no need of law. But man sins. For he has need of a law, because he yields to emotions and when he transgresses the law, he becomes liable to punishment. Hence, the same deed which is done at the instigation and direction of God, brings honor to Him, while it is a crime and sin to man. Therefore it is right that the guilty be punished whether here by the judge or on the other side by the King of kings and Lord of lords. For they have sinned against the law, not as principals, but as accessory instruments, which God can use as He will more freely than the father of a family may drink water or pour it out upon the ground. And although He impels men to some deed which is a wickedness unto the instrument that performs it, yet it is not such unto Himself. For His movements are free. Nor does He do wrong to the instrument, since all things are His more than any artisan's tools are his own, and to these he does no wrong if he turns a file into a hammer or a hammer into a file. He instigates the robber, therefore, to kill even the innocent and those unprepared for death. For the hairs of our heads are numbered in His sight [Matth. 10: 30]. How much more our souls!

No one shall say here, "Why does He slay the righteous and innocent man at the hands of the robber?" He does not slay him, but gives him life. For He transports him hence to the abode of the blessed. It has been appointed that man shall die once. He, therefore, summoned this man at the time when it seemed suitable to Him. Nor should any one say, "The robber, therefore, is innocent, for he killed at the instigation of God." He sinned against the law. "But," you will say, "he was forced to sin." I grant that he was forced to sin, but for this purpose, that the one should be translated, the other nailed to the cross. Here the champions of free will, the logical opponents of Providence are under a delusion. They stop when they have said, "If the robber killed at the instigation of God, he is wrongfully punished," when they ought always to go on, as Providence Itself never rests, and to say, "The robber smote at the instigation of God to this end that the smitten might pass hence to heaven, or, if he too is wicked, to hell, and that the robber might be sentenced to the cross by the judge." For the same Providence does all this. It not only influences and impels men until murder takes place, but goes further, and forces the judge by the law, goads him with the sting of conscience, drives him by the example of cruelty to bind the robber and raise him upon the cross. The answer, therefore, is ready, when the opponents of Infinite Providence say, "If there is no freedom of decision in man, we are forced to admit that thefts, murders, and all kinds of crimes are committed by Divine Providence. For, I say, I recognize Providence as caring for and doing all things." But do not stop, when you have said, "Providence influenced the robber." Go on, and say, "He influenced the robber, but He also influenced and roused the judge against the robber, that an example may be made, and the wicked mind that had been hidden may be revealed to the world." In short, God instigated the killing, but He instigates the judge just as much to sacrifice the slayer to justice. And He who instigates, does it without any suspicion of crime. For He is not under the law. But he who is instigated is so far from being free from guilt, on the contrary he does practically nothing without being bespattered with stains, because he is under the law.

After this preamble I proceed to the subject of election. This I will first define, then expound the definition, finally present confirmatory evidence from Paul and others. Election, then, is the free disposition of the divine will in regard to those that are to be blessed. This definition contains the generic term disposition, which I take in the sense of decree, determination, or even appointment, though otherwise it means also decision or resolution, which I do not wish to use as the generic term, because they are generally subject to necessity. For a decision is adopted in regard to some action when some necessity shows itself which bids us adopt the decision that the situation demands, not the one we are most inclined to. "Disposition," therefore, is more appropriate to the divine authority and majesty, which have no need of long deliberation. And as legislators and princes can freely dispose of things in accordance with what is fair and just, so the Divine Majesty is free to determine what is in accordance with Its own nature, which is the essence of goodness. Therefore to "disposition" I have added "free," that we may understand that this disposition is free, not dependent upon nor following our arranging and disposing.

And this I want understood thus:—The view of Thomas Aquinas* upon predestination, if only I remember his doctrine correctly, was this:—God, seeing all things before they take place, predestined man's fate at the time when by His wisdom He saw what he was going to be like. This opinion pleased me once, when I cultivated scholasticism, but when I abandoned that and adhered to the purity of the divine oracles, it displeased me very greatly. For St. Thomas believes that God's disposition in regard to us follows our own disposition. After He saw by His wisdom what we were going to be like, that is, how we were going to act and decide, then and then only, did He pronounce his decision regarding us. What else is this than making God's decision and disposition like unto the judgment and decision of a human judge? He does not pronounce judgment until he has heard the case, because he cannot see before that what the right and wrong of the matter in question is. Therefore, he must de-

*See Thomas Aquinas, *Summa Theologiae*, Pars I, Quaest. XXIII, art. 5, 1: *Ergo videtur quod praesentia meritorum sit causa praedestinationis.*

Marginal notes:
Election defined
NO DOUBLE PREDEST.

Aquinas
(read Helm)

pend upon the exposition of the case. Such a judge they make out God to be for us, who in this fashion make predestination to follow judicial examination. Moreover, they inadvertently bring God's goodness and omnipotence into danger. For if God before the creation of the world saw what Adam, Cain, or Judas was going to be like, and did not take measures to prevent them from falling into crime, He would seem to have forgotten His goodness. If, on the other hand, He could not prevent the fall which he foresaw, though He would gladly have done so, His power does not keep pace with His will, and accordingly His omnipotence is called in question.

Besides, if predestination followed our decision, we should be or become something of ourselves before God determined about us, and I have shown already what a groundless contention that is. And though I am well aware that the Deity's attributes, namely, wisdom, knowledge, prudence and the rest, are such that whatever is one of them is also the other (for that which is deity is absolutely simple everywhere, with all its endowments and powers), yet there is a sort of natural order in these things, that is, they are naturally grasped one after another by the human understanding, which is not made to see all things together at one glance, as God sees them. Thus those who follow Thomas's opinion can easily say, that, though we know wisdom, or prescience in their nomenclature, it does not actually precede predestination, yet adapting ourselves to the natural order of our perception, we make wisdom the basis of predestination. In saying this, I claim, they are disputing with words when they maintain that naturally, that is, according to our understanding, wisdom predestines after having foreseen our actions, though actually this sequence does not exist. For both I, or rather Paul, himself and I with Paul, hold that predestination is the free disposition of God with regard to us, and without any respect to good or evil deeds. Of this somewhat later when we come to the confirmatory illustrations.

To come now to another part of the definition, this disposition is the work of will as its principal cause, not of wisdom, though the Divine Will never acts blindly without wisdom, as man's will is always blinded by passions so that it pursues and seeks what the mind and understanding disapprove. For among God's endowments there is no discord. The Deity is simple.

Hence nothing can be done by Him to which all His attributes do not equally contribute. For they are yet one simple and indivisible thing, however much distinctions are made between them in our understanding. Yet to no one attribute or another is attributed what belongs to all, just as certain special characteristics are attributed to the individual persons, though they belong to all three. Thus the creation of the whole world as well as of man is attributed to wisdom, though providence and will had no less a part in it than wisdom. Care and provision for things are attributed to providence, though wisdom and will are no less concerned in them than is providence.

Election and predestination to the life of the blessed are attributed to will, though wisdom and providence equally contribute thereto. But meanwhile a special work is attributed to each, that the attributes of the Deity may be the clearer to us, and the works proceeding from Him better known. For is not His wisdom manifested in the creation of the whole world, and does not the creation of all things rouse the greater wonder and admiration when we see they were made by infinite wisdom, aided, to be sure, by goodness, justice, righteousness, power, foresight, and inclination or will, though wisdom, as the mistress, as it were, claims the credit of the work for herself? Although the handmaids are such that they did no less labor than the mistress herself, they cannot get the glory of the creation of the world for this reason especially, because wisdom is the first requisite for such work. So in destining men to salvation, the Divine Will is the first power, but attended by the handmaidens wisdom, goodness, righteousness, and the other attributes. Therefore it is attributed to will, not to wisdom, (otherwise God's gift and disposition would seem to depend upon our acts, as I indicated) not to righteousness, (for everlasting bliss would then be again the result of the works of righteousness), nor to divine bounty. Thus, whichever way you turn among the individual attributes of God, the work of election belongs to will, as chief mistress here.

The last part of the definition is, "with regard to those who are to be made blessed." Thus election is attributed to those only who are to be blessed, but those who are to be damned are not said to be elected, though the Divine Will makes a disposition with regard to them also, but He rejects, expels and

close or reprob. see p. 188

repudiates them, that they may become examples of His righteousness. Election, therefore, is the free but not blind disposition of the Divine Will, as the principal cause, though not alone, but accompanied by majesty and authority, and applying to the blessed, not the damned.

Now I pass on to the testimony of Scripture, by which not only the definition of election is confirmed, but the whole matter of Providence is set before our eyes. "Miseror," says the Lord to Moses, Exod. 33: 19, "quem voluero; et benignus sum ei cui voluero." For that is the meaning in Latin—[in English: "I pity whom I have willed and am kind to whom I have willed"] —of those Hebrew forms of expression which we render by "I will shew mercy on whom I will shew mercy," and "will be gracious to whom I will be gracious," though the Hebrew seems to be more forcible than the Latin. For what else is it to say, "I will shew mercy on whom I will shew mercy," than to make a fixed proclamation after the fashion of rulers, "I bestow mercy according to my pleasure; not according to the prayers of suppliants nor the misery of those that wail, but according to the gift and grace of election." For even the impious sometimes supplicate for help.

This view will be more clearly understood, when we weigh the words of the Lord Himself when He encouraged Moses—"I will harden Pharaoh's heart," He says, "and multiply my signs and my wonders in the land of Egypt. But Pharaoh shall not hearken unto you," Exod. 7: 3, 4. And this language He repeats often, not threatening by hyperbole, as some people say, but admonishing and telling man beforehand the secrets of His ordination by which He had decreed to make clear to the world by Pharaoh's rebelliousness and wickedness his rejection and damnation, which He had ordained in His heart before He created the world. For the Lord says also, Exod. 9: 16,* "And in very deed for this cause have I raised thee up for to shew thee† my power; and that my name may be declared throughout all the earth." By this we are clearly given to understand that the Lord shows both His power and His righteousness to the world by means of such examples of boldness and obstinacy. For

*The text has 17.
†Zwingli reads tibi, "to thee," following the Hebrew and not the Vulgate.

when He hardens them so that they resist Him, there is no doubt that He does it simply to set them up before the world as examples of His righteousness.

On the other hand, it is plain, that when He makes Moses leader of the people and David king, when He shows mercy on the thief dying upon the cross and on Peter not only abandoning his Lord in time of danger but wantonly denying Him, He puts forth examples of His goodness. Whence also St. Paul says, "Whom he will he pitieth, and whom he will he hardeneth," [Rom. 9:18]. What else does he show by these words than that election and rejection are the work of God's free will?

These first proofs from Scripture, then, confirm the second part of my definition of election, namely that the disposition of election is the work of will. Paul also speaks in the same passage in these words, "When Rebecca was with child from our father Isaac, and the twins had not yet been born" (so far were they from having done either good or evil, that the purpose of the divine election might remain inviolate, coming, as it does, not from works but from the one who elects), "it was told unto her that the elder should serve the younger," etc. [Rom. 9:10-12]. By these words of Paul in the first place all controversy about the merit of our works is done away with. In the second place the view of the followers of Thomas is refuted, according to which they believed that election was not determined by God until He had seen what kind of people the individuals were going to be. For Paul says distinctly that so far is it from being true that election has to do with our disposition or determination, that Rebecca's twins were elected before they were born. Nay, they were elected according to the inviolable purpose of God before they were conceived, in fact before the world was made. Then he says with equal distinctness that election does not come from works but is due to Him who elects. By this we understand first that the disposition of God is free, not depending upon any secondary consideration or cause, which is the second part of our definition. Secondly, we see that the merit of our works is overthrown. For either free election must fall or our merit must. For if blessedness is bought by works, it is no longer given free. If it is given free, it is not the reward of good works, as the same Paul plainly says in Rom. 11:6.

Since, all the same, the Holy Scriptures so often promise

blessedness as the reward of our works, it happens that the untrained fall into the evil of contention. Hence that strife about free will and merit which arising long ago still continues, one side seeing that Providence and the free gratuitous election of God are the essential thing, the other side declaring that it is freedom of will and the reward of good works. This evil strife could be concluded immediately, if men would once turn to the contemplation of the Deity as the safest bulwark of religion. The supreme good is the Deity. All that is, is from Him, and, being from Him, needs His power in order to be and exist. On the other hand, the Deity needs no one's help, exists by His own might, rejoices from native goodness that whatever is, shares His bounty, wishes well to all, cares for all, is the light of all knowledge, nay is the only source of understanding. Hence whatever we see live, understand, and act, lives, understands, and acts in Him.

How, therefore, can we give the credit for anything to ourselves, who do not even exist, much less live or act without Him? Since, therefore, nothing is or exists by its own power, nor lives, nor acts, nor understands, nor deliberates, but the present power of the Deity does all these things, how could human will be free? To be and to live undoubtedly precede the power and act of understanding. Since, then, even the poets of the heathen recognize that they depend upon the Deity alone, why, alas, do not the cultivators of true piety rise to the height of seeing that all the activity of all their faculties and powers is from the same source whence the whole universe flows?

And there is no reason why the fact that Holy Scripture still holds out rewards for our works, should be a stumbling block, since we have already heard that through the bounty of the Deity it happens, as with human things, that what truly belongs to the originator and master-builder is credited to the instrument. Thus remission of sins, as I have said, is attributed to the apostles who only proclaim it, when God alone can pardon sins and by His Spirit give us the sure consciousness of pardon granted. So to external things, namely, sacraments and symbols, is attributed what nothing but the Divine Power can give, to baptism which is the first pledge and bond of membership in the Christian army, is attributed the washing away of sins, when atonement is made only by the blood of Christ, and grace given only by His bounty; to the eucharist is attributed the atonement itself when that was made only at the time when the God-man Christ was sacrificed for human nature, while in the eucharist there is nothing but the calling to mind of this atonement and thanksgiving for it. Although the gift and bounty of the divine goodness are extolled therein, they are not brought to us by the power of the symbols, except in so far as the symbols and the words of the preacher proclaim them. For it is alone the Spirit that draws the mind to that fountain by which the soul, that has pined away through despair over its sins, is refreshed and renewed in youth. For if the celebration could do anything of this kind, Judas would have returned to his senses, and not have gone off to betray his leader, scorning the fellowship of his companions. Nay, those very blood-thirsty villains who brought Christ to the cross or vilified Him as He hung upon it, would have changed their purpose and kept their wicked hands off from Him, if external things brought faith or remission of sins. For they saw not only represented by symbols but accomplished before their own eyes that by which the sins of the whole world were atoned. But nothing of the sort happened. Only those repented whom the Spirit illumined within so that they recognized that this was the Saviour, and whom the Father drew to come to Him and accept Him.

Since, furthermore, externals can do nothing more than proclaim and represent (and when faith is brought into activity by them, certainly a faith is thus brought into activity which was there before), and since faith is a gift of the Holy Spirit, it is clear that the Spirit operated before the external symbols were introduced. Nevertheless, Christ Himself does not disdain to call the bread His body, which to quote Augustine's words, is only the sign of His body.* And holy men, following the example of their master,† represent the eucharist as all that for which we return thanks in that celebrated service of praise. They call it the body of the Lord, because in it is commemorated the fact that Christ took upon Himself flesh and died for us. They call it the remission of sins, because we return thanks for the forgiveness of our sins through the death of Christ. They

---

*Augustine says: "The Lord hesitated not to say, 'This is my body,' when he was giving a sign of His body." Against Adimantus, chap. 12, §3.

† ἀρχηγόν.

call it the food of the soul, because He who alone is the sure pledge of our hope is praised in it. Not as if the material bread were the material body of Christ, or as if, when eaten and digested, it washed away the poison of sin, or as if the material bread or the material body of Christ could feed the soul, but because the Divine Goodness is so pleasant and friendly to us that It deigns to present even to our senses certain shadowy forms of internal and spiritual things, which are called by the same name as the things themselves for the reason that they are the sacraments and representations of the real things.

Hence also the holy Fathers* said that the sacraments consisted of two things, the sign and the thing signified, the visible and the invisible, the perceptible and the spiritual. Not as if, to take the eucharist as an illustration again, the bread of the Supper were at once sign and thing signified, bread, namely, and the material body of Christ, as certain men ignorant of real piety and learning think, but because the bread is a sign, and the thing itself is Christ who was really delivered up and made an offering for us, and this thing is proclaimed, preached and believed by those who celebrate the Lord's Supper, yet the bread is but a symbol of this thing which is presented to the senses, the thing itself is present to the mind. Not as if the bread were at once material and visible bread and the material but invisible body of Christ, but because the bread is material and visible, while that which feeds the soul, namely the fact that God gave His Son wholly for us, is invisible, and the bread is a sign of this invisible thing. Not as if the bread were at once material and natural bread and spiritual power, but because the natural bread typifies the spiritual renovation of the mind, and unless

*Thus, e. g., Augustine says: "In sacraments it is always considered, not what they are, but what they exhibit; since they are signs of things; being one thing, and signifying another." (Contra Max. Arian., Bk. II, c. 22, §3). Again he says: "How is the bread His body? And the cup, or that which the cup contains, how is it His blood? These things, brethren, are therefore called sacraments, because one thing is seen in them, another is understood. That which is seen has corporal form, that which is understood has spiritual fruit." (Sermon 272). And again: "Discoursing on signs, I make this remark, that no one must fix his attention in them on what they are, but rather that they are signs, that is, they signify something. For a sign is a thing, which, besides the form it presents to the senses, causes something else external to itself to come into the mind." (De Doct. Christiana, Bk. II, c. 1, §1).

this has first taken place, he who is about to celebrate the supper approaches it to his danger; for it is written:—"Let the man prove himself," etc.

It is no wrong, therefore, that godly men* spoke thus by periphrase† both because they followed the example of their teacher, Christ, and because they saw that the divine benefits could not be worthily proclaimed by any word painting. But it is wrong for us to be so dull as to attribute to a material thing what belongs to God alone, and to turn the Creator into the creature and the creature into Creator. Clear and sure knowledge of the truth is not a thing to let itself be deceived by the artifice of words. Thus it ought not to be a stumbling block to us that that is promised as the reward of works which is bestowed gratuitously by the Divine Goodness. For this comes not from the nature of the thing, but from the Divine Goodness, which disdaineth not to let that be attributed to us which is really its own alone. To our merit, therefore, is credited what is received only as the gift of divine bounty. This will be made clearer by the illustration of faith, and when I have treated that, the subjects of election and of providence will both be rendered plainer.

REGARDING FAITH

"Faith," says the Apostle [Hebr. 11:1], is the essence of things hoped for and the evidence of things invisible." For thus I translate word for word the Greek ἔστι δὲ πίστις ἐλπιζομένων ὑπόστασις πραγμάτων ἔλεγχος οὐ βλεπομένων. In this definition I translate ὑπόστασις by "essence," not by "substance," for the reason that "substantia" in Latin is more readily ambiguous than "essentia," like ὑπόστασις in Greek, which word the heretics once distorted so cleverly that Jerome said* poison lay hid in it. I have no objection however to the term "substantia." The meaning of the Apostle is, therefore, that

---

* θεσπίους ἄνδρας.

† καθ' ὑπεροχήν.

‡Jerome, in Letter XV, 3, writes: "I ask them (the Arians) what three hypostases are supposed to mean. They reply three persons subsisting. I rejoin that this is my belief. They are not satisfied with the meaning. They demand the term. Surely some secret venom lurks in the words." Migne, *Patrologia Latina*, XXII, 356; also Schaff, *Nicene Fathers*, Second Series, Vol. VI, p. 19.

faith is the essence or substance of things hoped for, that is, the essential thing to the soul, not a cursory notion that pops lightly into a mind that wavers and believes or thinks now this, now something else.

It is the firm and real confidence of the soul by which it trusts wholly in the things to be hoped for, that is, in the thing for which solely and only it hopes without fear of disappointment. Thus "things hoped for" is a periphrase for the Supreme Deity in whom alone hope is rightly placed. Yet the Apostle said "things hoped for" in the plural number, after the fashion of the Hebrews, who much like the Germans, use the plural number for amplification. They use אלהים [Elohim], that is, gods, for one God, not, by heaven, as if they desired to introduce the notion of a plurality of gods, but because in this way they honor and magnify the name of the Deity according to the idiom of their language. Intentionally I did not want to translate:—"Faith is that firm and real thing in the soul by which it is led to God, in whom it hopes without fear of disappointment," though this is the sense of the words. For those words ἐλπιζομένων ὑπόστασις, that is, "the essence of things hoped for," have still another force, namely, they emphatically express the idea, "Faith is that real and firm quality in our souls which was given by Him who is the reality and object of our hope." I therefore translated indefinitely "essence" or "essential fact of things hoped for," that both meanings might be included.

Secondly, I used "evidence" to translate the Greek ἔλεγχος, the word most often used by Greek writers for "demonstration, evidence, and certainty," such as rises upon a firm foundation from reasoning. So I translated "evidence," to indicate a certainty clear, sure and plain to us. And this unshaken evidence and certainty explains, as it were, the previous part of the definition, namely, that faith is a real and substantial thing, that is, the clear light and certainty of the soul.

Finally I used "things invisible" as the translation of πραγμάτων οὐ βλεπομένων. How thoroughly are these words misunderstood by many. Some twist them so far that, whatever tale they bring forward in which you refuse to have faith, they say: "You must believe. For the things of faith are not visible." In this way any lie which a hypocrite invents can be thrust upon us by this definition. Hence all this license to lie.

At one time, fictitious stories of saints are brought forward, which they declare must be believed even if all history cries out against them, because "faith is of things invisible." At another time, wonders sufficiently miraculous in themselves and made more miraculous by the clumsiness and shamelessness of the liars, are defended as credible by the same shield, though they were never known in art or literature or history, for "faith is of things invisible."

Others, like the sacramentarians, (those are justly called sacramentarians, who attribute to the sacraments what they do not contain, and by high-sounding but false and made-up promises, lead men away from simple trust in the one God to belief in the power of symbols. Therefore if any one hereafter finds "sacramentarians" in my writings, I want him to understand that class of men who attribute to symbols what belongs only to Divine Power and to the Holy Spirit, personally working in our souls, which symbols and the external word only proclaim and represent), the sacramentarians, I say, either not understanding or not wishing to understand the usage and meaning of our Lord's words, twist this language so far as to venture to assert that the things themselves are really and materially conveyed by the sacraments by virtue of the words joined with the elements, and they defend their error by saying, "Faith is of things invisible." "You do not see grace in baptism," they say, "but it is certainly conveyed by virtue of the words, as soon as the clergyman has said, 'I baptize thee in the name of the Father and of the Son and of the Holy Ghost.'" When you demand proof of this proposition, they say: "Faith is of things invisible."

They fail to notice that baptism is not given to any one unless he first confesses that he has faith, if he is a grown person, or unless he has the promise in virtue of which he is counted a member of the Church, if he is a child. Thus this thing which the sacramentarians maintain is conveyed invisibly by the sacrament was actually conveyed before. For he who confesses faith had it before he confessed it and, therefore, before he was baptized. For confession precedes immersion. Thus the faith which was given by the light and gift of the Spirit was there before the candidate was admitted to the sacrament, or if he did not have faith, it is certainly not brought to him by baptism.

For neither Judas nor Simon the sorcerer, who were without faith when they were baptized, received faith by baptism. But if an infant is to be baptized, since he cannot himself confess faith, he must have the promise which counts him within the Church. The promise is, that the Gentiles, when they have obtained the knowledge of God, and true religion, shall be just as much of the church and people of God as the Hebrews. This all the prophets heralded and Christ Himself most plainly promises. "They shall come from the east and from the west, and shall recline with the God of Abraham and Isaac and Jacob."* And "The last shall be first," and "The vineyard shall be given to other husbandmen," and "There shall be one shepherd and one fold."

Since, therefore, the children of the Hebrews have always been counted with the Church with their parents, and the divine promise is sure, it is clear that the children of Christians belong to the Church of Christ just as much as their parents. This promise is not conveyed in baptism, but he to whom it has been previously given is baptized, that by a visible sign he may bear witness that he is of the number of those who through the goodness of God are called the people of God. Here surely nothing new is brought in, but that which has been previously given is recognized by a religious rite, and the name is given when the symbol and pledge have been received.

So, too, in regard to the Eucharist they err from ignorance, when they assert that the material body of Christ is conveyed by the words, "This is my body." "The word conveys," they say, "we must believe the words." And, when you point out the contradiction with other words of Christ, as, "The flesh profiteth nothing," and, "Hereafter I shall not be in the world," and others of this kind, they defend themselves with this weapon, "Faith is of things invisible; these things take place in some inexplicable and incomprehensible way." As if any juggler and even the Roman pontiff could not say of any juggling of his own, "This that I promise takes place, but invisibly and incomprehensibly. For faith is of things invisible and incomprehensible!" Cannot the Roman pontiff just as well defend the doctrine that the bread is transubstantiated into the body of

*Matth. 8: 11; cf. Matth. 19: 50; 21: 41; John 10: 16. But the word "God of" is omitted in the Greek as well as in the Vulgate.

Christ, by saying in the same way, "This happens incomprehensibly and invisibly, for faith is of the invisible," as the sacramentarians, when they say that the natural body of Christ is conveyed, defend themselves on the basis of this statement that faith is of things invisible?

All the detrimental errors of this kind come from not seeing that the part of the definition of faith, "things invisible," is a Hebrew periphrase for the one God, whom they call "things invisible" in the plural number after their own fashion of amplification. For they constantly bestow upon God this epithet, "unseen and not visible," as in Col. 1: 15, "Who is the image of the invisible God," and in I Tim. 1: 17 ["Now unto the King eternal, immortal], invisible, the only wise God," etc. Hence arises that kind of periphrase by which "things invisible" is put for God, the Creator of all things, and "things visible" is put for the creation. Thus, Rom. 1: 20, "For the invisible things of him from the creation of the world are clearly seen, being understood by the things that are made, even his eternal power and Godhead," and II Cor. 4: 17-18, "For our light affliction, which is but for a moment, worketh for us a far more exceeding and eternal weight of glory; while we look not at the things which are seen, but at the things which are not seen; for the things which are seen are temporal; but the things which are not seen are eternal." Here in both places "things invisible" is put by periphrase for God Himself and all His power, which is nothing else than Himself. For nothing invisible is offered man to look at save God alone. Thus, also in this passage "things invisible" is a periphrase for God, so that this is the meaning of the definition of faith:—"Faith is that real and unwavering thing given man by the Deity in whom alone he has the right to hope, by which he firmly and surely trusts in the invisible God."

So faith is, furthermore, πληροφορία, that is, full, clear and sure knowledge of God and hope in Him. And this is the meaning of the Apostle, as the whole epistle indicates, especially the part where before our definition he says, "Let us approach with true hearts, with πληροφορία, that is, with sure, evident, and fixed faith" [Hebr. 10: 22]. This is also shown by the fact that the apostle exhorts us to bear adversity through faith, and declares that all who suffer shipwreck in faith have been driven from the haven of happiness, and, finally, because he interprets the words of the prophet, "The just man shall live by faith," to mean that the life of the just man is regulated by faith in God, since faith is so efficacious, present and life-giving a medicine that he who drinketh of it is saved and secure.

Since, therefore, faith is that light and security of the soul by virtue of which it knows that its recognition of the one true God is its salvation and horn of plenty, and that this God is so rich that He has all things and can do all things, and is so bountiful and kind that He gives willingly and delights to give (for He delivered up His son to us, that we might become sharers in His riches),—since, I say, faith is this light and food of the soul, nothing else can happen than that faith should be to the just man, that is, the man who thus has faith and security in regard to the goodness of God and his inheritance therein,— that faith should be his life and strength, through devotion to which he is defended against all adversity. But this power is not from man (for otherwise every one would wish to have the greatest faith possible), since all have not faith, but is from God alone. Paul attributes it to the Holy Spirit [Gal. 5: 22]. For those who are of the earth, have the thoughts of the earth, but those who have been regenerated from above have the thoughts of heaven. Surrender man to himself, and whence will he acquire faith and get it for himself, since his thoughts and desires are of the earth? It is, therefore, God's gift alone.

Since, therefore, faith is God's gift (for none cometh to Christ save him whom the Father hath drawn thither [John 6:44]), how is it that everlasting bliss and salvation from sin are attributed to faith in so many passages of Scripture? For if faith is a gift, and forgiveness of sin is attributed to faith, then one gift is thus attributed to another. To return to our path, then, we ought to examine and see just to whom faith is given. For we have already concluded that it is the free gift of God. Faith is given to those who have been elected and ordained to eternal life, but so that election precedes, and faith follows election as a sign of it. For Paul says, Rom. 8: 30,* "Whom he did predestinate (or ordain), them he also called; and whom he called, them he also justified (or absolved); and whom he justified, them he also glorified." This statement of Paul brings

*The text has v. 29.

a wonderfully clear light into our argument. For he wishes to show that the decision and ordination of God are the origin and cause of our being given everlasting glory. When this decision or ordination had been made, man was called by God, not only with that general summons which makes the external preaching of the apostles, but also with that call by which the Spirit takes the elect, so to speak, by the ear, so that they desire to listen to what God orders or promises. "And whom he calls, them he also justifies" or absolves from sin. For the Hebrews use the word justification instead of absolution.

Now, what other justification is there than that of faith? For Christ and the apostles make the whole aim of their teaching to show that there is no other justification or absolution than that of faith. Those who have faith are heirs of the everlasting glory. By all this we learn that faith is given to those who have been elected. And those who have faith are justified, that is, absolved, so that no damnation awaits them. Not as if faith were a work to which forgiveness of sins was due as a reward, but because those who have faith in God know beyond all question that God has become reconciled to them through His Son, and the record of their sin has been blotted out [Col. 2:14], for it is only sin which precludes and shuts us out from entering upon the heritage. If that be taken away, we return into favor with God, just as bodies of water rush together if the space or barrier between them be removed.

When, therefore, the mind of man has been so taught by God as to know that His Son was made an offering for our sins, it is so charmed by the taste of the Divine Goodness as to trust in that only and alone which has wiped away the poisonous effect of sin. Finally it becomes so devoted to God only and alone that it is just as ready to die as to live for Him. Then there is nothing which can damn the soul of man. For, however much the Roman pontiff hurl his anathema, the sure knowledge of faith will presently leap forth as its champion with the weapon, "Thou knowest God is thine. For His Son is a pledge of the reconciliation of His goodness and righteousness. The accusation this man now brings is, therefore, a slander. Who shall bring anything to the charge of the elect, especially when he who is accused knows by what covenant and faith he has God as his bondsman?" Let sin accuse him, which is so in-

timately connected with us that if we boast of freedom from it
we are vain fools; straightway the light of faith takes up the
defense, declaring that sin is not such that on its account God
refuses His kindness, if only we frankly confess our fault and
are ashamed of it. For the sins of the whole world could not
prevent Him from leading His Son to the altar to atone for
them. Let the devil accuse us; faith will charge forward with
all its strength, and will not only rout the enemy, but so turn
him to flight that however often he return, accompanied by
seven others worse than himself, he cannot win the day. For
he that hath real faith trusteth the Lord, and feareth not what
all the assaults of flesh will do unto him.

He, then, who is thus protected by the shield of faith,
knows that he is elect of God by the very security based on his
faith. And this is the pledge by which the Spirit binds our souls
to Himself, so that we give to Him alone our love, our reverence,
and our trust. This is that bread which he that eateth shall
neither hunger nor thirst. This is the water which he that
drinketh shall be refreshed and revived forever. And he who
has not this certainty so that he feels it stand forth dauntless and
immovable, in the veins of his soul, as it were, nay leap also to
meet any adverse fortune, he, I say, should pray daily, "Thy
kingdom come," and, "Lord, increase our faith." For they that
possess the light and power of this faith are sure that neither
death nor life can take from them that treasure for which they
have sacrificed all to buy it. And their election is such that it is
known not only to God but also to the elect themselves.

There follows now another piece of testimony, by which
we learn that faith is given to the elect only, so that we shall not
believe that that is really faith which some men pretend to have,
when they confess God in prosperity, but desert and betray Him
when temptation comes. In the Acts of the Apostles, chapter
13: 48, it is written, "and as many as were ordained to eternal
life believed." Lo! those who were destined and ordained to a
life of happiness believed. It is plain, therefore, that those who
believe know that they are blest. For those who believe have
been elected. Election, therefore, precedes faith. Hence those
who have been elected and do not come to a knowledge of faith,
like infants, attain everlasting happiness none the less. For it
is election which gives the happiness, and this is so absolutely

free that no account is taken in it of our works or merits, as I think has been firmly enough established above. Also they who hear the message of faith and accept it not are destined and ordained to everlasting punishment. For those who believed the preaching of the apostles had been ordained to eternal life. On the other hand, those who did not believe, as Christ says Himself [Mk. 16 : 15], when the Gospel has been preached and heard (for the words, "preach the Gospel to every creature," precede this), are damned altogether, and unbelief is just as sure a sign of this as faith is of election. Accordingly, be it said in passing, the divine oracles ought to be carefully examined, for they speak by synecdoche when they say of the believers that they only shall be saved. For only those believers are comprised under this law who have heard and believed.

So it is with the damnation of the unbelievers. Those only are understood who have heard and not believed. About the others we cannot pronounce an opinion, because we do not know about the election of any, partly because Paul promises that, if uncircumcision [the heathen] do the works of the law, it shall become circumcision (for they show the law of God written upon their heart), and because Abraham, Isaac, and Jacob, the Virgin Mother of God, Peter and Paul were elected of God when they were still infants and had not faith, nay before the world was made. It is not, therefore, a universal rule that he who has not faith is damned, but him who has heard the doctrine of faith expounded and remains and dies in unbelief, we can perhaps count among the wretched. For many have not believed immediately upon hearing, but only when laid hold on by the Spirit and drawn to belief, like Paul. Therefore we may pass judgment only on those who remain in unbelief to their death. Although some give plain signs by their cruelty or lust that they are rejected of God, yet, since so often the worst men have returned to the right way, we ought not to condemn any one before his end, or his passing away, as the poet says.* And in this way are recon-

*Zwingli is here thinking of a passage in Ovid's *Metamorphoses*, III, 135, which reads: *Ultima semper expectanda dies homini est, dicique beatus Ante obitum nemo supremaque funera debet, i. e.,* "The approach of your last day always attend, And call none happy till his death and end." It is based on the famous remark of Solon to king Croesus, as given by Herodotus, see his *History*, I, 32.

ciled these two statements, "He that believeth not is damned"*
and "If the uncircumcision doeth the righteous works of the law,
its uncircumcision is turned to circumcision," etc., or "For
when the heathen who have not the law do by nature what is in
accordance with the law, they are a law unto themselves, though
they have not the law; for they show the work of the law written
upon their hearts," etc. [Rom. 2: 14, 15]. For nothing prevents
God from choosing from among the heathen men to revere Him,
to honor Him, and after death to be united to Him. For His
election is free.

I certainly, if the choice were given me, should prefer to
choose the lot of Socrates or Seneca, who, though they knew
not the one Deity, yet busied themselves with serving Him in
purity of heart, than that of the Roman pontiff who would offer
himself as God if there were only a bidder at hand, or the lot of
any king, emperor or prince, who serves as defender of such a
little tin god. For though those heathen knew not religion in
the letter of it and in what pertains to the sacraments, yet as
far as the real thing is concerned, I say, they were holier and
more religious than all the little Dominicans and Franciscans
that ever lived. These for a long time have been so far from
humbling themselves and giving God the glory for their holiness that there is no need of the touchstone of the Word of God
to detect their hypocrisy. Their boldness, luxury, unrestrained
recklessness, unbelief and cruelty show that their hearts are
without God so completely that no one is so ignorant and boorish
as to fail to see it clearly.

Therefore, when the gaining of eternal salvation is attributed to faith, that is attributed to the secondary thing and the
seal, as it were, which belongs to the primary and the instrument. Faith is the sign of the election by which we obtain real
blessedness. If election as a blossom had not preceded, faith
would never have followed. So also merit is attributed to works,
which even if they are of faith, like the works of Abraham, yet
do not merit salvation. This is set forth by Paul so strongly in
Romans and Galatians that there is no need of further confirmation of it now. And when Scripture says, "Do this and
thou shalt live" [Luke 10: 28], "If thou wouldst enter into life,
keep the commandments" [Matth. 19: 17], we ought to

*Mark 16: 16 and Rom. 2: 26.

understand that these things and things like them are said by synecdoche, that is, they put the effect for the cause. For, as justification and salvation are attributed to faith, when they belong only to the divine election and bounty, while faith so follows election that those who have it know, by seal and pledge as it were, that they have been elected, so those who do the works of faith give proof to themselves and others when they act bountifully and from love of God and their neighbor, not from vain glory, that they worship God, that is, that they have faith. For it is just as certain that where faith is, there are good works also, as it is that a furnace gives out warmth when a fire has been kindled in it.

Accordingly merit, about which we dispute so much in these days, is a name rather than a thing, that is Divine Bounty suffers Its gifts to be called the reward of merit, and shows Itself so altogether friendly to us that it suffers that which belongs to Itself alone to be ascribed unto us. Forgiveness of sin It attributed to the apostles, also the blessings of miracles which can belong to nothing but the power of God. No wonder, then, that that is promised as a sort of reward for good works which belongs only to God's greatness and excellence. For it is He who not only moves us to action, but gives us life, and not only gives it but preserves it. Thus will the human heart more effectively aspire to love of Him, when He thus makes us sharers and heirs of what is His, and not only enriches us, but advances us in honor, when He promises to our works what He gives from His own bounty.

Free will or merit can, therefore, in reality not be maintained, though no one can deny that they are named and mentioned in the Holy Scriptures, but assuredly only as the names of things which belong to God only, but are given to us as a sort of gracious accommodation, proving his friendship, or loans, as it were, given to us chiefly because all things are of Him and to Him. For nothing can be lost to Him, and pious men recognize in this sharing on God's part, His goodness rather than their own. Hence it is evident that there is no hyperbole in statements like, "The hairs of your head are numbered," [Matth. 10:30], "not even a sparrow, two of which are sold for a farthing, falls to the ground without the knowledge of your Father" [Matth. 10:29], and others of the sort, as a certain genius at word-tinkering* has tried to persuade the world in our time.

On the other hand things like the following are exaggerations and hyperboles—"If thou wouldst enter into life, keep the commandments" [Matth. 19:17], "He who doeth the will of my Father, is my brother," etc. [Matth. 10:50], and all the other promises made to our works. They are true only by consequence, so to speak, if you insist. For we are made brothers of Christ not by our actions, but by recognizing and embracing Him in consequence of election. For who would do anything without cause and purpose? Faith, then, is not acquired by deeds, but works by faith. For those who do the will of God, show by their deeds as the fruit thereof that they are filled with God. But if you consider the thing rather than words, the kind of promise by which the divine wealth in things pours out upon and attributes to us what belongs only to Itself is really a hyperbole.

I will add this one thing. When Paul writes to the Romans [Romans 10:17] that faith comes from hearing [the Word] he attributes in the same way to the nearer cause that is better known to us what belongs only to the Spirit, not to external preaching, as the sacramentarians are apt to contend. And this is so true that it is not only gathered from such testimony in the Holy Scriptures as, "No one cometh to me except my Father draw him,"† and, "To another is given faith by the same gift of the Spirit," and the like, but is also learned by experience. For we see daily certain men hear the preaching of the Gospel, yet not believing any more than before.

Paul's meaning, then, is only that it is necessary, as far as is shown by Scripture examples, that the Word be preached, in order that then God, who giveth the increase, may plant the seed of faith by means of this tool, as it were, but with His own hand as the immediate cause. For the apostle's work also is from the hand of God, but indirectly, the internal drawing is the work of the Spirit acting directly.

The sum total of the whole matter is that all things which have to do with man, either as to his body or as to his soul, are so completely from God as their only real cause, that not even the

*Erasmus of Rotterdam.
†John 6:44; and I Cor. 12:8 ff.

work of sin is from any one else than God, though it is not sin in Him, as I said early in the discussion. When we attribute anything to the nearer instrument or cause, it really comes from these, if you look at the matter closely, no more than the harvest from the husbandman. If that came from him, what would hinder his taking care to have his granaries always overflowing with plenty? Why should he not keep want afar off? No, it is Another who furnishes all things, however much the farmer may not withdraw his hand from the plow and rest. Thus whatever we do or think is of God, the Doer and Disposer of all things.

And let not this question about infants trouble anybody, —since all the elect were elected before the creation of the world, and the infants of the faithful are of the Church, there is no doubt that when these infants die, they are received into the number of the blest according to election, which the Apostle says* remains sure. Are we then all elect while we are infants, or not? I am speaking of us who are born and live within the Church. For we are sons of the line of Isaac, the heathen, of the line of Ishmael. If we are all elect, and election remains sure, however we live or believe after we are grown up, we yet attain salvation. For he who has once been elected, remains always elect. If not, those who die in infancy and have not been elected are sentenced to eternal punishment, without having deserved anything of the kind, since they have been delivered from original sin through the mediation of Christ, and they have themselves done no wrong.

In order that what I mean may be clearly understood, I raise, for the sake of an illustration, the following question:— Jacob and Esau, when infants, were both counted, as belonging to the Church. For both had been introduced into it by the symbol of circumcision. Since, then, Esau had been rejected by the will of God before he was conceived in the womb, would he have been received into the number of the blest, if he had died in infancy, or not? If he would have been received, rejection was not permanent, consequently neither is election. For Esau had not been elected, and would have had to be elected afterwards. If he would not have been received among the saints, to be counted within the Church and to have been

*Romans 9: 11.

marked with its sign would have profited nothing. Thus to be counted within the Church would be no sure sign that we are the sons of God.

Nevertheless, this question seems to be of the class of those which seem to be begotten of curiosity rather than of piety (for we ought rather to recognize what is done by the Lord as rightly and properly done than to demand reasons why He did so), yet, since there is no godlessness in contemplating with wondering admiration the things which we unequivocally acknowledge as done rightly by the Lord, and then in searching from experience for the reasons why they were done or were so done (for the Deity Himself gives the reasons why He created the sun and the moon*), it will not be irreligious to satisfy the minds of those who, while not without religion, are endowed with so meagre an appreciation of things that they find a casual stumbling block, not in religion itself, in which they remain steadfast, even if ignorant of much that is clear to others, but in the light or knowledge, which is not the least part of the contemplation of God's works. And this stumbling block, although not able to injure faith, yet often keeps the intellect troubled. For though to believe that there is only one Deity and to trust in Him belongs to all who have true religion, yet the knowledge of the ways and characteristics of the Deity belongs only to the experienced and those endowed with a clear understanding, nay to those more intimately taught by God. So, then, I answer, that neither Esau nor Jacob could have died in infancy, however much they were under the general law of mortality. For before the creation of the world Divine Providence had just as much determined about their acts and life as about their creation and birth. For if the hairs of our head are numbered, if nothing can escape Divine Wisdom, if Providence is nowhere at rest, if Goodness neither neglects nor postpones anything, it is clear that what follows life and existence is just as much regulated as the bestowal of these. For among causes, these two are the chief, the efficient and the final. And since nothing can be done by Divine Wisdom without reference to its end, it follows that nothing is created by Divine Wisdom of which the end and all the attending circumstances to the end have not been foreseen and settled long before they take place. Life and activity,

*Gen. 1: 16.

therefore, are just as much arranged by Divine Providence for every man as are his birth and generation.

On the other hand, death and the cutting of the thread of life are just as much ordained as creation and the course of life. For these are properly the end. Hence it is to be inferred that no one dies in infancy whose fate has not been determined from eternity, and no power can effect that he for whom this or that limit has been fixed can overleap it. The fifteen years that the Lord granted to Hezekiah [II Kings 20:6] as an addition had been put down as an addition before the establishment of the world. For what has once been arranged remains fixed forever. Hezekiah's end, therefore, had been so arranged that the years should be added in this way, and only after them should Atropos* really cut the thread which she had only threatened to cut before.

Since, then, neither Esau could have died in infancy, because the Lord had arranged differently in his case, nor that little son of David, whom he begot in faithless and wicked adultery, could have lived, because the Lord had determined to slay him, it is evident that when the infant children of the faithful die, it is a sign of their election and summons to the glory of the blessed. For they are taken away that wickedness may not stain their souls, that is, that they might not by a wicked life betray their rejection to the world, as they would do if they had been rejected.

Those who survive and become intractable and rebellious like Esau, are saved for this, that their rejection and casting out may be made manifest by their godless life. But those who survive and remain pious and obedient to God, like Jacob, are saved for this, that by their good deeds the kindness of God and their own election may be made evident. Meantime, as long as they are counted within the Church as infants or young children, and we cannot tell how they are going to turn out, whether they be destined to life or death, we follow the same rule of judgment as with grown persons, namely, that they are of the Church and are elected of God, as long as they do not by monstrous deeds of shamelessness show that they are unregenerate. As there are among grown persons many who are not discovered by us to be unregenerate until they betray it by

*One of the three goddesses of Fate.

great wickedness, and, on the other hand, many who after living some time in wickedness, return to the right way, and by repentance and honesty of life show that they have been elected by the Lord, so, in general, all the children of Christian parents (for of these we have the clear promise of the Word) are included by us in the number of the sons of God. Meantime God either shows their election by an early death or by a longer life of integrity, so led in consequence of faith, or makes plain their rejection by their long, but profligate life.

Thus there are none of whose election we are more sure than of those children who are taken away young, while still without the law. For the life of men is sometimes not really, but only in appearance, upright, but in children who are born of believing parents, there can be no blemish. For original sin has been atoned for by Christ [Rom. 5:15] (for as in Adam we all die, so in Christ we are all restored to life, we, that is, who believe or who are of His Church according to the promise), and no stain of wicked deeds can defile them, for they are not yet under the law. And since no cause but sin separates from God, and they are without all sin, it is clear that no one is so incontrovertibly known to be among the elect as those children who finish their days while young. For dying is just as much a sign of election in them as faith is in grown people. And those who are unregenerate and have been rejected of God do not die in this condition of innocence, but are preserved by Divine Providence that their rejection may be made known by their wicked life. That this is true all that precedes proves, unless one denies Providence, and with such I have nothing to do. So much about man, how he and all the details of his life are just as much regulated by God as are the things without minds and souls.

SEVENTH CHAPTER

A Confirmation of all that precedes by examples.

It is now evident enough that God is not like man. For man's plans often turn out so unsuccessfully that he says, "I didn't think of that," or "It did not succeed this way, let us try another." God can form no plan without full knowledge. Therefore, what He determines upon remains unchanged, because He foresees everything so that nothing can happen to interfere with or prevent what He undertakes. His decrees remain unalterable, because He is Himself unalterable and unchangeable. Hence we may infer that what God once was towards His creatures, He is also today, so that if He ever showered His goodness upon the good and pursued the wicked with righteousness, He maintains the same attitude today also in the freedom of His will. Therefore, as He once was toward the elect, so He is now, and likewise toward the rejected. As He was in the beginning toward all His creatures, so is He still toward all.

First, then, I will bring forward illustrations by which it will be shown that the things lower than man do not happen by chance but are regulated by Providence, although the deluge in the time of Noah seems to have fallen upon and overflowed things as if nature (as the philosophers call it) had brought it on. For it is said that the floodgates of heaven broke loose and rain fell continuously for forty days. Yet no nature did this, but the Author of all things, who is the real nature and power of all that is. He could not only have commanded the rivers to swell and overflow their banks and drown everything without any rain, but could have destroyed everything with one word, nay have reduced everything to nothing by withdrawing His power. But He preferred in this way, by rain, namely, to put a new aspect upon the world. When we have comprehended that He had decided upon this, we see without any trouble that whether He brought on the rain naturally, according to the order of things once established, or whether He called it forth out of the natural course, it did not rain by accident when the world was submerged. How much less does it rain by accident when the earth is moistened for the good of man! For though we grant that all things above and below worked together in natural course at that time to produce all that quantity of water, yet this had preceded: Divine Providence, when It created the world, foresaw and arranged things so that everything should take place in proper course and time. Things were bound to happen, therefore, according to the way Divine Providence had determined from eternity to punish mankind, which was to become very bad at Noah's time, by submerging it in the flood. Hence it follows,—whether things above had been so arranged

as to pour out that quantity of water in natural course at that
time, or whether the water was sent down by a new miracle,—
it follows, I say, that either event was so patent to Divine Providence when It created the world that It so regulated the course
and order of things above that they should pour out all that
water at the time when the wicked were to be destroyed, or so,
that while things above kept their own special course, a new
miracle should overwhelm the evildoers with water.

When at the prayer of Elijah rain was given after so long
a course of years, a little cloud not bigger than a man's hand
appeared, then grew as clouds are wont to do, and poured out
such generous showers that all things were restored [I Kings
18: 44, 45]. If this rain was accidental or given by the power
of nature, not by Providence, who could have made Elijah sure
of its coming, when he promised rain so persistently, especially
in so weighty a matter in which he had brought forward the
rain as witness that his Lord who had given the promise was
God? Since, then, the rain fell by the Providence and arrangement of God, it is immaterial to us whether it was poured out by
a combination of natural forces adapted to do this at the time
or by a new miracle, provided we understand that before the
foundation of the world Providence so foresaw all things and
had all things so clearly before It, that It knew that the conjunction of the natural forces which should produce all that abundance of water would coincide with the wickedness of the world
which It wiped out by the waters at the time of Noah.

So also with the plentiful showers that were brought on
after the long drought. For whether these things occurred in
regular course or out of course, the warning and prophecy about
them show that they were done by Providence. For if they
happened in regular course, if a flood in natural course coin-
cided with the wickedness of man, Divine Wisdom and Providence are reflected from them. If the waters were poured forth
out of course, again we see both these, Righteousness as well as
Power. For God does miracles out of the ordinary course of
things, that the astronomers* and those who, like them, wage
war against the sovereignty of the Deity like the giants, may not
be able forever to attribute everything to some force of nature,
but may be compelled to recognize a greater force than visible

*Zwingli refers to the end of the world, predicted for the year 1524.

things possess, whether they will or no, when they see fire fall from heaven and suddenly engulf five cities by its flames [Gen. 19: 24], or the sun at one time stand still in mid course [Josh. 10: 13], when Joshua, Israel's leader, needs light to pursue the enemy, or at another time lay aside its light and be darkened, when Jesus, the Saviour of the world, overcomes the enemy by His death.

If, then, those rains, by which the flood and the refreshment of the earth were brought about, were poured forth by Providence, why should we attribute any rain to some natural force? Does that Providence which is the essence of being sometimes wake and sometimes sleep? If, on the other hand, rain is brought on by chance, why is rain alone poured forth by chance and not all things? If everything comes by chance, Providence is done away with, and if Providence is done away with, the Deity also is done away with. For if anything goes by chance, then everything must go by chance. For if Providence were idle in one single thing, It would not be Providence. It must apply to all things, because the power of the Deity is over all, and if it were not over all, He would not be the Deity. And if His power were over all, and not also His providence, all the attributes of the Deity would not be equal, and accordingly the Deity would not be the Supremely Simple. Hence, if one shower is poured out by Providence, all are poured out from the same source. Rains, therefore, are just as much showered upon the world by appointment of the Deity now as they used to be, and so with droughts, with abundance of harvests and with scarcity.

It is, therefore, clear that the movements and arrangements of the things above are ordered by Providence, not by nature, unless you take nature for the Deity, by antonomasia.* If Elijah's rain was given in accordance with an arrangement of heavenly bodies determined before, not by a new miracle, it must have been given by Providence, who before the creation of the world saw that this arrangement of the stars and this pressing need of mankind would coincide. If it was given by a new miracle, this was done by Providence. For who can do miracles but He who can regulate and rule all things? Though eclipses, earthquakes and lightnings were accounted as miracles when the world was still ignorant, they have been found to take place

*That is, the substitution of a general for a specific term.

in natural course, that is, according to the arrangement of heavenly bodies, as nearer and better known cause, and this discovery has taken away abnormal wonder at them, though they are just as much brought about by the power of the Deity alone as are those miracles which take place out of the natural course of events. And they are more wonderful as the result of an established order which maintains and performs its functions forever than are those things which are done only for the moment and occasion. Although, therefore, showers poured out in natural course, that is, according to an order established in the beginning, seem to be produced by agencies nearer and better known to us, yet they are just as much the work of Providence as when they occur miraculously.

I will give an illustration from our own time. The astronomers threatened a flood and the general break up of the universe for the year fifteen hundred and twenty-four, and the preachers, especially among the Christians, are still proclaiming that the end of the world is upon us. The one based their calculations upon the conjunction and clashing of the heavenly bodies, the others upon the wickedness and corruption of the times, and when the latter have invaded human society the preachers become more certain that the divine vengeance is at hand, than any astronomers are from their scheme of lucky and unlucky years. That year has gone by and left the earth for us still further to dwell upon, and though there were freshets in some places, the streams of Switzerland were lower than for many years. But there is reason to fear that this jungle of wrongs, suppression of public justice, pride, luxury and the utter shamelessness of all evil will bring on a far more destructive deluge than one in which the bodies of men and brutes should be drowned. In this the preachers predicted much more correctly than the astronomers. Meanwhile they despise each other vigorously, when they ought, on the contrary, to have more regard for each other. When the astronomers saw the stars in a sinister and threatening position, they ought to have looked with admiring wonder upon the wisdom of the Deity, which from the creation of the firmament had so regulated the course of the heavenly bodies that a fatal calamity should be threatened by them at the period when all things had become thoroughly corrupt. The preachers are right in disparaging the wanton and unrestrained divination of the astrologers, but they ought not to scorn the benefits of astronomy any more than they should the stars themselves. For as these are instruments by which the Divine Power pours Itself out, so the knowledge of their course is nothing else than the knowledge of the course of the divine activity. Hence the preachers, as far as I can see, should respect astronomy as highly as any branch of knowledge.

The disturbances by which the world is shaken at present are not caused by chance or by the anger of the stars, but by Divine Providence, which so orders all things that the preachers are able to threaten divine vengeance, and the astronomers to foretell coming calamity. Both of these things are manifested by the goodness of God, that the way to repentance and salvation be opened more clearly before us. So far, therefore, is it from the truth that the stars run outside of the course appointed for mortals that rather since the foundation of the world their power and course have been adapted to the course of human affairs. And when we now see that these have been such that the might of the stars has evidently been angry with mortals, corresponding to the wrath of God, and the stars are nothing but instruments of the Divine Power, it is clear that they are continuously under the sway and rule of God's beck and call, and never do anything at random. For if any one thing were done by them at random and without God's providence, by the same fact everything would take place at random. For he who thinks that Providence neglects one single thing, does away with Providence altogether, as has been shown before. And if the theologians and the astronomers will both reflect upon this, there will, I hope, be no more quarrels between them hereafter. The one class [astronomers] will refrain from trivial divination, and the others [theologians] will not decline to defend Providence, because they failed to regard these as instruments of the Divine Power, so constituted by the Divine Wisdom that they are ever obedient to the call of the Deity, and, stopping with the stars themselves, things without life, and not reverencing their author and mover, have limited Providence too boldly.

The astronomers, may, therefore, give warning according to the fixed and indubitable axioms of their science, that is, propositions and principles demanding immediate acceptance, but they may not set limits to things, partly, because many trivial things have crept into their science, and partly because the Deity, the soul of the stars, regulates them at His will, and through them works what He will, and gives them what He will, not what we wish or teach is given them. On the other hand, the theologians can more plainly recognize Providence when they regard the stars not as some special thing apart from the Deity but as the instruments of His power.

So much about the movements of the heavenly bodies. In these I want included the celestial phenomena, the constellations, as they are called, the lightning flashes and thunderbolts, what goes down and comes up, the changes of the wind, earthquakes and storms, and everything above or below that takes place by the influence of the heavenly or upper bodies, because all these things which come from the heavens are done by the providence and immediate power of the Deity.

Nor should we think that the stars do, at God's command and ordination, to be sure, many things that it is still not necessary for God Himself to know or pay attention to. As if that power which is the Deity could be wearied or could wear out under excessive labor, so that we must spare it, lest by seeing, ordering, and doing all things, it became weary and need some Atlas to put his shoulders under the burden, while it takes breath. Such is the nature and power of the Deity that it consists of activity and is absolutely foreign to rest. For where rest is needed, there is need of taking breath. Where taking breath is necessary, there labor is oppressive. Where labor is oppressive, fatigue follows. Where there is fatigue, there is also weakness, and this must be absolutely foreign to the Deity. Divine Power is not, therefore, exhausted by doing, surveying, and arranging all things. It delights in it, loves it, is used to it, that means, its nature requires it. For when it is made clear in regard to chance happenings that the Deity takes account of them, as I shall presently show, will there be anything from which He can withhold His hand?

The name "chance happenings" is inconsistent with real religion. For nothing can happen by accident of fortune, if all things are regulated by Providence. Furthermore, when I have shown that the things which are believed to be accidental proceed from the direct action of the Deity, I hope that though the name "chance happenings," or, as the new school says, "contingent happenings," remain, it will be plain that the things which are attributed to fortune or chance are the work of God in reality.

In approaching this matter, I shall first bring forward illustrations from the realm of inanimate things or things without intelligence, where yet the evident work and care of the Deity are discoverable, and afterwards illustrations that have to do with man. When the hatchet of the prophet's pupil slipped from its shaft and fell into the river [II Kings 6: 5], it was, at first sight, an accident. But when the prophet teacher threw in the piece of wood to bring back the metal and it obediently floated back from the bottom, we see both from the strangeness and the greatness of the miracle that the metal fell in for the purpose of making plain the prophet's holiness and his close relationship with God.

The straying asses [I Sam. 9: 3], in search of which Saul had left his father's house, show clearly enough that they went astray at the ordination of God, since the son sought asses and found a kingdom that he had not sought, and the father got not only the asses he was troubled about but a king for a son, which he had never thought of. Will the ass that stood with the colt [Matth. 21: 2] at the cross roads for the use of the poor be believed to have been driven thither by chance, when the King of kings and Lord of lords mounted it to enter Jerusalem, according to the words of the prophets? Shall we say that the small cords which Christ gathered at random in the temple [John 2: 15] and made into a scourge lay there at random, since with them He drove the money changers from the sacred edifice? Shall the fig tree [Matth. 21: 19], which, sterile by nature or worn out with bearing, stood there with nothing but leaves, be thought to have been planted accidentally all those years before, since Christ cursed it with such indignation as an everlasting illustration of His detestation of hypocrisy? The fish certainly had not kept away from Simon's net all night by accident, when they rushed into it in crowds after Christ came [Lk. 5: 4-6] and bade him be of good cheer. For they were the instruments for the great miracle, by which such a vast quantity of fish was caught. The five barley loaves and two fishes [John 6: 9] were not at hand by chance, nor the honey in the honeycomb, with the portion of cooked fish left over [Lk. 24: 42], since in both cases the miracle which followed bears witness to Providence. But I shall be overloaded with abundance of testimony rather than refuted by the want of it, so full of illustrations is everything. I pass by the clear testimony of Scripture, by which we see that everywhere the things we say occur by accident are done and regulated by Providence. I pass on, therefore, to the illustrations which have to do with man.

The case of Joseph is altogether of such a kind that more than anything else it shows the hand of Providence in all things. It is no accident that as a boy he was clothed with the coat of many colors. For afterwards it was more surely recognized, although it had been so soaked with the blood of goats that it presented the appearance of a garment torn by a wild beast. He has a dream; it is no accident, for he rouses the hatred of his brothers against himself in consequence of his interpretation, and foretells what was some time to come true. He falls unwittingly into his brothers' wicked machinations; it is no accident, for when he relates the crime to his father [Gen. 37: 2], he displays the magnanimity of his nature and incites his brothers to doing what God had determined. When on his way to see his brothers as they pastured their herds in the fields, he loses his way and is brought back to the path; it is no accident, for thus is manifested the alertness of the still young lad and the care of Providence which gave him a guide to set his wandering steps in the right road. What need of lengthy detail? He is thrown into the pit, drawn out, sold, the Ishmaelites pass by. What is accidental in these things? We see clearly that the traders, a class of men not always useful, took their journey to the best advantage through the region in which they bought a Joseph, a man who was one day to be the father of his country. He is charged with adultery, and languishes among prisoners. Others have a dream which becomes the occasion of his deliverance. He shows by his interpretations that even dreams are never so vain that they are not sent by Providence for some purpose.

Now, to say nothing of the physicians who easily discover the constitution of the body from dreams, to say nothing also of those kinds of dreams by which something important is told or taught or by which the drunkard condemns his drunkenness or the passionate man his rage or lust, if we got nothing else from

dreams than the fact that remembering them we discover that
the soul is immortal (for since it does not rest even in sleep,
but fashions phantom shapes, even as animals also do, which,
though it [the soul] generally discovers them to be vain, yet
cling to the memory afterwards, while they vanish for the
animals, by which manner is it not proved that real being is
ours, that is, substance whose nature is unresting and unwearying?)—if, I say, we brought away from dreams this advantage
only, it would be enough to show that not even such a trifling
thing as a dream makes its appearance without Providence.
Thus Joseph's whole life is nothing else than a testimony to
the fact that all things are done by Providence. There is no
event in it which has not been shown to have taken place at its
own good time by command and ordination of God.

But, having made this little digression about dreams, I
know that there will be people who say that this reasoning is too
thin and even vain, chiefly on the ground that some dreams are
so trivial and others so vile that it seems wicked to drag Providence down to such low things. Let them have this answer:—
Since Providence Himself has condescended (for nothing is too
much for His kindness; consider in detail the humanity which
the Son of God actually put on)—condescended, I say, to declare important things by dreams, why should any one venture
to accuse me of boldness, when I attribute dreams as well as
everything else to Providence, especially when in this matter the
argument from one to all, from the individual to the universal,
is sound? For it is a logical argument:—Providence has once
been found to have decreased the harvest by drought and again
to have restored it by rain; therefore Providence always has a
care for the harvest. Therefore He never neglects the things
that pertain to this care, whether He wills to withhold or to pour
out abundantly. For one instance of neglect would utterly do
away with both the clear vision and the power of Providence,
as has been sufficiently shown above.

Then again, from what dreams can it be said that nothing
results, even if we look only at the foolish telling or thinking
about the dream, nay a vain effort to remember it? The man
who tells a vain dream to others sometimes interrupts serious or
harmful discourse, and this God uses for some good purpose,
although we may sometimes not discover the good until later,

sometimes never. Or he gives himself or others occasion for repeated reflection. So the man who recalls a dream, brings his
attention to something good or bad which Providence wishes
him to think about. And if he seeks in vain and cannot bring
up again a dream that has disappeared, this also happens not
without profit, calling him from harm or relaxing him for the
lighter things of life. For all these things tend to advance or
stimulate men's plans and thoughts, and deeds follow plans.

See how things, whose importance we do not rightly estimate, are not necessarily of no consequence. We fancy that the
swarms of bugs, lice, and fleas, since these are hateful to man,
are unworthy of Divine Providence, but if we consider the decayed matter from which they are produced for the purpose of
delivering us of it without harm, we shall see that cruel plagues
are sometimes averted by these insignificant things. The insects produced from the decayed matter of the wild fig tree
soften the figs unto ripeness.* These facts have been discovered
to be such. Others though not equally understood are equally
sure, namely that from rottenness and decay are produced
things into which these pass and are thus prevented from
causing greater harm.

Every one admits that this is the proper view of worms,
flies, gadflies, roaches, spiders, locusts, and that kind of little
insects, namely, that they are produced from poisonous rottenness that would do harm unless it passed into the little beast
which is made to deliver man from it without injury. Since,
therefore, the things outside of man are thus changed and purified for his good, how much more are the things within man,
namely, thoughts, dreams, visions, counsels, interests, and in-
differences, not without purpose but always taken up or allowed
to drop for some good end!

I do not regard this as pointing to our being unduly careless of ourselves, though this itself is from the Deity. On the
contrary, we ought to understand that a man does all things
according to his election or rejection. He who has been rejected
of God directs all his schemes to getting riches and pleasures,
and, wishing to acquire or striving to retain the name of a good
man, he conceals all his wrong doings by hypocrisy or parades

*For the correct interpretation see Driver in "Cambridge Bible," *The
Book of Amos*, p. 207f.

them with polish and adornment as virtues. Who will regard plans of this kind a little thing? They are as much greater than works as the cause is superior to the work that follows from it. For unless planning goes before, no works will follow. If anything is accomplished without the thought of the doer, it is not credited to him, so much higher is purpose reckoned than achievement. We grant that the works of the unregenerate and accursed are done by Providence, shall we deny this of their plans? Now, if we grant the plans, why should we not with equal propriety attribute all that belongs to the plans to Providence?

He who has been elected of God turns all his zeal towards acquiring real virtue, not counterfeit, not on his own account, but to the glory of God and the good of his neighbors. He devotes his efforts to their advantage, not his own. It is his highest pleasure to give glory to God or win advantage for his neighbor. Whatever he listens to, thinks upon, undertakes, he manages skillfully, is undaunted and does not retreat. Whatever happens, he recognizes must happen so, and understands that by these events the goal at which he is aiming is to be attained. Who would deny that all his designs and thoughts and efforts are from God, since he regards and reverences the Deity in all things, even when he sins through weakness, he interprets even his sin to the glory of God, as will presently be made clear in the case of David?

Nothing, therefore, is done or achieved which is not done and achieved by the immediate care and power of the Deity. I pass by willingly and knowingly both the dream which the Midianite told to his fellow soldiers on awaking [Jdg. 7: 13], and the chance coming of the reconnoitering Gideon to him. In these things we see that the dream which in form was most absurd did not come by accident, and that Gideon, without his own knowledge to be sure, but not without God's providence, came upon that place where he found evident hope of accomplishing his whole purpose.

Bathsheba seems to have gone accidentally to bathe and David to have been an accidental spectator thereof [II Sam. 11: 2], but when we hear the tragic end of the story, are we not seized with wondering horror? David had violated the wife of his most faithful champion, and, having inflamed rather than satisfied his lust, formed the wicked design of destroying the innocent husband who had no thought of vengeance, and of thus being able to satisfy his desire for the woman to his heart's content. Everything proceeded according to his wish, so that the prophet expressed in two words the greatness of the crime, which no words were adequate and strong enough to describe fully—Thou hast ravished and killed. Then David, coming to himself, was so humbled and cast down that this great fall was a bar to any self-exaltation on his part that might have led to his death. David was elected of God, and was a man after His own heart. Therefore, this great sin turned out well for him. But what other thought can we believe that he had all his life than this:—"The Lord, thy God, willed that thou shouldst fall into this sin, that thou mightest recognize that thou art but a man. He gave thee first the gift of prophecy, He gave thee strength, greatness of soul, a crown, a kingdom, riches, and promised thee a Saviour. All this might have turned thy head if He had willed, but He is kinder to thee than thou wouldst thyself have been. He has humbled thee by this monstrous crime, that thou mightest not think of thyself as something greater than man. Thus does thy God make thee an example of His bounty and His mercy." For so long as the world lasts when we want to encourage any one who sees himself a sinner, we shall hold up before him the case of David as an illustration of pardon, like a mirror or painting from which he may learn the readiness of the Lord to show mercy. Shall we say, then, that all these things happened by accident, when they furnish such instructive examples?

I will add another illustration to corroborate the above. In the last chapter of the second book of Samuel is written, "And again the anger of the Lord was kindled against Israel, and he moved David against them to say, Go, number Israel and Judah" [II Sam. 24: 1]. No passage can be adduced to show more plainly than this that not only our deeds and works but our thoughts and plans are suggested and inspired by the Lord, whether they be good or whether they be evil.

What sort of man Jeroboam was from his early years until he divided Israel and brought in idolatry, I do not need to expound. But however wicked and reckless he was, he was yet installed as it were in royal power by the prophet Abijah, when he cut his cloak into twelve parts and gave ten to the future king of the ten tribes [I Kings 11: 30, 31]. Since, therefore, he had set up golden calves to be worshipped, why did God not only suffer but order him to seize the kingdom? It so pleased Him. He was going to reject Israel. He undertook this affair, therefore, with these methods, that we might see that things are done according to His will and not according to our decisions.

Be it enough, therefore, to have brought forward all these examples in proof of the fact that everything that is done, whether we call it accidental or premeditated and determined upon, is done by the immediate providence of God, whether it has to do with inanimate things or with things endowed with life, mind and understanding—however much we, being immersed in such deep darkness of ignorance, on account of the gross sluggishness of the flesh, fail to see all this clearly. And if to any it is given to look at these things from a somewhat higher point of view, good Lord, what delight they feel, when they detect everywhere the wisdom and goodness of the Deity, so that the contemplation of the universe, beautiful as it is, is a sordid thing beside the delightfulness that meets them when they mount to God, and consider the architect of the structure of the universe! For what wondering admiration do you think enters the pious heart, when (to offer several confirmatory illustrations of this gracious dispensation also) it considers the aforesaid Jeroboam who was ordained by God to separate Israel into two kingdoms, and presently abandoned him whom He had installed, after he had set up golden calves to be worshipped! This thing first brought Israel and then Judah to destruction, for it was an unworthy deed to lead men away from the true God to idolatry, but it would have been an ill considered plan on God's part to raise a man like this to the throne who was going to revolt against him, unless He had determined to use his treachery for the thing that he was preparing.

When, I say, piety considers what follows, so far is it from passing judgment against God that it even wonders and extols His ways. Supreme Goodness had determined to give up the Jewish race at last and choose the nations given over to idols That downfall, therefore, which It was going to bring upon Israel, It paved the way* for, by means of Jeroboam. For

* παρασκευάζεται.

from this point Israel began to totter until she fell into the Babylonian and Roman captivities. But the peoples of the Gentiles, put in her place, then triumphed in the knowledge of the Deity. When the religious heart sees this so clearly, is it not carried away with a wonderful joy?

Consider also the value of the lesson that by this deed a warning is set before our eyes showing whither dissension and division lead and how sure a sign it is of an angry God and impending loss of freedom when violent and irreligious men are set over affairs. If we had looked at this lesson, we should long have had a clear view of the pitiable downfall of the Christian cause. When effeminate and reckless men rule the Church, and boys, not to say anything worse, govern kingdoms, what sign is lacking, not of a tottering but of an already falling Christianity? What hope is left us? How often has any people remained in safety after discipline and religion have collapsed? The preachers are at the head of religion. These have now become "fawning tails" [Isa. 9:15], to use the words of the prophet. The magistrates as guardians of justice are the maintainers of good order. May I perish if you can go through Europe and find that there have ever been any rulers more corrupt, unjust, and violent than those of today. But I talk to deaf ears. They do not listen to a warning, nor look at wholesome lessons, nay, nor attend to an accusing conscience that trembles with fear.

These things are, therefore, sure signs of the wrath of God and that He is going to visit us with dire punishment as He did those of old. The poet says* that "nothing can be said which has not been said before," but I believe that nothing is done which has not been done before. Since, then, the Deity is always of the same character, what madness is it not to see that in equalling the ancients in our sins we are also bound to meet equal punishment! So useful to us would be the lessons of ancient times if we would only look at them. But godlessness drags us elsewhere.

*Zwingli was probably thinking of the words of Terence: *"Nihil dictum quod non dictum prius,"* see Terence, *Eunuchus*, Prol. 10. But the form of his sentence seems to be influenced by a saying of Cicero: *"Nihil tam absurdum dici potest ut non dicatur a philosopho,"* for he writes: *"Nihil dici perhibet Poeta posse, quod non olim quoque dictum sit."*

But I return to my subject. This much good followed the insurrection of Jeroboam that the Jews then began to be an example of faithlessness and afterwards of divine rejection, and the door was opened to the Gentiles for the knowledge of God. For after the Babylonian captivity the Jews never came to their own, and finally under the Romans were utterly ruined on account of the crucifixion of Christ.

That God made man to let him fall fills many with wonder, but when they consider that matter more deeply and see how at the time He determined to fashion man, He also determined to redeem him through His Son (for as soon as He began to think of fashioning man, He saw how he was going to fall, to speak as we must after the manner of men), they at once understand that it was an inestimable blessing that man was so made that he could fall. Otherwise the Son of God would never have put on human nature. Thus good always follows from the works of God, even though the beginnings may not be free from some marked crime.

Jacob lamented that his son Joseph had been torn to pieces by wild beasts, when his brothers had committed their capital offence against him. But what a glad ending came to the matter as a whole! The father believed he would be killed by his grief, but to him and to all his many descendants that event became a source of life which in the beginning had been so wicked. Nor is God acting unjustly and violently when He afflicts the father with grief and the son with disaster.

Who would accuse the husbandman when of the forest which he maintains he keeps part for timbers and beams and posts, with which to build a house, and uses part to feed a fire? Is not the use of both parts profitable and advantageous, nay, even necessary to the owner? Indeed, is not the part which is consumed in the fire more necessary than that which goes into the building? So the pitiable misfortunes of Jacob and Joseph, most righteous of men, do not convict God of cruelty and violence, partly because all things are His more completely than the wood is the husbandman's, partly because all His works turn out happily, not at the time we desire, but at the seasonable time which He alone knows.

Herod perpetrated an atrocious deed when he slaughtered the young and wailing children [Matth. 2:16], but two blessings came therefrom for us,—first, that in Christ's escaping the plot, we see that God was guarding and leading, and that it is vain to fight against God, and, secondly, that an illustration was left us that impotent anger, cruelty, and fear of losing the kingdom raged in vain. Would that the princes of this century would oftener take that to heart!

In short, two sparrows which are bought for a farthing [Matth. 10: 29], are not separated so that one falls to the earth without God's providence, and this we see applies to all the chance events, as we call them. Again, the hairs of our heads are numbered [Lk. 12: 7], and this applies to the smallest and humblest and most indifferent of all things. Nothing, therefore, however worthless in our judgment, is of too little value for God's providence to have a care for it. Nothing can escape Him. As the householder who has his house filled with all kinds of goods and arms and furniture and instruments of the most varied assortment, yet knows where each thing is and in what condition, whether worn, bright or covered with rust, whether whole or broken, now brings out one thing to use and leaves another put away so that none can complain that it is used too much or too little nor can find fault with the householder that he uses the thing already worn oftener than that which is going to pieces from disuse; so God, the householder of the whole universe, must know all the things that are in His house and cannot neglect to look after them. He knows how one is dull through idleness and, as Cato says, perishes from lack of use. He knows how another is worn out with constant labors and calamities and yet uses him more and more. He employs one constantly for His glory and His work, then puts him aside, and takes into His hand* another, yet cannot be accused meanwhile of any injustice or lack of knowledge. Milo is banished,† Cato suffers defeat, David is prevented from entering his kingdom, Caleb, easily the bravest of all the Hebrews, is the last to meet his fate. Thus it pleases Providence to use until they are used up and consumed; while, meantime, Clodius and Piso, Manasseh and Absalom decline through pleasure and riotous living, and are ruined with the rust of idleness. Peter's

---

* ἐυχειρίζεται.

†This is Titus Annius Milo, banished from Rome in 52 B. C., in spite of Cicero's defense.

mother-in-law and Timothy,* both constant in the work of the Lord, fall ill with fever; Herod and Nero, both unclean with all lewdness, revel in health. Thus is Providence that disposes all things free to use the one constantly for the general good, setting up a pattern of living virtue and showing what a great thing virtue is and how it is acquired, or to show others as a sink and sewer of vices into which they all discharge their foul filth.

A man complains that he has been confined to his bed many months and learns shortly after how much good it brought to him or how much harm he has escaped. A house is burned but a better one is raised in its place, and he to whom this disaster happened is humbled by it. Girls dance, some to learn to move their limbs with proper grace, others to advertise by unseemly gesture to an admirer that their chastity is for sale. Cato becomes drunk for a month, to relieve the burden of his cares and thoughts. Anthony prolongs last night's intoxication, to plunge into lust and riot and destroy himself. Caesar seizes a monarchy, Brutus destroys one, the first sending headlong to ruin the Roman power already tottering to its fall, the other to tear out the tyranny of a Tarquin and make room for justice in a future democracy. So God uses for good all deeds both good and ill, though with the distinction that He turns to good for the elect even the evil they do, and the contrary for the rejected, while we meanwhile complain through impatience or ignorance. Thus all things happen, because all things are done by His dispensation and command.

EPILOGUE

Now that, having been borne over a vast sea of wonderful things, which we have just touched with the tips of our oars, because our fear made us fly rather than sail, we see at length some harbor, it is time to haul in the sails. I will, therefore, gather up the gist of all the above into a brief epilogue in the form of aphorisms as it were. And I will do it in such a way that one proposition will seem to follow necessarily from the other.

*Paul speaks of Timothy's infirmities, I. Tim. 5: 23, but there is no reference to fever.

If the Deity exists (and He must exist, for there is one first principle of all things, and this we call God), Providence also must exist.

Now this Deity or First Principle must be intelligent, good, and powerful. For unless He were intelligent, how could He create intellects or produce works in certain shapes? If He were not good, how could He exist by virtue of His own excellence? The cause of destruction and decay is to have had in one's constitution something unsound and defective.

And He must exist of Himself. For if He depended upon something else, that something else would be the supreme. I am speaking of the supreme above which nothing exists or can be imagined. If He were not powerful, He would not be the supreme good nor intelligent. For intelligence is power and moral excellence, and the good is nothing but the moral excellence, and moral excellence is nothing but right working. In general, unless that supreme thing which is God were supreme moral excellence and power, it would not be God.

That intelligence must be supreme just as much as the power. Intelligence is not supreme unless it knoweth all things. So also power is not supreme unless it means the ability to do all things, as far as lawful ability is concerned. The ability to do ill or to supplant one's self or to turn like a foe upon one's self or to be inconsistent with one's self is weakness, not power.

Since, therefore, He knows all things, He has the ideas of all things within Him, and since He can do all things, power over all things is at His command. Since, at the same time, He who knows all things and can do all things is as truly and simply good as He is intelligent and powerful, we have Providence at once before us. For He who knows all things and can do all things would not be good, unless He cared for all things in accordance with His wisdom and power.

And as He cares for all things, it must be that all things are of Him and in Him. Indeed it follows from His goodness and power that all things are of Him, through Him and in Him. For the things he cares for are certainly His. If they were another's, there would be two deities at the head of the universe. But in admitting that Providence is at the head of all things, we ought not to understand this in so confused a manner as certain of the theologians do, who, while recognizing Provi-

dence with their lips, yet in speaking of man allow him some
freedom, albeit very little, which little they insist upon having to
some extent defined.

But we ought to recognize Providence as so broad of scope
and so complete that, if there were anything which escaped Its
notice or could evade It, the Deity would either not be supreme
intelligence or not be supreme power. For in whatever quarter
He failed to know anything, at that point there would be a lack
of supreme and perfect wisdom, and at whatever point He could
not do anything, therein there would be a lack of supremely
effective excellence. If, on the other hand, He passed by anything knowingly and of His own will, or neglected anything
from idleness and laziness when He had the power to do it, He
would not be the supreme good. The latter must be so good
that absolutely no good can be imagined which is not from it,
in it and, in fact, itself. For as the Deity exists of Himself, so
there is nothing else which is of itself and not of Him. To be of
the universe is, therefore, to be of the Deity. Hence the opinion
of those philosophers is no absurdity who said that all things are
one, if we only understand them rightly, namely, in the sense
that to be of all things is to be of the Deity, in that all things are
endowed and maintained by Him. Hence nothing can be
neglected by Him. For, since all things are of Him and in Him,
there can be nothing of Him or in Him which is either unknown to or esteemed lightly by Him. His wisdom and goodness forbid it. From this we may infer that nothing so humble
exists that it has not existence from Divine Providence, and
nothing so humble can be thought of, nay dreamed of, that it is
not thought of by Divine Providence. That we, however, disregard many things, are ignorant of many things, in short,
despise many things, comes from the fact that we are not the
Deity. To Him nothing is mean, because He cannot be influenced by loathing. To be subject to loathing, is to be miserable. The Deity cannot be miserable, and therefore cannot be
influenced by loathing for anything.

And since Providence cares not only for things themselves
and their end, but also for the series of things, namely, the
course of action, life, performances, thoughts, and what leads
to or attends their end (for unless He did so, He would again
fall under suspicion of lack of knowledge or lack of good will),

it is clear that there is nothing, however worthless in our judgment, that is not thoroughly worthy in its kind and valuable in His sight.

How much more is that rarest of all works, man, not pitiable, as far as his kind is concerned! For, being endowed with intellect, he is raised in dignity above all the things that have sensation. For all except man are without the intellect which is chief among the prime endowments of the Deity. Since, therefore, man has it in common with the Deity, albeit as a loan, he is as much nobler than other creatures endowed with sensation, as the light is than darkness, the bird than the reptile, the soul than the body. Man so made that he can fall is, therefore, not the work of inattention or displeasure upon God's part, and we must hold the same view of the angels. For, since these two alone share with the Deity that intellect which is the supremely divine endowment, and nothing is so weak and lowly that it is not thoroughly good and valuable in its kind, man must have been made by Divine Providence most perfect in his class. What we thoughtlessly put down as misfortune is, therefore, really a blessing. The ability to fall has been implanted by the Deity. Therefore it was for the sake of some marked good.

Now, since the fall brought disaster, the fall itself was evidently not a blessing, nor can the disaster which followed from it be called a blessing either. But when we consider that which dawned upon man in consequence of the fall, namely, the knowledge of righteousness, which could not be learned except by gazing upon the face of unrighteousness, and this God could not show in His own person, we see that the fall was imposed upon our race for our good, that we might learn by the fall and by erring what could not have been done by earnest striving and endeavor.

Hence we may infer that man's nature was so constituted by the Deity that he should learn more clearly by his own fall what the true, the right, and the holy were. But if Divine Goodness had not provided a remedy for the fall of man at the time when It saw he was going to fall in this way, he would have been created with his endowment of intellect to no purpose. For what would have been the use of an intellect to him, if he was to perish like cattle or to be carried off to condign punishment?

But since man has been endowed with mind, it is clear that he was so endowed in order to have intercourse with the Supreme Mind. But all hope of such intercourse would have been cut off, if Providence had not provided a remedy for the fall. Nay, it would have been a random work for Providence to make man, unless He had determined to redeem him, at the time He saw he was going to fall. The counsels of God are everlasting. Therefore the plan of redemption is just as eternal as that of creation.

The election of God, therefore, stands secure and immovable, though he ordained to take the elect to Himself by means of His Son. For when righteousness was to be learned through its opposite, unrighteousness, and unrighteousness had not yet been born, though righteousness existed from everlasting, it could have been forced out prematurely through transgression of the law, and when it came forth, it had no real vital force. Whatever was born of it, therefore, must have the same condition, so that in the innermost heart of Providence the redemption must have been conceived as early as the creation of man.

If now election and redemption are co-eternal, election remains sure, even though the elect fall into such monstrous sins as characterize the godless and rejected. Only to the elect they are an incentive to regeneration, to the rejected a reason for despair. David, Paul, Mary Magdalene, the thief, and others are witnesses. Therefore, for the same reason, the course of our lives is foreseen and arranged from eternity, so that Esau, though mortal, yet under the guardianship of Providence, could not die until by his heinous crimes he had given proof of his rejection, and Abel could not possibly have been saved, since Providence had ordained to transport him hence as a spotless victim, sacrificed by the murderous hand of his brother.

Therefore, all the fortunes of life are to be borne with equanimity, but we must not explain Providence so as to say, "I will, therefore, indulge my inclinations. If I am elect, I shall attain felicity however I live." Men who speak thus give evidence either that they are not elect or that they have not yet acquired faith and the knowledge of God. For those who have the knowledge of God know that life must be ordered according to God's will, and those who have faith know that they are elect. And the elect, knowing this, cannot help seeing that they must refrain from whatever the law forbids. All things, therefore, work together for good to the elect, all things that have to do with them are done by Divine Providence, and there is nothing trivial enough to be trivial in God's dispensation and activity. Though the Catabaptists, who pretend to be so directed by the Spirit that if they stand still suddenly or go forward suddenly, they put it down to the Spirit, are not wrong (for we do not live, much less move, without the action of the Deity), yet however much things of this kind are done by God's impulse, they are, nevertheless, done to publish the rejection, hypocrisy, and folly of these people.

In a word, the proper recognition of God's providence is to the pious and God-fearing the greatest and most helpful antidote against the evils of both prosperity and adversity. For if riches, beauty, good health, children, honors and office fall to our lot, and we recognize them as given by the blessing of Providence, what a sense of rest and also of responsibility is called forth in our hearts! The first, when we see that even the good things of the body are given by the Deity and may be enjoyed, the second in that we can never guard enough against dispensing in a miserly manner what we have so generously received. From the one spring feelings of thankfulness, from the other watchfulness and the strictest integrity of life.

If, on the other hand, poverty, ugliness, illness, childlessness, lack of appreciation and defeats fall to our lot, and we attribute them to Providence, what comfort it brings us amid such hard lines! With what high spirit, think you, such a man rises above the world and scorns what is below him! Having said to himself, "These things are given me by Divine Providence. The cup must be drained, therefore, and the battle won by endurance with undaunted soul. You are God's tool. He wills to wear you out by use, not by idleness. Oh, happy man, whom He calls to His work!", he is ready to lay down his life, seeing that the whole world can promise nothing but varied misfortunes and hardships. Would not our friend gladly and willingly suffer the whole world, if he possessed it, to be taken from him again? Who would not give up a farm whence there was no return but profitless toil? To this point the religion of Providence leads. For when we see the things we are in the habit of calling goods of fortune, so variable and uncertain that they cannot remain in any fixed place, we shall, unless unbalanced in mind, bend all our efforts to standing firm ourselves and not tossing about with them, just as a ship seeks shelter from the blast behind some headland, gets ready and casts anchor there. Hence, what can strengthen us against the buffetings of these misfortunes but the contemplation of Providence? It suggests to the stoutest heart the thought, "Believe not that these things happen by accident. They are done at my command. They had to be. They could not be otherwise. If you bear them bravely, you will win a splendid triumph, not in the eyes of those who applaud even the most wicked, if he only achieves some bloody deed, but in the assembly of the blest, where of all the righteous, and brave, and wise, and learned, and pious, that have been since the foundation of the world, not one fails, where recklessness cannot sell itself for bravery, hypocrisy for religion, chatter for learning, empty oratory for wisdom. For there assemble only those who have sought the real gold of virtue, not dross. There presides a master of the contest whom none can deceive, and who himself cheats and deceives none. But if from idleness or despair you shun toil, none will be more disgraced than you. For the leader whom you betray cannot be deceived. He knoweth the secret recesses of the human heart. Your guilt cannot be denied or put upon some one else. For He sees written upon our foreheads, whatever we have done, and knows all the types of all things, so that no change or falsification in the superscription of the laws is possible. No hiding place can conceal the murder done by Cain and Romulus, the crime of David or Aegisthus. Hence, though before men you can give your sin another name, you cannot before God."

Balaam's example can give the strongest support to the wavering against this instability, through which our souls fail to put sufficient trust in the knowledge of Providence. Balak had summoned him to curse the people of Israel, and made him no mean promises. But God forbad him to undertake or utter anything against this people [Nu. 22:12]. See what conflicting emotions rend his soul! God says that his prophecy and curse shall have no force, and he believes God without question. On the other side are pressing upon him the king, heaping up promises, and greed like a dropsy forever thirsty and forever drinking, and they pull the man in different directions, so that however vigorously he declares he will not go, yet his greed urges him just as vigorously. At length God allowed him to set out, but on this condition, "Thou shalt contrive nothing against Israel." When they came to the real scene of action, what efforts are made both by the king and the prophet! They gaze now upon part, now upon the whole, of the Israelite army in vain attempts to bewitch it. But whatever is devised by the one in his fear of losing his kingdom or by the other in his fear of losing his reward, the cursing comes out according to the command and providence of God, not the desires of man.

Thus, I say, we struggle and waver in the matter of Providence. When It presents Itself before our eyes so plainly that we are forced even against our will to see It, regard It, and execute Its commands, we yet bid ourselves to hope for results according to our own desires. This recklessness sometimes goes so far that it promises us the treasures of the Indies even in spite of the Deity. But however we clamor and whatever we devise, the plans of God remain unchanged. Tyrants scheme, and restless peasants, far less skillful and happy in plotting than they, also scheme, the one to strangle the sprouting germ of the Gospel, that the boundless extortions with which they keep up every lewdness and luxury may not be brought to light, nor the distinction between right and wrong be seen, lest the wiles of their crooked lives and words be discovered, and they be no longer able to cover up their violence with the name of righteousness, if ever the people understand what force and right are, the others to see how under pretense of championing the Gospel they can aim at unrestrained wantonness rather than at the liberty of a free man. Does not greed urge them on as much as it did Balak and Balaam? But what purpose will finally succeed? Certainly not Balak's, however much he rages and fears for his kingdom, for the camp of Israel will be safe under the protection of the Lord; nor the purpose of Balaam boiling with greed, for the Gospel of Christ seeketh not wantonness nor wrong. But the purpose of the Lord will be victorious, in accordance with which He has determined to cleanse His Church of the worst rubbish, not to introduce it therein.

But, "why," you say, "did the Lord allow Balaam to set out, when He was going to bring his journey to naught?" That we poor fools might see that plans are vain when formed at the instigation of greed. For though they advance for a time towards success, they yet fail in the end. And also that we might see that this enmity between the flesh and the spirit can never be composed nor any agreement be reached that shall prevent either from working against the other according to its obstinate rebelliousness or its steadfast perseverance respectively. The angel blocks Balaam's way, the ass balks, and dashes her rider's foot against a wall. Why are these things done in this way by Providence, especially when he might have destroyed the rebellious prophet with one word? We might just as well ask why He made man to suffer so many hardships. Nay, why does He not take him to the realms above, as soon as he is born? But why do I say as soon as he is born? Why does He suffer him to be born, especially since there is hardly any distress equal to that of the birth of man?

Trees are things of beauty, but since they do not move, they are not of so high a class as the things that move. So the world was not made for no one to use it. And to whom has the use of it been assigned? To man. If he, as I showed early in my remarks, had never come into the world, would not that great work be in vain? Who would turn all these things upside down with building and tearing down, plowing and sowing? Man's course and constitution, then, have been so ordained by Providence that he tarries a while in this world like the fruit on the trees, and as that, when ripe, is gathered and stored away, so he, after the vicissitudes of this world, is stored in the heavenly granary. Meantime the flesh rebels. This must, therefore, be restrained, now by blows, now by gifts and rewards. By the one is offered to it the taste of future blessings, by the other that of future woes. Hence the terror or the comfort that visions bring. At one time, angels bring their comfort, that man may see how he is regarded by the Deity. Then again, the doings of evil spirits and goblins display their terrors, that man may not be indifferent to the warnings of the Deity and go over to the side of the perverted spirits.

In general, if we do not assign the will of the Deity as the reason why everything has been made, we say either that it was enough for God to delight in Himself without any created things, since they are of no use to Him, or that there is no Deity.

For that anything should owe its origin to any one in a sort of random way only argues imperfection in him, and if the Deity is imperfect, He is no Deity. Both of these notions are equally wicked and foolish. For this also is altogether incontrovertible, either Providence cares for all things and is nowhere idle or listless, or there is no Providence at all. And if there is no Providence, there is no Deity. And how wicked and foreign to man that is, everybody can see. For to what end would he in that case have been endowed with a soul? To what end understand and know the true, the right, and the holy? If we lived and died like cattle, we should not be endowed with intelligence nor with aspirations towards the right and just. But since we are such, there is an object for which we are such. That, therefore, must be something beyond all the things in this world. Nay, unless the supreme good is supreme intelligence and supreme moral excellence, it will not satisfy the human mind. It is clear, therefore, that by ascending in this way from our intelligence we arrive at the Deity, and when we have reached Him we have searched out Providence also. I pray that He may show Himself more and more to them that worship Him and are eager to see Him, and after the exile of this world vouchsafe to them the blessing of companionship with Him. Amen.

Therefore, to conclude at last, do you, Most Christian Prince, and ye other brethren who serve under the banner of Christ, turn often to the contemplation of Providence. There you will find rest and deliverance from all storms and blasts. It may be that all that I have said may seem to have been said hurriedly, and, as it were, cursorily, and that I have made larger use of argument than of the testimony of Scripture, though this is not lacking on occasion and is, indeed, the foundation for the whole argumentation which can in no wise be shaken.

I hope, however, that I have offered to beginners and the inexperienced something to help them to a clearer appreciation of the subject. I was forced to write and to read over my words in sections. Hence it is that on reading them over I find numerous repetitions, which yet I have not wished to expunge. For experienced men know what happens to those who are every moment distracted by the call of new duties, so that I doubt not you will take it all in good part. Do you, excellent

Prince, continue to live up to your reputation, and may Divine Providence preserve you safe and sound to His Church. I frankly recognize that you demanded this service of me, that either some elucidation or my folly might come to light.

ZURICH, August 20, 1530.

VI.

A Short and Clear Exposition of the Christian Faith Preached by Huldreich Zwingli, Written by Zwingli Himself Shortly Before His Death to a Christian King; Thus Far Not Printed by Anyone and Now for the First Time Published to the World. Matth. 11: "Come Unto Me," etc., 1536.

(Written July, 1531.)

[CHRISTIA- | NAE FIDEI A HULD- | RYCHO ZVINGLIO PRAE- DICA- | tae, brevis et clara expositio, ab ipso Zuin- | glio paulo ante mortem eius ad Regem | Christianum scripta, hactenus a ne- | mine excusa et nunc primum | in lucem aedita. | Matth. 11. | M. D. XXXVI. | 88 octavo pages, numbered by leaves 2-43. Signed p. 58, Tiguri Mense Julio, Anno 1531; pp. 59-85, containing an appendix: De Eucharistia et Missa, pp. 86-88 blank. Printed also in *Opera Zwinglii*, Tom II, fol. 550*b*-564*b;* Schuler and Schulthess ed., Vol. IV, pp. 42-78. A German edition, printed by Froschauer without date, but apparently in the same year, had the follow- ing title: *Eyn kurtze klare sum vnd erklärung des Christenen gloubes, von Huldrychen Zwinglin geprediget, vnd vnlang vor synem tod zu eynem Christenen Künig geschriben.* At the end: *Getruckt zu Zürich by Chris- toffel Froschouer.* 144 octavo pages, numbered by leaves; on pp. 3-6 a dedication of Leo Juda to Werner Steyner. A copy of this edition is in the library of Union Theological Seminary, New York City. A partial modern German translation in *Ulrich Zwingli eine Auswahl aus seinen Schriften*, Zurich 1918, pp. 797-816. The following English translation, made by Mr. Henry Preble, was revised by the editor.

As early as 1526 Zwingli had commended the reform of the Church to King Francis I of France, in the letter prefixed to his Commentary on the True and False Religion. From the beginning of the year 1530 the French ambassadors Paisrigault and Maigret were in negotiation with the magis- trates of Zurich, both for the purpose of avoiding a religious war and in the hope of luring them into an alliance with France. These ambassadors appeared to favor the Reformation. In the hope of opening a wider field for the Reformation in France, Zwingli entered into the scheme and prepared an outline of the advantages to be gained by the cities of Protestant Switzerland making an alliance with the French King for fifteen or twenty years for the defense of the Christian religion.

When Maigret asked Zwingli to send the King an exposition of his teaching, in order to remove the prejudice against it which had taken possession of the King's mind, Zwingli complied with his request. This exposition was taken to Paris in the summer of 1531 by Rudolph Collin, delegate of Zurich. Simmler in his collection of manuscripts, Vol. XXIX, has a note upon a copy of this book to the effect that the original copy written by Zwingli still exists in the Royal Library in Paris. "At the suggestion of Master Maigret, Royal Ambassador to the Swiss, an exposition of the Christian Faith was written by Zwingli in the month of July, 1531. It was published by Bullinger in the month of February, 1536."

Because Zwingli in this pamphlet counted among the saints in heaven even heathen of noble character and called them blessed and holy, the pamphlet caused great offense to the theologians of his own time as well as to those of later times. Luther was among the most severe in branding this view as infamous, while few besides Bullinger and the Swiss Reformers praised it.

A copy of the "Exposition," at one time belonging to the library of J. J. Breitinger, the distinguished antistes of Zurich, 1613-43, contains some additions, taken from an autograph ms. of Zwingli. These, noted at their proper places by Schuler and Schulthess, have been retained.

H. Bullinger, Zwingli's successor, who after Zwingli's death published the booklet in 1536, prefixed to it this prefatory note:

TO THE PIOUS READER GREETING.

Though that most faithful herald of the Gospel and most steadfast champion of Christian liberty, H. Zwingli, was clear, careful, and transparently plain in all he said, yet in this pamphlet he surpassed himself, as it were, and sang a sort of swan-song upon the true faith when near his death. He sets forth lucidly and briefly what true faith and pious religion are. He also makes answer to slanderers who defame the evangelical faith and preaching, and furnishes unto all Christian kings and princes a kind of complete defense of the true faith and religion. I was not willing to deprive you of so rich a treasure; do you receive in candid spirit what is offered with sincerely good purpose. The whole work has been copied from the autograph manuscript of the author himself. This I state, because the pamphlet comes out five years after its author's death. It has all been faithfully copied. Farewell. Zurich, in the month of February, of the year 1536.]

PREFACE

OF ALL the things that are rising up in this tumultuous age, nothing comes forward more auspiciously than inauspicious falsehood, most pious King, either because the evil spirit is always trying to crush out the life of every good seed at the start, or because the heavenly husbandman of souls as it were sharpens and promotes virtue and faith by means of vice and faithlessness, just as the Spartans, having taken some town by storm with much expenditure of toil and blood, ordered it not to be utterly destroyed, that they might not lack a grind-stone and stake,* as it were, by which to train their soldiers. So also the Lord suffers us to be tried and troubled in manifold ways that we may prove our mettle to Him. For how can one become brave and temperate save in the midst of perils and an abundance of luxury? In the same way the truth that has begun to raise her head becomes brighter and rises higher under the attacks of falsehood. For as this thrusts at her from all sides and pours out all its poison upon her, she is forced to shake herself free, wipe off the stains and defend her limbs, and thus it comes to pass that the mask of falsehood and the charming face of truth herself are more and more displayed and show themselves as they are. But enough of preface.

The fear has befallen me that, by the more than empty and lying insinuations of certain faithless persons, your clemency may be sorely tried, for I know it cannot be really provoked. The more faithless they are, the more they do not report but mangle the truth to many. And they report us in countless ways as treading religion under foot and treating with scorn the holy office and dignity of kings and magistrates. How true all that is I beg your fairness to pronounce when you have heard me set forth to the best of my ability the sources of our faith, the laws and customs of our churches, and our reverence for our rulers.

And there is nothing so well within a man's power as the task to set forth his faith. For since faith is, as the apostle defines it, that power of the soul, that assurance and certainty, with which one trusts unwaveringly in the unseen God, who can be so dull and slow as not to know how to set forth whether he has trust in a thing or not, especially as faith is the daughter of truth? Every man trusts in that which he knows to be absolutely true. And since God alone is true, if any one feels and experiences that he recognizes this, how shall he not be

*The Spartan soldiers learned to fight by attacking a stake set in the ground.

able to set forth this trust in a few words? This, then, is my
thought in regard to God and divine things:

[CHAPTER I]

REGARDING GOD AND HIS WORSHIP

I.   All the things that are are either created or uncreated.
The one and only uncreated thing is God, for there can be but
one uncreated thing.   If there were several uncreated things,
there would be several eternals, for the uncreated and the eternal
are so closely allied that as one is so is also the other.   For if
there were several eternals, there would be several infinites, for
these are so like unto and allied with each other that whatever is
eternal is also infinite and whatever is infinite is also eternal.
Now, since there can be only one infinite (for as soon as we
admit two infinite substances each becomes finite), it is certain
that the one and only uncreated thing is God.   On this depends
also the origin, source and foundation of the first article of our
faith, that is, when we say, "I believe in one God, the Father
Almighty, Creator of heaven and earth," we confess and declare
that we have an infallible faith, since it is one resting securely
upon one only Creator.   The heathen and the unbelievers who
trust in created things are forced to confess that they may be
deceived in their faith or belief, seeing that they trust in
created things.   But they that trust in the Creator and Source
of all things, who never began to be, but called all other things
into existence, these cannot be convicted of error.   This also is
certain, that nothing which is a created thing can be the object
and basis of that unwavering and indubitable power which is
faith.   For whatever has begun to be at some time was not.
When, therefore, it was not, how could anyone have trusted in
what did not yet exist?   Things, then, that have had a beginning cannot be the natural object or basis of faith.   Only the
eternal, infinite, and uncreated Good, therefore, is the true basis
of faith.

Hence, all that confidence falls to the ground by which certain people lean thoughtlessly upon even the most sacred of
created things or the most holy of sacraments.   For that in

which one should trust with absolute assurance must be God. But if one should trust in a created thing, then the created thing would have to be the Creator, and if in sacraments, then the sacraments would have to be God, so that not only the sacrament of the Eucharist, but baptism and the laying on of hands also would be God. How absurd that is to learned, to say nothing of pious men, not only the learned but any one endowed with intelligence can judge. In order, therefore, to help the theologians reach the truth, I shall gladly hold this torch before them. When they say, created things are to be employed but only God enjoyed, they say nothing else than what I also say, if they do not unthinkingly put a foreign meaning into their own words. For if God alone is to be enjoyed, He alone also is to be trusted, for that is to be trusted which is to be enjoyed, not that which is to be employed.

II. From this, most gracious King, you see clearly that we do not dismiss the saints nor the sacraments, nor move them from their place, as some men say that we do, but that we keep and guard them in their proper place and dignity, that no man may use them wrongly. We do not insult Mary, the Virgin Mother of God, when we forbid that she be adored with divine honors; but when we would attribute to her the majesty and power of the Creator, she herself would not permit such adoration. For true piety has one and the same character among all men and is the same in all, because it originates by one and the same Spirit. It cannot even be imagined, therefore, that any created being should at the same time be pious and suffer the worship due the Deity to be offered to himself. So also the Virgin Mother of God will as much the less accept the worship due the Deity as she is high above all created beings and reverently devoted to God, her Son. It is a mark of insanity in godless men and demons when they allow divine honors to be paid to them. This is proved by the images of demons and the arrogance of Herod, of whom the first, by teaching worship of themselves, deceived the world to its destruction, and the second, not refusing the divine honors offered him, was struck with phthiriasis,* that he might learn to recognize the feebleness of man.

* φθειρίασις, i. e., the *morbus pedicularis*, or the louse disease; see Josephus, *Antiquities*, XIX, 8, 2, who relates of Herod Agrippa that his

But we venerate and cherish the sacraments as signs and symbols of sacred things, not as if they were themselves the things of which they are signs. For who can be so ignorant as to say that a sign is the thing it signifies? In that case the word "ape," which I write here would place before the eyes of Your Majesty a real live ape. But because the sacraments signify real things, which really and naturally happened at some time, I say they represent these things, call them to mind and, as it were, set them before our eyes. Understand me correctly, I beg, O King! Christ by His death atoned for our sins. The Eucharist is a commemoration of this thing, as He Himself said—"This do in remembrance of me." By this commemoration all the benefits are presented which God has vouchsafed unto us through His Son. Furthermore, by the symbols themselves, namely the bread and wine, Christ Himself is, as it were, presented to our eyes, so that not only the ears but the eyes and the mouth see and perceive the Christ whom the soul has present within and rejoices in. This, therefore, we say and teach is the legitimate worship of the saints and the sacraments, which Christ Himself transmitted and taught us. "If ye are the children of Abraham," He said [John 8: 37], "do the works of Abraham." This is, therefore, the example that we ought to follow in the case of all saints and holy men. Thus, if any of the prophets or holy men gave us divine warnings to drink, as it were, we should receive what has been given and set forth to us by the divine Spirit with the same religious devotion with which they received and imparted it. If they adorned religious devotion by sanctity of life, we should follow in their footsteps and be pious, holy, and innocent as they were.

In regard to baptism He says, "Baptize them in the name of the Father and of the Son and of the Holy Ghost" [Matth. 28: 19]; in regard to the Eucharist, "This do in remembrance of me" [Luke 22: 17]; and by the mouth of Paul, "We are all one bread and one body of the faithful" [I Cor. 10: 17]. It is not hinted here, either in regard to the worship of the saints or

flatterers called him a god, and, not rebuking them, was struck by a disease which ended his life after five days' suffering. See also Acts 12: 23. Only tyrants and great persecutors are reported as having been struck by this loathsome, but fabulous, disease, so e. g., Antiochus Epiphanes, see I Macc. 6: 9; and Herod the Great, see Josephus, l. c., XVII, 6, 5, and Farrar, Life of Christ, New York, 1894, p. 34.

in regard to the institution of the sacraments, that they have the power and grace which belongs to God alone. Since, then, the Deity has never conferred on created things the power which we attribute to them, it is clearly frivolous for us to teach that either the saints or the sacraments remove sins and bestow grace upon us. For who remitteth sins save God alone? Or from whom is every perfect gift, as St. James puts it [James 1: 17], save from the Father of lights and of all good? We teach, therefore, that the sacraments should be cherished as sacred things signifying the most holy things, both such as have been done and such as we ought to do and show forth. Thus baptism signifies both that Christ has washed us by His blood, and that we ought to put Him on, as Paul teaches [Gal. 3: 27], that is, live according to His example. In like manner the Eucharist signifies both all that has been given to us by divine bounty through Christ, and that we ought in gratitude to embrace our brethren with that Christian love with which Christ has taken us to Himself, cared for us, and secured salvation for us. But whether the natural body of Christ is eaten in the Eucharist will be discussed at length later.

To sum up:—This is the fountainhead of my religion, to recognize God as the uncreated Creator of all things, who solely and alone has all things in His power and freely giveth us all things. They, therefore, overthrow this first foundation of faith, who attribute to the creature what is the Creator's alone. For we confess in the creed that it is the Creator in whom we believe. It cannot, therefore, be the creature in whom we should put our trust.

III. I hold further in regard to God this view:—Since we know that God is the Source and Creator of all things, it cannot be that we should understand that there is anything either before Him or along with Him that is not from Him. For if there could be anything which was not from Him, He would not be infinite, for He would not extend to where that other was that was outside of Him. Hence, though we see that in the Scriptures God is called Father, Son, and Holy Ghost, these are not different creatures or gods, but these three are one, one essence, one existence,* one force and power, one knowledge and providence, one goodness and kindness,—the names or

* οὐσία.

persons are three, but they are all and each one and the same
God. This God we know is by nature good, for whatever He is,
He is by nature. Moreover that is good, which is gentle and
righteous. Gentleness without righteousness would be no longer
gentleness, but carelessness or fear. On the other hand, if you
do not temper righteousness with goodness or equity, it becomes
the utmost injustice and violence. Since, therefore, we recognize
that God is by nature good, we confess at the same time that He
is mild, gentle and bountiful, as well as holy, righteous, and
inviolable. Since, then, He is righteous, He must abhor contact with evil. Hence we may argue that inasmuch as we poor
mortals are not only defiled with sin but saturated with evil, we
can have no hope of fellowship and friendship with Him.

Again, since He is good, He must just as much temper all
His thoughts and acts with equity and goodness. This was the
cause of His clothing His only begotten Son with flesh, that He
might not only show to, but bestow upon, the whole world
these two things, redemption and renewal. For, since His goodness, that is, justice and mercy, is inviolable, that is, firm and
immutable, His justice required atonement, His mercy pardon,
and pardon a new life. Therefore the Son of the most high
King put on the cloak of the flesh and came forth to be made a
victim (for in His divine nature He could not die) to placate
unchangeable justice and reconcile it with those who even in
their own innocence did not dare to come into the presence of
God, because of their consciousness of guilt. And this He did
because He is gentle and merciful, and these virtues could just
as little suffer rejection of His creation as justice could permit
freedom from punishment. Righteousness and mercy were
mingled together, therefore, that the one should furnish the
victim and the other accept it for the atonement of all sins.
From what class of beings, then, was this victim to be chosen?
From the angels? But what did the transgression of man
concern them? From men? But they were all guilty before
God, so that whichever one of them had been marked out for
the sacrifice would have been unable to accomplish it on account
of his defilement. For the lamb, which typically represented*
this victim, had to be altogether sound†, pure and clean. The
divine goodness, therefore, took from itself that which it would

* τυπικῶς promittebat   † ἄμωμος.

give to us. It clothed its own Son with the weakness of our flesh, that we might see that its bounty and mercy were equally supreme with its holiness or righteousness. For what has He left ungiven who giveth us Himself, as the divine Paul has said [Rom. 8: 32]? If He had made an angel or a man the victim, what He gave would have been outside of Himself. There would, therefore, have been something greater left, which He might have given, namely, Himself, but which He had not given.

When, therefore, supreme goodness intended to bestow the supreme gift, it gave the most precious thing it could bring out of its treasure chest, namely, itself, that the heart of man, ever eager for something greater, should not even have a way left to wonder how this angelic or human victim could be so great as to be sufficient for all, or how one could put unshaken trust in a creature. The Son of God has, therefore, been given to us as a confirmation of His mercy, as a pledge of pardon, as the price of righteousness, and as a rule of life, to make us sure of the grace of God, and to teach us the law of living. Who could worthily extol the greatness of this divine goodness and generosity? We had deserved to be disowned, and He honors us with being chosen. We had destroyed the way of life, and He has restored it. Thus, then, we have been redeemed and renewed by divine goodness so completely as to be acceptable through His mercy, and to be justified and blameless through His atoning sacrifice.

[CHAPTER II]

REGARDING CHRIST THE LORD

IV.   I believe and teach that this Son of God Himself took on human nature in such manner that His divine nature was not lost or changed into human nature, but each nature is in Him so truly, properly and naturally, that nothing has been diminished of His divine nature, so that He should not be truly, properly and naturally God. Moreover, His human nature has not passed over into divine nature so that He should not be truly, properly and naturally man, save only as far as inclination to sin is concerned. Thus, in general, in so far as He is

God, He is God with the Father and the Holy Spirit in such manner that none of His divine attributes has suffered because of the assumption of human feebleness, and, in so far as He is man, He is thus man that He has whatever belongs to true and literal human nature, so that nothing has been taken from it on account of the union with the divine nature, save the disposition to sin.   Hence it is that both natures so reflect their own character in all their words and deeds that the religious mind sees without trouble what is to be credited to either nature, however rightly the whole is said to belong to the one Christ. "Christ hungered," is said rightly [Matth. 4: 1], since He is God and man; yet He did not suffer hunger according to His divine nature.   "Christ cured diseases and ailments" [Matth. 4: 23], is said rightly; yet these things belong to divine power, not to human, if you weigh them properly.   And yet no division of person follows on account of the difference of natures, any more than when we say a man thinks and sleeps.   Here, though the power to think belongs to the mind only, and the necessity of sleeping to the body, yet the man is not on that account two persons, but one.   For unity of person is brought about even from very different natures.   In general, I confess that God and man are one Christ, just as one man consists of a soul endowed with reason and a dull body, as Saint Athanasius has taught. He took up human nature into the unity of the hypostasis or person of the Son of God, not as if the humanity taken on were a separate person, and the eternal divinity were also a separate person.   The person of the eternal Son of God assumed humanity into and by virtue of its own power, as holy men of God have truly and clearly shown.

V.   And I believe that this humanity was conceived of the virgin, made pregnant by the Holy Spirit, and was brought forth by preserving her perpetual virginity,* that He, who from

---

*Zwingli still believed, with the Catholic Church, in the perpetual virginity of Mary. Birth from a virgin was necessary, according to him, (see *De vera et falsa religione, Werke*, III, 686-7), because (1) the divinity does not tolerate any taint. But, if a virgin had conceived through human agency, would not the birth have been tainted? (2) The sacrifice had to be without a taint, but natural birth is tainted. The perpetual virginity of Mary was necessary to remove even the suspicion of taint. He tries to prove the latter from Isa. 7: 14 and Ez. 44: 2, by a very artificial exegesis. See also his sermon "Von der ewig reinen Magd Maria," *Werke*, I, 391-428.

eternity was born Lord and God from a father without mother, might be born into the world as deliverer and healer of souls from a virgin mother, in order that a holy and spotless offering might be made to Him unto whom all altars, loaded with animals, smoked to no purpose, and men might repent of sacrificing beasts and turn to the offering of their hearts, when they would see that God had prepared and offered to Himself a victim in the form of His own Son.

VI. I believe that Christ suffered, being nailed to the cross under Pilate, the governor, but that the man only felt the pangs of the suffering, not the God, who, as He is invisible*, so is also subject to no suffering† or sensation. "My God, why hast thou forsaken me?" [Matth. 27: 46], is the cry of pain, but "forgive them; for they know not what they do" [Luke 23: 34], is the voice of the unimpaired divinity. And He suffered for the expiation of our sins by the most ignoble sort of punishment, that He might leave no depth of humiliation untried and unsounded.

VII. If He had not "died and been buried," who would believe that He was a real man? Therefore the apostolic Fathers added in the creed, "descendit ad inferos," i. e., He descended to those below, using the expression as a circumlocution to signify real death. For to be reckoned with those below is to have gone from the land of the living, and shows that the efficacy of His redemption extended even to those below. And this St. Peter hints at when he says [I Pet. 3: 19 f.] that the Gospel was preached also to them that are dead, that is, to those below who following the example of Noah from the foundation of the world, believed the warnings of God, when the wicked were scornful.

VIII. On the other hand, if He had not risen again from death to life, who would believe that one who had been put to death, so that there was no life or force left in Him, was a real God? I believe, therefore, that the real Son of God really died as far as His human nature was concerned, that we might be made sure of the expiation of our sins. I believe, that He also really rose again from the dead, that we might be sure of everlasting life. For in all that Christ is, He is ours; all that He accomplished is ours. For God so loved the world that He gave

---

* ἀόρατος.   † ἀνάλγητος.

His only begotten Son to quicken us into life [John 3:16]. When, therefore, He rose again, He rose again for us, beginning by it our own resurrection. Hence also Paul calls Him "the first fruits of them that sleep" [I Cor. 15:20], that is, of the dead, for when He lives, being dead, He shows that we also live when we die, for this is the signification of the word "to rise again" in Hebrew—to remain, persist, endure. Hence Paul reasons as to both alternatives thus: If Christ rose again, that is, lived when He was believed to be dead, and took up His body again, there is for us a resurrection of the dead. Behold, most learned King, the strength of the reasoning lies in this, that Christ is ours, and that every activity of His is ours. Otherwise, "Christ rose again; therefore we also rise again," would not follow any more than if one argued, "The king has power to free from punishment him whom the judge has sentenced; therefore every one has this power." Hence this would not follow either, "Since Christ did not rise again, neither shall we rise again," for Christ can live and rise again by His own power, which we cannot do by ours. But, [since Paul argues] if Christ had not risen again, there would be no resurrection for us, it is clear that He made the power of His resurrection ours and all men's. This is what holy men had in view when they said* that Christ's body nourishes us unto the resurrection, by which they simply wished to show that when Christ, who is wholly ours, rose again, we were thereby made sure that we also live in the spirit when dead in the body, and shall some day live again with the same body.

IX. Furthermore, in that this same Christ of ours has ascended into heaven and taken His seat at the right hand of the Father, as I believe unhesitatingly, He promises that we also who hasten thither as soon as we die, shall one day enjoy everlasting bliss there also in the body. And as He sitteth there until He shall come for the general judgment of the whole world, so our souls and those of all the blessed are with Him without bodies until the aforesaid judgment, at the beginning of which we shall all put on again the garment of the body that we have laid aside, and with it depart either to the everlasting marriage of our bridegroom or to the everlasting torments of the enemy, the Devil. Here I will set forth two things to you, as I think

*e. g., Irenaeus, see p. 53, note †.

about them, most gentle King.

[CHAPTER III]

PURGATORY

The one is, that, since Christ did not experience the torments of the regions below, as St. Peter teaches, Acts. 2 : 27, but having gone through death ascended to heaven, we also, when freed from the bonds of the body, shall go thither without delay, hindrance, or new torment, if only we have had sincere faith; and that those who hold the threat of the torments of the fire of purgatory over mankind, already miserable enough without that, have dared to feed their own greed rather than the souls of the faithful. For, in the first place, they utterly make void and destroy Christ's mission. For if Christ died for our sins, as He Himself and the apostles imbued with His spirit taught, and as the nature of our religion compels us to confess, according to which mankind is saved by the grace and goodness of God, how could it be admitted that we should be compelled to make atonement ourselves? For if those are at variance with Christ who put their trust in works, as St. Paul tells us, how much more do those cast off and bring to naught Christ who teach that men's sins are to be atoned for by their own torment? For if good deeds cannot win blessedness, but torment wins it, the goodness of the Deity is called in question as if He delighted in afflictions and tribulations, and were averse to gentleness and kindness. Secondly, if Christ does not take away the penalty and punishment due to sin, why was He made man? Why did He suffer? The distinction some theologians make, that we have been redeemed from guilt but not also from punishment, is a frivolous invention, indeed, one insulting to God. For not even a human judge inflicts punishment where there is no guilt. As soon, therefore, as guilt is remitted by God, punishment is done away with. Third, since Christ himself taught that those who believe have eternal life and those that trust in Him who sent Christ to us come not into judgment but have already passed from death into life, it becomes evident that this delay in torment, which the Papists put upon souls departing hence, is a baseless invention.

[CHAPTER IV]

THE PRESENCE OF CHRIST'S BODY
IN THE SUPPER*

The other thing which I have undertaken to set forth here is this,—that that natural, material body of Christ's, in which He suffered here and now sitteth in heaven at the right hand of the Father, is not eaten literally and in its essence, but only spiritually, in the Lord's Supper, and that the teaching of the Papists, that Christ's body is eaten by us having the size and the exact qualities and nature it had when He was born, suffered, and died, is not only frivolous and stupid but impious and blasphemous. For, in the first place, it is certain that Christ took on, excepting always the inclination to sin, a real humanity consisting of body and soul, just as we do. From this it follows that all the characteristics and endowments that belong to the nature of the human body were most truly present in His body. For what He took on for our sake was derived from us, so that He is wholly ours, as I have said before. From this two incontrovertible corollaries follow, one, that the characteristics which are present in our body are also present in Christ's body, the other, that whatever there is in Christ's body, that was corporeal, belongs also to our bodies. For if anything which has to do with the nature and character of the body were in His body but lacking to ours, He would seem to have assumed that not for our sake. For what reason? Because there is nothing in the realm of body except man that is capable of everlasting blessedness. Hence that point which I touched upon before, that Paul proves our resurrection from Christ's and Christ's from ours. For when he says, "If the dead rise not, then is not Christ raised" [I Cor. 15:16], how can this reasoning be sound? For, since Christ is God and man, who would not at once make answer to

*Zwingli seems not to have intended to put into this defense of his position this section upon the presence of Christ's body in the Supper and upon the power of the sacraments, in its entirety, for he added in the margin the note, "You are not to go on with the account here, but to put in something else that seems appropriate in place of this." But this is what Bullinger attached to this Defense by way of appendix along with the statement on the Eucharist. The credit of this observation belongs to J. J. Breitinger.

Paul, "Your reasoning is crooked,* theologian? For Christ's body can and should rise again, being united with divinity, but ours, being without divinity, have not the same power." But Paul's reasoning has its strength in this that whatever Christ's body has, as far as nature, endowment and characteristics of body are concerned, it has for us, as our archetype as it were, and it is ours. Hence, "Christ's body rose again; therefore our bodies will also rise again," and "We rise again; therefore Christ also rose," follow logically. From these sources drew Augustine, that pillar of theologians, when he said that Christ's body must be in some particular place in heaven in virtue of its character as real body.† And again, "Christ's body which rose from the dead must be in one place."‡ Christ's body, therefore, is not in several places any more than our bodies are. And this view is not mine, but the apostle's and Augustine's and that of faith in general, which, though we had not witnesses to the fact, would suggest that Christ became in all things like ourselves. For He took on human weakness for our sake, and was found as man in character, that is, in endowments, characteristics and qualities. By all this, most glorious King, it is made clear to you incidentally, I think, how unfairly they brand me as a heretic in respect to the sacrament of the Eucharist, when I have never taught a single word that I have not drawn from the divine Scriptures or the holy theologians.

But I return to the subject, since from that reasoning which rests upon the holy Scriptures it is established that Christ's body must in a natural, literal and true sense be in one place, unless we venture foolishly and impiously to assert that our bodies also are in many places, we have wrung from our opponents the admission that Christ's body, according to its essence, in itself, naturally and truly sits at the right hand of the Father,

---

* παραλογίζῃ.

†See Augustine, *Letters* 187, c. 13, §41: "Doubt not that Christ is wholly present everywhere as God, and is in the same temple of God as indwelling God, and in some one place in heaven on account of the measure [or limit] of a true body." Migne, *Patr. Lat.*, XXXIII, 848.

‡The whole sentence reads: "For the body of the Lord in which He rose can be contained in one place [or rather, according to the reading of Gratian, Peter Lombard, and Thomas Aquinas, when quoting the passage, *must be in one place*]; his truth is spread abroad everywhere." See Com. on John, tract, 30, §1.

and it is not in this way in the Supper, so that those who teach the contrary drag Christ down from heaven and the Father's throne. For all the learned have condemned as exploded and impious the opinion which some* have ventured to maintain, that Christ's body is just as much everywhere as His divinity. For it cannot be everywhere unless in virtue of being infinite in nature, and what is infinite is also eternal. Christ's humanity is not eternal; therefore it is not infinite. If it is not infinite, it must be finite. If it is finite, it is not everywhere. But putting aside these things, which I have introduced in order not to fail to meet the demands of philosophical argumentation, if you should happen to come upon such, O King, let me come to the impregnable testimonies of Scripture.

I have made it plain enough before that whatever is said in the sacred Scriptures of Christ is said in such way of the whole and entire Christ that even if it may be easily detected to which of His natures the thing said applies, yet Christ is not divided into two persons, however much each nature possesses its own peculiarity. For having two natures does not sever unity of person, as is clear in the case of man. And again, even if the things that belong to Christ's divinity are attributed to His humanity, and, on the other hand, the things that belong to His humanity to His divinity, yet the natures are not confused, as if the divinity had degenerated and been weakened to humanity, or the humanity changed into divinity. This will be made more transparently clear by the testimonies of Scripture:

"And she brought forth her first born son . . . and laid him in a manger" [Luke 2: 7]. That Christ who is God and man was born of a virgin, no one denies on account of the unity of person. And therefore I hold that she is properly called ϑεοτόκον, i. e., the mother of God. Yet His divine nature none but the Father begot, as in the case of man, also, the mother brings forth the body, God alone the soul. Nevertheless, the man is said to be generated by his parents. Furthermore, that He who occupies and fills the heavens and the realms below was laid in a manger applies to the human nature in like manner. But when these things are attributed to the whole Christ,—His being born and laid in the manger—no difficulty arises, and that

*Namely the Lutherans, who teach the ubiquity of Christ's body.

because of the conjunction and union of the two natures in one person.

"He ascended into heaven" [Mark 16: 19]. This equally applies to the humanity, in the main, though the humanity was not carried there without the divinity; indeed the latter carried and the former was carried. This humanity, as has been said, remains circumscribed forever; otherwise it would cease to be true humanity. But the divinity is unlimited and uncircumscribed forever; hence it does not move from place to place, but is everywhere and remains the same forever.

"Behold, I am with you even unto the end of time" [Matth. 28: 20], applies in the main to His divinity, for His humanity has been borne to heaven.

"Again, I leave the world, and go to the Father" [John 16: 28]. Truth itself compels us to take this of Christ's humanity, in the main, and indeed literally. For it is God who is speaking, and what He says must be true. Which nature in Him, then, leaves the world? Not the divine, for that moveth not from its place, not being contained in a place. Therefore, the human leaves it, and since it has left the world, you will understand, O King, as regards natural, substantial, local presence, it is not here. The body of Christ is, therefore, not eaten by us, literally or in substance, and all the more not quantitatively, but only sacramentally and spiritually.

"I shall not be in the world hereafter," for that is the equivalent of: καὶ οὐκ ἔτι εἰμὶ ἐν τῷ κόσμῳ, "and now I am no more in the world" [John 17: 11], an expression which absolutely dispels any cloud of uncertainty, so that He is not to be looked for in the world according to His humanity in literal, substantial, bodily presence, but only in a spiritual and sacramental sense.

"Ye men of Galilee, why stand ye gazing up into heaven? This same Jesus, which is taken up from you into heaven, shall so come in like manner as ye have seen him go into heaven" [Acts 1: 11]. In this passage we have Him plainly taken up from the disciples into heaven. He has gone away, therefore, and is not here. But how has He gone away? In a bodily and literal sense, and as He really is by the essence of His humanity. When, therefore, they say, "shall so come," He means in bodily and literal sense and in substance. But when shall He so come?

Not when the Church celebrates the Supper, but when she is to be judged by Him at the end of the world. Therefore the view is irreligious that maintains that Christ's body is eaten in the Supper in a bodily, literal, substantial and even quantitative sense, because such view is opposed to the truth, and what is opposed to the truth is impious and irreligious. These few brief remarks will be enough, I think, to enable your wisdom, which in its ready skill can estimate the whole from one of its parts, to see that out of the mouth of the Lord we are forced to consider how Christ's body is present in the Supper. Oecolampadius and I have treated the matter at length elsewhere and in many writings to various people, indeed, have waged long war, but it would be distasteful to repeat all this. But truth is carrying off the victory and breaking through daily more and more. Now that I may set forth what it is to eat spiritually and sacramentally, I shall make a digression.

To eat the body of Christ spiritually is nothing else than to trust in spirit and heart upon the mercy and goodness of God through Christ, that is, to be sure with unshaken faith that God is going to give us pardon for our sins and the joy of everlasting blessedness on account of His Son, who was made wholly ours, was offered for us, and reconciled the divine righteousness to us. For what can He refuse who gave His only begotten Son?

To eat the body of Christ sacramentally, if we wish to speak accurately, is to eat the body of Christ in heart and spirit with the accompaniment of the sacrament. I wish to set the whole matter, before the eyes of Your Highness, O King. You eat the body of Christ spiritually, though not sacramentally, every time you comfort your heart in its anxious query:—"How will you be saved? You sin daily, and yet are daily hastening towards death. After this life there is another, for how could this soul be destroyed with which we are endowed here and which is so solicitous about the hereafter? How could all this light and knowledge be turned into darkness and forgetfulness? Since, then, the life of the soul is everlasting, what sort of life is coming to my dear soul? A happy or a miserable life? I will examine my life and search out what it deserves, to be happy or miserable." Then when you see such a host of things that we men are in the habit of doing from passion and desire, you shudder and as far as your own righteousness and integrity are concerned declare yourself in your own opinion unworthy of everlasting happiness, and straightway despair of it. When, I say, you comfort your troubled heart thus:—"God is good; he that is good must be righteous and merciful and equitable, for righteousness without equity or mercy is the height of injustice mercy without righteousness is indifference, wantonness and the destruction of all discipline. Since, therefore, God is righteous, His righteousness must receive satisfaction for my sins. Since He is merciful, I must not despair of forgiveness. I have an infallible pledge of both of these in His only begotten Son, our Lord Jesus Christ, whom He has given to us out of His mercy to be ours. And He has sacrificed himself to the Father for us, to appease His eternal righteousness. Thus we are sure of His mercy and of the atonement for our sins made to His righteousness by none other than His own Son whom He has given to us out of love." When with this confidence you cheer up your soul, tossed on the floods of fear and despair, saying, "Why art thou sad, my soul? God, who alone bestows blessedness, is thine, and thou art His. For when thou wast His work and creation, and yet hadst perished by thy sin, He sent His Son to thee, and made Him like thee, sin excepted, that, relying upon the rights and privileges of this great brother and companion, thou mightest dare even to demand everlasting salvation as thy right. What devil can frighten me so that I shall fear him, when He is at hand to help me? Who shall take from me what God Himself has bestowed, in giving His Son as pledge and surety?"—When you comfort yourself thus, I say, you eat His body spiritually, that is, you stand unterrified in God against all the attacks of despair, through confidence in the humanity He took upon Himself for you.

But when you come to the Lord's Supper with this spiritual participation and give thanks unto the Lord for His great kindness, for the deliverance of your soul, through which you have been delivered from the destruction of despair, and for the pledge by which you have been made sure of everlasting blessedness, and along with the brethren partake of the bread and wine which are the symbols of the body of Christ, then you eat Him sacramentally, in the proper sense of the term, when you do internally what you represent externally, when your heart is refreshed by this faith to which you bear witness by these symbols.

But those are improperly said to eat sacramentally who eat the visible sacrament or symbol in public assembly to be sure, but have not faith in their hearts. These, therefore, call down judgment, that is, the vengeance of God, upon themselves by eating, because they hold not in the same high esteem, in which it is rightly held by the pious, the body of Christ, that is, the whole mystery of the incarnation and passion, and even the Church itself of Christ. For a man ought to test himself before he partakes of the Supper, that is, examine himself and ask both whether he so recognizes and has received Christ as the Son of God and his own Deliverer and Saviour that he trusts Him as the infallible author and giver of salvation, and whether he rejoices that he is a member of the Church of which Christ is the head. If as an unbeliever he unites with the Church in the Supper, as if he had faith in these things, is he not guilty of the body and blood of the Lord? Not because he has eaten them in the literal, material sense, but because he has borne false witness to the Church that he has eaten them spiritually when he has never tasted them spiritually. Those, therefore, are said to eat merely sacramentally, who use the symbols of thanksgiving, to be sure, in the Supper, but have not faith. For this they are in more terrible condemnation than the rest of the unbelievers, because those simply do not acknowledge Christ's Supper, while these pretend to acknowledge it. He sins doubly who without faith celebrates the Supper. He is faithless and presumptuous, while the mere unbeliever is destroyed through his unbelief like the fool through his folly.

Furthermore, there has for some time been a sharp controversy among us as to what the sacraments or symbols do or can do in the Supper; our opponents contending that the sacraments give faith, and bring to us the natural body of Christ, causing it to be eaten in real presence. We hold a different view not without authoritative support. First, because none but the Holy Spirit giveth faith, which is confidence in God, and no external thing giveth it. Yet the sacraments do work faith, historical faith; for all festivals, trophies, nay, monuments and statues, work historical faith: that is, call to mind that a certain thing once took place, the memory of which is thus refreshed, as was the case with the festival of the Passover, among the Hebrews and of the *seisachtheia, i. e.,* removal of debts,* among the Athenians, or that a victory was won at a given place, as was the case at Ebenezer [I Sam. 7: 12]. In this way, then, the Lord's Supper worketh faith, that is, signifies as certain that Christ was born and suffered. But to whom does it signify this? To the believer and the unbeliever alike. For it signifies to all that which belongs to the meaning of the sacrament, namely, that Christ suffered, whether they receive it or not, but that He suffered for us, it signifies to the pious believer only. For no one knows or believes that Christ suffered for us, save those whom the Spirit within has taught to recognize the mystery of divine goodness. For such alone receive Christ. Hence nothing gives confidence in God except the Spirit. No one cometh to Christ except the Father draweth him. Furthermore, Paul also decides this whole quarrel by one sentence when he says, "But let a man examine himself, and so let him eat of that bread, and drink of that cup" [I Cor. 11: 28]. Since, then, a man ought to examine his faith before he approaches the table, it cannot be that faith is given in the Supper, for it must be there before you draw near.

I have opposed a second error on the part of our adversaries. They say that by the symbols of bread and wine the natural body of Christ is brought before us because this is the force and meaning of the words, "This is my body." But what I have said above about the words of Christ that showed that His body was to be no longer in the world, contradicts this view. Moreover, if the words could do that, they would bring before us Christ's body that was capable of suffering. For when He spoke these words, He still had a mortal body. Therefore, the apostles would have eaten His mortal body, for He did not have two bodies of which one was immortal and exempt from physical sensation, the other mortal. If, then, the apostles had eaten His mortal body, what would we be eating now? Of course, His mortal body. But that body is now immortal and incorruptible which before was mortal. If, then, we would now be eating His mortal body, He would, again, have a mortal and at the same time immortal body, and since this is impossible

*One of Solon's measures to relieve the situation at Athens. See p. 53, note *.

(for it cannot be mortal and immortal at the same time), it would follow that He had two bodies, one mortal, which we would eat as well as the apostles, the other immortal, which would sit on the right hand of God, and not to move thence. Otherwise we would have to say that the apostles, indeed, ate His mortal but we eat His immortal body. Anyone can see how absurd that is.

Finally, I opposed our adversaries in their assertion that the natural, substantial body of Christ is eaten in real presence, because piety denies that also. When Peter perceived that there was divine power in Christ in the marvelous catch of fishes, he said, "Depart from me; for I am a sinful man, O Lord. For he was amazed" [Luke 5:8]. Now, do we long to eat Him physically, like cannibals? As if anyone's love for his children were such that he wished to devour and eat them! Or, as if among all men those were not adjudged the most savage who feed upon human flesh! The centurion said, "I am not worthy that thou shouldest come under my roof" [Matth. 8:8]. But Christ Himself bore witness of him that He had not found such faith in all Israel. Therefore, the greater and holier faith is, the more is it content with spiritual participation, and the more thoroughly that satisfies it, the more does a religious heart shrink from bodily manducation. Ministering women were wont to show their adoration by bathing and anointing Christ's body, not by eating it. The noble counsellor Joseph and the pious, secret disciple, Nicodemus, wrapped it in linen and spices and laid it in a sepulchre, but did not eat it physically.

[CHAPTER V]

THE VIRTUE OF THE SACRAMENTS

These difficulties, therefore, O King, plainly show that we ought not, under the guise of piety, to assign to the Eucharist or to Baptism qualities that bring faith and truth into danger. What then? Have the sacraments no virtue?

First virtue:—They are sacred and venerable rites, having been instituted and employed by Christ, the Great High Priest. For He not only instituted Baptism, but Himself received it, and He not only bade us celebrate the Eucharist, but celebrated it Himself first of all.

Second virtue:—They bear witness to an accomplished fact, for all laws, customs, and institutions proclaim their authors and beginnings. Since, then, Baptism proclaims by representation Christ's death and resurrection, these events must indeed have taken place.

Third virtue:—They take the place of the things they signify, whence also they get their names. The passover or passing by, through which God spared the children of Israel, cannot be placed before the eye, but a lamb is placed before the eye instead of this event as a symbol of it. Neither can the body of Christ and all that was accomplished in it be put before our eyes; the bread and wine are set before us to be eaten in place of it.

Fourth:—They signify sublime things. Now the value of every sign increases with the worth of the thing of which it is the sign, so that if the thing be great, precious, and sublime, its sign is, therefore, accounted the greater. The ring of the queen, your consort, with which Your Majesty was betrothed to her, is not valued by her at the price of the gold, but is beyond all price, however much it is gold, if you regard its material—for it is the symbol of her royal husband. Hence, it is even the king of all rings to her, so that if she should ever name her ornament separately and appraise it, she would doubtless say, "This is my king," that is, "this is the ring of my royal husband with which he engaged himself to me, this is the symbol of our inseparable alliance and trust." So the bread and wine are the symbols of that friendship by which God has been reconciled to the human race through His Son, and we value them not according to the price of the material but according to the greatness of the thing signified, so that the bread is no longer common, but sacred, and has not only the name of bread but of the body of Christ also, nay, is the body of Christ, but in name and significance, or, as the more recent theologians say, sacramentally.

The fifth virtue is the analogy between the symbols and the thing signified. The Eucharist has a two-fold analogy, first as applying to Christ, for as bread sustains and supports human life, as wine cheers man, so Christ alone restores, sustains and makes glad the heart bereft of all hope. For who can pine

away in despair any longer when he sees the Son of God made
his own, and holds Him in his soul like a treasure which cannot
be torn from him and through which he can obtain all things
from the Father? It has a second analogy as applying to us,
for as bread is made of many grains, and wine is made of many
grapes, so the body of the Church is cemented together and
grows into one body from countless members, through common
trust in Christ, proceeding from one Spirit, so that a true temple
and body of the indwelling Holy Spirit comes into existence.

Sixth, the sacraments bring increase and support to faith,
and this the Eucharist does above all others. You know, O
King, that our faith is constantly tried and tempted, for Satan
sifts us like wheat, as he did the apostles. But how does he
attack us? Through treachery in the camp, for he busies himself with trying to overwhelm us through the body as through
an old wall of our defense ready to tumble down, setting up the
scaling-ladders of the desires against our senses. When, therefore, the senses are diverted elsewhere, so as not to give ear to
him, his schemes are less successful. Now in the sacraments
the senses are not only made deaf to the wiles of Satan but bound
over to faith, so that like handmaidens they do nothing but what
their mistress, faith, does and directs. Hence they aid faith.
I will speak plainly. In the Eucharist the four most powerful
senses, nay, all the senses, are as it were, reclaimed and redeemed
from fleshly desires, and drawn into obedience to faith. The
hearing no longer hears the melodious harmony of varied strings
and voices, but the heavenly words, "God so loved the world
that He gave His only begotten for its life." We are present,
therefore, as brethren, to give thanks for this bounty to us. For
we do this rightly at the command of the Son Himself, who on
the eve of His death instituted this thanksgiving, that He might
leave us a lasting memorial and pledge of His love towards us.
"And He took bread, and gave thanks, and brake it, and gave
unto the disciples," uttering from His most holy lips these holy
words, "This is my body" [Luke 22: 19]. "Likewise also He
took the cup," etc.—when, I say, the hearing takes in these
words, is it not struck and does it not give itself up wholly in
admiring wonder to this one thing that is proclaimed? It hears
of God, and His love, and the Son delivered up to death for us.
And when it gives itself up to this, does it not do what faith

does? For faith is that which leans on God through Christ. When, therefore, the hearing looks to the same thing, it becomes the handmaiden of faith, and troubles faith no more with its own frivolous imaginings and interests. When the sight sees the bread and the cup which in place of Christ signify His goodness and inherent character, does it not also aid faith? For it sees Christ, as it were, before the eyes, as the heart, kindled by His beauty, languishes for Him. The touch takes the bread into its hands—the bread which is no longer bread but Christ by representation. The taste and smell are brought in to scent the sweetness of the Lord and the happiness of him that trusteth in Him. For as they rejoice in food and are quickened, so the heart, having tasted the sweetness of the heavenly hope, leaps and exults. The sacraments, then, aid the contemplation of faith, and harmonize it with the longings of the heart, as without the use of the sacraments could not be done at all so completely.

In Baptism, sight, hearing, and touch, are summoned to the aid of faith. For faith, whether that of the Church or that of him who is baptized, recognizes that Christ endured death for His Church, rose again, and triumphed. The same thing is heard, seen, and touched in Baptism. The sacraments, then, are a sort of bridles by which the senses, when on the point of dashing away to their own desires, are checked and brought back to the service of the heart and of faith.

The seventh power of the sacraments is that they fill the office of an oath of allegiance. For "sacramentum" is used by the Latin writers instead of "ius iurandum," i. e., "oath."* For those who use one and the same oath, become one and the same race and sacred alliance, unite into one body and one people, and he who betrays it is false to his oath. When, therefore, the people of Christ by eating His body sacramentally become united into one body, he who without faith ventures to obtrude himself upon this company betrays the body of Christ, as well in its head as in its members, because he does not "discern," that is,

*The following may be quoted as examples: "We are called to the service (militiam) of the living God then, when we respond to the words of the oath (sacramenti)," see Tertullian, *Ad Martyres*, Bk. I, chap. 3, in Migne, *Patrologia Latina*, I, 697; also "If thou keep thy allegiance (sacramenta) in the heavenly warfare, doubt not that thou wilt be crowned in the triumphal camp of the eternal king," see Leo the Great, Sermon XXII, 5, in Schaff, Nicene Fathers, 2nd Series, XII, 131.

does not properly value the body of the Lord, either as having been delivered up by Him for us, or as having been made free by His death. For we are one body with Him.

We are forced, then, whether we will or no, to acknowledge that the words, "This is my body," etc., are not to be understood literally and according to the primary meaning of the words, but symbolically, sacramentally, metaphorically, or, as a metonymy,* thus:—"This is my body," that is, "this is the sacrament of my body," or, "this is my sacramental or mystical body, that is, the sacramental and vicarious symbol of that body which I really took and exposed to death."

But it is now time to pass to other things, lest I offend Your Majesty forgetting to be brief. What I have said, however, is so certain, most brave King, that no one, however many have tried to rebut it, has thus far been able to affect it one jot. Therefore, be not troubled if they that are more ready with their tongues than with substantial Scripture, cry out that the view is irreligious. This they boast, indeed, in bold but empty words, though when they come to facts they are more empty than a cast-off serpent's skin.†

[CHAPTER VI]

THE CHURCH

I believe also that there is one holy Catholic, that is, universal Church, and that this is either visible or invisible. The invisible, as Paul teaches,‡ is that which comes down from heaven, that is, which recognizes and embraces God through the enlightenment of the Holy Spirit. To this Church belong all those that believe throughout the whole world. And it is called invisible not as if they that believe were invisible, but because it is not evident to human eyes who do believe. The faithful are known to God and themselves alone. And the visible Church is not the Roman pontiff and the rest of them

† μετωνυμικῶς.

†For the Latin proverb, *leberide sunt inaniores*, i. e., "they are more empty than a cast-off serpent's skin," see Erasmus, *Adagia*, chil. I, cent. I, prov. 26; also chil. I, cent. III, prov. 134.

‡Phil. 3: 20; but perhaps a slip for Rev. 21: 2.

that wear the tiara, but all throughout the whole world who have enrolled themselves under Christ [through baptism]. Among these are all who are called Christians, even though falsely, seeing that they have no faith within. There are, therefore, in the visible Church some who are not members of the elect and invisible Church. For some men eat and drink judgment unto themselves in the Supper, yet all the brethren know them not. Since, therefore, this Church which is visible contains many rebellious and traitorous members who having no faith care nothing if they be a hundred times cast out of the Church, there is need of a government, whether of princes or of nobles, to restrain shameless sinners. For the magistrate carries the sword not in vain [Rom. 13:4]. Since, then, there are shepherds in the Church, who, as may be seen in Jeremiah [23:4ff.], have also the rank of princes it is clear that without a temporal government the Church is crippled and incomplete. So far are we, most pious King, from rejecting government and thinking it should be done away with, as some men charge us with doing, that we even teach that it is necessary to the completeness of the ecclesiastical body. But hear our teaching about this briefly.

[CHAPTER VII]

GOVERNMENTS

The Greeks recognize these three kinds of governments with their three degenerate forms: Monarchy, which the Latins call "regnum, kingdom," where one man stands alone as the head of the state under the guidance of piety and justice. The opposite and degenerate form is a tyranny, which the Latins less fittingly call "vis" or "violentia," "force" or "violence," or rather, not having quite the proper word themselves, they generally use "tyrannis," borrowing the word from the Greeks. This exists when piety is scorned, justice is trodden under foot, and all things are done by force, while the ruler holds that anything he pleases is lawful for him. Secondly, they recognize an aristocracy, which the Latins call "optimatium potentia, the power of the best people," where the best men are at the head of things, observing justice and piety towards the people. When this form degenerates it passes into an oligarchy, which the Latins call literally "paucorum potentia, the power of the few." Here a few of the nobles rise up and gain influence who, caring not for the general good but for private advantage, trample upon the public weal and serve their own ends. Finally they recognize a democracy, which the Latins render by "res publica, republic," a word of broader meaning than democracy, where affairs, that is, the supreme power, are in the hands of the people in general, the entire people; and all the civil offices, honors, and public functions are in the hands of the whole people. When this form degenerates, the Greeks call it σύστρεμμα ἡ σύστασις, that is, a state of sedition, conspiracy, and disturbance, where no man suffers himself to be held in check, and instead each one, asserting that he is a part and a member of the people, claims the power of the state as his own, and each one follows his own reckless desires. Hence there arise unrestrained conspiracies and factions, followed by bloodshed, plundering, injustice and all the other evils of treason and sedition.

These distinct forms of government of the Greeks I recognize with the following corrections: If a king or prince rules, I teach that he is to be honored and obeyed, according to Christ's command, "Render unto Caesar the things that are Caesar's and unto God the things that are God's" [Luke 20:25]. For by "Caesar" I understand every ruler upon whom power has been conferred or bestowed, either by hereditary right and custom or by election. But if the king or prince becomes a tyrant, I correct his recklessness and inveigh against it in season and out of season. For thus saith the Lord to Jeremiah, "See, I have . . . set thee over the nations and over the kingdoms," etc. [Jer. 1:10]. If he listens to the warning, I have gained a father for the whole kingdom and fatherland, but if he becomes more rebelliously violent, I teach that even a wicked ruler is to be obeyed until the Lord shall remove him from his office and power or a means be found to enable those whose duty it is to deprive him of his functions and restore order. In the same way we are watchful and on the alert, if an aristocracy begins to degenerate into an oligarchy or a democracy into a σύστρεμμα, mob. We have examples in Scripture, from which we learn what we teach and demand,—Samuel endured Saul until the

Lord deprived him of his kingdom along with his life. David returned to his senses at the rebuke of Nathan, and remained on the throne under much trial and temptation. Ahab lost his life because he would not turn from wickedness when Elijah reproved him. John dauntlessly unbraided Herod when he felt no shame at his incestuous conduct. But it would be a long task to bring forward all the examples in Scripture. The learned and pious know from what source we draw what we say.

To sum up, in the Church of Christ government is just as necessary as preaching, although this latter occupies the first place. For as a man cannot exist except as composed of both body and soul, however much the body is the humbler and lower part, so the Church cannot exist without the civil government, though the government attends to and looks after the more material things that have not to do with the spirit. Since, then two particularly bright lights of our faith, Jeremiah and Paul,* bid us pray to the Lord for our rulers that they may permit us to lead a life worthy of God, how much more ought all in whatever kingdom or people to bear and to do all things to guard the Christian peace! Hence we teach that tribute, taxes, dues, tithes, debts, loans, and all promises to pay of every kind should be paid and the laws of the state in general be obeyed in these things.

[CHAPTER VIII]

REMISSION OF SINS

XI. I believe that remission of sins is surely granted to man through faith every time he prays for it to God through Christ. For since Christ said unto Peter that forgiveness was to be given seventy times seven times [Matth. 18: 22], that is, an indefinite number of times, it cannot but be that He Himself always pardons our faults. And I have said that sins are remitted through faith, by which I simply mean to say that faith alone makes a man sure of the remission of his wrongdoings.

*Zwingli was probably thinking of Jer. 29: 7 and I Tim. 2: 2. He discusses the latter passage in his treatise, "De vera et falsa religione," see Zwingli's *Werke*, Vol. III, 1914, p. 873f.

For though the Roman pontiff even should say hundreds of times, "Thy sins are forgiven thee," yet the heart will never be at rest and sure of its reconciliation with God unless it sees and believes beyond all doubt, nay feels, that it has been absolved and redeemed. For as none but the Holy Spirit can give faith, so also none other can give remission of sins.

The restoration, satisfaction, and expiation necessary to our guilt has been obtained in God's sight through Christ alone having suffered for us. For "he is the propitiation for our sins: and not for ours only, but also for the sins of the whole world," as the apostle and evangelist related to him says [I John 2: 2; John 3: 36]. Since, then, He has given satisfaction for sin, who, pray, become partakers of that satisfaction and redemption? Let us hear His own words: "He that believeth on me," that is, "that trusteth in me, that leaneth on me, hath everlasting life" [John 6: 47]. But no one obtains everlasting life, unless his sins be taken away. He, therefore, that trusteth in Christ, hath his sins remitted. As, therefore, no one knows about anybody whether he believes, so no one knows whether any one's sins have been remitted, save only the one who through the light and confidence of faith is sure of pardon, because he knows that God has forgiven him through Christ and is sure of this remission so that he has not the slightest doubt about the pardoning of his sins, because he knows that God cannot deceive or lie. Since, therefore, He has said from on high, "This is my beloved Son in whom I am well pleased," [Matth. 3: 17], or "through whom I am reconciled," it cannot but be that all who trust in God through Christ, His Son and our Lord and brother, know that pardon for their wrong doings has been given them. Hence all such words as the following are frivolous:—"I absolve you," and, "I assure you of the pardoning of your sins." For though the apostles preach the remission of sins, yet none obtains this remission except the believer and the elect. Since, therefore, the election and the faith of other men are hidden from us, however much the spirit of the Lord makes us sure of our own faith and election, it is also hidden from us whether another's sins have been remitted. How, therefore, can a man assure another man of the remission of his sins? All that the Roman Pontiffs have invented in this matter is fraud and fables.

[CHAPTER IX]

FAITH AND WORKS

But since I have come to touch upon the subject of faith, I should like to explain briefly to Your Majesty what my teaching is about faith and works. For there are people who slander me rather unjustly as forbidding good works, though I really teach upon this subject as upon all others nothing but what the divine Scriptures indicate and what common intelligence suggests. For who is so inexperienced as not to say that works should proceed from intention, or that works without intention are not works but accidents? Faith is in the human heart what intention is in action. Unless intention precedes the deed, whatever results is thoughtless and aimless. Unless faith occupies the stronghold and commands the whole action, whatever we do is without merit and vain. For even we human beings look more at the faithful purpose in any work than at the work itself. If faithful purpose is not there, the value of the work is naught. If anyone perform some great work for Your Majesty, but not from faithful purpose, do you not straightway say that you owe no thanks to the doer because he did not act from his heart? Or rather you straightway feel that in whatever anyone does for you without faithful purpose some perfidy lies hidden, so that he who does a service without faithful purpose is always suspected of some perfidy and seems to you to have acted for his own interests and not for yours. So also in regard to our works this is the rule and order. Faith must be the fountain head of works. If faith is there, the work itself is acceptable to God, if it is not there, the whole result is unbelief and in consequence, not only unacceptable but an abomination to God. Hence St. Paul says, Rom. 14: 23, "Whatever is not of faith is sin," and some of our own people have declared, in paradoxical fashion,* that all our works are an abomination. By this they have meant to say nothing else than what I have already said, "If the work is ours and not faith's, it is unbelief, which God abominates." Now faith, as I have indicated above, is from the Spirit of God alone. They, therefore, that have faith, look in all their works to the will of God as to a model to follow. Hence, not only are

* παραδόξως

those works rejected which are done contrary to the law of God, but also those which are done without the law of God. For the law is the permanent will of God. What is done, then, without the law, that is, without the word and will of God, is not of faith. What is not of faith is sin. If it is sin, God abhors it. Hence it appears that if anyone does without faith a work that God has commanded, *e. g.*, alms, that work is not acceptable to God. For when we inquire as to the source of alms which do not result from faith, we find that they are begotten of vain glory or the desire to receive more in return or some other evil passion. And who would not believe that such a work is displeasing to God?

It is plain, therefore, that those works which are done without the will of God are also done without faith, and since they are done apart from faith, are sins in Paul's judgment, and since they are sin, God abominates them. Whatever, therefore, has been given out by the Romanists, without the authority and testimony of the divine Word, as pious, holy, and acceptable to God, like fictitious indulgences, the extinguishing of the fires of purgatory, forced chastity, a variety of orders and superstitious customs, which it would be tiresome to enumerate: all this is sin and an abomination in the sight of God.

Furthermore, as to those works which are done according to the law of God, as when we feed the hungry, clothe the naked, comfort the captive, it is a difficult question to decide whether they have merit. Our opponents quote Scripture to prove that they have merit:—"If any one shall give another a cup of cold water in my name, he shall not lose his reward" [Mark 9: 41]. But the word of the Lord bears witness just as much that there is no merit:—"When ye have done all these things say, 'We are unprofitable servants' " [Lk. 17: 10]. For if our works merited blessedness, there would have been no need of the death of Christ to satisfy the divine righteousness. It would not be grace when sins are pardoned, for every one could win merit. Paul discourses upon this irrefutably in Romans and Galatians. For it must be true that "no man cometh unto the Father but through Christ" [John 14: 6]. Therefore, only by the grace and bounty of God, which He pours out upon us abundantly through Christ, does everlasting happiness come.

What, then, shall we say to the above passage of Scripture about the reward promised for a draught of cold water and to like passages? The following: The election of God is free and by grace. For He elected us before the creation of the world, before we were born. Therefore God does not elect us because of works, but elected us before the foundation of the world. Hence works have no merit, and when He promises a reward to works He is speaking after the manner of men. "For what dost Thou reward, O good God," says Augustine, "save thine own work? For inasmuch as Thou makest us to will and to do, what is there left for us to claim for ourselves?" But since men are, on the one hand, incited to good works by promises, and, on the other, are so kind and noble that they say to those to whom they have done a kindness, "I owed you that; you have deserved well," or some other like phrase, so that the man who receives the kindness may not be relegated in his own eyes to the ranks of beggars (for one who loves another desires to guard against his feelings being humiliated), so God also raises up all the more by His bounty those whom He loves that they may not despise Him, but cherish and honor Him, and He attributes to us what He Himself does through us, rewarding it as ours, though not only all our works but all our life and being are of Him. From this it follows that God is in the habit of speaking to man in the language and fashion of men. As men give something to those who have deserved well and call their gift a reward, so God also calls His gifts a reward and recompense. It is manifest, then, that the terms "merit" and "reward" are found in the divine Scriptures, but in the sense of "bountiful gift." For what can he merit as a reward who by grace exists and by grace receives all that he has?

At the same time this must be noted, that works are by no means omitted by pious men because, properly speaking, we do not gain merit by works. On the contrary, the greater our faith, the more and greater are the works that we do, as Christ himself testifies, John 14: 12, "Verily, verily, I say unto you, He that believeth on me, the works that I do shall he do also; and greater works than these shall he do," and "If ye have faith like a grain of mustard seed, and shall say to this mountain, Move hence, and take up thy abode in the sea, it will obey" [Matth. 17: 20; Mk. 11: 23]. Hence they are unfair to me who, because I take great pains to preach faith, say that I teach that no good works are to be done. Indeed, making truth a laughing stock, they slander me thus:—"This is the teaching for us, my friends. We are saved by faith alone. Hence we shall not fast, nor pray, nor help the needy." By such slanders they simply betray their own unbelief. For if they knew what a gift of God faith is, how effective its power and unwearied its activity, they would not scorn that which they have not. For that trust with which a man depends on God with all the powers of his soul, can think and do naught but what is divine, or rather, cannot help doing what is pleasing to God. For since faith is an inspiration of the divine Spirit, how can it rest idle or sit down in slothful ease when that Spirit is perennial activity and work? Wherever, then, there is true faith, there are works also, just as where there is fire there is also heat. But where there is no faith, works are not works but an empty imitation of works.

Hence we may infer that those who so persistently demand a reward for our works, and say that they will cease working the works of God if no reward awaits the works, have the souls of slaves. For slaves work for reward only, and lazy persons likewise. But they that have faith are untiring in the work of God, like the son of the house. He has not merited by works his being the heir of the estate, nor does he toil and labor for this, that he shall become the heir, but when he was born, he was the heir of his father's possessions through birth, not through merit. And when he is untiring in work, he does not demand a reward, for he knows that all things are his. So the sons of God who have faith know that by divine birth, that is, the birth of the Spirit, and by free election they are sons of God, not slaves. Since, then, they are sons of the house, they ask not what reward awaits them, for all things are ours, who are the heirs of God and joint heirs with Christ. Freely, therefore, gladly, and without weariness they labor, indeed there is no work so great that they do not believe it is accomplished by His power in whom we trust, not by our own.

And, since there are in the Church these two diseases, unbelief and weakness of faith (for there are some who absolutely do not believe, those, namely, who in the Supper eat and drink judgment unto themselves, like Judas and Simon Magus; and there are those who have a languid faith, those, namely, who thoughtlessly waver when any danger threatens, whose faith is choked by the thorns, that is, the cares and interests of this world, and put forth no fruit or holy work), I urge the believers, as Christ, Paul and James, did, if they are really believers, to show by their works that they are such, for we say that faith without works is dead, a good tree bringeth forth good fruit, the children of Abraham do the works of Abraham, nothing avails with Christ save the faith which worketh by love [Gal. 5: 6].

Thus I preach the law as well as grace. For in the law the elect and the believers learn the will of God, the wicked are terrified by it, that either through fear they do something for the good of their neighbor, or betray their own hopelessness and faithlessness. But at the same time I admonish men that those works count for nothing which we perform with human skill under the idea of serving God, for they certainly are no more pleasing to Him than it would be to you if anyone wished to serve you, O King, in some way that you did not like. If, then, you must be served according to your own will, how much are we not to bring before the face of God works which He has not commanded and does not like! We open up the source, therefore, from which good works flow when we teach faith. On the other hand, when we urge works, we are as it were demanding the payment of a debt which would not be paid without compulsion.

[CHAPTER X]

EVERLASTING LIFE

XII. Finally I believe that after this life, which is rather captivity and death than life, a glad and happy life will come to the saints or believers, and a gloomy and wretched one to the wicked or unbelievers, and that both will be unending. And in regard to this matter I maintain against the Catabaptists, who contend that the soul sleeps with the body until the day of judgment, that the soul whether of angel or of man cannot sleep or be at rest. For such an idea contradicts all reason. The soul is a substance so instinct with life that it not only lives itself, but also quickens whatever habitation it dwells in. When an angel takes on a body, either one of air or one specially created, he presently gives it life so that it moves, works, acts and is acted upon. As soon as the human soul enters a body, this straightway lives, grows, moves, and performs all the other functions of life. How could it be, therefore, that the soul when released from the body should lie torpid or sleep? Philosophers give the name "activity" or "action" to the soul, from the live and wide-awake, that is, unceasing character of its power of action. This force the Greeks* express by a more significant word, calling it ἐντελέχει,α that is, perennial power, operation, effective and prolonged action. The visible things in the world are constituted by Divine Providence in such order that the human mind can rise from them to the knowledge of the invisible. Fire and air occupy the place among the elements that the soul occupies among bodies. As air is everywhere present throughout the body of the universe, so the soul permeates the whole human body. As fire is nowhere present without actual operation, so the soul is everywhere in operation. This is also seen in sleep, for we dream and remember our dreams. Sleep, therefore, is a function of the body, not of the soul. For the soul meanwhile invigorates the body, renews it, and restores the waste, so that it never ceases working, acting, and moving, as long as it is in the body. As, therefore, the fire is never without light, so the soul never grows old nor becomes inactive, nor dies, nor sleeps. It is ever alive, awake, and active.

So far we have been philosophizing about the soul. Now we must come to the testimony of Scripture by which we prove that the soul never sleeps. "He that believeth on me cometh not into judgment but passeth from death into life" [John 5: 24]. He, therefore, that believes in this life, already perceives how sweet is the Lord, and obtains a beginning of the heavenly life and a certain taste thereof. If, then, that soul which lives in God here presently slept when it had gone out of the body, the life of a Christian man would be more desirable in this world than when he had left this world; for he would be asleep then, while here he is awake and in conscious enjoyment of God.

"He that believeth in me hath everlasting life" [John 3: 36]. But life would not be unceasing ("everlasting" is used here for "unceasing") if this life of the soul which it leads here be interrupted by sleep hereafter.

*Especially Aristotle, who coined the word.

"Father, I will that where I am there also shall be they that attend upon me" [John 17: 24]. If then the Holy Virgin, Abraham, and Paul are with God, what kind of a life is it in heaven or what is the nature of the Deity if there be sleep there? Does the Deity also sleep? If He sleeps He is no Deity, for whatever sleeps is exposd to change, and sleeps in order to refresh its weariness. If the Deity becomes weary, He is no Deity, for the Deity is unconquerable by any toil or labor. If the Deity does not sleep, it is just as inevitable that the soul also should not sleep as it is that the air should be clear and transparent when the sun shines on the earth. Foolish, therefore, and vain is this notion of the Catabaptists, who are not satisfied to have deluded men, but must defile the sure and infallible utterances of the living God. I could add many more proofs:—"This is life everlasting, to know thee," etc. [John 17: 3], and "I will receive you unto myself; that where I am, there ye may be also" [John 14: 3], and similar passages, but brevity forbids.

I believe, then, that the souls of the faithful fly to heaven as soon as they leave the body, come into the presence of God, and rejoice forever. Here, most pious King, if you govern the state entrusted to you by God as David, Hezekiah, and Josiah did, you may hope to see first God Himself in His very substance, in His nature and with all His endowments and powers, and to enjoy all these, not sparingly but in full measure, not with the cloying effect that generally accompanies satiety, but with that agreeable completeness which involves no surfeiting, just as the rivers, that flow unceasingly into the sea and flow back through the depths of the earth, bring no loathing to mankind, but rather gain and joy, ever watering, gladdening and fostering new germs of life. The good which we shall enjoy is infinite and the infinite cannot be exhausted; therefore no one can become surfeited with it, for it is ever new and yet the same. Then you may hope to see the whole company and assemblage of all the saints, the wise, the faithful, brave, and good who have lived since the world began. Here you will see the two Adams, the redeemed and the redeemer, Abel, Enoch, Noah, Abraham, Isaac, Jacob, Judah, Moses, Joshua, Gideon, Samuel, Phineas, Elijah, Elisha, Isaiah, and the Virgin Mother of God of whom he prophesied, David, Hezekiah, Josiah, the Baptist, Peter, Paul;

here too, Hercules, Theseus, Socrates, Aristides, Antigonus, Numa, Camillus, the Catos and Scipios; here Louis* the Pious, and your predecessors, the Louis, Philips, Pepins, and all your ancestors who have gone hence in faith.† In short there has not been a good man and will not be a holy heart or faithful soul from the beginning of the world to the end thereof that you will not see in heaven with God. And what can be imagined more glad, what more delightful, what, finally, more honorable than such a sight? To what can all our souls more justly bend all their strength than to the attainment of such a life? And may meantime the dreaming Catabaptists deservedly sleep in the regions below a sleep from which they will never wake. Their error comes from the fact that they do not know that with the Hebrews the word for sleeping is used for the word for dying, as is more frequently the case with Paul than there is any need of demonstrating at present.

[CHAPTER XI]

ON THE CATABAPTISTS

And since I have come to speak of the Catabaptists, I should like, O King, to sketch for you in a few words the doctrines of that sect. They are mostly a class of rabble, homeless from the want of means, who make it their business to win old women by pompous discourses upon divine things to extract from them the wherewithal to support themselves, or to gather in considerable alms. In general, they make pretense of the

*These words, "Hic Ludovicum Pium" and "Ludovicos, Philippos, Pipinos," are omitted by Bullinger; they have been added from Zwingli's autograph manuscript.

†It was especially this passage that called forth Luther's wrath against Zwingli, which he poured out in unrestrained abuse in his book: *Kurz Bekenntniss D. Martin Luthers vom heiligen Sakrament*, MDXLIV. In it he declared that Zwingli had altogether become a heathen, though Luther had previously expressed a similar opinion in his sermon on Genesis XX, in which he said: "That cannot be denied that there are very pious Christians among the heathen," and again, "I would rather hold to this opinion, in order to allow God's grace to enter among the heathen." See Luther's *Werke*, Weimar edition, Vol. XXIV, p. 364f.

same holiness of which Irenaeus, Bishop of Lyons writes in connection with the Valentinians and Nazianzenus [Gregory of
Nazianzus] in connection with the Eunomians.* Then, in reliance upon this, they teach that a Christian cannot be a magistrate; that it is not lawful for a Christian to put even a guilty
man to death even by process of law; that we must not go to
war even if tyrants or godless persons and robbers resort to force
and plunder, slay, and destroy every day; that an oath must not
be taken; that a Christian should not exact duties or taxes; that
all things should be held in common; that the souls sleep with
the bodies; that a man can have several wives "in the spirit"
(having, however, carnal intercourse with them); that tithes
and revenues should not be paid, and hundreds of other things.
Nay, they daily scatter new errors like tares amid the righteous
seed of God.

Although they have left us, because they were not of us,
there are yet people who impute all their errors to us, though
we fight against them more fiercely than any one, and teach
the opposite of their teaching in all the above named matters.
Therefore, most excellent King, if I am reported to Your
Majesty from any quarter as wishing to abolish magistrates,
saying that an oath ought not to be taken, and teaching the rest
that the Catabaptist scum spits out upon the world, I beg and
pray, by the truth to which men say you are so devoted, that
you will believe nothing of the sort of us, that is, of those who
are proclaiming the Gospel in the cities of the Christian
alliance.† For we do not rouse tumult nor weaken the authority of magistrates or laws, nor do we advocate any man's not
keeping his faith and paying his debts, however much certain
people accuse us of these things not merely by secret denunciation but in public writings. We do not reply to them for this
reason particularly, that the world is already full of fiercely controversial books, and facts themselves are every day making
plain what lies those people write who are scattering such
reports about us among the people, not caring for the glory of

*See Irenaeus, "Against Heresies," Bk. I, chap. VI, §3, in Migne,
Patrologia Graeca, XLVIII, 642, Bk. III, §4; tr. Schaff, *Nicene Fathers*,
I, 324; and Gregory of Nazianzus, "Orations," XXVII, §9, in Migne, l. c.,
XXXVI, 22.

†The Swiss and German cities of the Burgher Rights are meant.

Christ but for their own glory and for their bellies.

Now this Catabaptist pest has crept in principally at those places where the true teachings of Christ have begun to take root, so that you can more easily see, O King, that it has been brought in by the evil spirit, in order to choke the wholesome seed at the start. We see cities and towns that had made a fine beginning in receiving the Gospel, after being infected and hindered by this pest, come as it were to a standstill, so that, because of their confusion, they were unable to attend to sacred or civil affairs. Therefore, I warn Your Majesty (begging your pardon, for I know how you are surrounded by excellent counsels, but counsel does not provide against what is not foreseen. If this evil occurred to the minds of your advisers, they would easily make provision against it, I know, but since they are doubtless unaware of the danger, I think you will not take my warning amiss),—since it cannot but be that also in your kingdom some sparks of the reviving Gospel are flashing forth, I warn you not to suffer the good seed to be choked by the Papists whose influence has grown unduly, for then instead of this good seed you would find the Catabaptists' tares growing up where you least suspected it, and such disorder in all things appearing throughout your kingdom that it would be very hard to discover a remedy.

This is a summary of my faith and preaching which I hold by the grace of God, and I stand ready to give an account of it to any man, for there is not one jot of my teaching that I have not learned from the divine Scriptures, and I advance no doctrine for which I have not the authority of the leading doctors of the Church, the prophets, apostles, bishops, evangelists, and translators—those of old, who drank from the fountain-head in its purity. This will be admitted by those who have seen and examined my writings.

Accordingly, most holy King* (for what hinders me to call "most holy" him who is the most Christian King?), gird yourself to receive with due honor the Christ who is to be born anew for us and brought back to us. For I see that by the providence of God it has come to pass that the kings of France are called "most Christian," since the restoration of the Gospel of

---

*Whatever in this peroration differs from Bullinger's edition has been restored according to the autograph manuscript of Zwingli.

the Son of God was to take place in your reign—a king whom friends and enemies alike all proclaim to be gracious by nature. For a Christian prince must be of gracious and affable nature, of just and intelligent judgment, of most wise and brave mind. God has made you very rich in these endowments, that you might shine upon this age, and yourself rekindle the torch of the knowledge of God. Go on, then, with these heroic virtues, seize shield and spear, and attack unbelief with dauntless and intrepid courage and with that body of yours conspicuous for all grace. Thus when the other kings shall see you, the most Christian king, championing the glory of Christ, they will follow you and turn out Antichrist. Permit the doctrine of salvation to be preached in purity in your realm. You are strong in men of wisdom and learning, in resources, and in a people inclined to religion; you will not, therefore, suffer their hearts which are so devoted to God and yourself to be led astray into superstition. There is no reason to fear here that the slanderers will cry out their falsehoods to oppose truth. Not only your subjects but the outside allied nations will wage holy and righteous wars. Not only the people but preachers also will take the oath of allegiance without hesitation, though the Papists have thus far refused to do so. Even the preachers will pay their dues and taxes, so far are they from being inclined to teach that they should not be paid. They will leave every man his own rights and privileges. If mistakes are made, they will censure them, but they will not create any disturbance because of temporal things, for they recognize the ordinary judge in these things, however much they may criticise and censure him when he does wrong.

Believe me, indeed, believe me, magnanimous Hero, none of those evils will come to pass which the Papists threaten. For the Lord protects His Church. Oh that you might see with your own eyes the States of certain princes who have received the Gospel in Germany, and the security, happiness, and faithfulness of their cities. Then you would say because of the results: "I doubt not that what has come to pass is from God." Examine the whole matter in the light of your faith and wisdom, and pardon the daring with which I have disturbed Your

Majesty in boorish fashion.   The situation demanded it.
Zurich.*

Your Majesty's most devoted,

H. ZWINGLI.

APPENDIX ON THE EUCHARIST AND MASS†

There are some things which in the above exposition I touched upon lightly; these I will now treat of in a fuller exposition.   And I shall especially prove that the Papists depart from truth when they proclaim that they offer Christ for sin in the Mass.   For as He offered Himself once on the cross and again to the Father in heaven, so He won and obtained remission of sins and the joy of everlasting happiness, and he who boasts that he offers Him to the Father can in no way more completely reject or deny Christ.   This I shall try to make clear as follows:

First, I ask the opponent, who among men offered up Christ when He was hung upon the cross?   They can only answer that no man offered Him up; He was offered up by Himself.   To this the prophets, Christ Himself, and His apostles bare witness.   He was offered up, because He Himself willed it.   "No man taketh my life from me," and "I have power to lay it down, and I have power to take it again" [John 10: 18].   "I lay down my life for my sheep" [John 10: 15], and "The bread that I will give is my flesh, which I will give for the life of the world" [John 6: 51].   Through the eternal Spirit He offered Himself up unspotted unto God.

If, therefore, Christ was then offered up by none other than Himself, I ask secondly, whether there is any difference between that real offering of Himself to death and the offering by which the Papists offer Him up.   If they say there is no difference, it will follow that Christ must endure suffering and pain, nay, must die today also when He is offered up.   For so it is written in Hebr. 2: 14, "that through death he might destroy him that had the power of death, that is, the devil;" in Rom. 5: 10, "we were reconciled to God by the death of his Son."   "Where

*The month and year are lacking in the autograph manuscript.

†This is what Bullinger added as an appendix to Zwingli's confession. See the note on p. 248.

there is a testament, there must also of necessity be the death of the testator" [Hebr. 9:16], that is, if one is to hand over a legacy by testament to anyone, the testator must die. And our testament or legacy is the free remission of sins, as we see in Jer. 31:35, and Hebr. 8:12. When the divine goodness bequeathed this to us, it was necessary that He should die through whom the pardon of our sins had been bequeathed to us. It follows, therefore, that if the Papists now offer Him up, Christ dies even now. For if they offer Him up, sins are taken away by the offering; if sins are taken away, death must intervene, for "without shedding of blood is no remission," Hebr. 9:22, and Rom. 6:10, "for in that he died, he died unto sin." It is, therefore, altogether apparent that if the Papists offer up Christ for the remission of sins, as He offered Himself up, they also slay Him, for without death sins are not abolished.

But if between their offering and that by which Christ offered Himself up there is some difference, I ask what it can be? They will answer, no doubt, in the old way, that there is this difference, that He actually offered Himself up, while they now offer Him up spiritually. Therefore it was necessary then for Him to die, but now, since their offering is a spiritual one, death is not required. I reply that in so difficult a matter no ambiguous nor obscure form of expression must be allowed to pass unchallenged, lest forsooth we be led away from the truth through not understanding the force of the expression. I ask, therefore, when they say that they offer Him spiritually, what they understand by this word "spiritually,"—whether they mean their own spirit, so that the meaning is, "We offer up Christ spiritually, that is, we consider in our hearts and recall the memory of Christ's having offered Himself up for us, and we give thanks for it." If this is the way they understand "to offer up spiritually," meaning to offer up Christ in their hearts, they do not differ at all from us, but they differ from themselves by more than τρὶς διὰ πασῶν, i. e., "three times the octave" So far are they from offering up Christ in this way that it is they themselves who, already offered up to Him in faith, now offer Him up visibly in the Supper also.

If by "spiritually" they understand the spirit of Christ, in the meaning, "We offer up Christ spiritually, that is, we offer up the spirit of Christ," this is contradicted by the words of Christ that I quoted above, "No man taketh my life," etc., for no man has power over Him. For He offered Himself up through the everlasting Spirit, that is, He delivered His life and body over to death, by the will and order of the eternal Spirit or counsel. No one but Himself, therefore, can offer up Christ in this way.

But if they understand "spiritually" as follows: "We offer up the real body of Christ spiritually, that is, in some inexplicable manner, so that while it is real body it is not the actual, natural body, but according to a fashion of its own a spiritual one, which fashion is unknown to us" (for that is about* the way they speak), I will show that they simply string together words which cannot be consistent. For since it is evident that Christ's body is a real body, so that it remains one and the same body in fact and in number before it died and after it rose again, although from being mortal it became immortal and from being animal it became spiritual, that is, divine, pure, incapable of suffering, and in all things obedient to the Spirit, it yet never so changes and passes over into spirit as not to be really natural and actual body, corruptible and frail to be sure before death, but after the resurrection incorruptible, strong and everlasting, yet always one and the same body. I am speaking of real body, then, and ask whether they say that real body is offered up, but in an inexplicable way. They answer, "Yes, certainly." I ask further why they venture to say that the manner is inexplicable when the first line of division between all things and all substances is that they are either body or spirit. This division is so far reaching that it even includes God, and the angels and all spirits. For "God is spirit," John 4: 24. Though, therefore, my question is about what is, not about how it is, as they themselves say with the philosophers, that is, though I first ask what is offered up, and only afterwards ask how it is offered up, not with the desire as it were to demand the reason of the doings of God, but because they do not make proper answer as to the thing or substance, I will now show that they do not any more make proper answer as to how it is. But that the cloudy mists of sophistry may not be displeasing to Your Majesty, I will explain very clearly and plainly what I have said because of contentious persons.

I ask of the Papists first in regard to the thing, "What do

*"Ferre" in the text must be a misprint for "fere."

you offer up for sin in the Mass?" They answer, "The body of Christ." I say, "Is it the true and real body?" They answer, "Yes." I say, "If you offer up the true and real body, two utter absurdities follow. First, you take upon yourselves a work which belongs to the Son of God alone. For He offered Himself up, as has been said before. For no one can offer up anything greater than himself. The priests of the Old Testament used to offer up animal sacrifices, and these were as much below the priests themselves as a brute is lower than a man. But each one offered up the highest sacrifice he could when he dedicated and bound himself over to the Lord, that is, when he devoted his whole heart to God, and surrendered his whole life and all his actions to His service. Hence also the apostles nowhere teach us to offer up anything else than ourselves. Christ, therefore, is offered up by Himself alone. For on this account did the chief high priest alone enter the holy of holies and once only in the year, as a figurative representation, that Christ alone was to make expiation for sin.

The other absurdity is that if you offer up Christ for sin, you slay Christ, for sin is not abolished save by death. For a seed of corn, unless it die, bringeth forth no fruit [John 12: 24]. If, therefore, you slay not, you produce no fruit; if you slay, you crucify Christ again, when He died once for all and cannot die any more, as the apostle teaches truly and undeniably in the epistles to the Romans and the Hebrews. See, most wise King, into what straits, into what difficulties and quicksands the Papists suffer themselves to be drawn through their greed. Christ alone can offer Himself up. The offering takes place only at the time the victim is slain. Sin is abolished only at the time the expiation is made, that is, at the time the victim that has been sacrificed is accepted by God with smiling approval. It follows, therefore, that no man can offer up Christ, much less can the Papists. This also follows, that if they offered up Christ they would be slaying Him. But since Christ cannot die any more, it follows that even if the Papists would like to slay Christ, in order that they might receive money for His blood, yet they cannot slay Him. For death can have no more dominion over Him. But all this will become clearer to Your Majesty when I have adduced the testimony of the apostle.

Hebr. 1: 3, "Who being the brightness of his glory, and

the express image of his person, and upholding all things by the word of his power, when he had by himself purged our sins," etc. Behold, most excellent King, who He had to be who purged our sins. The brightness of the everlasting sun, that is, the supreme light, the image, that is, the likeness and antitype of the everlasting Deity, that is, of His substance, which has its being through itself and gives being unto all things. He is almighty, as one whose commands all things obey. What impudence is it, then, for us to maintain that men offer Him up for sin, when He has purged away sin by offering up Himself!

In the same epistle, Hebr. 5:5, "So Christ also glorified not himself to be made a high priest, but he that spake unto him, Thou art My Son, this day have I begotten Thee." What an irreverence, then, and insult to God is this that a man should make himself high priest, when not even the Son of God took this honor upon Himself but received it from His Father!

In the same epistle, Hebr. 7:26, "For such a high priest became us, holy, guileless, undefiled, separated from sinners, and made higher than the heavens," etc. What created being now will dare to take upon himself to boast that he is high priest, when that high priest who is to abolish sin must be holy and free from all blemish?

In the same chapter [v. 24], "But he, because he abideth for ever, hath his priesthood unchangeable." Hence He can always save and deliver them that come through Him to make supplication to God, living ever as He does to intercede for them. What folly is it to choose substitute priests for Him who gives up neither His office nor His life! Christ is the everlasting priest, our everlasting advocate before God. Why, then, do we make other advocates for ourselves? Is Christ dead? Has He abandoned our cause? Behold, most brave King, how they deny Christ and insult God who thus make themselves priests.

In the same chapter [v. 27], "Who needeth not daily, like those high priests, to offer up sacrifices, first for his own sins, and then for the sins of the people; for this" (sacrificing for the people), "he did once for all, when he offered up himself." We see here that Christ was offered up once for all. What vileness, then, to do what has already been done and finished! Since He, in that He was offered up once for all, perfected the atonement for sin, and this endureth for ever through Him, he who boasts that he offers Him up does the same thing as if he boasted that he created the world. For that, when once created endureth forever; so also redemption, once obtained through Christ, equally endureth forever. For the works of God are not like the works of men to fall to the ground unless they happen to be renewed and made over.

In the same epistle, 8: 1, "Now in the things which we are saying the chief point is this: We have such a high priest, who sat down on the right hand of the throne of the Majesty in the heavens," etc, What presumption is it, therefore, to make one's self a high priest or minister, when He alone is our high priest who sat down on the right hand of God!

In the same epistle, 9: 11 and 12, "But Christ having come a high priest of the good things to come, through the greater and more perfect tabernacle, not made with hands, that is to say, not of this creation; nor yet through the blood of goats and calves, but through His own blood, entered in once for all into the holy·place, having obtained eternal redemption." What arrogance, therefore, to take upon one's self the work of the Son of God, when He offered up His own blood, and alone did it, and thus to boast, being a man subject to sin, that one is offering up the same blood which He offered up once for all, but so abundantly and generously that the redemption won endureth forever! For God is everlasting. He who redeemed also created. I will quote from this epistle one more proof in which all that I have said is seen as on a tablet.

In the same epistle, 9: 24, "For Christ entered not into a holy place made with hands, like in pattern to the true; but into heaven itself, now to appear before the face of God for us: Nor yet that he should offer himself often, as the [Levitical] high priest entereth into the holy place year by year with blood not his own; else must he often have suffered since the foundation of the world; but now once at the end of the ages hath he been manifested to put away sin by the sacrifice of himself." See how being offered up involves suffering! What dullness, then, not to see that when Christ is offered up He also dies! And since He can have died only once, He can have been offered up only once. But, once offered up, He purifies forever the sanctified, that is, those destined for everlasting life. He who

reconciles the Father to us must sit in heaven.   Hence also the
Church that through Christ possesses and obtains all things is
called the true Church of Christ.

But why should I trouble Your Majesty with more words,
since it is clearer than the sun that no one can offer up Christ
but Himself, and, secondly, that He can be offered up once
only?   For if the offering up of Him were repeated, it would
show that His own doing it was not sufficient.   Thirdly, if He
were offered up, He would suffer again.   It is, therefore, established that the Papists deny Christ and make void His work.

But since the ancient theologians, who drank in and
treated of the Christian religion in greater purity and simplicity,
very often call the Eucharist an offering (for the word "Mass"
was not heard until after the time of Augustine),* some one
might raise the objection, "Why, then, did they call it an offering if it is not really an offering?" especially since in the judgment of all they spoke more learnedly and to the point than
later writers.   I answer, "The more learned and religious anyone is, the less he wanders from the truth whatever words he
uses."   For learning, like a lamp, lights up and makes clear to
the sight whatever is said, but religion forbids that anything at
variance with the truth should be accepted on account of the
apparent meaning of the words.   It takes to heart the warning
in Saint Augustine's rule, and says, "Even though you do not
grasp the words, and do not know the real meaning of the divine
utterance, yet it is certain that God's utterances are every way
consistent, and however much they seem to have a different
meaning in different passages, yet they never do contradict
themselves."   When they seem to us at first sight to contradict
themselves, this is due to our being deceived by our ignorance of
language or feebleness of religious feeling.   When, therefore,
they call an offering what cannot really and literally be an
offering, we must first appeal to our religious consciousness.
Religion denies, as I think has been said strongly enough, that

*What is regarded as the earliest instance of the use of the word
"mass," in Latin *missa*, is found in the letters of Ambrose, who, referring
to events of the year 385 A. D., writes: "The day after, which was Sunday, after the lessons and the sermon, when the catechumens were dismissed,
I was teaching the creed to certain candidates . . . I however, remained
at my ministrations and began to celebrate the mass."   See Letter 20, §4, in
Schaff, *Nicene Fathers*, 2nd Series, X, 423.

there can be any other high priest than Christ. Therefore, not even the Pope, however great he is, if we are to estimate him at his own valuation, can offer up Christ. While this is firmly established by religion, she is seconded by her handmaid, learning. "Go to," she says to righteousness, "It is nothing new for things to get names from their inventors, or authors, or from what they represent." This useful quality in words the learned call "metonymy," that is, "the substitution of the name of one object for that of another." For instance, when Paul says, "When Moses is read, the veil is upon their eyes,"* where "Moses" signifies the law that is, the entire Old Testament, simply because Moses brought out the law according to God's will and command. Also when the lamb which was eaten at the Supper is called the Passover, though it only signifies the passover. So also the Eucharist was learnedly and religiously called an offering by the ancients, not because it was one, but because it signified that offering in which Christ, by offering Himself up in that one offering, made perfect and redeemed forever those who have been sanctified, that is, have been elected of God. But you might call this that I say a thing made up by me if you did not find that Augustine expresses the same view in the letter to Boniface which is numbered 23.

AUGUSTINE.

"We often say in ordinary parlance when Easter is approaching, 'tomorrow or the day after is the Lord's Passion,' although He suffered so many years ago, and, in general, that Passion took place once for all time. On Easter Sunday itself we say, 'This day the Lord rose from the dead,' although so many years have passed since His resurrection. But no one is so foolish as to accuse us of falsehood when we use these phrases, for the reason, that we give such names to these days on the ground of a likeness between them and the days on which the events referred to actually occurred, the day being called the day of that event, although it is not the same, but one corresponding to it by the revolution of the same time of the year, and it being said, on account of the celebration of the sacrament, that a thing is done on that day which was done not on that day but long ago. Was not Christ offered once for all in His own

---

*II Cor. 3: 15. The Vulgate as well as the "Textus Receptus" together with the modern English versions have "heart" instead of "eyes."

person as a sacrifice, and yet in the sacrament He is offered to the nations not only all through the solemnities of the Easter day, but also daily among our congregations, so that the man who, being questioned, answers that He is offered as a sacrifice in that ordinance is strictly true. For if sacraments had not some likeness to the things of which they are the sacraments, they would not be sacraments at all. In most cases, moreover, they do in virtue of this likeness bear the names of the realities which they resemble. As, therefore, in a sense the sacrament of the body of Christ is the body of Christ, and the sacrament of the blood of Christ is the blood of Christ, so the sacrament of faith is faith," etc.*

From these words of Augustine Your Highness easily discerns that the Eucharist is called a sacrifice or offering exactly as the Resurrection and Passion of the Lord are so called, which days, inasmuch as they signify and call to mind real things which took place once, receive the names of those things. It is established, therefore, that the Papists are entirely mistaken when they make the Mass or Eucharist a real offering, seeing that it is only the likeness and commemoration of an offering. This also is established, that they are foolish and ignorant who think that sacraments and festivals of praise are not properly called by the names of the things which they signify, however much they are not these things. When, therefore, the Papists strive to make the thing itself out of the symbol, they only succeed in showing all men that they are themselves uneducated and ignorant.

I pass over in silence the other errors into which they fall in regard to the Mass, or rather which they invent and devise with perverted ingenuity:—the way they traffic in it and make it a matter of revenue, which is not only an attack upon the holiness of our religion but upon common honesty. (For who among the heathen have ever pursued filthy lucre so sordidly as openly to defile religion?) I also pass over that they promise the redemption of the soul from purgatory through it, when neither any fire of purgatory exists as they think, nor any offering which can reach God save that through which Christ sacrificed and offered Himself up upon the altar of the cross. I pass

*Letter 98, in Migne, *Patrologia Latina*, XXX, 363f, §9; translated in Schaff, *Nicene Fathers*, 1st Series, I, 409f.

over their saying that Christ's body is eaten by an unbeliever just as much as by a believer; that the Mass is equally effective whether performed by a reprobate or by a pious and holy man; their speaking so ignorantly of the body of Christ as to say that it is eaten in the Supper in the proportions in which it hung upon the cross and lay in the manger, and hundreds of other declarations as foolish as they are impudent. Meanwhile they say that I am a heretic if I do not assent to all their madness, and they weave together extraordinary lies to bring my teaching under suspicion in the eyes of those to whom a report of them may come. As if I denied that Christ was in the Supper, denied His omnipotence, denied His words, and other things of that kind. But do you, most gracious King, hear a brief statement of my opinion as to how the body of Christ is in the Supper.

I believe that Christ is truly in the Supper, nay, I do not believe it is the Lord's Supper unless Christ is there. Proof:— "Where two or three are gathered together in my name, there will I be in the midst of them" [Matth. 18: 20]. How much more is He there where the whole Church is gathered together for Him! But that His body is eaten in the dimensions that they say is absolutely at variance with the truth and with the spirit of faith. With the truth, because He said, "I shall be no more in the world" [John 17: 11], and, "the flesh profiteth nothing" [John 6: 63], as far as eating is concerned, that is, in the way the Jews then thought and the Papists now think he must be eaten. And it is inconsistent with the spirit of faith, because faith (I speak of grand and true faith) embraces in itself love and religious feeling or reverence and fear of God. And this religious feeling shrinks from that carnal and crude manducation just as much as any one would shrink from eating a dearly beloved son. Proof:—The centurion, whose faith Christ proclaimed as greater than any in Israel, out of the reverence of faith said to Him, "Lord, I am not worthy that thou shouldest enter under my roof" [Matth. 8: 8], and Peter, when at the draught of fish he bids Jesus to depart from him [Luke 5: 8], on account of the fear that had taken possession of him, shrinks in consequence of this same reverence from His bodily and visible presence.

It is clear, then, that the heart and faith, that is, the truth, which is the one light of the mind, and religious feeling, by which we seize hold of, revere, and worship God, shrink from such crude manducation as that in which the men of Capernaum and the Papists say that they eat the body of Christ. For, as Augustine holds, when the men of Capernaum said "How can this man give us his flesh to eat?" and "Is not this the son of Joseph?" [John 6:52], they thought that His body was offered them to eat as meat from the market is eaten, as, namely, it stood before them as perceived by the senses, in its special form and height.* And what else do the Papists maintain when they say that Jesus is eaten in the proportions in which He hung upon the cross and lay in the tomb? For truth and the heart shrink from such manducation, and religious feeling and faith have too holy a regard and love for Christ to desire to eat Him in this way.

I maintain, therefore, that the body of Christ is not eaten in the Supper in the carnal and crude fashion they say, but I believe that the real body of Christ is eaten in the Supper sacramentally and spiritually by the religious, faithful, and pure mind, as also Saint Chrysostom† holds. And this is a brief resume of my view, or, rather not mine but the truth's own, in this controversy.

I want, however, to subjoin the order of service which we use in celebrating the Supper, that Your Majesty may see that I do not alter or make void the words of Christ, or distort them into a perverted meaning, and that I preserve entire in

---

*Augustine, Homilies on the Gospel of John, Tract XXVII, 5: "They indeed understood the flesh just as when cut to pieces in a carcass, or sold in the market, not as when it is quickened by the Spirit." (Schaff, *Nicene Fathers*, 1st Series, Vol. VII, p. 175.)

†Zwingli may have been thinking of the following passage in Chrysostom's *De Sacerdotio Libri VI:* "When you see the Lord sacrificed and lying [on the table] and the priest standing by the sacrifice, and praying; and all [the communicants] red with that precious blood; do you think yourself to be still among men, and to stand upon the earth? and not rather to be translated direct to heaven? And casting out of your soul all fleshly thoughts, you look around upon the things in heaven with a clear soul and a pure mind. Oh! wonderful! Oh! the loving kindness of God! He who sits above with the Father is at that time held in the hands of all, and gives Himself to those that desire the gift, that they may embrace and lay hold of Him. *But all do this by the eyes of faith.*" See Migne, *Patrologia Graeca*, XLVIII, 642, Bk. III, §4; tr. Schaff, *Nicene Fathers*, 1st Series, IX, 46f.

the Supper the things that ought to have been preserved in the
Mass, namely, prayers, praise, confession of faith, communion of
the Church or the believers, and the spiritual and sacramental
eating of the body of Christ, while, on the other hand we omit
all those things which are not of Christ's institution, to wit,
"We offer efficaciously for the living and the dead:" "We offer
for the remission of sins," and the other things that the Papists
assert not less impiously than ignorantly.

HERE FOLLOWS SUBSTANTIALLY THE ORDER OF
SERVICE WE USE AT ZURICH, BERNE, BASEL,
AND THE OTHER CITIES OF THE CHRISTIAN
ALLIANCE:

First, in a sermon of appropriate length is preached the
goodness of God which He has shown us through His Son, and
the people are directed to the knowledge of this and thanksgiving for it. When this is finished a table is placed in front of the
choir, so-called, before the steps; this is covered with a cloth, the
unleavened bread is placed upon it, and the wine poured into
cups. Then the pastor comes forward with two assistants, and
they all turn towards the people, so that the pastor or bishop
stands between the others, having on only the usual garb worn
by men of standing and ministers of the Church. Then the
pastor begins in a loud voice, not in the Latin tongue, but in
the vernacular, so that all shall understand what is going on,
"In the name of the Father, and of the Son, and of the Holy
Ghost." The assistants respond in the name of the whole
Church, "Amen." The Pastor:—"Let us pray." Now the
church kneels.

"Almighty and everlasting God, whom all creatures rightly
worship, adore, and praise, as their Maker, Creator, and Father,
grant unto us miserable sinners that we may in sincere faith
render that praise and thanksgiving which Thy only begotten
Son, our Lord, Jesus Christ instructed us to do, through that
same Jesus Christ, Thy Son, our Lord, who liveth and reigneth
with Thee, God, in the unity of the Holy Spirit world without
end. Amen."

Then the assistant who stands on the left reads, "What is

now read is written in the first Epistle of Paul to the Corinthians, eleventh chapter,—'When ye come together therefore into one place, this is not to eat the Lord's supper,'" [v. 20], and the rest as far as, "not discerning the Lord's body" [v. 29].

Then the assistants and the Church respond, "Praise be to God." The Pastor, "Glory to God in the highest." The Deacon, "And on earth peace." The Sub-deacon, "To men a sound and tranquil mind." The Deacon, "We praise Thee, we bless Thee," and the rest to the end of this hymn, the assistants reciting it alternately, verse by verse, the Church understanding the whole and admonished at the beginning that each man is to say over in his heart and consider in the sight of God and the Church the things that are said. The Deacon says, "The Lord be with you." The assistants respond, "And with Thy spirit." The Deacon, "What is now read is written in the Gospel of John, the sixth chapter." The Church responds, "Glory be to Thee, O Lord." The Deacon, "Thus spake Jesus, "Verily, verily, I say unto you, he that believeth on me hath everlasting life. I am that bread of life. Your fathers did eat manna," etc., to the words, "the words that I speak unto you, they are spirit, and they are life." After these words the Pastor says, "Glory to God who deigns to forgive all our sins according to His word." The assistants respond, "Amen." The Pastor, "I believe in one God." The Deacon, "the Father Almighty, Creator of heaven and earth." The Sub-deacon, "And in Jesus Christ, His only begotten Son, our Lord," and the rest to the end of the Apostles' Creed, so-called, the ministers repeating it alternately in loud voice just as they did before the hymn, "Glory in the highest."

Invitation of the pastor to the worthy celebration of the Supper:—"We now desire, dear brethren, in accordance with the custom instituted by our Lord Jesus Christ, to eat this bread and drink this cup, as He commanded should be done in commemoration, praise, and thanksgiving, because He suffered death for us, and poured out His blood to wash away our sins. Therefore, let every man examine and question himself, as Paul suggests, as to how sure a trust he puts in our Lord Jesus Christ, that no one may behave like a believer who yet hath not faith, and so become guilty of the Lord's death, and sin against the whole Church (which is His body) by thus showing contempt for it. Accordingly fall upon your knees and pray, 'Our

Father which art in heaven,' " etc., to the end. And when the ministers have responded "Amen," let the pastor again pray.

Prayer: "Lord, God Almighty, who by Thy spirit hast united us into Thy one body in the unity of the faith, and hast commanded Thy body to give praise and thanks unto Thee for that bounty and kindness with which Thou hast delivered Thy only begotten Son, our Lord Jesus Christ unto death for our sins, grant that we may fulfil this Thy command in such faith that we may not by any false pretenses offend or provoke Thee who art the infallible truth. Grant also that we may live purely, as becometh Thy body, Thy sons and Thy family, that even the unbelieving may learn to recognize Thy name and Thy glory. Keep us, Lord, lest Thy name and glory come into ill repute through the depravity of our lives. We always pray, 'Lord, increase our faith, that is, our trust in Thee, who livest and reignest God world without end.' " The church responds, "Amen." Then the pastor speaks the sacred words with the following actions:—

"The Lord Jesus the same night in which He was betrayed to death took bread" (here the pastor takes the unleavened bread into his hands); "and when he had given thanks, he brake it, and said, Take, eat: this is my body, which is broken for you; this do in remembrance of me." (Here the pastor hands the bread to the ministers who are standing about the table, and they immediately take it with reverence, divide it between them, and eat. Meanwhile the pastor continues): "After the same manner also he took the cup, when he had supped," (here the pastor takes the cup into his hands), "gave thanks and said, Drink ye all of it. This cup is the new testament in my blood; this do ye, as oft as ye drink it, in remembrance of me. For as often as ye eat this bread, and drink this cup, ye do shew the Lord's death," (ye praise Him and thank Him) "till he come."

After this the assistants carry round the unleavened bread, and each person takes a piece of the bread with his own hand, and then passes the rest to his neighbor. If any one does not wish to handle the bread with his own hand, the minister carrying it round hands it to him. Then the assistants follow with the cups and hand one another the Lord's cup. Let not Your Majesty shrink from this custom of offering and receiving the elements, for it has often been found that men who had accidentally taken seats next each other when they yet felt enmity and hatred towards each other, have laid aside their angry feelings through this participation in the bread or wine.

Another assistant reads again from the pulpit out of the Gospel of John, while the congregation is eating and drinking the sacrament of the Lord's body and blood; beginning at the thirteenth chapter. When all the cups have been brought back, the pastor begins, "Fall upon your knees," for we eat and drink the sacrament of the Supper sitting and silently listening to the word of the Lord, and when all kneel, the pastor begins, I say:

"Praise, O ye servants, the Lord,* praise the name of the Lord." The Deacon: "Blessed be the name of the Lord from this time forth and for evermore" [Ps. 113: 2ff.]. The Subdeacon: "From the rising of the sun unto the going down, etc.," and so again the assistants go through alternately this psalm which the Hebrews say used to be said by their ancestors after eating. After this the pastor exhorts the Church in these words:

"Be mindful, dearly beloved brethren, of what we have now done together by Christ's command. We have borne witness by this giving of thanks, which we have done in faith, that we are indeed miserable sinners, but have been purified by the body and blood of Christ which He delivered up and poured out for us, and have been redeemed from everlasting death. We have borne witness that we are brethren. Let us, therefore, confirm this by love, faith, and mutual service. Let us, therefore, pray the Lord that we may keep His bitter death deep in our hearts so that though we daily die to our sins we may be so sustained and increased in all virtues by the grace and bounty of His Spirit that the name of the Lord shall be sanctified in us, and our neighbor be loved and helped. The Lord have mercy upon us and bless us! The Lord cause His face to shine upon us and be gracious unto us! Amen."

The pastor again prays:—"We give thanks unto Thee, O Lord, for all Thy gifts and benefits, who livest and reignest God world without end. Amen." The pastor: "Go in peace. Amen." Then the Church separates.

Here you see, most wise King, how nothing is lacking which is required for the proper, apostolic celebration of the Eucharist,

*Zwingli has "dominum"—"praise the Lord,"—where the King James version translates "domini," i. e., "of the Lord."

as far as the substance of things is concerned, but that the things which are suspected of having been introduced from greed of gain are omitted.

But if any one complain, that we have no right to use a new form of celebration even if some errors have crept into the Mass, for when we venture to do this, it is just as if any one in a kingdom or city, disregarding the laws of the state, should enact special laws for himself, living according to which he would throw the rest into uproar and sedition, and therefore we should rightly be called heretics, for errors can be tolerated for a time even according to the example of the apostles until the general council of the Church decrees something else, let him, I pray, consider that this case of kingdoms and cities and laws is by no means parallel with the case of the divine laws and the liberty of truth and faith and the rights of the Church. For whatever human laws command applies to the arrangement and regulation of external affairs, but what the divine law enjoins strikes the conscience so that as soon as it understands the divine will it condemns itself unless it acquiesces and obeys. For by the law cometh knowledge of sin, and the more we detect that we are sinning against the Holy Spirit, the less can the conscience assent to and tolerate insult to the Creator.

Since, therefore, we have learned under the tuition of the Holy Spirit that there is but one offering and that made by the Son of God, and have pointed that out to the great men in the Church, that whatever was wrong might be corrected, and yet they have more and more not only contended but raged against the truth, the power of the pontiff, that had been seized by violence ought not to stand in the way of anyone's defending the truth and clearing away the disgraceful dishonor to the Son of God. For what reason would there be, alas, to have regard for a pontiff of the Church who did not reverence that on which the Church is based and built? The Church is based upon faith in God which lays hold of His word. When the pontiff does not believe God's Word, how can he rule the Church? Can faith be increased or retarded according to the notions of men? Or, when the Lord said, "Do unto others as ye would that they should do to you," is one to postpone accepting this law until the heads of the Church decree its acceptance? This law has certainly to do with human affairs merely, though to offer up the Son of God is an insult to God Himself.

Finally it is the right of the Church to believe and live according to the inspiration of the divine Spirit, as Paul commands, "Quench not the Spirit" [I Thess. 5:19]. For who does not immediately reject the nonsense of indulgences when he understands that they are a lying invention? Faith waiteth not for the judgment of another, but rests upon her own. When, therefore, she sees these terrible blasphemies against the Son of God, she feels that they are not to be tolerated but to be abolished or abandoned at the very first possible moment. Thus, then, the Mass of the Papists has been abolished among us by desertion and defection. For when the people fled from it, having recognized its error, and some of the officiating priests shrank away, while some feared an attack from the crowd, the Mass was so thoroughly deserted that we found it necessary to cast about for a simple and Christian form of celebration. When this had been perfected, the Council of our city appointed a conference between us and the Roman bishops. Learned men among them came, but declared that they could not confer upon so difficult a matter without a council (though three years later they themselves appointed a conference at Baden with much corruption).

Our Council, therefore, having heard what was brought before them pro and con from the divine Scriptures and other writers, voted that no man should be compelled to perform or to hear the Mass. Then the Roman party attempted bribery, and violence began to be resorted to, and forced by this, our illustrious Council passed this decree, "No one shall celebrate the Mass in our city after the Popish fashion henceforth forever, unless he maintains from the Holy Scriptures that it has a right to be preserved." Thus, I say, the Popish Mass was abolished, and the Lord's Supper instituted. Our example has been followed by many princes, nobles, peoples, and cities in Germany, and by countless individual priests, monks, magistrates and private persons throughout the world. Nothing, therefore, has been done among us at variance with reason, nothing at variance with the authority of the divine oracles, upon which we rely and stand dauntless in the face of all assaults, sure that He who is on our side is stronger than any

opposing power whatever. But we have dismissed the Mass,*
and pray that Your Majesty be strong mightily in God.

*It is a pity that the play upon words involved in *"missam missam
facimus,"* though of doubtful taste, seems incapable of reproduction in
English. The nearest approach seems to be that given above.

ADDITIONAL NOTES

p. 4, 1. 30.

The passage in Gellius, *Noctium Atticarum Libri XX*, is as follows: "It must not be omitted, that in the books of the old lawyers *morbus* is distinguished from *vitium: vitium* is perpetual, whilst *morbus* is subject to variations." See *The Attic Nights of Aulus Gellius*, translated into English by the Rev. W. Beloe, London 1795, Vol. I, p. 241.

p. 71, 1. 11.

Zwingli said at Berne *(Werke*, (Schuler and Schulthess ed.) II, 1, 146): "We know from Luke 2: 52, that Christ grew according to his humanity. From this we learn that his humanity was not like his divinity infinite and immeasurable, but according to his human nature he was finite and subject to limitation."

p. 76, 1. 7.

For Zwingli's explanation of Ephes. 5: 27 see his *De Canone missae epicheiresis*, in his *Werke*, ed. Egli and Finsler, II, 571.

p. 78, 1. 18.

The book referred to is Luther's *De votis monasticis*, 1521, (see *Werke*, Weimar ed. Vol. VIII, pp. 577-669), and the sermon from John 3: 16, *Sic deus dilexit*, held on June 9, 1522 *(Werke*, Weimar ed., Vol. X, pt. 3, No. 29, pp. 160-169.)

p. 81, 1. 6.

Eck was probably thinking of §15 of the Bull *"Exsurge Domine,"* which condemned the following statement of Luther: "If they believe and trust that they will receive grace, this faith alone makes them pure and worthy [to come to the sacrament of the Eucharist]." See Jacobs, *Martin Luther*, 1898, p. 419, who gives the full text of this bull in an English translation.

p. 82, 1. 26.

The sacraments are visible signs of invisible grace. This definition goes back to Peter Lombard, who defined a sacrament as "a visible form or sign of an invisible grace," see his *Sentences*, Bk. IV. It is based in turn on Augustine, who defined a sacrament as "visible signs of divine things, in which the invisible things themselves are honored," *De Cat. Rud.* XXVI, §50.

p. 85, l. 13.

The reference here is to the *Corpus Juris Civilis* of Justinian, more definitely the *Codex Justinianus*, Book I, chap. 1, which is entitled: *De summa trinitate et de fide catholica et ut nemo de ea publice contendere audeat.* In §4 of this chapter occurs the sentence quoted by Eck: *Nam injuriam facit iudicio reverentissimae synodi, si quis semel iudicata ac recte disposita revolvere et publice disputare contendit.* See *Corpus Juris Civilis,* ed. Mommsen, Vol. II, p. 6.

p. 98, l. 18.

De saeculari potestate is Luther's tract, *"Von weltlicher Oberkeit,"* see his *Werke,* Weimar edition, XI, 245-281. In it he wrote: "They do nothing but skin and scrape. They pile one duty upon the other, one tax upon the other; here they let go a bear, there a wolf, so that there is no right, faithfulness or truth found among them, and they act worse than robbers and rascals. Their secular government lies prostrate as deeply as the government of the spiritual tyrants."

p. 98, l. 27.

Augustine speaks only of the possibility of punishments in the life beyond *(Enchiridion ad Laur.* 67; *De Civ. Dei.* 20, 18), and believes that these are referred to in Matth. 12: 32, and perhaps also in I Cor. 3: 11f., hence purgatorial fire is not incredible.

p. 102, l. 19.

Zwingli himself gives as his reason for declining this safe conduct: "I know that all who adhere to the Popish Church cry out, that I am a heretic, therefore, no safe-conduct should be given to me, but, if it were given, it should be done that it might be broken, and they might get me into their power," *Werke,* ed. Schuler and Schulthess, II, 2, 463.

Index

Scriptural Citations

Genesis
1:16. 205
2:16–17 . . . . .7, 14, 15
3:10. 16
3:15. 17
4:1. 17
5:3. 8
5:28–29 17–18
6:3. 8
6:5. 8
8:21. 8–9
17:7. 20
17:10–12 20
17:10–14 90
17:14 . . . . .11, 75
19:24 210
37:2. 215
41:33 135

Exodus
3:13–14 147
7:3–4 187
9:16. 187
10:4ff 46
12:11 . . . . .52, 89
29:24 115
33 24
33:19 187
34:28 157

Numbers
11:31ff 46
14:31 9
22:12 230

Deuteronomy
6:8. . . . . 12n
6:15. 168
17:12 69

Joshua
10:13 210

Judges
7:13. 218

I Samuel
7:12. 255
9:3. 214
21:13 95

II Samuel
11:2. 218
12:13–14 100
24:1. 219

I Kings
8:1. 80
8:14. 80
8:39. . . . . .26, 77
11:30–31 219–220
12:28 103
18:44–45 209
19:11 46

II Kings
6:5–6 214
20:6. 206

II Chronicles
35:1. 89
35:17–18 89–90

Job
11:18 78

Psalms
1:6. 9
14:2. 14
28:3. 68
31:1. 181
32:1. 73
34 95
35:18 64
37:18 9
51:5. 74
111:4 91
113:2ff 290
116:10 92
118 93

Proverbs
15:11 43
27:2. 102

Ecclesiastes
7:20. 77
9:1. 77

Song of Solomon
1:5. 77